CALLED UPON

A NOVEL

BETHANY LEE

NEW YORK

LONDON • NASHVILLE • MELBOURNE • VANCOUVER

CALLED UPON
A NOVEL

Published in New York, New York, by Morgan James Publishing. Morgan James is a trademark of Morgan James, LLC. www.MorganJamesPublishing.com

ISBN 978-1-63195-202-9 paperback
ISBN 978-1-63195-203-6 eBook
ISBN 978-1-63195-204-3 hardcover
Library of Congress Control Number: 2020908204

Morgan James is a proud partner of Habitat for Humanity Peninsula and Greater Williamsburg. Partners in building since 2006.

Get involved today! Visit
www.MorganJamesBuilds.com

I don't know how long I'd been there, balled up in the fetal position and staring at my friend's lifeless body. Time was a slippery concept since the world had tipped upside down and dumped me into this terrifying new reality.

Trembling, I slowly reached out to touch her hand. She no longer had the feel of warm, thriving flesh but that of meat just pulled from the freezer to be thawed for dinner. Her shirt molded stiffly, unnaturally, around her torso, and the bright crimson made a gruesome contrast to her bluish lips—lips which were forever fixed into an openmouthed grimace. Her eyes stared into nowhere, and ice crystals gripped her lashes like teardrops too frightened to fall.

I quickly reclaimed my hand and held it steady against my chest, shamed by the proof of life thumping under my fingertips. How easily it could have been me lying there like that. Maybe if I'd been the hero that night in the woods, I'd have two bullet holes in my chest and she wouldn't. Maybe it would've been better if she and I had never become friends at all. Then nature would have run its course; I would have disappeared, she'd have spent the summer miserable but alive, and all the others none the wiser.

But who was I kidding? I knew there was only one reason that she was dead and that I was alive: I had been *called upon*, and she had not.

How could I have been so naïve? I'd wanted so badly to believe that I belonged, that I was special, I had been willing to chew and swallow just about anything given to me. What's more, I'd flat-out shrugged off all of the flashing warning signs. Shouldn't my mother's pleading eyes have been warning enough?

But despite the lies I'd been told and the lies I had believed, there was no point denying that I was special. I had an astonishing gift, a talent for which people would kill. *Had* killed. I had the power within me to change the world, save it even. But looking down at my friend's body, I couldn't help but question if the one thing that made me special was also the one thing that made me an extremely dangerous weapon.

CHAPTER 1

KAITLIN

The way I saw it, I had three options. The most obvious choice, given my age and gender, would be to yell—to make a mighty stink right there in the café in front of everyone. And if I really wanted to raise some eyebrows, I could toss a few four-letter grenades into my tirade . . . the juicier the words, the better. I'd never tested my mother with a public temper tantrum before, but I guessed she would give in to any demand, no matter how ludicrous, just to calm the storm.

My second option, inspired by Gandhi himself, was cold defiance. Folding my arms at my chest and lacing my ankles tightly around the legs of my chair, I could hold my breath until my lips turned a victorious shade of blue. If Mom somehow managed to uproot me, which I seriously doubted she could, I could play it like a toddler being forced into the bathtub and go completely limp.

If all else failed, there was always the crying option. Simple. Classic. Elegant. I'd ask what I did wrong and why she wanted to get rid of me for the summer, meanwhile leaking gallons of "why, oh, why, don't you love me?" tears. I could sniffle and moan, and even pretend to gag a little. That'd get her.

As I weighed my three options, Mom slowly stirred the straw around her Diet Coke and braced herself for my counterattack, in whatever form it might take. Her lips were turned under, and her eyes were heavy and troubled. Was she worried about my reaction? Or was the worry deeper?

My parents weren't stupid or anything. Obviously they noticed that my phone never vibrated with texts, and the extent of my social life was tagging along on their weekly date night, but could they know how bad it truly was?

I mean, I'd tried to put on a brave face for them—glossing my lips into a smile and prancing around the house like there was no place I'd rather be. In the privacy of my own bedroom, however, I let it all out. I secretly recorded my loserdom into the fibers of my pillow as I cried myself to sleep each night.

Had they figured it out? Is that why they were shipping me away for the summer—to bring a little pine-scented sunshine into my pathetic life?

I was too old for summer camp. I was pretty sure that my bra size would be greater than or equal to that of any camp counselor I could have had, so singing campfire songs with cheeks bulging with toasted marshmallows was absurd. But after considering my alternative summer plans—snipping away at my split ends, hiding in the stacks of the public library, and eating cookie butter straight from the jar—I discarded options one, two, and three and came up with a fourth option: acceptance.

"Okay,"—I shrugged—"I'll go."

Mom's jaw dropped far enough to give me a complete visual of her tongue, that little dangly thing at the back of her throat, and her complete digesting breakfast. It was scrambled eggs and toast, I'll have you know. "I'm sorry, what? You'll . . . go?"

"That's what I said."

Mom's eyes darted around the café, as if seeking verification from the baristas and patrons alike that I had, indeed, agreed to summer camp. She then straightened her posture, peeled open a pouch of mayonnaise, and dabbed it across her turkey avocado sandwich. "Well, that could've been worse," she mumbled.

Suddenly, I felt annoyed. I mean, Mom had just ambushed me with the news that I'd basically be spending the whole summer using tree bark as toilet paper and, brilliant me, I'd let her off the hook without a word of protest . . . almost. "So, how long have you and Dad been conspiring about this? Months? Years? Or is this whole camp idea a sudden spark of genius?" I couldn't resist. I was a slave to my fourteen years.

"For crying out loud, Kaitlin. We thought camp would be fun and a good way to get you out of the—"

"Mom," I interrupted, avoiding the reminder of my life as a houseplant, "I'm only joking." Kind of. "But just so I know, this isn't some youth correctional camp or anything, is it?"

Mom scooped a barbeque potato chip into her plastic spoon and launched it at my shoulder.

"Fat camp?" I countered, teasingly. The fact that I weighed only slightly more than a cocker spaniel only escalated my mother's chip assault. I ducked beneath the table and only surfaced when my mother's ammunition dwindled to the bottom-of-the-bag crumbles. "So tell me about this camp place you're sending me."

Mom shrugged. "Well, it's called Camp Overlook. There will be lots of outdoor activities, like hiking and fishing and crafting, but you may find the whole setup a little alternative."

"Alternative?" I mouthed, mentally sifting through all of the thirteen hundred reasons why *alternative* could be a problem.

"Well, I don't exactly know what you should expect, but don't worry, the brochure said that camp will be an enriching and enlightening experience."

"So basically, you're telling me you have no idea what I will be doing at camp?" I paused dramatically, pursing my lips and giving my mom the ol' stink eye. "For all you know, this camp could be run by a bunch of granola-faced tree-huggers, and all we'll do is sit around smoking pot and eating bran muffins. Or maybe it's a tattoo camp, and I'll come home with gang symbols inked all over my arms. Or better yet . . ."

"Whoa there. Your father and I wouldn't send you just anywhere. We feel really good about this place. You'll just love it." Somehow, the pinched expression on her face wasn't very reassuring.

I would miss her, too.

"Oh geez. I'm sure I'll be okay." Though careful not to sound too enthusiastic, I thought this Camp Overlook place didn't sound that bad. I actually liked the mountains and didn't mind roughing it once in a while. Heck, maybe a few toasted marshmallows, or tattoos, were exactly what the doctor ordered.

I swigged the remains of my drink and eyed Mom's full plastic cup hopefully. As she pushed it toward me, the sun filtered through the window and lightly powdered her face. I was immediately hit by the irony of how beautiful she was and how beautiful I was not. Like Mom, I had wavy honey-colored hair with natural blonde highlights and eyes that opted hazel or green depending on the sun or color of my shirt. We were both on the shorter side, although slender enough that we looked taller than we actually were. But even though my facial features resembled hers, my nose was just a little too round, and my skin had just one too many freckles; I barely missed the cutoff.

"We really need to get going on this camp thing, though," Mom interrupted my thoughts, snapping her fingers in front of my face. "I need you to vacuum your room and pack your duffle bags tonight so we can leave first thing in the morning."

"I'm sorry, what? Tomorrow! We are leaving tomorrow? Holy freakin' cow, school just let out two days ago!"

With that, the front entrance to the café swung open and a dark and heavy sensation washed into the room. My first thought was Dementors, obviously, but the real source of my blackened mood was far worse. A group of girls from my ninth-grade class, led by none other than the fabulous Mia Bethers, giggled their way in, smothering any trace of self-assurance I might have felt the moment before. I tilted my head downward and feigned a sudden interest in a dried ketchup mass under our table.

"Isn't that Mia?" Mom asked, nudging my knee. "Wow, she's all grown up now."

Mia was the captain of the JV dance squad. She was cute, popular, freckle-free, and the leading reason my life as a teenager was a complete disaster. Did I mention that she used to be my best friend?

"Oh yeah," I nodded, trying to play it cool. "She's a little different now, but still really . . . cool."

Mom's eyes widened as though a beam of light had shot down from heaven and impregnated her brain with the smartest idea known to man. "I know! You should go say hi to her. You could invite her to dinner tonight! We'll make homemade pizza and chocolate malts just like old times!"

"I don't think so, Mom."

"Why not? You two used to be so cute together. Remember when you were in primary school and you had all those sleepovers and how you used to spend all of your recess time hanging upside down on the monkey bars?"

Of course I remembered that time. We *had* been cute together. All that, however, was before the "incident" and before Mia made it her life's mission to see to it that nobody at our school would touch me with a ten-foot pole. "It's just that we've gone our separate ways. She has new friends now. I wouldn't want to . . ."

"Come on, Potato Bug? Give it a shot. For me?" Mom looked at me with so much hope, so much concern, so much denial. With this sudden camp stuff, Mom tiptoed across the truth, admitting that I wasn't quite fitting in at school but not acknowledging the extent of my exile. Was I really ready to fess up to everything and force my mom to face the reality that her beloved daughter was actually the most detested girl in all of Colorado? Could I be that cruel?

"Fine. I'll say hi to her," I said abruptly. Before I could process the consequences of what I was about to do, I stood up and marched to the service line where Mia and her stupid friends were waiting to order. One of them gasped as I tapped Mia on the shoulder. The others erupted into giggles. Mia turned around slowly, her brown eyes stone cold, but a polyester grin stitched across her face.

"Er . . . hi, Mia," I said.

"Er . . . hi, Kaitlin," she mimicked and stood there unhelpfully, waiting for me to say something else.

It took a second. "Um . . ." was the best I could do.

"Ummm . . ." she mimicked, though trying to sound like a bovine with a brain injury. Her friends cackled because apparently she was, *like, totally hilarious.*

Then silence.

Mia, still grinning, reached out to my hair and gently ran her finger from my scalp all the way down to the end. This gesture might have seemed friendly coming from someone else, like she was about to compliment my long beachy hair or something, but I knew better. I clenched my fists and debated whether to slap her hand away or flee back to the safety of my mom. Both routes were rife with possible unfavorable outcomes, so I just stood there, like an idiot, and waited to see what would happen next.

With her other hand, Mia pulled a bright pink wad of chewing gum from her mouth and attached it to the bottom of my hair. I cringed as she scrunched it into the surrounding hair and then pulled back to admire her handiwork. One of her friends slipped her a low five, while another one pulled out her phone, pointed it at my face, and snapped a picture. Great, looked like I was going to be the star of another horrendous GIF.

"I guess that's all I had to say." I turned around and trudged back to our table, my feet having turned into ten-pound blocks of cement. I was humiliated by how I'd been treated, of course, but more embarrassed that my mother had just witnessed *a day in the life*. If she hadn't known how bad it was for me before, she certainly did now.

Mom's eyes flickered with sadness and protectiveness. When I was a child, she reserved this expression for my fevers and paper cuts, scrapes, and bruises. Now the look surfaced whenever my mom perceived emotional boo-boos. Like in sixth grade when she saw that someone had written "barf bag" in permanent marker on my backpack or just yesterday when she flipped through my ninth grade yearbook and saw that no one had signed it.

I hated that look.

So I did the same thing I did the other times Mom looked at me like that. I crinkled my nose and forced a smile. "We probably should go now. Like you said, my room really needs to be vacuumed."

Mom paused for a moment as if trying to process my complete dismissal of what had just happened. But then she rearranged her face into this weird, unnatural smile and squished my nose with the tip of her finger. "Right you are, Potato Bug. And why don't we stop by the salon on the way home? Your hair could use a little trim before camp."

I nodded, swallowing the lump in my throat.

We discarded our trash and pretended not to notice the taunting eyes and the whispers that followed us out of the café.

"Dad might be starting a new contract this week, so it will be just you, me, and the open road. We'll pack all sorts of junk food, listen to music, and have so much fun together. Girl time!" my mother said, her voice an octave higher than usual. She was trying hard to pretend the pain away.

"Can't wait," I said, already imagining the hours of Christina Aguilera and Mariah Carey CDs I'd have to stomach on our trip to Camp Overlook. Had I known that the car ride would ultimately lead to my disappearance, Mom's sorry taste in music would never have crossed my mind.

ASHLEY

"How come these pregnancy books always compare the size of a fetus to produce?" Jade giggled as she read aloud from Ashley's library book. "Last week your baby was the size of a crab apple, and this week he's the size of a lime." She placed the book down on her lap and frowned dramatically. "Don't you get hungry every time you read about your growing uterus?"

"That's twisted, Jade. Only you would think of it that way." Ashley grabbed the book from Jade's lap and flung it onto the bed next to a pile of stuffed animals.

"Just saying . . ." Jade shrugged.

"So if my baby is the size of a lime, how come I feel like there's a whole cantaloupe in there?" Ashley lifted her shirt and ran her fingernails up and down her lower belly, where a small taut bulge pushed above her jeans.

"The book said that retaining water is normal, so of course you feel bloated. You don't look it, though. You're three months along, and no one would, like, ever guess that you are pregnant. Except for that natural prenatal glow," she added.

"Yeah, it's called acne. My hormones are attacking my face. Talk about kicking a girl when she's already down."

"Girl, your face fits in perfectly with the rest of the sophomore class." And Jade was right. At this point, people were far more likely to see Ashley as a victim of adolescence than motherhood. "So, when are you going to tell that loser, Luke, about the mess he got you into?"

"Are you kidding? I haven't even told my own mother yet."

"Ash, if you wait another month, she'll figure it out on her own."

"I know, I know. I guess I just want to have a plan before I tell her anything."

"I thought that's the mom's job, to make the plan."

Ashley stretched out on her bed, pulling her shirt back over her belly. "And my mom takes *that* job seriously. When I tell her I'm pregnant, she'll go all ballistic on me, and then she'll completely take over like she was the one pregnant. Knowing her, she'll quit smoking and send me to the grocery store for her midnight cravings."

"At least she'll foot the bill."

Ashley squinted at the ceiling and tried to follow the path of the fan as it stirred the air in the room. "With what money? I don't know a lot about private insurance, but I do know that getting pregnant on it is a big *no-no*. When my mom gets the hospital bills, she's gonna lose her mind."

"It's not like you got pregnant for kicks and giggles; accidents happen."

"Dropping a gallon of milk on the tile floor is an accident; this is a complete train wreck."

"Whatever. You're going to be, like, the cutest pregnant girl ever. You're gonna get super curvy; you'll be the first girl in school with a homecoming date."

"But Luke won't be asking me. I doubt he even remembers my name. I wasted my whole life for those ten stupid minutes." Ashley shivered at the memory of how casually Luke had handled her. It was not at all like what she imagined her first time to be.

"Your life isn't wasted. You just got a head start on things. Did you know that you're going to be the first person at our school to have a baby? The very first. That's, like, so cool."

"People will say I'm a slut."

"Just because they're jealous."

"I don't even know if I like babies. For sure I won't know what to do with it when it comes. I can change diapers, but that's about all I got."

Jade lay down on the pillow so she was facing her best friend. "You'll be a great mom, Ash."

Ashley huffed.

"Besides, you're forgetting how much fun a baby will be. They are so cute and so little. Their fingers are, like, smaller than Cheetos."

"Their fingers *are* little," Ashley conceded.

"If it's a girl, we can make her a bunch of bows and ribbons, and if it's a boy, we can dress him in jerseys and baseball caps. He'll be the cutest baby ever. And I'll babysit all the time. And I won't charge . . . unless there's, like, a poop situation."

"But my baby wouldn't do that."

"Never," agreed Jade and they both giggled.

CHAPTER 2

KAITLIN

I staggered out of the car and slammed the door behind me. The last twenty minutes of our drive took place on an unmarked dirt road, and our Toyota Corolla's decrepit shock absorbers threw in the towel midgame. I felt queasy from all the winding and bumping . . . but maybe the seven hours of nonstop mom music was really to blame. Nelly Furtado never did sit well with my digestive tract.

I took a moment to equalize before surveying my surroundings. Two mammoth mountains, the kind that looked like giant chopped pecans, split the earth open and stood on either side of us. Weathered pine trees peppered their jagged peaks, but healthy trees completely cloaked the mountain below the waistline. Camp Overlook was wedged snuggly at the base of the valley. "The guy who named this joint was either an idiot or had a really weird sense of humor," I told my mom as she popped the trunk.

The exterior of the lodge was also a little surprising. I don't know what I had been expecting, certainly not a lodge made out of Lincoln Logs and Elmer's

Glue, but this here was not it. A massive beamed entryway, flagstone siding, gargantuan windows—the building reminded me of a five-star ski lodge made exclusively for A-list celebrities, Fortune 500 CEOs, and people who had a heck of a lot more money than us.

"Shall we?" Mom asked, raising her brows at me, signaling that she was also a little surprised and impressed by my summer accommodations.

We dragged my three duffle bags through the paved parking lot and up a set of slate stairs. Thunk. Thunk. Thunk. "Wow, Kate. Your bags weigh a ton. What on earth did you pack?"

The truth was that I may have been a bit overzealous while packing my summer reads. I'd practically dumped my whole bookshelf into one bag and my mother's bookshelf into another. I didn't know how much extra time I'd have on my hands, but if these past few years were any indicator of my future social demands, then a few books would be crucial.

We opened the oversized front door and hauled the bags across the bright hardwood flooring. A large stone fireplace framed by a heavy copper mantel accentuated the left side of the room, and a leather seating area took up the other. Mom and I kept the place balanced by walking a straight line to the reception desk, where a slender black woman in dark-framed glasses and a strategically tight sweater sat behind a white laptop. Her smooth black hair was secured in a stylish ponytail. Her long perfectly manicured fingernails clicked hastily along the keyboard. I'd see her more as a high-end fashion magazine executive than a camp counselor.

"Welcome to Camp Overlook, Kaitlin. I am Tanji," she said in a dry English accent, not so much as glancing up from her computer.

"How did you know it was . . . er . . . that I am me . . . er . . . that I am Kaitlin?" I fared just fine around Mom and Dad, but placed in a conversation with a stranger, a peer, or especially a guy . . . well, I became a babbling idiot.

"You're the last one to check in. The other campers, the ones who were on time, are getting settled in their bunks right now." She shoved a bunch of forms my mother's way. "I'll need you to sign and date where I have marked. Have all fees been paid?"

"Um . . . just one more to go," Mom said.

Tanji tapped a few keys on the computer and nodded. "Oh, I see. Yes, that's right." Then, for the first time since we arrived, Tanji looked up at me. "Why don't we get you in for your physical while your mother finishes up the paperwork?"

I nodded, though not exactly processing what Tanji had said. Instead, I was mesmerized by her eyes; I'd never seen anything quite like them. Behind the lenses of her glasses, her irises were gray. But not your everyday, mix-black-paint-with-white-paint gray. They were the color a candle makes when capped right after the flame is extinguished—the trapped air swirling around with chalky, translucent smoke. They were beautiful yet unsettling at the same time.

"Physical?" Mom asked Tanji, pulling me out of my trance. "I wasn't aware that there would be a physical. No one told me that."

"Yes, standard procedure for all camp participants. Turn to page four; I'll need you to sign the medical release form."

Mom fumbled through the papers, eyed me hesitantly and, after what looked like some excruciating soul-searching, bit her lower lip and signed.

"Of course, I'll make copies of all written agreements for your personal and legal records," Tanji said smugly and then placed her hand between my shoulder blades. "This way, Kaitlin." She steered me toward the back of the lodge and around the corner, and then, unwilling to compromise the integrity of her cuticles, tapped a door lightly with the tips of her knuckles. An older man, with a pot belly and fluffy gray hair sticking this way and that, opened.

"Aw, Miss Kaitlin! We've been waiting for you. What a joy to meet you! How are you this fine afternoon?"

I liked this man instantly. Minus the lab coat and stethoscope, he reminded me of a grandpa . . . the kind that teases you, gives you Werther's Originals from his tweed coat pocket, and takes you fishing. "Pretty good, I guess."

"Excellent, excellent. I am Dr. Forsythe. Come on in my office, and we'll get this darned examination over with. Thank you, Tanji."

She smiled using only the lower portion of her face and closed the door behind her. "Sparkly personality, that one," he joked.

I chuckled appreciatively.

"Have a seat." He thumbed through a stack of charts and retrieved a file with my name on it. While reading my info, he absentmindedly hummed a Christmas carol. "Looks like your shots are all up to date . . . ho-oh-ly niiight . . . no major illnesses . . . aaaall is caaalm . . . I see you have an allergy to penicillin . . . aaall is briiight . . . mind if I get your height and weight?"

I giggled. "Only if you'll do Little Drummer Boy next."

Dr. Forsythe did all the standard check-up stuff—took my measurements, did an eye exam, listened to my heart, and then asked a handful of health questions, nodding profusely after all of my answers.

"Are you currently taking any prescription or over-the-counter medications?"

"Naw."

"Do you smoke, drink alcohol, or engage in any other risky underage behavior?"

"No."

"Do you have or any of your family members have a history of cancer, heart disease, diabetes or other blood disorders?

"Not that I know of."

"Digestive problems?"

"Er . . . no."

"Do you suffer from depression or anxiety?"

"Just normal teenage stuff, I guess."

"Do you regularly experience unusual or unsettling dreams?"

I hesitated. My mind rushed to the incident in sixth grade, but that was over three years ago. "Nope."

"Are you in any sort of physical pain or discomfort right now?"

"Right now, as in this very second?" I asked. "Should I be?"

The doctor chortled. "Of course not. It's just a rudimentary question."

"Okay. Well, I'm feeling normalish."

"Excellent, excellent. Now, if you wouldn't mind rolling up your sleeve, I'll need a little Cream of Kaitlin Soup."

"Huh?"

"Blood," he winked.

"Oh." I offered my arm and averted my eyes, focusing on the crow's feet around the doctor's gentle eyes instead of the needle in my arm. Thirty seconds later, Dr. Forsythe gently wrapped gauze around my inner elbow and snipped away the excess.

"We're all done here, camper. You're a beacon of health and beauty, so I don't expect many run-ins with you this summer. But if you ever do get a cough, sprain an ankle, or simply fancy urinating in a cup, you know where to find me." He gave my hand a hearty shake and opened the door to let me out.

Walking back into the reception area, I saw Tanji hand my mom what looked like a receipt. Mom caught sight of me and, with a startled expression on her face, quickly tucked the receipt into her purse. "Oh . . . I was just . . . this is just . . ." She caught sight of my bandage and then frowned. "Looks like they sucked your blood."

"What? Oh, yeah. Doc said I tasted like Seven-Up; warned me to bathe regularly in mosquito repellent."

Tanji cleared her throat and folded her arms impatiently. "I'll help Kaitlin with her bags if you are ready to say your goodbyes."

Mom instantly began fanning her face and blowing out short puffs of air, a clear signal that things were about to get extremely emotional and exceptionally wet. I scrambled to keep the mood light. "Are you staying in town for a while? You could do a little hiking, mix with the locals?"

"No. I'll get a motel room tonight and drive back home tomorrow morning. Dad will be missing me. Plus, Grandma wants to help reorganize our kitchen pantry on Wednesday . . . even though it's fine how it is. That woman, I swear." She blew a wisp of hair out of her eye and then placed her hands on my shoulders. "Write me all the time. About new people . . . activities . . . about everything."

I nodded.

"You'll be okay, you know? You'll have fun. Make some friends. You'll be safe. Everything will be fine." Then the tears came. She sniffled and then folded me in her arms, holding me for what seemed like an eternity. "I love you so much, Potato Bug. You are my sweet baby girl."

"I love you, too," I said and broke the seal, fully expecting to hear a pop.

"Like I said, write lots of letters and have lots of fun." She kissed my forehead and quickly turned away. I sniffed away my own tears in the making as the giant doors closed behind her. If one had to have a mother, she'd be the one you'd want.

I turned to Tanji, who already had two of my duffle bags slung around her arms and didn't look happy about it. "Congratulations, Kaitlin. You might win for camper with the most stuff."

"Er . . . yeah. Thanks . . . I mean . . . sorry."

"I'll lead." She marched toward the back entrance, her ponytail bobbing from left to right, her globular bosoms remaining spectacularly stationary. I grabbed my other bag and raced outside to catch up.

Tanji kept several paces ahead of me as we moved quickly along the pathway. After several minutes of silence, she stopped abruptly and motioned to our left. "Down that path there is the amphitheater, where you will have many of your classes and the majority of your nighttime activities."

"Classes?" I asked, feeling a little gipped.

Tanji ignored me. She pointed to a one-story building to the right of us, which looked a lot like the lodge, but landscaped like an alpine Versailles, and was emitting a mouth-watering aroma. "That's the dining hall. The food is magnificent; our chef trained at Le Cordon Bleu and has led the kitchens of several of New York's premier restaurants."

I ducked out of the way as she swung her arm to the left. "Over that way are the tennis and basketball courts. The pool is just down the trail; it's heated with a hot tub. The stables are next to the pool." Le Cordon Bleu? Tennis Courts? Did my parents take out a third mortgage to pay for this place? It hardly seemed possible that they could have afforded it on my mom's abysmal salary and my dad's on-again off-again work situation. I hoped I was on scholarship, because man, this place was bonkers.

"As you can see, the bunkhouses are spread out all around the main facility. Your bunk is named Pine Oak." She pointed to a small cabin just up the slope. Though partially veiled by a clump of trees, it had obviously seen better days. The khaki exterior paint was peeling in chunks, and the front door seemed likely to fall off its hinges if I sneezed or just looked at it the wrong way. I was strangely relieved by this. I'd had a vision in my head of how camp was supposed to be— rugged, dusty, sloppy-joeish, and my cabin was the first and only thing that had met my expectations.

"Here you are," Tanji said as we reached the cabin. She dumped my personal belongings on the ground and left me to my own devices without saying goodbye. Consequently, I withheld my congratulations to her for managing the slope in stilettos.

From within the cabin I could hear the high-pitched buzz of giggling and gossiping. A surge of anxiety made its way down my spine and trickled to all the nerve endings in my body. I imagined a room full of Mia Bethers' clones just waiting to pounce and shred what remained of my self-esteem into tiny bite-size pieces. Honestly, I'd feel safer sharing a bunk bed with a lesser evil . . . like Pennywise or Hannibal Lecter.

I closed my eyes and said a silent prayer that my cocampers wouldn't be able to smell the loser on me. I prayed that no one would know or care who I was before this summer. Maybe, just maybe, I could ride out the summer in peace and quiet—no one could possibly know about the incident, after all. And as for the viral GIF, I was hardly recognizable in it. What were the chances someone would put two and two together?

And then, for one reckless moment, I tinkered with the idea of making friends. But no. I hadn't exercised the *socially acceptable* muscle for quite some time and was bound to be repulsively awkward and complicate my life even further. No, it would be best if I did everything within my power to fly under the radar this summer.

I inhaled deeply and slowly let the air stream from my lips. Then I pushed open the cabin door with my backside and yanked my duffle bags in one by one. My arrival had a silencing effect on the room, like I'd entered wearing only my underpants and a slice of bologna on my head. I slowly turned around to face the thunderous silence.

Five sets of eyelashes blinked curiously back.

PARKER

Parker hated his father. While other guys his age were spending the summer at the pool trying to look cool for girls, Parker was cooped up in the library studying trigonometry, biochemistry, and political science. While other guys sat idly watching sports on TV, Parker brushed up on his Arabic and read books on horticulture.

Parker was a nerd, and it was his father's fault.

When Parker wasn't studying, he was at the lab. In fact, he logged more hours there than anyone of the other counterparts. His eyes burned from hours spent staring at the computer screen, and his hands ached from relentless data entry. By necessity, Parker had grown accustomed to, even friendly with, his paper cuts. Every day, his fingers grazed the edges of hundreds of pages of information as he searched to make sense of messy equations. Equations for which he hoped he would be the solution.

But Parker's father didn't even blink at his hard work. Never a "Good job, son" or a "Keep it up, son." Parker would've settled for a "Pass the salt, son." His father regarded him as idly as a piece of furniture, if he regarded him at all. The most Parker ever got from his father was an occasional hopeful look. The "wouldn't it be great if" look.

That occasional hopeful look angered Parker beyond belief.

And drove him.

Parker pushed himself even harder to learn more, to be more. More lab hours, more books, more practice; that he could do. When push came to shove, however, Parker knew that only one thing mattered to his father—him, Parker, being *called upon*.

And that was completely out of Parker's hands.

Which, unsurprisingly, made him hate his father even more.

CHAPTER 3

KAITLIN

I felt completely paralyzed. I tried to smile, which no doubt made me look constipated. I tried to say something, but only a peculiar gurgling sound came out.

One of the girls in the cabin snorted in amusement—a boyish-looking girl with short black hair and a sinister hoop laced through her nasal septum. Another girl lurched at me. I jumped backward but realized sheepishly that she was only aiming for my duffle bags.

"Here, let me help you with those," she said and began dragging my bags across the cabin floor. I was positive that she was an angel sent by the Almighty Himself. Not only was she helping me out, which no mortal teenager had ever stooped to do, but her flawless skin, cascading brown hair, and symmetrical features positively reeked of divine perfection. I couldn't decide whether to fall to my knees and worship her or to hate her beatific face with every fiber of my being.

"Your bed is right under mine," she said. "Hope you don't mind the bottom bunk; there's nothing else left." Not only was I on the bottom, but the foot of the bed was mere feet from the entrance to the bathroom. The angel creature shrugged. "Nothing says good morning like the flushing of toilets?"

Don't be awkward. Don't be awkward. "At least I'll make it to the toilet on time if I ever need to . . . er . . . pee in the middle of the night."

Again, a distinct snort from the nose piercing from the next bunk over. The angel pretended not to notice the snort or my luminous remark. "I'm Molly," she said.

"Urm, Kaitlin," I replied and did a quick panoramic of the cabin.

Three bunk beds skirted the wall. The two end bunks, one of which was mine, were turned perpendicular to the other at the wall's crease. Next to the bathroom entrance sat an oak dresser and a rickety oblong table whose functionality looked akin to that of the cabin door, that's to say "iffy."

I started unpacking my books into the only empty dresser drawer when "Hi, I'm Syrup!" crackled wetly into my eardrum. I turned my head to find myself nose to nose with a round-faced girl whose eyebrows had been severely over tweezed in the middle. "Well, my birth name is Maple, like the leaf, but I like Syrup so much better, don't you? It was my birthday last week. When's yours?" Without warning, she wrapped her arms around my shoulders and swayed me from side to side. She smelled like yogurt.

"Nice to . . . er . . . meet you."

"Yup!" she replied and rotated my body to the right. "See that girl at the table? Her name is Aya. She's my bunkie. Get it? Bunkie? She has the top, and I have the bottom. Get it?" I nodded vigorously in hopes that Syrup would stop needling my appendix with her elbow.

Aya looked up from her letter writing and gave an apologetic smile. She had thick, choppy hair, high cheekbones, and narrow eyes on which she'd exhausted a whole eyeliner pencil, I'm sure. Despite this, I could clearly see her eyeing my book collection in the same way a dog would eye a frying pan full of bacon.

The top bunk bed next to mine harbored the snorter, who didn't bother introducing herself, but did bother peeling off a fingernail tip with her teeth and blowing it onto the cement floor next to my foot. Below her, a petite girl with a curly red bob and cappuccino skin tacked a sparkly Polaroid collage of her friends to the wall next to her bed. "I'm Sierra, and I'm from Texas," she announced, as if any information I learned thereafter was only secondary in importance.

These girls, omitting the snorter, seemed harmless enough. Still, instead of risking another embarrassing social blunder, I smiled diplomatically, if not awkwardly, and quietly finished unloading my books. Then I peeled off my jacket and dropped it onto the bed.

Something clanked softly against the bed frame.

Surprised, I reached into the jacket's side pocket and pulled out a disposable flip phone wrapped in a charger cord. Mom must've slipped it in there during our marathon goodbye hug. A sticky-note was attached:

Hi, Kate. I know that cell phones aren't allowed at camp, and maybe you don't even get reception, but I thought you should have one in case of an emergency. Keep it charged and tucked away so it won't get confiscated. Call me if you need to, but I'm sure there will be no reason because everything will be fine. Really. I miss you already. Mom.

I glanced around the room to make sure no one had spotted my contraband and quickly tucked the phone under my mattress. Then, I covered the bed in clean sheets, unrolled my sleeping bag, and tucked my baby blanket deep within.

Tink. Tink. The angelic Molly slid down from the top bunk, the delicate balls of her feet hitting the cement floor like a fairy tiptoeing across ice. She tucked her thumbs into her pant pockets and smiled at me with hopeful chocolate-drop eyes. "It's almost five o'clock. Do you want to walk to orientation with me?"

I scanned the room to be certain she wasn't talking to someone else, almost hoping that she was. I felt painfully ill equipped for even the most basic social interactions. "Uh . . . me? Oh. Okay. Sure." I kicked my remaining belongings under the bed and followed her outside. As we walked down the dusty trail, I racked my brains for something brilliant—but not strange would do just fine—to say. Unfortunately, "So, uh, where are you from?" was all I had to offer.

"I'm from Virginia," she replied, waving a dust cloud away from her face.

"That's a long way to travel just for summer camp."

"Tell me about it. I was on the plane for hours. I was exhausted and smelled like airplane food by the time I got here. I hate, hate, hate traveling. Hate."

"Why didn't you just go to camp back east?"

"My parents thought I should see the Rocky Mountains. They said that they're pretty spectacular compared to the speed bumps in Virginia."

"And what do you think . . . of the mountains, I mean?"

"They're okay. Truthfully, I'm a city girl. Hand me a credit card, and I can navigate any mall. Hand me a compass, and I'm about as useful as a spleen. And I hate dirt," she added, importantly.

I couldn't have been more opposite. The malls depressed me because: a) my family operated on a Walmart budget and b) malls were prime hunting ground for my blood-thirsty peers. The mountains were different, though. My family went camping at least twice every summer, and some of my best memories were fishing with my dad or reading books by the lake with my mom. It didn't matter to the mountains whether my clothes were Anthropologie or Ross Dress for Less. The mountains didn't laugh at me or cyber bully me. I felt safe there, like my real self was just fine.

But I didn't articulate these thoughts to Molly. Of course not. I wanted her to think we were two peas in a pod. "Yeah, dirt sucks."

"I'm glad we're on the same page," said Molly. "You know, we should totally stick together this summer. Then I won't look like such a loner chilling by the pool instead of going on hikes and doing, you know, nature stuff."

"Yeah. Down with nature," I said and quickly changed the subject. "So, um, what's up with the girl with the nose ring?"

"Oh, her. I think her name is Claire. When she got here, she chucked her bags at the cabin wall one by one, muttering some pretty salty stuff about her mom. Since then, she hasn't done much but sit on her top bunk and shoot death glares at the rest of us. We've all done our best to steer clear of her; the girl's got issues."

"Sounds like her mom gave her as much of a choice about coming here as my parents gave me," I said.

"If that's the case, you seem to be handling it better."

"Yeah, well, I'm saving up my tantrums for when my parents do something really bad, like ground me from my flat iron."

Molly chuckled at my joke a little too hard. I mean, it wasn't even that funny. Why was she being so nice to me?

"So you were forced here against your will?" she asked.

"I wouldn't go so far as to say that. I mean, they sprung it on me, but I didn't put up much of a fight. How about you?"

"Are you joking? I was packed and ready to go before the school year ended."

"Huh? But I thought you don't like camping?"

As our path merged with the camp's main trail, a stampede of boys passed us by, two of them glancing backward and high-fiving each other, no doubt congratulating themselves on the tall goddess next to me. I suddenly felt an ulcer burrow a hole through my stomach and leak belly juice into the crevices of my lower organs.

"I didn't know"—*swallow*—"that guys would be here, too." As if learning how to socialize with my own gender wasn't taxing enough.

"Why do you think I packed my bags so quickly?" Molly grinned.

We followed the other campers into the dining hall, me lagging several feet behind Molly, and found seats at a beautiful acacia table with a rustic floral centerpiece that would make even Martha Stewart blush with pride. The table also happened to be in the dead center of the room. I got the distinct impression that Molly wanted to be seen. Ironic. All I wanted to do was crawl into a dark corner and shovel spoonful after spoonful of cookie butter down my throat.

As the rest of the campers trickled in, I was reminded of a bag of gourmet jellybeans—a colorful assortment of girls and guys with a dozen flavors of ethnicity. Some campers teetered on the brink of puberty while others had noticeably been there, done that. While a few kids chatted and made friends with those around their table, many others sat stiffly, like me, unsure how to acclimate. Even though I was sitting by Molly, I felt more like a loner-flavored jellybean than ever. I didn't trust Molly's friendship. It was too easy. She was too pretty and too nice to me. Or maybe I didn't trust myself not to screw it up.

Molly nudged my leg and motioned to a table at the back of the room. There, a bunch of guys played "football" with a tightly folded piece of paper as they waited for orientation to begin. "The one in blue," she mouthed, and I could instantly appreciate why he'd captured her attention. The boy was gorgeous—in a rugged, Hemsworth sort of way. He had a sharp jaw line, perfectly symmetrical nose, and husky-dog eyes—noticeably blue, even from across the room. And while he was currently seated, I could tell he packed some serious height when stretched to full capacity.

The blue-eyed boy held his fingers together in a U-shape and waited for the football to glide on through, but he looked up just in time to catch the two of us gawking at him.

I veered back into my chair and wiped the corners of my mouth in case I'd drooled. Molly, on the other hand, tucked a strand of hair behind her ear and pitched him the most flirtatious smile I'd ever seen. "I'll have that boy eating out of the palm of my hand by the end of the week," she muttered, and I absolutely believed it. He and Molly could not have made a more perfect-looking couple had cupid matched them himself.

Our roommates joined us at our table just as a man in designer sunglasses and an expensive tailored suit strode across the dining hall to a podium at the front of the room. He waited for the room to quiet before leaning into the microphone.

"Welcome to Camp Overlook," he said, smoothing the sides of his already gelled-stiff hair. "My name is Mr. Leavitt, but you may call me Director Leavitt as I will be overseeing all of the functions of Camp Overlook. I think most of you have already met the assistant camp director, Tanji Robinson." He motioned to the back of the room, where Tanji gave a half-hearted wave.

"You've also had the pleasure of donating blood to our resident doctor, Kenneth Forsythe." The doctor, who was standing next to Tanji, saluted proudly.

"You have not yet, however, been introduced to the head of outdoor activities and classroom instruction, Margaret Stratlin. She's taken a break from her work with Greenpeace in hopes of making your summer memorable, so please give her a warm welcome." Mr. Leavitt stepped aside for a frizzy-haired blonde woman in a green, organic-looking sweater.

"And I'm thrilled to be here!" she exclaimed, pumping her fist in the air. The sound system screeched, and she jumped away from the microphone with a giggle. "And you should be excited, too, because this summer is going to be super-duper awesome! Now, I've made out a complete summer schedule for each of you. You'll be attending all of your classes and scheduled activities with your cabin mates, so treat 'em nice; there will be no escaping 'em."

She continued, "All campers will meet at twelve and six for lunch and dinner. Breakfast is at your leisure. You'll also have several hours of scheduled free time during the day. Take advantage of the sports facilities, the stables, the recreation room, and the hiking trails. Just remember to use the buddy system, and *always* stay on the designated paths. If you have questions, you can come see me anytime. Till then, I will have your daily schedules delivered to your bunks after dinner." Margaret flashed the peace sign and backed away from the podium just as Director Leavitt stepped back up.

He cleared his throat. "You may have noticed the absence of counselors in your cabins. Camp Overlook is founded on trust; we feel confident that you will honor our trust by abiding by the curfew, abstaining from drugs and alcohol, refraining from intimate relations, and adhering to the strict no cell phone policy. We ask that you communicate with your families by letters only; we want your camp experience to be untainted by technological distractions.

"Now I'd like to introduce you to our camp security guard, Philip Stitchler." Director Leavitt motioned to a bony-looking man lurking in the doorway to the kitchen. He had a long pointy nose and crooked smile, and I imagined that his breath smelled like rotting vegetables. "Phil will be pacing the grounds every night to ensure your safety and see to it that you are following the rules. If the rules are violated, the consequences will be swift and severe."

Phil smiled, if you could call the weedy upturn of his chapped lips a smile, and I shivered. I found it strange that the man supposedly in charge of our protection gave me such a rabid case of the heebie-jeebies. I couldn't pinpoint exactly what was so creepy about him, maybe his oily hair or his long, bony fingers. Whatever it was, my blood curdled to cottage cheese at the thought that Philip would be prowling around our cabins at night.

After orientation, the kitchen staff paraded into the dining room with our dinner. Thank heavens meatloaf was on the menu and not some foreign delicacy that I couldn't pronounce. I found it difficult to trust a mess hall chef trained at "Le Cordon Bleu."

"This food is good! Good! Good! Good!" Syrup declared from the other side of me, her mouth overflowing with sirloin chunks and her torso wiggling from left to right. Aya quietly slid a napkin to Syrup from across the table, but the nose-ringed Claire's reaction was less discreet. She dropped her fork against her plate and threw her cloth napkin at Syrup's face. "Didn't your mom teach you manners, or is she also a barnyard buddy?" Claire stormed from the dining hall.

The table went quiet, everyone staring at Syrup. She giggled nervously, clearly shaken, and pulled a chocolate-flavored Chapstick from her pocket. She traced her lips over and over until it looked as though a melted fudgesicle had attacked her face. I patted her knee reassuringly.

Just then, a white object shaped like a flat, miniature football grazed my shoulder and plopped into my garlic mashed potatoes. I looked around and saw the blue-eyed boy smile and turn away. "What the . . ."

"It's a note!" Molly yipped.

I scraped away the potato gunk and unfolded the paper.

To the cute girl with the long hair, it began.

Ha! It wouldn't take a rocket scientist to know that I was not the note's intended target. I forwarded it to its rightful recipient, Molly, and we read it together.

I couldn't help noticing you noticing me before orientation. If you're open for free time tomorrow, maybe we could check out the lake together. Meet me at the Arrowhead trailhead 2:30. Bring your friend. Jake (with the blue eyes).

Molly gave me a discreet low five. "Out of the palm of my hand," she whispered triumphantly.

———

"Do y'all think Director Leavitt would go out with a younger woman?" Sierra asked, sticking a small gold rhinestone onto her drying red toenail. "The man is a pure specimen of hotness."

"Dating him would be against the law," Syrup replied knowingly. She was lying on her bed, pointing and flexing the toes of her gigantic monster-feet slippers. "He's a grownup and you're, what, fifteen?"

"Eww," Molly concurred. "Mr. Leavitt might be good-looking for an older guy, but he seems to have the personality of Shredded Wheat. His orientation was a snooze fest." She flipped her wet hair forward and wrapped a towel around her head. Even in the absence of makeup and hair, she still managed to look airbrushed. Her skin reminded me of a wedding cake draped in rich, caramel fondant—smooth and flawless. I touched my own face but quickly dropped my hand in disappointment.

"Okay, then, so forget Mr. Leavitt. What about Security Phil? Wasn't he dreamy?" Sierra's joke elicited a unanimous groan from everyone in the cabin. Apparently, I wasn't the only one revolted by Overlook's night patrol.

Molly scooted next to me on my mattress and put her hand on my shoulder. "Did you see Jake staring at me all throughout dinner? It was so obvious. He's all about me."

"Yeah, totally," I said, yawning. It had been a long day, and I was counting down the minutes until lights out.

"You're coming on the hike with us tomorrow, right?"

"I don't think so, Molly. I don't want to be the third wheel."

"I'm sure there will be other guys there, too. Why else would Jake tell me to bring a friend?"

I shrugged. Truth be told, the thought of hanging out with boys liquefied all of the solids in my digestive tract. "I'm sure you'll do fine without me."

"You want to see the lake, don't you? But you know that you're not allowed to hike by yourself. Here's a thought"—she leaned in close—"maybe you could take Claire as your buddy. Wouldn't that be fun?"

I looked up at Claire, who was on her top bunk reading some hardcore music magazine with a *cross-me-and-die* expression on her face. "May I remind you that you don't even like to hike?" I said. "Remember?"

"Come on, Kaitlin. Puhleeeze!" She pouted her perfectly glossed lips and batted her meticulously separated eyelashes. While her feminine wiles did little to weaken my resolve, I knew if I were of the male population, I'd be toast.

I shook my head.

"But Kaitlin, it's for the greater good."

I was pretty sure she wasn't talking about helping the starving children in Darfur. "Sorry, Molly."

"You're my friend, aren't you? I'd do the same for you in a heartbeat." Of all the words to use, she chose the f-word. Friend. No one had referred to me as that in several years. The word was a siren song, alluring and beautiful, beckoning me to do something that would surely lead to my demise.

"Fine. I'll go," I huffed and reached down into my duffle bag for my anti-anxiety drug of choice. I unscrewed the lid and wrapped my plastic spoon in a gorgeous gob of cookie butter.

Syrup swooped in from nowhere, seized the spoon from my hand, and shoved it into her mouth. "You know this stuff will kill ya, right?" She held the butter on her tongue for a moment, then swished it around, allowing the mixture to burrow cavities into her every molar and bicuspid, and then gulped loudly. I stared in alarm as Syrup helped herself to two more bites and then passed the jar to Aya, who cringed her overly lined eyes and forwarded the jar and spoon to Sierra.

"On a diet?" Sierra inquired, taking a heaping spoonful to prove that she, herself, wasn't.

"It's not that," said Aya quietly. Her already pale skin had a sudden greenish tint to it. "It's just that I haven't felt very good tonight. Maybe it was the meatloaf."

"Did you blow chunks or what?" asked Syrup, a bizarre hopeful glimmer in her eyes.

"Oh, uh . . . no," said Aya. "I mostly just feel weird, like something isn't quite right. It's hard to explain."

"That's where it all begins," said Claire mysteriously from her top bunk. We all looked up, surprised. We hadn't realized that she'd been paying attention. "Next thing you know . . ." she made a gruesome slicing sound while running her index finger across her neck.

"And what's that supposed to mean?" asked Sierra with some difficulty, as her mouth was sticky with cookie butter.

"Like I'd tell *you*, Fire Crotch," Claire snapped. She flipped the page of her magazine and then rolled over, exiting the conversation as quickly as she had entered it.

Sierra scowled, Molly patted a dab of moisturizer into her face, and Aya gently massaged her neck with a confused and worried expression on her face. With that, I snatched back my cookie butter and hastily screwed on the lid. It was half gone and, when it came to cookie butter, one could only be so generous . . . even with, *dare I say it*, new friends.

ASHLEY

Ashley waddled up the driveway wearing a loose-fitting T-shirt and unbuttoned jeans. Despite the wardrobe adjustment, the clothes still felt clingy and uncomfortable in the warm, scratchy air. It was unfair how quickly the transformation had taken place. One day, her clothes fit reasonably well, and the next day, they didn't. One day, her belly button was cute and concave, and the next day it actually looked like a button. No way around it. Ashley was starting to show. It wouldn't be long now until the entire sophomore class was lit up about the girl who had gotten herself knocked up.

Ashley swung open the front door and tossed her keys onto the front room couch. She veered into the kitchen but jumped backward abruptly at the sight of her mother, Janice, sitting rigidly at the kitchen table.

"Mom! You scared me. Why aren't you at work?"

Janice had a very serious expression on her face. She patted the chair next to her. "You ready to talk?"

"'Bout what?" Ashley said quietly, inching forward.

"I've been waiting around for two weeks, thinking that surely you'd come to me on your own. You weren't planning on doing this all by yourself, were you?"

"Doing what?" Since Ashley had already committed to the innocent act, she might as well follow through.

"This!" Janice exploded. She lifted Ashley's T-shirt, exposing her daughter's swollen belly. "Now sit down and let's talk!"

Ashley did what she was told.

"What's wrong with you—getting pregnant at sixteen? So irresponsible, so selfish! I taught you better than this . . . at least I thought I did. Obviously, I messed up somewhere."

"No, Mom," Ashley looked at the floor. "You're a great mom."

"What a mess," Janice stood up and paced the room. "Did you think about who's going to pay for this child? Did you?"

"Insurance will help, won't it?"

"Our insurance is nonsense! I've told you that over and over."

"Maybe the government has some sort . . ."

"Of program? Yeah, right. The second I noticed your little screwup, I made a bunch of phone calls. Guess what I learned? I learned that I make just enough money that we don't qualify for any of those programs. But when your dad died, he left us all this debt and no life insurance policy. Even though we don't have a penny to spare, the government likes to pretend we do. God bless America."

"I'm so sorry, Mom." And Ashley was. She'd known better, and she hated disappointing her mother.

"You were going to be something, Ashley. With your grades and test scores, you could've been a lawyer or an architect or anything you wanted. Now, you'd be lucky to be promoted to manager of Taco Mania without a degree."

"I can still go to college, Mom. I still really want to. It will just be trickier with a baby."

"That's what I said, too." Though Janice was only in her early thirties, her hair was wiry with grays, and her lips were pulled downward by thin etched lines.

Tears now dripped from Ashley's cheeks onto the table below, the sight of which seemed to moisten Janice's mood slightly.

"Have you seen a doctor yet? No, of course you haven't. We need to find an obstetrician; I'll make some calls. Then we'll get you prenatal vitamins and find you some suitable maternity clothes."

Ashley nodded, her chest heaving too violently to speak.

"Oh goodness gracious, child, come here." Ashley stood up, and Janice pulled her into a rigid embrace. "It was that Luke kid, wasn't it?"

Ashley nodded, her chin bobbing on and off her mother's shoulder.

"Is he going to open his wallet?"

Ashley shook her head, her throat still too pinched with emotion to speak.

Janice sighed again and brushed her calloused hands through her daughter's hair. "Look, I know this seems pretty horrible right now, and it is, but I'll fix it. I'm always fixing things for you."

Just as Ashley had predicted, her mother was taking charge of the situation, but not as predicted, Ashley felt relieved. Lighter. She wasn't alone in this. She could do it with help. Ashley melted into her mother's arms and absorbed the small sum of comfort they offered.

"By the way, Ashley, you'll be giving this baby up for adoption."

CHAPTER 4

KAITLIN

I was awake for at least ten minutes before I even considered opening my eyes. This was the first time in months that I had the luxury of getting up when my body, not the alarm clock, mandated, and I was planning on milking the moment for what it was worth. Granted, it was only 7:30, hardly a respectable sleep-in time in anyone's book. Still, it felt positively delicious slowly stretching and breathing in the musty cabin air with the knowledge that I had no immediate place to be.

"Kaitlin, you awake?"

That's when my ten minutes ended.

With all the energy I possessed, I cranked one eye open. From the top bunk, Molly's head dangled over me. I blinked and swatted the wisps of her hair out of my face.

"Yes! You *are* awake," she sang. "I'm starved. Wanna get breakfast?"

I half gurgled, half groaned as I rolled out of bed and closed the bathroom door behind me. Brilliant, I'd roped myself a BFF from a time zone several hours ahead of my own. And she was gorgeous. And she hated nature. But I guess I didn't have the luxury of being picky.

After showering and getting ready for the day, and then a satisfying breakfast of poached eggs, English muffins, and freshly squeezed orange juice, Molly and I made our way down the main path till it forked into several smaller trails. Most of the paths led to other bunkhouses, but we took the trail that led us through a narrow gap of pine trees and kept going till we reached the top of the amphitheater. We climbed down tiers of wooden seating to the bottom row, which faced an unlit fire pit. This was the location of our first summer class.

Sierra, Aya, and Syrup were clustered together at the edge of the row. A meter over, on the other edge of the row, sat Claire, all alone. Molly shook her head decisively and sat down by Syrup, giving me no choice but to take the spot directly next to the camp grouch. Claire scooted away from me several inches and, while I couldn't be sure, I think I heard the subtle gnashing of teeth.

Margaret, the instructor of the class, hippity-hopped her way down the tiers behind us, her hair, frizzy as the day before, springing upward with every step. "Goooood morning, ladies! You all look beau-ti-ful this morning, as does the weather. Don't you just want to drink the air up in one giant gulp?"

Like a bee in a field of poppies, Margaret buzzed from person to person and pollinated each of us with a leather-bound journal and a ballpoint pen. But her smile brightened, if possible, when she reached Claire. "Oh! I didn't know you'd be back this year! What a treat to see you again!"

Claire snatched the journal. "I bet it is."

I was taken aback. I'd assumed that everyone at camp was here for the first time. The other roommates exchanged looks, equally surprised.

Margaret backed away from Claire like a wounded hamster. "Uh, anyway . . . this class is called Meditation and Self Actualization. Every day, you'll have the opportunity to meditate and write in your journals. You can write about anything you want—your experiences at camp, the relationships you are building, dreams you've had . . . there are no wrong avenues to explore. We will meet once a week to discuss your entries or just chit chat about boys, or chocolate, or what-ev. I will collect your journals at the end of class and will return them to your bunks the next day. I know that some of you might want your thoughts to remain private. Rest assured, I'll keep everything you write strictly confidential." Margaret zipped her lips and threw away the imaginary key.

Aya raised her hand shyly. "If we're not being graded on our journals, why do you have to read them?"

"Awesome question! I read them to make sure that you're having a positive experience at Camp Overlook and to gauge how much personal progress you're making this summer. But essentially, I read them because I care."

Claire huffed loudly.

"Is there anything you want to add, Claire?"

"You don't give a steaming turd about any of us or our personal progress, and you know it." Claire glared at Margaret so fiercely that I watched for her head to explode.

But it didn't. Instead, Margaret's eyes softened with kindness and understanding. "Of course I care. That's the whole point of the journals."

"Well I, for one, am excited to get started," Sierra piped up, giving Claire a good old-fashioned stare down. "Journaling will be fun, even if some of y'all can't express yourself without flames shooting from your nostrils."

Several of us nodded in agreement. I think we all felt defensive when Claire challenged Margaret. It was like pinching off the wings of a colorful butterfly.

Margaret smiled and rolled out a yoga mat. "Now, before you write each day, you should take fifteen to twenty minutes to mentally prepare. I am going to demonstrate a few breathing and stretching techniques to help relax your bodies and clear your minds." She proceeded to huff and puff and contort her body in ways that gave us simply too much information about her personal anatomy. After thoroughly scarring us for life, she set us loose to write our first entries before our next class.

I wouldn't advertise it, but I was actually looking forward to this journaling project. I was good at writing, I liked it, and was grateful for the excuse to have an hour or two of alone time. I bade my roommates farewell and made my way up the wooden tiers. I spotted a poorly maintained trail sloping up the west side of the valley and hiked it for several hundred yards, pushing aside prickly weeds and plants, until I found the perfect spot on top of a crusty boulder. From so high, I could pick out stray campers here and there—a girl carrying a tennis racquet, a boy hanging out at a picnic table reading a book, another hobbling to the lodge for some reason or another.

Claire was easy to spot because of her hunched, stormy stride. As she marched forward, she pulled her journal from her pack and, without a second thought, lobbed it into the air. The journal sailed through the sky and landed in a thick tangle of bushes in the distance. I resolved then and there never to be caught on the receiving end of that belligerent arm.

But down to business. I forewent Margaret's stretching exercises and cracked the spine of my new journal. My pen glided across the page as I described Molly and my other bunkmates. I wrote about the mountains, camp meatloaf, and I may have mentioned the blue eyes of a certain male camper, even if he was miles out of my league. I kept writing until riled by the sound of campers heading in groups toward their next classes. I shut my journal and ran down the slope to meet Molly at the lodge for Rocky Mountain Wildlife.

Following class, lunch, and a ridiculous hour-long beautification ritual, Molly and I met Jake for our hike. He was leaning casually against the trailhead marker, his hair strategically disheveled and his eyes taking on an even deeper blue when paired against the mountain sky. By his slick posture and the slight smirk on his face, I suspected he knew exactly how good he looked.

Just as Molly had guessed, he was accompanied by two friends. I recognized them as the "football" players from the dining hall: one, a baby-faced boy—good-looking enough—with curly blond hair and a rounder physique, and the other, olive-skinned and dark brown eyed, slightly shorter than the other two, with wisps of brown hair peeking out from under his green backward baseball cap.

Molly strolled confidently over to the boys and offered her hand to Jake. "What's up? I'm Molly," she said in her best *you should see me in a bikini* voice.

"Jake," he grinned, revealing a crooked canine tooth, which, on him, didn't look like a flaw at all. "This is my buddy, Garrett." He gave his tow-headed friend a playful shove. "And that's Max," he gestured to his dark-haired friend who was just barely out of range.

"So, Molly," Garrett prodded, "Does your friend have a name, or should we just call her 'Exhibit B'?"

I felt the sudden urge to pull a cowardly lion and sprint to the safety of our cabin. The last time I had a non-school related conversation with a boy was in sixth grade about who could spit the farthest. I looked at Garrett. "Er . . . ah . . . " I rubbed my nose.

"This is Kaitlin," said Molly helpfully, putting her arm around my shoulder. "The coolest girl I know." An unearned complement being that we had only known each other for twenty-four hours.

"What's up, Kate? Thanks for hanging out with us," Jake smiled.

Hot prickles exploded under my skin. He smiled at me. He called me Kate. I liked it.

"I hope you girls are in shape," said Garrett, motioning toward the trail. "I hear it's a steep one."

"I'm ready. I even wore my hiking clothes," Molly adjusted her fanny pack, drawing special attention to her shorts, high-waisted but so short that her back pockets peeked out below the hemline.

The boys took note.

"Great then. Let's kick this mountain in the butt!" Garrett led the way, Jake followed, and Molly took his side, leaving me to fend for myself next to Max.

Molly and Jake flirted mercilessly all the way up the trail. She kept grabbing at his bicep and squealing outrageously every time she encountered a flying bug or heard the rustle of a nearby bush. And Jake slurped it all up, laughing loudly at her nonhilarious jokes and gallantly protecting her from the flying bugs and rustling bushes.

Watching the shameless hormone slinging gave me that same guilty feeling I got when watching steamy love scenes while at the movies with my folks. I lowered my eyes and tried to focus on the nooks and crannies of the trail. Max, sensing my discomfort, and perhaps commiserating, tried to engage me in conversation. It was a welcome distraction, though I'd surely fail to hold up my end of the dialogue.

"Nice day, huh?" he observed politely.

"Yep . . . I mean, yes . . . I think . . . er."

"How do you like camp so far?"

"It's good. There are . . . um . . . pinecones everywhere. I really like pinecones. Except the ones with sap on them, because they're, er, really sticky." *Oh my gosh, Kaitlin! Shake it off!*

Max was kind enough not to comment on my idiocy. "What classes did you take today?"

"Uh, Meditation and Self-Actualization with Margaret and then Rocky Mountain Wildlife with Tanji."

"Tanji, huh? I could swear that woman wouldn't know a moose from a mountain lion."

"Well, er, she wasn't the most spirited teacher in the world, but she did seem to know her stuff. Forward and backward, actually. Learned a lot. So . . . uh . . . how about you? What classes did *you* take?"

"We had Ropes and Knots by some counselor name Julio and then Dr. Forsythe taught a first aid course in the dining hall."

"That sounds . . . uh . . . neat."

"Yeah, if you like practicing CPR with dudes."

"No you didn't!" I exclaimed, forgetting to insert an awkward filler word.

"No, we actually didn't," he laughed, flipping his baseball cap forward. "I kid. The teacher gave us manikins and mouth guards. I just pretended my manikin was a Scandinavian super model, and the time just flew by."

"How romantic," I teased, surprised by my boldness.

"Helga thought so. She was practically begging for more by the end of class."

"Probably begging for you to use your toothbrush more often."

"Fair enough," Max laughed good naturedly. "So where are you from?"

"I'm from Colorado. A city called Aurora right outside of Denver."

"So, your drive here didn't take too long, then?"

"Naw, just a day, with an overnight stop at a motel. Not bad at all. So, uh, where did you come from?"

"California. I live just a few miles from the beach. I was going to spend the summer surfing with my friends but the 'rents won some sort of online raffle thing. The prize was a free summer stay for me at Camp Overlook, airfare and expenses included. The crazy thing is that they couldn't even remember entering the raffle. But they couldn't refuse a deal like that, so here I am, not an ocean in sight."

"Bummer, dude."

"Yeah, I was pretty mad at first but, I don't know, I might be having a change of heart. You're right about the pinecones; they're just awesome." He smiled teasingly, and suddenly, my awkwardness returned full force.

Lucky for me, the terrain was much steeper over the next half mile, and everyone was too winded to attempt conversation. We pushed upward but paused at a wide switchback to rehydrate and take in the view. Now, I was no stranger to beautiful mountains—I lived a hop, skip, and a jump away from some of nature's best—but the valley view from where we stood was something else entirely. It was the kind of spectacle for National Geographic covers, simply jaw-dropping in its vastness. "This must be what heaven looks like," I whispered.

"Funny, I thought heaven looked like a basketball court and a bottomless bowl of Ramen Noodles," Jake philosophized.

"Heaven, in my mind, has always been and will be a nude beach at sunset," said Garrett wistfully.

"Look there, it's our bunkhouse." Molly pointed to what appeared to be a small khaki Lego in the distance. She squinted and squished the cabin between her thumb and index finger.

From this position, it made sense why Camp Overlook was called Camp Overlook. From here, we had a bird's-eye view of all of camp—the pool, the lodge, the cabins, people parading as ants, everything. The vista extended far beyond the campground, though. A cascade of water gushed down the opposite mountain and slithered saucily through the valley. Trees huddled for miles, lathering the mountainsides with a rich green frosting.

I unzipped my hoodie and knotted it around my waist. Feeling the distinct sensation of someone's eyes on me, I quickly looked up and to see Jake watching me. And he was concentrating hard. Counting my freckles maybe? Decoding my ethnic makeup (a mixture of German, Scottish, and Native American, in case you were wondering)? My cheeks boiled, so I wiggled my nose and turned to face southward. That's when I noticed the building.

"What's that?" I said, pointing to the large structure rising above the trees a good distance south of camp, maybe ten miles away. Even from far away, the building looked strikingly like Camp Overlook's lodge but much larger. A bunch of satellites and antennae crowned the building, but its most notable headpiece was a bright blue helicopter.

"I didn't even know that place was there," said Garrett. "Looks like we've discovered the destination of our next adventure."

"I doubt we'd have time to make it all the way there and back in our three hours of free time. It's, like, fifty miles away," Molly panted, the notion of another long hike seeming to do her in.

"Who said anything about hiking it during the day?" Garrett rubbed his hands together mischievously. "I packed an extra set of flashlights for just such an occasion."

"And be subject to the wrath of Security Phil? Forget about it." Molly crinkled her lips as though she had an unpleasant taste in her mouth.

"Well, guys, I think the lake is just over that ridge. Ten more minutes and we're there," said Jake, entirely disinterested with mystery buildings and forbidden midnight hikes. Following his lead, we stowed away our water bottles and pressed forward till we reached the lake.

It wasn't a massive lake, smaller than a football field, but it was picturesque all the same—pines surrounding the shoreline, their silhouettes reflecting in the glistening water. Garrett, as if summoned by a force greater than himself, dropped his pack, ripped off his shirt, and hurled himself into the freezing-looking water. He surfaced with a yelp and tossed his head from side to side. "Oh, baby, that's refreshing! Care to join me, ladies?"

"Are you kidding?" cried Molly. "There are raw fish in that water."

"Raw fish," said Max quietly and smacked his forehead.

"How about you, Kaitlin? Swimsuit optional," Garrett's teeth chattered wickedly.

"Pass, but thanks," I yelled back.

"But lookie what I found!" he pulled a cobalt blue sneaker from the water. "If one can find such a magnificent shoe in this lake, imagine what other riches await? Diamonds, pearls, exotic imported cars . . ."

"No!" Molly and I yelled in unison.

"I have a better idea; why don't we take the canoes for a spin?" Jake motioned to the boats moored twenty yards down the shoreline. We agreed that the canoes sounded fun and walked down the beach, leaving Garrett in the freezing water to fend for himself. We found a pile of lifejackets and oars in the hollow of one of the canoes.

"How about a race?" Jake suggested as he helped Molly into a bright orange life preserver. He fastened the front clips of her jacket and smiled into her eyes.

"I'm game," Molly smiled back.

"Alright, then, me and Kaitlin versus you and Max."

My stomach flopped. Me and Jake. In a boat. Alone. Even my life preserver wouldn't be able to keep my head above water on this one.

Equally unenthused by this turn of events, Molly folded her arms and stuck out her lower lip. Max gave her a reassuring fist bump. "What do ya say we take these jokers down? Do you want the bow or stern?"

Molly hesitated. "I'll take the back of the boat?"

"Um, I've got the bow," I said to Jake and climbed unsteadily into the canoe. Jake pushed the boat into the water before climbing in himself.

Garrett, whose lips had turned an impressive shade of blue, swam between our two canoes and treaded water. "I guess that makes me the ref then." He cleared his throat and spoke in a deep official voice. "The first team to make it around the first buoy and then back to shore again will be the winners of the first unofficial Camp Overlook Canoe-apalooza. The prize, you ask? Bragging rights for the summer and the honor of giving me an hour-long full-body massage, preferably from the lady champion. On your marks, get set . . . GO!"

Jake and I had a rocky start. I hadn't been canoeing in several years, so it took me a moment to figure out how to position the oar and which direction to paddle. Then Jake and I struggled to unify our forward strokes. After some trial and error, and a lake full of laughing trout, Jake and I finally began gliding smoothly across the water. We beamed at each other in light of our newly discovered compatibility. My face muscles froze in the smile position long after Jake looked away.

Molly and Max were having less luck. Their canoe kept turning around in leisurely circles. Molly cursed—calling her oar names like "stupid piece of tree" and my personal favorite, "splinter of my life"—while Max chuckled and passed along a few good-natured steering tips. Soon enough, however, they were both laughing and had forgotten the competition all together. As Jake and I rounded the buoy, Molly and Max had floated several yards to the left of where they'd originally begun.

We reached the finish line triumphantly. Jake jumped to his feet in the canoe and executed a victory dance, complete with the floss and the rhythmic dusting of his shoulders. The canoe rocked ferociously, and I tried to counter-distribute my weight to keep us afloat.

"And I give you the Canoe-apalooza champiooooons!" Garrett proclaimed and swam next to the winning canoe, gripping the side. "I'll take that backrub any time, babe," he double clicked his tongue at me.

"Sure," I looked at my invisible watch. "Will a quarter to *never* work for you?" I reached into the water and gave Garrett a playful splash. Was I flirting? With boys? *Me?*

"I was actually feeling a kink in my neck right this minute. Man, I'm sore." Garrett pulled up on the side of our canoe and attempted to hoist his body inside. We were already off balance thanks to Jake's wobbly victory dance, but Garrett's extra weight did us in. The canoe listed to portside and then completely dumped Jake and me into the bitter-cold lake. I gasped as my life preserver popped me to the surface.

Molly and Max rolled with laughter from their canoe. "Hey, Garrett! Was a dip in the lake part of the prize package, too?" Max joked.

"Sorry, guys," called Garrett from beside the capsized boat. "I was getting lonesome in the water all by myself. You can't blame me."

"I am going to kill you, Garrett," Jake yelled and shook out his hair like a waterlogged husky.

"So, so cold," I sputtered, trying to catch my breath from the shock of the water.

Our life preservers made the swim back to the shore awkward and slow, and we had to crawl through the muck when the lake got shallow. Jake helped me get to my feet and allowed his fingertips to linger on mine for a few seconds longer than necessary. "So, you and I make a pretty decent team, eh? Do you want my jacket? I took it off before we got in the canoes."

"Uh . . . no thanks. My jacket is dry, too. I should be fine." My teeth chattered. I unbuckled my life jacket and wiped my face with my sopping wet T-shirt.

"If you say so." Jake pulled off his shirt and rung the water onto the ground. Droplets of lake water rippled down his skin, drawing attention to his deliciously wavy abdominal muscles. He wound the shirt into a tight roll and quickly snapped it at Garrett as he climbed out of the water.

"Dude!" Garrett whined, holding his arm dramatically.

Molly and Max pulled their canoe ashore. "Good run, guys," said Max. "We should probably head back to camp and get you three some dry clothes, though."

"What's the rush?" said Molly, mesmerized by half-naked Jake. He grinned and pulled his dry jacket over his bare chest. I put my jacket on, too, but within minutes it seemed just as soggy as the T-shirt below it.

As we hiked down the mountain, my tennis shoes squished and my clothes clung to my skin like drying wallpaper. Freezing cold and super perturbed, I silently began plotting ways to murder Garrett when suddenly I felt another jacket being slipped over my shoulders. It was big. It was cozy and smelled nice. It was Max's jacket.

———

Hallelujah. The cabin lights were off, and the only sounds left in the room were the rustling of sleeping bags and Syrup's rumbling snore. It had been a long day. I flipped on my flashlight and wrote Mom and Dad a quick letter about the campground, the lake, the food. I asked if Dad had gotten some work and if Mom had made the drive home safely. I didn't mention my new friends, not wanting to get their hopes up about my tenuous social skills, but I told them that I was enjoying myself and not to worry. I sealed the letter in an envelope and then opened a book, the best way to free my mind and offer my soul slowly to the sleep gods.

But the gods must've been in a picky mood because I just couldn't turn off my brain. I mean, I'd spent practically a whole afternoon with boys, cute ones, and I survived. Not only that, no one seemed to notice my extreme social impediment. Part of me felt like an impostor posing as a regular human girl, but maybe I wasn't posing. Maybe the kids at school were mistaken. Maybe I wasn't a freak at all. I found this thought endlessly reassuring. For the first time since I arrived at Camp Overlook, and frankly for the first time since the incident, I felt like I could breathe.

"Um, Kaitlin?" I looked up from my book to see Aya at my bedside, clasping her hands below her chin. Her thick black hair was braided into a loose ponytail, and the layers of black eye makeup had been washed away. She looked young, maybe only twelve. "Sorry to interrupt."

"It's no problem," I whispered and folded down the corner of my page. "What can I do for you?"

"I was wondering, and feel free to tell me no, but I was wondering if I could borrow something to read. I can't sleep."

"Yeah, of course." I wiggled out of my sleeping bag and stumbled to the dresser. I aimed my flashlight into the dark cavity of my drawer and let Aya thumb through my book collection.

"I should've thought to bring books," Aya said. "Why didn't I think of that?"

"Well,"—*yawn*—"I've got plenty to share."

"This is a good one," she said as she pulled out *A Tree Grows in Brooklyn*. "It's pretty sad about the dad. When she gets the roses from him on her graduation day . . . I think I cried for hours after that part." I could imagine gooey trails of black mascara streaming down her cheeks. "I guess it hit me so hard because I never had a dad to begin with. He died before I was born. He was pretty much a loser, though. That's what my mom says. I kind of miss him anyway. Is that dumb?"

"No way. It's not dumb. It actually makes perfect sense to me." Why Aya chose to shovel her family dirt on me was a mystery, but I couldn't lie, it felt good to be confided in.

"Shut up you two!" hissed Claire from her top bunk, flinging her pillow at sweet, innocent Aya's head. "How am I supposed to get any sleep with you two yapping like lapdogs?"

Aya, seemingly unfazed by Claire's shade, smiled at me and then goofily crossed her eyes. It was the first time I'd seen her be silly. She lifted the book up in the air, marking it as her final decision. She then picked Claire's pillow off the floor, handed it back up to Claire, who didn't say sorry or thank you, and climbed back into her sleeping bag.

PARKER

Parker didn't think all that much of Jason, either. He had reasons for this. There was the *my father likes you more than he likes me* reason, of course. Parker saw the way his father looked at Jason, with so much pride, love even. The guy wasn't even his own son!

Another reason not to like Jason, he was too pretty. Guys should never be as pretty as him, and Parker thought it a form of false advertising. When one would look at Jason's exterior package, they'd assume that something special was inside, but in reality, Jason had about as much personality as boiled eggplant.

Lastly, Jason had no manners.

"Moving in!" Jason pushed Parker's textbooks aside to make room for his own on the library table.

Case in point.

"You could've just asked," Parker mumbled, scooting his books and laptop to the farthest end of the table.

"The last time I asked you to move over, you told me to shove my books up my . . ."

"I had important things to study. You sitting next to me would have been a distraction."

"You assume that *your* studies are the most important. They are not."

"And yours are?"

"I'm studying the law. The information I learn will benefit thousands, maybe millions."

"That's what my father would like you to think," Parker yawned melodramatically.

"Your father is a genius."

"My father is a jackass."

Jason put his finger close enough to Parker's face that Parker could have leaned forward and taken a bite. "Your father," he said through gritted teeth, "will do more for humanity than all the greats combined—King, Mandela, Theresa, Einstein, all of them. You should be ashamed of yourself, Parker."

"Listen, I don't have to listen to you singing the praises of a man I know to be deeply flawed. I really should get back to studying."

"No, you listen to *me*, Parker. At this very moment, Douglas is studying the ins and outs of economics, and Keisha is getting her piloting license. Julio is seconds from mastering three different Middle Eastern languages, and Sam is reading his fourth book on quantum physics. Tomorrow morning, I will be on equal footing with every single one of them and they with me. Do you get what I'm trying to tell you? What we know matters. What you know doesn't."

"Just because I haven't been *called upon* yet . . ."

"Parker, if it was going to happen, you'd already be seeing the signs. Face it, you're nothing more than a useless counterpart."

"I hate you," Parker said.

"You don't hate me; you want to be me."

"Why would I want to be a tool like you?" Parker grabbed his textbooks and computer, shoved them in his backpack, and stormed out of the library.

Yeah, there were lots of reasons Parker didn't like Jason, but the main one was that Jason was an idiot.

CHAPTER 5

KAITLIN

We arranged our towels along the edge of the pool and stripped down to our bathing suits. In harmony with her painted toenails, Sierra sported a bright red bikini with shiny gold beading. My swimsuit, which I'd purchased on clearance at Target, was emerald green and slightly less bedazzled. Aya blushed as she stepped out of her shorts, unveiling a conservative black one piece. I couldn't tell exactly whether she was embarrassed by showing too much skin or embarrassed by showing too little.

The air hovered at a steady sixty-five degrees, still too nippy for the pool, but the hot tub looked nice. We lowered our bodies into the water and breathed in the heavenly scent of simmering chlorine. I'd take this over yesterday's dip in the lake any day.

"So, where's Molly right now?" Sierra asked me, her eyes closed and head relaxed against the hot tub wall.

"Oh, she's at the rec room playing foosball with Jake."

"Figures." Sierra made a sour face. "No offense, I know y'all are tight, but girls like her always choose hanging out with boys over their friends."

"Oh, it's okay. She told me that Jake asked her, like, as a date thing," I explained. In truth, I felt a mixture of jealousy and relief that I wasn't included in his invitation. "So, where's Syrup?"

"She's busy flipping rocks over in search of bugs, I think. That girl's a riot; cracks me up," Sierra chuckled.

"Well, I'm glad I'm here with you guys. I needed to get out of the stuffy cabin for a few minutes." Aya's voice sounded brittle, as if it might shatter into a billion pieces if she sneezed or coughed.

"Are you feeling any better today?" I asked.

"I don't know, maybe. I didn't fall asleep until after two last night, and when I finally did, it was crappy junk sleep, if you know what I mean. "

"Was Syrup snoring again?" Sierra asked. "I was so tired from our late night that she could have snored the Star-Spangled Banner and I wouldn't have woken up."

"Syrup was definitely snoring," Aya forced a feeble giggle, "but she wasn't the problem. I kept waking up, my mind reeling, from these weird dreams. It would take me another half an hour to fall back asleep, but then I'd have another dream and wake back up."

I reached over to turn on the jets. "What were you dreaming about?"

"Something about numbers, I think. And maybe robots. I don't even remember now. You know how it goes with dreams."

"Well, I sure as heck remember my dream from last night," said Sierra, snickering wickedly at the recollection. "It involved me, Claire, some pliers, and a certain nose ring. Y'all, it was glorious."

I laughed guiltily. "Yeah, it got a little heated between you two a few nights ago."

"That was nothing compared to what happened yesterday. Y'all know how I stood up for Margaret at our meditation class? After that, Claire stared me down, like literally, the rest of class. And she was smiling in a cheeky *I know something you don't know* way. So at the end of class, I asked what her problem was, and you know what she said? She said, 'What's *your* problem, lab rat?' She called me a lab rat."

"I've heard much worse coming from her mouth," mused Aya.

"It was just rude. Like, how was I supposed to take that? Lab rat," Sierra repeated, shaking her head.

"I saw Claire throw her journal into the bushes yesterday. Maybe she's mad that Margaret is analyzing her thoughts," I theorized.

"Margaret isn't some crazy psychologist, she's a dorky camp counselor. She could sip thoughts from my brain with a straw and a paper umbrella, and I still wouldn't care."

"I feel bad for Claire," said Aya, who let her hands float along the foamy surface of the water. "She doesn't have any friends here. She's probably really lonely."

"I don't feel sorry for her at all," said Sierra, lifting herself out of the spa so that only her legs were dangling in the water. "She doesn't have to dress like an Emo freak and treat everyone like they are less than. She's a witch, and I hope she leaves camp early."

I didn't like Claire and was maybe a little afraid of her, but I felt bad for her, too. It was hard being a loner, even if it was by her own doing. I knew I should reach out to her, but befriending someone like Claire would drain whatever social cred I'd earned over the last few days.

"Aya," I asked, turning to face my young friend, "have you seen Dr. Forsythe yet? He might be able to do something or to give you something to help you feel better."

"I was hoping this'd go away by itself, but it *has* been three days . . ."

"I'll go with you to see him if you want, for a little moral support."

"Well, okay, if you think he could help out." Aya sent me a grateful smile, and my conscience was temporarily appeased. We dried ourselves off, said goodbye to Sierra, and went to the lodge. Dr. Forsythe seemed pleased to see us and had Aya sit on the examining table.

"Brleeehh!" she recoiled as Dr. Forsythe pulled the tongue depressor from her throat.

He gave a hearty chuckle. "You think I'd be able to hold it in after the hundreds of throat swabs I've done. I apologize for laughing at your expense, Miss Aya. Unfortunately, I find the gag reflex a little amusing. Yours was particularly good."

Aya and I exchanged a look and then giggled ourselves. Aya's shoulders lifted, and her cheeks regained a touch of color. Dr. Forsythe had a way of making you feel like you had a belly full of hot chocolate.

"I'll get this culture analyzed to rule out strep. Truth be told, the symptoms you described—nausea, fatigue, headaches—seem more viral to me. Medicine would do little but mask your symptoms. I recommend drinking lots of fluids and taking naps during the day."

Aya frowned.

"Be of good cheer. At least you'll have an excuse to ditch a couple of Tanji's riveting lectures on Rocky Mountain Biology. Doctor's orders."

We giggled again.

"There's one other possibility we shouldn't dismiss. In situations like these— leaving one's family and friends for the summer, sleeping in a new bed, having new experiences—it's not uncommon for one to catch a minor case of the blues."

"Huh?" said Aya.

"Depression, my dear."

"But I don't feel sad, just exhausted."

"Did you know that depression often manifests itself through physical symptoms? Like tummy troubles or sleeping disturbances. You mentioned both of these problems."

"Well, yeah."

"I am certainly not diagnosing you with depression at the moment, but I'm hesitant to rule it out. I suggest that as you put effort into resting your body, you also pay attention to your mental health. Listen to your mind. After waking, try to remember your dreams and how they made you feel. Writing is an excellent therapeutic tool, so I suggest you record your thoughts into the journal Margaret gave you. Between resting, hydrating, and writing, I imagine that you'll feel better within the week. If not, please see me again."

He turned to me. "Miss Kaitlin, I leave Aya in your care. Make sure she doesn't push herself too hard, and for heaven's sake, try to keep a smile on her face. If by chance you find yourself with similar symptoms, please stop by my office, and we'll talk about it. I care deeply about the well-being of my little campers. More than you know."

"It's getting too hot. It's gonna catch on fire. Watch it! Watch it! Ohhhhh!"

I lifted my gooey fireball out of the flames and blew it out with three frantic puffs.

"Told you so," said Garrett, who had been harassing everyone at the bonfire with advice on toasting the perfect marshmallow.

"I don't mind my mallows crispy," said Max. He sandwiched my marshmallow between his two graham crackers and pulled the sticky mess off of my roasting stick. He quickly restocked my poker. "There you go, a fresh start."

"Thanks," I said and lowered the new marshmallow above the glowing embers, a smidgen higher that time.

The night began with all Overlook campers huddling together on the tiers of the amphitheater while the leaders lit the summer's first camp bonfire. We sang a bunch of dorky campfire songs and then migrated closer to the fire, warming our hands and stuffing our faces with s'mores.

Jake and the boys had made a point of sitting with Molly and me. It was like they'd officially crowned us their girls for the summer. The five of us joked around, swapped funny stories, and even poked good-natured fun at each other's expense. The whole time I felt like I was outside my body, hovering above the fire, and watching myself in awe. Is that really *me* down there? Did I *really* just wink at Jake? Did he *really* tell me that my eyelashes were the longest he'd ever seen? And was it just me, or were the other campers watching us, envying us, maybe wanting to join in our fun?

My excitement reminded me of the day I got my first training bra. Sure, I felt a little awkward and nervous at first, but mostly I was thrilled. I had entered the changing room a caterpillar and come out a double-A-sized butterfly. Likewise, I'd come to Overlook a "dork" but now, just look at me, I was part of a clique— the cool kids' clique. And it felt amazing. But C-cup amazing. This must've been how my nemesis, Mia Bethers, felt every day while roaming the halls of our high school with her squad of good-looking friends. The sense of belonging was powerful and exhilarating.

"There you go again!" cried Garrett, interrupting my thoughts. "There-you-go-a-gain!" He clapped in time to his words, like an exasperated schoolteacher.

I looked down at my second marshmallow. It was on fire.

Jake blew it out this time. He took me in with those incredible eyes of his and laughed. "You seem to have a knack for sticky situations."

"Your face is a sticky situation, Jake," Garrett retorted.

"Oh yeah, well your mama is a sticky situation."

"Did you know that marshmallows are fat-free?" said Molly, licking the edge of her s'more. "That means I can eat as many as I want and not gain a pound."

"I hear that cooking the tar out of 'em also lowers the calorie count," said Max. "At least Kaitlin seems to think so."

I gave Max a little shove. "Oh, really? Well, I hear that eating burned marshmallows lowers your brain cell count. At least Max seems to think so."

"Are you saying that your cooking has made me stupider?"

"Would that be possible?" I giggled.

"How many calories less?" asked Molly, in all seriousness.

"So, Kate," Jake said, placing his arm around my shoulder, "you missed a great game of foosball today. What could be more important than hanging out with us?"

"Kaitlin decided to go the pool during free time," Molly quickly volunteered. "Can't you see her fresh tan? She looks hawt."

"Well, we missed you. Next time, there will be no excuse. I mean it." Jake nudged me playfully with his hip.

Molly grabbed his arm and gently pulled him away from me. "And *next time* you won't let me win at foosball, right?"

"No, you won fair and square, Molly. I was too distracted by your beauty to play my A-game."

My stomach churned, and surprisingly not in response to the *gag-me-with-a-stick* flirtation between Jake and Molly. I didn't know that I had been invited to play foosball today. Did Molly forget to tell me? Did she forget on purpose? I tried to convince myself that it didn't matter; I wouldn't have bailed on Sierra and Aya even if a more enticing offer had come along.

I looked for my bunkmates in the crowd of campers. Aya wasn't there, obviously, as she was already in bed trying to catch up on sleep. Claire was also nowhere to be seen. She was probably in the craft room making voodoo dolls so she could cast terrible spells on us. But Sierra was sitting next to Syrup, a couple of tiers above us. Her head was parked between her hands as she watched our group longingly. I caught her eye and waved. She perked up, grabbed Syrup by the hand, and dragged her down the tiers. Apparently, she took my wave as an invitation to join us.

"Thank you, thank you, thank you!" she mouthed.

"Uh, sure," I said.

"Did you know that your marshmallow's all burned?" said Syrup, motioning to my stick.

"Oh, uh, thanks for letting me know." I shook the brittle mass onto the dirt.

Max leaned over and gave the girls a small wave. "Hey, I'm Max."

"Hi," Sierra squeaked. "This is Syrup, and I'm Sierra. I'm from Texas."

"Cool," said Max. "I like your accent."

"Thanks," she squeaked again.

"That over there is Garrett, and the ugly guy next to him is Jake." Garrett and Jake nodded, and I crossed my fingers that Sierra would maintain bladder control.

"So, what part of Texas are you fr—" Max begun, but paused distractedly as Garrett tossed a few empty soda cans into the fire. "Whoa. Is it that time already?"

"Time for what?" Sierra asked.

The guys just snickered. Garrett reached into his bag and pulled out three black garbage bags, handing one to Max and one to Jake. They pulled the trash bags over their jackets and pushed their heads and arms through the plastic.

"Ummmm . . . what are those for?" Molly asked nervously.

"Homemade ponchos," Jake grinned.

"But why?"

Just then, the fire emitted three deafening booms. Campers screamed as a gooey, sickly sweet substance shot out in every direction from the flames.

Reflexively, I ducked behind Max. Other campers dropped to the ground, covering their eyes with their hands. Too late. Every camper around the fire was now drenched in a warm, bubbly orange substance.

"What was in those soda cans you threw in the fire, Garrett?" Molly screamed, wiping goop out of her eyebrows.

Max, Jake, and Garrett doubled over laughing, crinkling, and shaking as they rolled around in their makeshift raincoats. It took them a good minute to regain enough composure to answer her question, but even still, their hysteria left them gasping for air. "They weren't empty soda cans," Garrett mustered. He clenched his stomach and rolled into a rigid ball. "They were cans of pork and beans! Paaaaah!"

"Gross!" screamed Molly, shaking the slop off of her arms. "I am covered in baked beans . . . and pork!" Her outburst only magnified the convulsing of the boys on the ground. She kicked each boy in the side, not hard but with anger and disgust, and stormed back toward our cabin. Sierra and Syrup followed close behind.

All around me, girls were whimpering about the bean shrapnel in their hair, guys were scooping up leftover bean puddles and slinging it playfully at one another, and everyone else, thinking along the same lines as Molly, was bolting up the wooden tiers in hopes of avoiding a line for the shower.

As for me, I stood there examining the damage done to my clothes. I looked like I'd been tie-dyed in soup. Bean avalanches had carved sticky trails down my jacket and pooled at my zipper. There were, like, ten beans down there. It was actually pretty funny.

I fought back the instinct to start laughing myself—I didn't want to give the boys the satisfaction—and put on my most fierce-looking face. I unzipped my hoodie and tossed it on the ground. Then I clenched my fists at my hips and peered sternly over the remorseless perpetrators still twitching in the dirt. "First of all, someone could have been seriously injured by your thoughtless prank. It was scary and rude and very dangerous! You are lucky someone wasn't hurt," I chided.

"Sure, Mom," Garrett snorted.

"Second of all, you can mark my words, boys, you have not seen the end of this. Molly and I will get you back so big and so ugly that after all the beans settle, you will be begging us for mercy."

"That's some big talk from such a little woman," Jake retorted.

"Bring it," challenged Max.

"Oh, we will!" I stared the guys down till they pulled themselves off the ground, high-fived each other like a group of proud athletes, and hightailed it all the way up the tiers, their garbage bag ponchos crinkling as they went.

I shook my head and then lingered by the fire to quickly roast a marshmallow to bring back to Aya. I pulled the hot marshmallow off the stick with a graham cracker and turned to grab my hoodie and head back to the cabin.

That's when I realized that I was the only one left at the fire pit.

It was an eerie feeling finding myself completely alone in the wilderness. It was so quiet and dark. I felt like the night sky could wash over me at any minute, and I'd be gone for good. The crackling fire, which seemed so fun and inviting only seconds before, now sounded loud and menacing. I wanted to run back to the cabin but was afraid to move, like traveling alone through the dark would make me even more vulnerable to wild animals and boogeymen.

What was even more terrifying than finding myself alone when I thought I wasn't, however, was finding myself with company when I thought I was alone.

Long, bony hands wrapped themselves around my shoulders, and I could feel the cold fingertips touch my skin one by one. My heart skipped a beat.

I would like to say that it was Jake or Max coming to escort me back to my cabin. It wasn't, though. It wasn't Molly or Sierra, either. It was probably the last person I wanted to be touched by in the dead of the night. It was Security Phil.

"Good evening, Kaitlin," he said, his hands still grasping me from behind. He knew my name. Why did he know my name?

"Um . . . I was just heading back to the cabin right now. My friends are waiting for me and . . ."

"You shouldn't be out here alone. You never know what sort of unsavory character might be roaming the woods at night." His voice was raspy. Or was it screechy? Whatever sound his voice made, it was making it directly in my ear. I could feel the revolting vapors of his breath in my brain.

"I'll remember that for next time." I was shaking, really shaking now.

"I know things about you, Kaitlin. Things you don't. Things you wouldn't want to know." Wasn't it Phil's job to patrol the camp and keep everyone safe? Right now, he was doing the complete opposite, threatening me and scaring the crap out of me.

"Please," I whispered. "Please, can I go to my bunkhouse now?"

"And I'll be watching you."

I didn't wait one second longer. I writhed out of his grasp and ran, I mean *ran*, up the tiers and all the way back to the safety of the cabin, all the while squishing the heck out of poor Aya's s'more.

ASHLEY

Back and forth. Back and forth. Back and forth. Ashley pushed her legs outward and then pulled them back in again. She liked the squeak the steel links made as they curved against each other. The moment of weightlessness when the swing paused and switched directions brought her back to a time when problems came in the form of melted ice cream and balled up roly-polies. That time was not long ago.

"My mom is making me give the baby up for adoption," Ashley said, finally, quietly.

"What!" Jade gasped from the swing beside Ashley's. "We've been at the park for, like, twenty minutes, and you're only telling me this now?"

"I didn't want to say it out loud."

"Why? Because you want to keep the baby or because you're relieved?"

"Maybe both." Ashley shrugged.

"I can't believe it! Adoption. It's, like, so completely obvious! Why didn't we think of it ourselves? Of course!" Jade bopped her forehead with the palm of her hand.

"I know. It would fix everything. I wouldn't have to drop out of school, I'd get to hang out on the weekends, the medical bills would be taken care of, college would be back on the table. It's the perfect solution."

"Then why are you crying?"

The tears felt cold as they streamed to the sides of Ashley's face. She lowered her legs and let her toes scrape the gravel beneath her. The swing slowed to a gentle sway. She sniffed. "Because I felt the baby move today."

"Cute!" Jade said, completely missing the heaviness of the moment.

"I felt my baby move. *My baby*. I made it and I am growing it, so I should keep it."

"Your mom can't make you give it up if you don't want to. You've told her how you feel, right?"

"Yeah. She told me that I don't really love the baby, that I want a doll to play dress up with." She sighed. "I don't know, maybe she's right. You and I keep talking about how fun a baby would be and how cute it would look in feety pajamas. There's more to a baby than those things. I can't give this baby everything it needs."

"Then adoption it is."

"But I felt him move."

Ashley and Jade sat quietly, their swings waving to the gentle cadence of the wind. Jade peeked at Ashley. "What did it feel like?" she whispered.

Ashley thought. "Pump your legs," she said.

"What?

"Pump. You know, in and out. Pump."

Jade obeyed, slowly climbing higher and higher in the sky.

"Harder," Ashley commanded.

And Jade leaned back and pushed her legs out, pulling back in with equal force.

"Now jump."

Instantly, Jade let go of the swing and sailed through the air. Her feet hit the ground, and she tottered palms first into the gravel.

"What did that feel like?" Ashley asked.

"Like a sprained wrist." Jade pushed herself up and brushed her dusty hands on her jeans.

"No, when you were flying. What did it feel like?"

"Um, well, it felt a little scary, but fun. My stomach felt all tickly and strange. It felt good."

Ashley nodded. "That's how it felt when the baby moved."

CHAPTER 6

KAITLIN

"Whoa!" Molly gripped the reigns of her horse so tightly that her knuckles took on the chalky color of toothpaste. "I don't know what to do! This horse is out of control!"

I smiled. Molly's horse was about as lazy as lemonade on a Sunday afternoon. The only thing out of control was Molly's respiration.

Claire whizzed past us on her brown mare. Because she'd certified the previous summer, the instructor had given her permission to gallop around the indoor arena. Claire had made a show of lapping us, each time inching a little closer to Molly's horse, probably trying to scare it into bucking. Claire wasn't exactly smiling, but with the jaunty way she bounced in her saddle, it seemed as though she was enjoying herself—whether it was because she loved riding or because she loved freaking out Molly was yet to be understood.

"I hate this, I hate this, I hate this," Molly chanted.

"It's just a horse," I said, stroking the mane of the chestnut creature beneath me.

"It's not *just* a horse," she trembled. "It's . . . it's like a symbol . . . a symbol of everything I am not."

"Okay?" I prompted.

"If you must know, when I was ten, my parents bought me and my little sister a horse to share. The horse was named Herbert, which was a stupid name for a horse, but whatever. They said that riding was a good sport for smart and responsible girls. Anyhow, Mom had bought us all these cute riding outfits—black helmets, matching riding boots, frilly white shirts. I looked great, and I was so excited for our first lesson.

"My sister went first. She was only seven, but she wasn't scared at all. She got on Herbert, and she did great. She's great at everything she does. When it was my turn, I wasn't scared, either. I put on my helmet and marched straight over to Herbert. The teacher helped me onto the saddle, but Herbert started freaking out for no reason. He bucked, just a little, but enough to knock me off. I didn't get hurt, but I cried for hours. I refused to ride him ever again."

"Your parents didn't make you try again?"

"No. They said that I was right; riding wasn't for me. They signed me up for baking lessons instead."

"Fun," I said, unsure whether to sound sarcastic or encouraging.

"You know, over the last few years, my sister has won sixteen medals on Herbert. My parents would drag me to all of her equestrian shows, and I'd watch as she'd jump and do tricks, just like a smart and responsible girl."

"Yes, but you can't frost a horse with chocolate and eat it. Well, I mean, technically you could, but I wouldn't."

"I quit baking classes, too."

"Oh."

Claire zoomed past us again, flouring Molly and her horse in another layer of dust. The horse tossed its head from side to side, and Molly began to panic, screaming like a banshee and sliding herself off the saddle. Her foot caught the stirrup, and she squirmed around until her bum hit the ground and her right leg was twisted awkwardly at the horse's side. It was all so dramatic and funny looking that I started to laugh. I couldn't help it. I dismounted my horse and helped Molly untangle her foot.

"I might have been killed, you know? If the horse had been running, it would have dragged me, and I would've hit my head, and I would've died."

"Molly, you *chose* to fall off the horse." I grabbed Molly's hands and pulled her to her feet.

"If I didn't fall, he would've knocked me off. I hate horses, and horses hate me."

I laughed a little harder. And then, when Molly realized how ridiculous she sounded, she began to laugh as well.

I squinted, licked my lips, and released my index finger. The paper football sailed through the air and glided seamlessly through Max's outstretched fingers. The table erupted into ovation.

"Field goal!" Jake exclaimed, pointing both arms in the air.

My back was slapped, my hair was tousled, and I was congratulated with a bunch of grunts and high fives. I jumped up on my chair and imitated Jake's canoe-rocking victory dance, even dusting my shoulders with a proud, rhythmic swagger.

"What has gotten into you?" Molly hissed in my ear as I slid back down in my chair. "You're like a whole different person than when I met you."

I took this as a compliment. A week into camp and I was finally feeling completely comfortable with myself amidst my new friends. This, teamed with my newly acquired football skills, were cause to flex, and flex I would!

The boys had invited themselves to sit at our bunk's dinner table this evening. Sierra, thrilled to be part of the in crowd, had fallen silent and simply basked in the glory of the "smokin' hot" guys. She didn't even touch her dinner. When Max asked her to pass the breadsticks, she giggled absentmindedly and handed him the water pitcher instead.

"Thanks," Max said in a confused tone. He paused for a moment and then poured himself a glass of water.

Claire snorted.

"So, Kaitlin, those were some pretty sick football skills. I wasn't aware that you were an athlete," teased Jake.

"Oh, there are a great many things you don't know about me," I said saucily. "For instance?"

"For instance," Molly piped in, a little snidely if you asked me, "did you know that Kaitlin still sleeps with a blankie?"

All eyes turned to me.

Okay, so I couldn't part with my blankie for the three months of camp. Sure, its vibrant pink threads had long since morphed into a dingy gray, but I still loved it, still needed it. The blanket got me through some pretty rough patches, including but not limited to the incident. I was practically indebted to it. I kept it tucked snugly into my sleeping bag and thought no one had noticed it.

"You know, I have a friend who sleeps with a stuffed rhino," said Max quietly, throwing Garrett a sly look and then smiling down at his plate.

Syrup raised her hand and started wiggling in her chair.

"Syrup," I called on her, mostly because her wiggling was making me feel uncomfortable.

"The horn on the rhinoceros is made of matted hair, not bone, like a gigantic dread lock poking out of its face."

"Thanks for sharing," Jake mumbled sarcastically.

"Animal Planet." Syrup pointed at Jake and double clicked her tongue.

"Alright, I admit it!" Garrett exploded, seemingly out of nowhere. He threw his hands into the air in exasperation. "So I have a stuffed rhino. Big deal! It brings me luck with the ladies."

"You might want to consider investing in a different good luck charm," suggested Jake. "I think the rhino is broken."

"Shut up; I get tons of girls," he said defensively. "And thanks for throwing me under the bus, Max."

"Hey man, I didn't say *who* had the rhino. You did that all on your own."

I smiled at Max gratefully. I wondered if he knew that he had deflected the attention away from me, saving me from extreme embarrassment. I suspected that had been the plan all along.

"And what are *your* deepest darkest secrets, Jake?" asked Molly, flipping her sumptuous brown hair behind her shoulder.

"Just that I like roses, long walks on the beach, cuddling, and lengthy emotional conversations about relationships . . ."

"Oh, stop!" Molly giggled and gave him a wimpy smack on the arm, as if his joke wasn't a complete cliché.

"Uh, Kaitlin?" whispered Max, careful that Sierra couldn't hear. "Would *you* pass me the breadsticks? I really like them."

I reached over Aya and passed Max the breadbasket. "Here you go."

"Thanks. Oh, and I think it's kind of cute that you still have a blankie. I just hope it gets a good washing every now and then," he winked.

It was the first time that I noticed that Max had a dimple.

I continued pondering on the dimple until Director Leavitt entered the dining hall wearing another designer suit and enough hair gel to fuel a rocket ship to the moon. He walked stiffly to the front of the room, which happened to be right in front of our table, and cleared his throat loudly. From so close, I could better appreciate his polished appearance: dark skin, smooth fingernails, orderly eyebrows, steel-colored eyes. Something about him was strangely familiar to me, but I couldn't quite put my finger on what.

"It's good to see you all again. I trust that everyone is having a great time at Camp Overlook." I realized that this was only the second time I'd seen Director Leavitt since camp had begun. What had he been doing all week? By looking at his crisp exterior, my first guess would've been aggressively grooming himself.

"I'm stepping in to inform you of a new development. Margaret, Tanji, and I have discussed it and we feel that your stalwart behavior over the last week has earned you a bit of a treat. Therefore, I would like to announce that we will be throwing a dance the second week of July," he said.

Molly reached for my arm and squeezed excitedly.

"It will be a masquerade ball and, by announcing this now, you should have plenty of time to prepare your masks. The craft room at the lodge is stocked with glue guns, sequins, and feathers for your masks. We've also brought in a rack of dressy clothes for you to choose from if you didn't bring anything suitable from home. Prizes will be awarded for creativity. Dates to the dance are optional, but I expect everyone to attend. That is all. Enjoy your dessert."

On cue, dining hall staff paraded into the room with platters of strawberry cheesecake and chocolate mousse. Our server lowered the silver tray so we could take our pick. I didn't hesitate before selecting the chocolate mousse. Sierra picked the cheesecake, and Molly passed altogether, a martyr for the cause of skinny jeans.

"Can I have one of each? Pretty please?" asked Garrett, blinking his baby-blues. When the server refused, Garrett pouted and snatched a ramekin of chocolate mousse off the tray.

"Y'all can have my cheesecake," ventured Sierra, standing up and passing her plate to Garrett. "I'm completely full."

"Thanks, Sierra. Don't mind if I do." Garrett helped himself to a hearty bite right then and there.

Sierra turned to me with a satisfied grin, which faded to a frown as she motioned to Molly, who was flirting with Jake viciously enough to give anyone within a five-mile radius a toothache. She leaned over my shoulder and into my ear. "That was completely rude of her to dog y'all out about your blanket. Just because she's pretty, she thinks she can say whatever she wants."

I had tried not to think about Molly's slip of the tongue, but Sierra was right. Molly had intentionally tried to embarrass me in front of Jake, and that was not the first time she'd done it. What was her problem, anyway?

Flush.

That was the noise that woke me up at 3:30 A.M. Aya emerged from the bathroom and closed the door behind her. It was dark, but I could see that her face was splotchy and swollen like she'd been crying.

"Rough night again?" I whispered groggily.

Aya just nodded.

"Anything I can do?"

"I wish," she flipped off her flashlight and climbed miserably back into her bed. I rolled over and quickly fell back sleep.

By sunrise, Aya's bed was empty and her belongings were gone. She was the first to disappear that summer.

PARKER

Parker was doggone sick of everyone telling him how great his father was. *Blah blah blah genius. Blah blah blah leader. Blah blah blah savior.*

All those who thought his father was something noble did not live with him. They didn't watch his father sneak away to the station to smoke cigars with Philip, who was basically the shadiest dude on the planet. They didn't see the snakelike smirk his father wore at home when his guard was down and his feet were up. They didn't see the indifference with which he treated his own son. What kind of father doesn't care about his own flesh and blood?

All people saw was a man with purpose. His father's powerful speeches and pleasant demeanor touched their hearts and blinded their eyes. Everyone wanted to believe that such a man was capable of only miraculous things.

Once upon a time, Parker had marched proudly behind his father as well. The greater good and the unfounded desire to please his father was the driving force behind the hours spent at the lab and his obsession with being *called upon*.

But no more. Today had been the final straw.

Parker had made a lunch appointment with his father with the intention of laying it all out on the table. He was going to tell his father that he, being *called upon* or not, was worth something. He was going to say that he was every bit as good as Jason and was more than just a run-of-the-mill counterpart. He was going to make sure that his father would leave their meeting seeing, really seeing, Parker.

But not even an hour after making the appointment, his father's secretary called Parker back. His father had to cancel. Someone was being *called upon*—someone who was most definitely not Parker. There was simply too much to do, and his father could not be bothered by trivial matters.

That was it. Parker would have to take more drastic measures to get his father's attention, even if it meant tearing down the man that everybody thought was so great.

CHAPTER 7

KAITLIN

The baked bean fiasco had not been forgotten, nor had my promise of revenge. Even so, Molly and I took our time in plotting the perfect retaliation. We let three weeks pass, just enough time for the boys to let down their guard.

They'd been easily distracted. Camp only got better with time. Aside from morning classes and daily journaling, our afternoons were filled with exploration and fun. We were given free rein over the trails that directly surrounded Overlook. Most campers opted to travel around by horseback, but I humored Molly, and we trekked by foot (she might argue that she was humoring me by hiking at all). Often, we picnicked at the lake. The guys came with us usually and usually, some way or another, Garrett ended up in the lake. We skipped rocks, canoed, and I even taught the crew to fish once. It ended badly—Garrett cast backward and hooked Jake by the jeans. I personally couldn't tell the snag apart from the existing designer rips, but Jake was angry enough to spit.

Again, Garrett ended up in the lake.

There were days when we went climbing and rappelling. One day, we ran obstacle courses, and the next we shot pellet guns. We had basketball and tennis tournaments, played pool and volleyball, and when feeling lazy, fried our brains with arcade games in the rec room.

Molly was a pretty good sport about all the activities as long as Jake was there. She watched from the sidelines, whatever the activity was, and cheered us on. I repaid Molly's sportsmanship in pool time. Whenever we went for a hike, I factored in two hours of sun worship afterward, and whenever I made a free throw on the basketball court, I calculated the number of freckles I'd sprout across my cheeks in the warm mountain sun.

Happily for Molly, the evening's activities usually required a little less physical exertion or athleticism. Overlookers gathered around the campfire at least three times a week, engaging in the type of rowdiness only acquired by an open flame and copious amounts of sugar. When we weren't at the fire pit, we were shooting pool in the rec room, stewing in the hot tub, having skit nights and lip syncs, and always, eating, eating, eating.

Occasionally, the five of us would sneak away from the other campers to the picnic table behind the lodge. We'd light a lantern and pull out some face cards. Poker was almost always the game of choice, and we'd gamble anything from Tootsie Rolls to Toblerones.

But through all the fun, Molly and I secretly debated how and when to serve the boys their just desserts. Molly pushed for property damage, still fuming about the pinto bean that had burrowed deeply in her left ear canal, but I argued for a more subtle revenge. The perfect prank was a delicate balance of creativity and mischief. It shouldn't cause harm or hurt, rather it should produce extreme annoyance followed by amusement and appreciation. Pranks were an art form.

As luck would have it, we stumbled across the perfect recipe for revenge when Molly woke up one day with a horrible case of the wiggles. She was in and out of the bathroom for three days straight. Embarrassed, but desperate, Molly finally visited Dr. Forsythe's office. With a chuckle and a pat on the back, Doc diagnosed her with a minor urinary tract infection. The medication he gave her relieved her discomfort, but with a funny side effect. It tinted her pee an alarming neon red-orange color.

It was then that we knew we'd struck gold.

We chopped up her leftover pills and funneled the dust into a bottle of red sports drink. Then we sat courtside as the boys played a vigorous game of basketball. By the end of the match, Garrett, Jake, and Max were practically begging for a swig of Molly's ice-cold electrolytes. She, being an exemplar of the Golden Rule, was too polite to refuse. It wasn't until several worried letters home and an enlightening visit to Dr. Forsythe's office that the boys realized they weren't suffering from a life-threatening pee disease, but rather a dazzling rebuttal from two very sassy young ladies. They were both aggravated and humbled by our prank and were no doubt planning a vicious counterattack. Molly and I waited with great anticipation. Mission very much accomplished.

Yes, besides my disturbing run-in with Security Phil, I liked it at Camp Overlook. I liked myself there. I was fun and carefree and hardly ever thought about Mia Bethers or the incident anymore. My past didn't define me there. The only thought that ever dampened my mood was that summer would one day turn to autumn, and I'd have to leave the comfort of this cozy little Overlook womb.

"It makes no sense! It's been over a month, and he still hasn't made a move," Molly whined, her arms dangling off the edge of her inflatable pool raft. She and I had been floating around the pool for the last hour—most of the time was spent ranting, and listening to rants, about Jake.

Guess who was doing the listening?

"No sense whatsoever," I mumbled, dabbing my shoulders with a gob of sun block. While freckles were an inevitability, my skin rarely burned. But I was trying to send a subtle hint to Molly. Itsy-bitsy teeny-weenie would've been generous in summing up the measurements of her stringy pink two-piece, and the sun would have a whole lot of surface area to work with if it fancied giving someone skin cancer. "Want some?" I asked, bouncing the SPF bottle in her line of vision.

"No thanks. I mean, he acts interested. He flirts like crazy and keeps talking about how cute I am. If he thinks I'm so cute, though, why doesn't he do something about it?"

I was ready to be done talking about Jake . . . like, now. "So, what are you wearing to the fiesta tonight?"

"Well, I was thinking either my pink sweatshirt or my blue sweater. I look good in both. Which do you think Jake would like best? I really need him to ask me to the dance tonight. There's only one week left for us to coordinate our outfits."

"I'll be your date," I suggested. "We could make matching masks and wear the same clothes and stuff. Then you wouldn't have to wait for Jake to get his act together."

Molly sighed. "Nah. Not that you wouldn't be a hot date, I'm just pretty sure that he'll ask me. Besides, I'm guessing that Garrett will ask you."

"Garrett?" I sputtered. "*What*? What are you talking about?"

Molly smiled slyly. "You and Garrett would make the cutest couple ever. You should totally go for him."

"Garrett is *not* my type." I shivered.

"Why not? If Jake and I weren't about to get together, I'd totally go for Garrett. He's so cute. But he wouldn't be interested in me—he likes you. He'll ask you to the dance for sure."

"And I'd say no."

"Oh, come on, Kaitlin. You have so much in common with him."

"Why are you pushing Garrett on me? I said I wasn't interested!" I didn't mean to explode, but if Molly thought that Garrett and I would make a great match, then I was insulted. Sure, he was outdoorsy, like me, but he was also overly emphatic about everything and extremely irritating.

Molly whistled. "Wow, salty. So Garrett is definitely out . . . but Max is pretty cute. You guys should date."

I growled.

"I kid," she said quickly.

Okay, I admit that I'd like to get asked to the dance; I was only human. At the same time, I was petrified of going on a real date. I wouldn't know how to act, and my nerves would take complete control of my body; I would surely revert to the *beginning of the summer Kaitlin*, and no one missed her. No, it would be better if I went to the dance stag.

"Kaitlin!" chirped a voice from outside the pool fence. I opened my eyes to see Margaret jumping up and down like a kangaroo on fire. She pulled open the gate and scuttled to the pool area carrying a small box. "I've been looking for you everywhere!"

"Is everything okay?" I asked.

"Oh yes, fine. It's just that this package came in the mail for you. There's a note that says that it must be opened today, and since you haven't been to the lodge to check your mail, I thought I'd deliver it myself."

"That's nice. Thanks." I paddled my raft to the pool's edge and reached out my arms to receive the parcel. "You didn't have to go out of the way."

"Actually, I wanted to. I've been meaning to tell you how much I love reading your journal."

I looked down at the package self-consciously. Obviously I knew that Margaret was reading my journal; I just tried to ignore the fact. Some of the things I wrote were insanely personal, and I didn't care to discuss them with her and especially not in front of Molly. "Uh, thanks."

"Well, the compliment doesn't come without a catch. I challenge you to dig even deeper, to push past your day-to-day activities and write about how you feel about life. I want to read about your emotions, your ambitions, and your dreams. I think you'll grow more as a writer and a person if you do."

"Okay . . . thanks," I said again.

"No prob. Is there anything else I can do for you while I am here?"

Luckily, I remembered the question I'd been meaning to ask Margaret for weeks. "When we were hiking up the Arrowhead Trail, I spotted a building several miles south of camp. It looks a lot like the lodge, and there's a helicopter on the roof. What is it?"

Margaret fluffed her frizzy hair. "Um, I think it's some sort of government building, but I'm not exactly sure. I could find out for ya if you want."

"It's no big deal," I said. "I was just curious."

"Alrighty," Margaret spouted. "Well, I've got loads to do—reading journals, preparing for the fiesta tonight, organizing . . . uh . . . things—but I'll see you two at dinner. Check ya later!" She waved her hand and practically sprinted from the pool area.

"That woman should seriously rethink her Red Bull consumption," observed Molly.

"Don't you think that was weird?" I pushed myself from the pool's edge to float nearer to Molly.

"What?"

"Margaret. She seemed really . . . on edge when I asked about that building. She got all fidgety."

"She just didn't know the answer to your question," said Molly.

"It's the only other building for miles. How could she not know? And why would a government building be out in the middle of nowhere?"

"Maybe it is a top-secret building where top-secret experiments happen," Molly wiggled her fingers the same way someone who was telling a silly ghost story would. I wondered, however, if she was onto something—all jokes aside.

"So what's in the box?" Molly removed her sunglasses and lifted her head off of her air pillow to get a better view.

"I don't know," I said—which was a lie. It was my birthday. A package from my parents was no surprise. I hadn't told anyone about my fifteenth birthday, not because I wanted to keep it a secret or anything, but because I didn't want people to think I expected them to make a big deal of me . . . even though I secretly hoped they would.

I pulled the strands of packing tape from around the package and lifted the lid. The package contained a new book, a fresh jar of cookie butter, packing peanuts, and a birthday card chastising me for not writing home more often. I patted the bottom of the box to make sure I hadn't missed anything.

"Kaitlin, is it your birthday?" Molly asked.

I nodded sheepishly.

"I can't believe you didn't tell me! What a brat! Happy birthday!" Molly proceeded to howl Katy Perry's birthday song at the top of her lungs. I groaned and pelted her in the chest with a handful of peanuts—but I wasn't all that sad that my birthday secret was out.

———————

"Ouch, ouch, ouch!" Garrett repeated as he tossed his steamy foil dinner from one hand to the next.

"That's why you use tongs to pull it out of the fire, Einstein," said Jake, who opened and closed a pair of metal tongs in demonstration.

"I like the hot-potato approach. It suits me." Garrett sucked his seared index finger like a melting Popsicle.

Dinner had been uprooted from the dining hall to the fire pit for Fiesta Night. Margaret, heinously misappropriating in a black mariachi suit, passed out sombreros as the campers arrived. As far as I could see, only two people were actually wearing theirs, Syrup and Garrett.

Molly looked both festive and seductive. She had braided her thick hair, coiled it into a low bun, and fastened the bundle with a red crepe paper flower—which contrasted nicely with her formfitting teal sweater. As predicted, the summer sun had turned her face Pepto-Bismol pink, but somehow the rosy cheeks only added brilliance to her perfectly proportioned face. Was I a bad person to look forward to the peeling stage of the sunburn?

Molly and I sat with the boys next to the fire and assembled our foil dinners. We wrapped sliced bell peppers, onions, and chopped steak in foil and tossed them into the smoldering embers of the fire. When the meat and veggies cooked through, we dumped the packets onto a heated tortilla, added guacamole, and—ta-da—campfire fajitas. Ole!

"I'm parched. Wanna grab a margarita with me, Jake?" Molly batted her eyelashes and motioned to the table where Tanji was mixing strawberry mocktails and rubbing her temples like the frivolity of the task was giving her a headache.

"Sure." Jake's eyes looked deliciously blue as he smiled down at Molly. "How 'bout you, Kate? Can I grab you a soda or a margarita?"

"A Coke for me and one for Max, too." I noticed that Max had just squashed his empty soda can and tossed it into the trash can. Max looked up from his fourth fajita and smiled gratefully.

Molly grabbed Jake's arm and pulled him toward the drinks, and Garrett, hypnotized by a girl with as much hair as curves (which is to say plenty), stood up and followed her through the crowd. I turned to Max. "I asked Margaret about that strange building today."

"Did you?" Max said, swallowing a chunk of steak.

"Yeah. She said it was some sort of government building."

"Huh, that's strange. I asked Tanji about it last week, and she said it was a rehab facility. But a government building makes more sense with the helicopter pad and everything."

"Margaret didn't seem a hundred percent sure that it was a government building. It's just that . . ."

"What?" said Max, leaning closer. He smelled good, and for a moment I lost my train of thought.

"Um, oh, it's just that Margaret seemed evasive about the question—like it made her uncomfortable."

"I got the same impression from Tanji." Max paused and formulated his thoughts. He looked at me right in the eyes. "Do you ever think that some things at Camp Overlook don't quite add up?"

"Yes," I said, thinking about my disturbing run-in with Security Phil.

"Like, why do the lodge, dining hall, and the pool all look as though they've been transplanted here straight from a resort in Aspen? I mean, there's marble flooring in a room that is used to teach campers to build latrines."

"I'm with you on that," I said. "But the cabins are old and rickety. Yesterday, Sierra sat down on a cabin chair, and one of the legs snapped in half—no warning. It was funny when it happened, but Dr. Forsythe said she had a fractured tailbone; then we all felt bad for laughing." I glanced up at Sierra, who was eating dinner with Syrup several tiers above us. Perched atop a blue rubber bum cushion, her face was wrenched in pure misery.

"So why spend all of that money on a mess hall and completely ignore our cabins? And why can't we call our parents? What if we had an emergency? And sometimes I think that my letters from home are being read before I get them. There was a page missing from my mom's last letter. And the envelopes sometimes look like they've been resealed."

I thought of the package I'd received earlier today. The tape did peel off way too easily. "What about our outgoing mail? Are they messing with that, too?"

"Don't know. Maybe I'm being paranoid." Max finished his last bite and crinkled his foil into a ball. He tossed it from hand to hand.

"So, got any theories on why Overlook is so bizarre?"

"Not really. You?"

"Actually, I do," I smiled mysteriously. "I bet that camp is really a meat farm. We are fattened up like hogs on Le Cordon Bleu cuisine and campfire fajitas, and when we've reached our optimal weight, we are taken to the slaughterhouse and ground up like beef."

"But who would eat us?" Max tossed me the foil ball.

"The underground cannibalistic society, naturally. I hear there are tons of 'em in the Midwest."

"You are a dark, twisted woman, Kaitlin," Max appreciated. "But may I propose a differing hypothesis?"

"Try me." I tossed the foil into the trash can.

"The camp staffers are not really people at all, but aliens—very curious aliens. They traveled from galaxies far away to study humans' obsession with hair. Every night, while we are asleep, they creep into our rooms, mess up our hair, and document our reactions when we wake up."

"I was wondering why I woke up covered in blue ooze this morning," I giggled.

Suddenly, Max's theory reminded me of Claire—not that she was an alien (although she did remind me of a certain creature from Predator)—but when she called Sierra a "lab rat." Was she just being a brat or was there *actually* something behind the insult? Again, I remembered the first day of class when Claire accused Margaret of being fake and then threw her journal into the bushes. Claire had been to Overlook the previous summer, so it was entirely possible that she knew something about camp that we didn't. I scanned the noisy campers for Claire but couldn't find her. She was probably alone in the bunkhouse rehearsing her poisonous glower-darts in front of the mirror. I decided not to dwell on Claire's whereabouts, being that mine were ever so much more interesting.

"What about the mail tampering, then?" I asked, returning to our flirtatious banter. "Are the aliens behind that, too?"

"Sure. The aliens are checking our mail to make sure our parents aren't sending us expensive hair products. That would flub up the whole experiment."

"There you have it," I laughed.

And Max was laughing, too. And we continued staring into each other's eyes and laughing until Max ran the back of his hand along my cheekbone. "You know, the firelight makes your freckles dance," he said.

I closed my eyes for a moment.

A loud whistle captured my attention. I opened my eyes to see Molly standing next to the bonfire with her thumb and index finger at her lips. "May I have everyone's attention please? Today is a very special day for a dear friend of mine. Kaitlin, will you please step forward?"

I felt lightheaded as everyone's eyes turned to me. Max nudged me upward, and I hobbled up to Molly. She placed a homemade birthday tiara on my head and kissed my blushing cheek. A few boys from the crowd whistled and shouted for her to do it again, and Molly shook her finger at them playfully. "You all know her and love her, so let's join together and sing 'Happy Birthday' to this beautiful, fabulous fifteen-year-old!"

As everyone sang, Jake and Garrett carried out a gigantic, two-tiered cake with "Happy Birthday, Kaitlin!" inscribed around the top in bright pink frosting. I made a wish and blew out the fifteen sparkling candles. My fellow campers cheered.

"Speech! Speech! Speech!" Max chanted from the front row. Other campers joined in. I cracked my knuckles nervously. "Um . . . er . . . I would like to thank all the people who made this moment possible. My mom, of course, for birthing me, Molly, for embarrassing me more that I have ever been embarrassed in my life, and thank you to everyone else for making camp so fun." I curtsied . . . *I know* . . . and scurried back to my seat.

It took me a minute to recover from being serenaded by my eighty-something peers, but soon enough, people were back in their cliques, enjoying the bonfire and fresh slices of cake. As I was no longer the focus of everyone at camp, I could relax and enjoy the moment.

"For the birthday girl," Max said, sliding the can of Coke that Jake had forgotten into one of my hands and a plate of cake into the other. He had finagled the slice with the most impressive frosting rose for me. I imagined he had to fend off a dozen sweet tooths for that coveted slice.

"Thanks, Max." I licked some icing off of my fork.

Molly and Jake joined us. "How'd you like that?" Molly twirled and bowed, obviously pleased with herself for pulling off the whole charade.

"You little stinker!" I exclaimed and punched her shoulder. "How did you get your hands on this cake? It's amazing!"

"After you left the pool today, I went to the dining hall and asked the chef if he was up for baking a cake. I had to pout and beg to get him to do it, but he gave in . . . just like they all do." I suspected that Molly was still wearing her string bikini at the moment of inquiry. "So, did you like the surprise or what?"

"Yeah, I really liked it," I admitted.

Jake put his arm around my shoulder. "Sorry I didn't get you anything. I just found out it was your birthday ten minutes ago. How 'bout I take you to the dance to make up for it?"

To say I was surprised by the invitation would be an understatement. I was blown away, ransacked, flabbergasted! Little dorky me getting asked to the dance by the hottest guy at camp? Mindboggling! "Um . . . Okay?"

Molly's party smile turned flat and forced. She looked as shocked as I felt. The hand beneath her cake plate twitched as she seemingly fought the urge to catapult the pastry straight into my face.

"Yeah, happy birthday, Kaitlin," said Max, whose eyes also held the faintest trace of defeat.

Garrett ran by and shoved a glow-in-the-dark football into Max's chest. "You guys in?"

"Game on!" Max called back. He threw the ball full force and pegged Garrett in the back. The guys ran to the meadow behind the campfire and began throwing the football back and forth.

I turned to Molly. "Look, just because he asked me to the dance . . ."

"Whatever. It doesn't matter. He probably just felt sorry for you or something," she retorted, still smiling but only with her mouth. Her eyes were fiery and fearsome. She turned and walked away.

Quite frankly, I would have preferred a birthday spanking.

ASHLEY

From the frantic tone in Ashley's voice, Jade assumed that something had gone horribly wrong with the baby. She hung up the phone, jumped in her car—no time for shoes—and doubled the speed limit to Ashley's house. Her friend was waiting on the front porch as the old pickup screeched into the driveway, and Jade opened the door and toppled out onto the pavement.

"Is everything okay?" she gasped, scurrying to Ashley's side.

"You tell me." Ashley thrust an ultrasound picture in Jade's face.

Panting, Jade scrunched up her face and squinted at the picture. "Hmmm, well, it looks like a big gray blob to me."

"Look harder."

"Okay," Jade took hold of the picture and concentrated. "What's this here?"

"That's a foot."

"So this must be the other foot," she said, pointing the center of the ultrasound.

"No, that's the baby's heart."

"Then what's this thing?"

"Another heart."

"Holy crap! Your baby has two hearts!"

"No, Jade; there are two babies up in there."

Jade gasped and grabbed onto Ashley's hand. "Twins! Ohm'gosh, ohm'gosh! Congratulations!"

"Are you kidding me! This is the worst thing that could ever happen! I don't know how to be a mother to one baby; how on earth am I going to figure out two?" Ashley, who had been crying for forty-five minutes straight, was finally out of tears and now on the verge of hyperventilating.

"Slow down, Ashley. Let's get you inside." Jade grabbed Ashley's arm and led her back into the house and to the kitchen table.

While Jade opened the fridge and pulled out a can of orange soda, Ashley dropped her head on the hard table and tried to even out her breathing. "Who is going to pay for all the diapers and clothes and cribs and baby food? Who is going to hold baby number one while I am feeding baby number two? I can't do this, Jade. I can't do this. Maybe I should just give the babies up for adoption like my mom said."

Jade popped the top of the can and placed it on the table in front of Ashley. "Where is your mom, anyway?"

"She had to go back to work after the doctor's appointment. She wanted to call in sick, but I told her I needed some time alone. Really, I just needed her to stop telling me what to do." Ashley took three deep rhythmical breaths and reached for the soda. "And I needed to talk to my best friend."

"Glad to be of service," said Jade and gave her friend's hair a playful tug. "So, are the babies, like, boys or girls?"

"Girls," said Ashley.

"That's great! You wanted a girl, right?"

"*A* being the key word."

"Can the doctors tell if the babies are identical or fraternal?"

"The ultrasound tech said the babies share some sort of sac or something, which means the babies are identical, I guess."

Ashley's cell phone began to ring. She fumbled in her bag and pulled it out. "That's probably my mom with another I told you so. I better get it. Hello?"

"Good afternoon," said a cheerful male voice on the other side. "May I speak with a Miss Ashley Campbell?"

"This is she," Ashley said, looking confused. "How can I help you?"

"Hi. My name is Dr. Kenneth Forsythe. I heard about your situation and actually, I believe it is *I* that can help you."

CHAPTER 8

KAITLIN

My curiosity had bubbled over the rim of sanity, and I was finally willing to take drastic, dangerous measures to get the tea on Camp Overlook's strange inconsistencies.

I was going to talk to Claire.

I danced around her all day, waiting for the right chance to pick her brain on her experience at camp last summer. But Claire's mood, like the day's rainy weather, was even more rancid than usual, which made me feel about as skittish as a turkey in November. Every time she caught me staring at her, I looked away or became infatuated with an object directly behind her. And when I finally mustered the guts to question her, a clumsy, forced cough came out instead. Claire yelled at me to cover my mouth if I was going to, and I quote, "eject my putrid germs" at her.

I sloshed up the muddy trail back to the cabin with my tail tucked between my legs. I was surprised when I opened the door to see that sometime during the day, someone (or some people—ahem Jake, Garrett, Max) had sneaked into our cabin and flipped everything in it upside down—our bunk beds, the dresser, desk, chairs, everything. Further, all of the roommates' belongings had been jumbled and redistributed into one another's duffel bags, and my book collection had been sacrilegiously de-alphabetized.

It took all of us hours of concentrated effort to sort through the mess and flip our furniture back to its locked and upright position. And even when everything was all cleaned up, I couldn't find my jar of cookie butter, my super-secret cell phone, or a very important half to my one and only pair of dry tennis shoes. Eventually, everyone left the cabin for dinner but me; I was still searching for my runaway shoe. I looked under the beds, picked through everyone's duffle bags, and even opened the back tank of the toilet. Nothing surfaced.

Just when I was making peace with the idea of trudging around camp in my mud-caked boots for the rest of the summer, I noticed that one of the dresser drawers was slightly ajar. I pulled the drawer open and snaked my arm behind it, relieved as my tennis shoe came back out with my hand. Just then, Claire flung open the door and tramped into the cabin, swearing profusely about the rain and her forgotten jacket.

Now was my chance. I swallowed hard and picked up Claire's black raincoat. "Uh, Claire?" I ventured, holding it to her.

"What are you, the freakin' lost and found?" She snatched it from me.

"You, um . . . went to camp last year, didn't you?"

She raised an eyebrow at me. "What's it to you?"

"Er . . . uh . . . it's just that sometimes I think that that this camp is a bit . . . weird, you know? Did you notice anything . . . abnormal last year?"

Claire's scowl morphed to an amused smirk in a matter of seconds. "So, that's the reason you've been staring at me like a hungry kitten all day? You wanted to ask if I thought camp was *a bit weird*?"

I decided to approach from a different angle. "Why did you call Sierra a lab rat? What does that mean?"

Claire froze in place. Her eyes darted around the room. "I don't remember saying that. I don't know what you're talking about."

"Remember, it was like the second day of camp, and we were at the amphitheater, and Sierra was defending Margaret, and then you called Sierra a lab—"

"Shhhhh!" Claire hissed and then motioned for me to come closer. "Look, we can't talk about this here. It isn't safe. Meet me at the fire pit after dinner, and we'll talk." She shoved her arms into her jacket holes and stalked out of the cabin.

A few minutes later, I sat down at the dinner table next to Molly, who rolled her eyes and rotated her body away from me. She'd been ignoring me all day, feathers still flying from Jake asking me out. Realistically, I doubted she'd ever forgive me. Since day one, she had all but peed on Jake—leaving no question that he was her territory. By accepting his invitation to the dance, I had flagrantly violated girl-code rule #1 and would suffer the consequences till the day I died.

Oh, well. It's not like Molly was my soul friend. She and I had nothing in common. She was so thirsty for attention, always dressing and behaving so that all eyes were on her. She hated the outdoors, and if she wasn't trying so dang hard to impress Jake, she'd never do anything even remotely adventurous. Also, I found her endless prattling and bragging about boys obnoxious. I mean, just stop.

But then again, alike or not, she was a friend. In my world, friends counted for a lot. In my world, friends were few and far between. I remembered how Molly came to my rescue the first day of camp. She was so nice, an angel, so willing to accept me. She helped me with my bags. She laughed at my jokes, not at me. And let's not forget the birthday cake . . . that big, beautiful, pink birthday cake. Who else would have thought to do something like that?

I quickly banished the memories from my mind. I would not be guilted out of going to the dance just because Molly had a thing for Jake. She didn't own him. She couldn't claim him just because she was prettier than me. And the fact that she suggested he asked me out because he felt sorry for me—that was mean and untrue (I hoped). I deserved to go to the dance with Jake. I had suffered for three years straight all because of a stupid incident that was completely out of my control. It was about time something went my way. I had every right to go to the dance with whoever I wanted, and my so-called friend Molly should get over it and move on.

So I pretended not to notice her snub and focused my smile on the rest of my friends at the dinner table. "Sorry I'm late, guys; I couldn't find my shoe."

"And when you found it, was it upside down or right side up?" Garrett asked, suppressing a snicker. Jake and Max also looked at me with mischievous eyes.

I debated whether to give them the lecture they'd obviously been looking forward to all afternoon, but decided against it. "Whatcha talking about?"

"Oh, I don't know. Since you girls didn't shoot hoops with us during free time, we thought something more pressing must've occupied your time."

"Nothing that I can recall," I said airily.

"So, these last few hours were spent . . ." Jake motioned for me to finish his sentence.

"Flossing my teeth," I said with an innocent smile. "Never underestimate the importance of good oral hygiene."

"Oh, come on!" Garrett bounced in his chair impatiently. "Don't you have anything to say to us? Anything at all?"

"Um, who won the basketball game? Is that what you're looking for?"

The guys groaned, and the server pulled up to our table with dinner—apricot glazed salmon with a rice pilaf and broccoli florets. I licked my chops and picked up my fork. Molly gasped as she stared down at her own dish. "I can't eat this. It's fish! I'm a fishatarian."

"I think a fishatarian would be a person who only eats fish," said Jake. "You know, like vegetarians only eat . . . vegetation and stuff."

"Whatever. All I have to say is that there is no way that this creature is entering my digestive tract."

"Great, 'cause I'm famished." Garrett skewered Molly's salmon and slapped it onto his own plate. Molly looked both repulsed and relieved by the thievery.

"Are you planning on starving, then?" asked Jake.

"Nope," said Molly. "I have beef jerky and a can of easy cheese in my duffle bag. It's low-carb and should sustain me just fine until tomorrow."

"I'm an Easy-Cheesatarian," said Max quietly, cheeks full and plate empty. If I hadn't witnessed his entire dinner devoured in four monstrous bites, I would've assumed that it had evaporated.

"So, what did you guys do after basketball today?" I asked.

"I spent some time moving all my stuff to the top bunk," volunteered Garrett. "My bunkmate moved out during the night."

"Who was your bunkmate?" I asked.

"Martin Larsen. He was the guy with the mole."

"Oh, yes, the mole guy," I recalled. Martin had a huge hairy mole in the dead center of his chin. If one was not too distracted by this extra appendage, one might notice that he also had a talent for saying things that made you feel extremely uncomfortable. For example, one day, he told me that I reminded him of his uncle, who had a karaoke fetish and ran an online hosiery company.

"One of our roommates up and left in the middle of the night, too," Molly chimed in. "I don't know if you remember Aya; she was super quiet. She'd been pretty sick, though. We weren't surprised when she went home. Maybe Martin got sick, too."

"Nah. Tanji told me that Martin was sent home because he snuck out at night with a girl," said Jake.

Garrett sputtered with laughter. "You're joking, right? No girl in her right mind would go near Martin. The guy was a weenie!"

Max and I exchanged a look. A girl sneaking out with Martin was about as likely as me swearing a lifelong oath against cookie butter. Tanji had lied.

After dinner, Garrett challenged the gang to an air hockey tournament, and we all agreed to all meet at the rec room in a half an hour. I opened my umbrella and called to Max before he got too far ahead. He joined me under my umbrella, and I quickly relayed to him my conversation with Claire.

"The plot thickens," he said. "Mind if I come with you to talk to her?"

"I was hoping you would. I might need a body guard."

"Afraid of a tiny nose ring?"

"Just the girl attached to it. I wouldn't be surprised if Claire set this whole thing up to mangle my body in a place where no one could hear me scream."

"Nah. Claire knows something and wants to talk it out—although a good body mangling might be fun to watch."

I playfully punched his arm and we started down the trail, still slick with the day's downfall. "So when you guys were busy feng shuiing our furniture today, you didn't happen upon a cell phone, did you?"

"Aha! You admit it! Just for the record, it was Garrett who went through your duffels with all of your, uh, underthings. I had nothing to do with it."

"Ew," I said. "But the cell phone? Did you see it?"

"A cell phone, huh? Naughty. How'd you pull that off?"

"My mom gave it to me in case of an emergency. I was hiding it under my mattress, but it's gone now."

"Hm. Well, I didn't see it, but Garrett would be the one to ask. I *did* see him with a suspicious jar of cookie butter before dinner."

"That little turd," I grumbled.

From the pocket of his rain jacket, Max procured a king-sized envelope of peanut butter cups. "This should more than make up for it."

"No way! I love these things!" I took the package and quickly tucked it into my own coat.

"Don't thank me—thank Garrett. I nabbed them for you from his stash."

"Even better."

We were quiet for a moment. We passed the stables and pool—careful not to slip down the muddy trail. Max finally sliced our silence in two. "So, you're going to the dance with Jake, huh?"

"It's no big deal," I said, grateful that he couldn't see me blush.

"It's a big deal to Jake. He's liked you since he tossed that note into your mashed potatoes."

"No, you're mistaken. That note was for Molly."

"No mistake. In fact, Jake called dibs on you after our hike to the lake."

"How chivalrous of him," I blushed again. Truth be told, I wasn't completely sure if I had feelings for Jake. I should. He was good-looking, and strong, and very cool. Sure, I liked him. Of course I did. Why wouldn't I? A gorgeous guy—a guy period—was interested in me. I should pull this freak occurrence close to my chest and run with it. But for some reason, I didn't want to talk about Jake right then. At all. I quickly flipped the focus to Max. "Who are you going to the dance with?"

"Me? Don't think I'll go."

"Too shy to ask a date?"

"It's not that," said Max, who perhaps took my teasing a little too seriously. "It's just that, um, I don't want to show anyone up on the dance floor. I've got some serious moves, and Garrett, especially, has very tender feelings."

I chuckled. "I'd love a demonstration—gotta know what I'll be missing when you're not there."

"Maybe another day, but trust me, you'd be moved to tears."

Max and I bantered playfully the rest of the way to the fire pit. The fact that we were marching to my imminent death slipped my mind until we caught sight of Claire waiting next to the unlit fire pit, no umbrella, a vape pen tucked between her top and bottom lip.

Max helped me down the slick tiers and we faced the bull head on.

"Hi. I'm Max," he said, his arm outstretched.

"I know." Claire looked at his hand the same way one would look at an aggressive form of cancer. "We only see each other every day."

"Fair enough. We've never really talked, though." Max shoved his rejected hand into his front pocket and smiled sheepishly.

"So now that we are here, what exactly do you want to know?"

"Er . . . um," I said.

"For starters, can you tell us what camp was like last year?" Max helped.

Claire blew a mouthful of vapor into Max's face "A lot like this year except that our days weren't mapped out down to our last piss, and we didn't have to take pointless classes like we do now. I don't know why they screwed with everything this year. They got it right the first time."

"So last summer was Overlook's first?"

"I'm pretty sure. At orientation, Leavitt made a big stink over us being the first people to enjoy the state-of-the-art facility. I guess he bought an old campground and added the lodge and pool and stuff."

"And you had fun?" Max asked. "Last year?"

"Actually, I did. Last year, everything was pretty cool. I had a lot of friends," Claire paused, waiting for us to challenge her. When we didn't, she continued. "I had a boyfriend, too—Sam. Met him the first day of camp."

Claire held her pen in one hand while unzipping her pack with the other. She fumbled through the bag and pulled out a crinkled Polaroid, holding it under our umbrella to keep it dry. Max and I leaned forward. In the photo, Claire posed cheek to cheek with a black guy with bright teeth and knowing chocolate-drop eyes. While last summer's Claire still had boyish hair and a nose ring, she somehow looked softer then.

"We went horseback riding almost every day and did the campfire thing with our friends at night. The leaders didn't care if we stayed out late or if we slept in until eleven the next morning—even Tanji had a shorter stick up her butt last summer. They *did* make us write in those stupid journals, but that's the only thing I didn't like about camp."

Claire dropped her vape and the photograph back in her bag and continued. "Sam got sick about two months into camp. Dr. Forsythe said he had mono. It sucked because all Sam could ever do was stay in his cabin and rest. I had to sneak into his cabin if I ever wanted to see him, and even then, he wasn't himself.

"One day, I went to visit him at his cabin, and his bunkmate said that he'd packed and left overnight . . . just like that. Gone." Claire looked away and cleared her throat. "He didn't even say goodbye . . . after everything. I wrote him a few letters, but he never wrote back. I was so pissed at him . . . until . . ."

"Until what?" I asked.

"Until it happened to other people. Two more people disappeared by the end of the summer. The leaders told us that one had gotten homesick and the other had a family emergency . . . but then I realized, mono is the kissing disease, right? So, why didn't I get sick? Not a sore throat, not a cough. I asked around and found out that the other two campers that went home had also been sick."

"Just like Aya," I said.

"Just like Aya," Claire nodded. "And what about your roommate, Max? The dude with the mole? Was he ever sick?"

"Don't know; could've been. I should've done a better job paying attention."

"So, you think Overlook is making the campers sick?" I asked.

"What I think is that we are the subjects of some psycho experiment, and it is the experiment that is making people sick."

"Lab rats," I whispered.

"Exactly," said Claire. "And I'll tell you what else—our parents are in on it."

"No way." I said definitively. "My parents haven't even cut the umbilical cord yet; there's no way they'd put me in danger."

"Ha! I bet they would for the right price."

"I'm sorry, what?" said Max.

Claire looked at us with a smug expression. "Look, when I got back from camp last year, I told my mom all about the disappearing campers. Instead of sympathizing with me, she told me to grow up—that I was being ridiculous and paranoid. We fought about it, but the issue eventually dropped.

"Anyhow, a few weeks before summer break, I ditched Trig and went home for some food. Mom was in her bedroom talking on the phone, and she was crying. I listened at the door and realized that she was talking to some douche from Camp Overlook—Leavitt, I think. She was begging him to take me back this summer, blubbering about how she knew that I was special, she just knew it. It was pathetic. She then said that she'd pay back all of the money they'd given her if they'd give me one more shot."

"Why would Director Leavitt pay for us to go to camp? What would he get out of it?" Max asked.

Suddenly, the image of Tanji handing my mother a receipt the first day of camp flashed in my mind. Was it really a check that Mom slid into her purse? I mean, it would make sense. My folks struggled just to pay the mortgage every month; sending me to camp would be a real stretch for them. And Camp Overlook—heated pools, fancy chefs, high-tech equipment—this place was downright extravagant. They could never afford to send me here without financial aid.

The sky began swirling around my head, and I quickly sat down. Max moved next to me and placed his hand on my shoulder. "There's got to be an explanation for this. Maybe if we asked Margaret . . ."

"That's the last thing we want to do," hissed Claire. "The second the staff realizes we're onto them, we'll disappear just like the others. Why do you think they're keeping tabs on us with journals? They don't give a crap about what we eat for breakfast or who has a crush on who. They just want to make sure that we're oblivious to their little experiment—that we're not a threat."

"That's a bit far-fetched," Max said.

"You don't know the half of it," Claire said. "Many of the letters I receive from home are crinkled all weird, like someone's been messing with them."

Max and I exchanged a look.

Claire persisted. "I bet our cabins are being bugged, too. That's why I thought we should meet out in the open."

"I'm sure you're just over thinking this. I agree with you about the mail, but bugging our cabins? That's crazy."

I agreed with Max. "If what you're saying is true, you would've disappeared the first week of camp. I saw you throw your journal away. I mean, you haven't exactly played the part of a *happy camper* this summer." I flinched instinctively, waiting to be punched or cussed out.

Claire didn't seem to notice, though. She slumped on the tier next to Max and laced her fingers around her knee. "I figured as much, so I went back and found the journal in the bushes, and I've been writing dutifully ever since— making up some BS about how I was pissed at my mom for sending me here when I wanted to spend the summer with my friends. Margaret and the rest of the mad scientists probably think I'm acting out because of my mommy issues."

"But you *are* mad at your mom," I pointed out.

"Yeah, I am! She screwed me over. Apparently, Leavitt agreed to let me come back if I was a good girl and ate all my vegetables. Mom surprised me with my packed duffles when I came home from the last day of school. She acted like she was doing me some big favor. She said I'd thank her when I came back home."

"And you didn't put up a fight?" I raised my eyebrows.

"Of course I did. I screamed that I never would come home because I'd disappear like the others. I said that she'd sold her soul to the devil by selling me to Overlook and told her that the little exchange had been a waste of money because I sure wasn't anything special. Then I flipped her off."

Max smirked. "How'd that go over?"

"She slapped me. That's the only time she had ever done that. So I got into the car and slammed the door. I didn't say a word to her the two-day drive here, and I don't plan to ever again. I haven't answered any of her letters."

"I don't get it," I said. "What could be so important about Overlook that your mother would send you here when you were clearly terrified?"

"I don't want to know if I have to disappear to find out. Those missing campers might be cut open, tortured, or worse—they're dead. Sam might be dead." Claire clasped her hands together to hide that they were trembling, but both Max and I saw.

"Have you seen that big building a few miles south of camp?" Max changed the subject before Claire started to cry.

She sniffed. "Yeah, but I don't know what it is. I'm sure it's connected to Leavitt; it looks just like the lodge. There's a third building, too."

"Another building? Where?"

"A few days ago, I went for a hike. I thought I knew where I was going—I do that a lot, go for hikes alone—but after about an hour, I'd lost the trail completely. Then it started getting dark and cold."

"That was the night of the fiesta, huh? I remember looking for you in the crowd."

"That's right," Claire recalled. "Anyhow, I started to panic and began searching for anything familiar. Finally, I heard some voices in the distance, but I didn't want to call out in case it was Leavitt or Tanji, so instead, I followed the voices until they led me to a building. I would've never seen it on my own; it was small and hidden behind a bunch of pine trees."

"Maybe it was a maintenance shed?" Max proposed.

"Why would a maintenance shed be in the middle of nowhere?" I asked.

"There's no way the building was for maintenance; it was too fancy-looking, and it had this satellite thing on the roof. Anyhow, I hid behind some trees and waited for someone to come out. After an hour or so, Phil—you know, that nasty security guy—walked out. He was on his walkie-talkie. I figured he was heading toward camp for night patrol, so I followed the light of his flashlight."

"Didn't he hear you following him?" I asked.

"Phil stopped a couple of times and looked around. I'm sure he heard me but must've thought I was an animal or something."

"Security Phil is disgusting," I said, knowingly. "He pulled me aside once and told me he had been watching me and that he knew things about me. Like, what could he possibly know?" I shivered at the memory. "I haven't slept well since. It must have been creepy following him through the woods."

"It was no big deal. I'm more freaked about disappearing than I am of little Phil and his big gun."

"But don't you want to find out what happened to Sam?" I asked.

"Duh," said Claire.

Max sat quietly and digested everything. "Obviously, there's something messed up going on here—I've thought so ever since the beginning of camp—and Kaitlin, that thing you said about Security Phil, well, that is horrendous. But we are letting our minds run away with us. There's no way that Director Leavitt is experimenting on us or plotting our deaths. There are too many kids here. Too many people know where we are. There's got to be an explanation for everything."

"Like?" said Claire, tapping her foot.

"Well, I don't know. But I think we should find out—if for no other reason than getting a good night's sleep. Claire, do you think you could find that building in the woods again?"

"Probably."

"Great. Let's check it out, see what it's used for."

"Now?" I asked.

"Not now. Everyone is waiting for us at the lodge. But soon. Maybe tomorrow night?"

"We're not supposed to leave the cabins at night. What if we get caught?" Someone had to play the role of the coward, and I was the obvious choice.

"Honestly." Claire rolled her eyes.

"We won't get caught. We'll just have to plan it out carefully." Max's eyes brimmed with intensity and purpose—a look that suited him well. I'd do anything for him at that moment.

"Okay," I relented. "Let's do it."

The lodge's rec room resonated with laughter and the flashing ping of electric arcade games. Scattered throughout the space, kids amused themselves with pool, darts, skee ball, and Pac-Man. Some shot free throws into a canvas-lined galley, while others worked their thumb muscles on the arcade machines. Max, Claire, and I surveyed the crowd until we spotted the crew hanging out at the air hockey table.

"Where have you guys been?" growled Garrett, tapping his wrist impatiently. "We almost started without you."

"Sorry. We were walking around the campground and didn't realize how much time had passed," Max replied. We'd agreed beforehand to keep our conspiracy theories to ourselves, at least for the time being.

"In this weather?" asked Jake.

"With her?" asked Molly, pointing at a sopping-wet Claire.

"Oh, yeah. I hope you don't mind if Claire enters the tournament, too," said Max.

Out of sheer politeness, we had invited Claire to join us. Never in a billion years had I imagined that she'd actually accept. Not only did she, but I think I saw a hint of the same happy smile that graced her face in her photograph with Sam. Who would have thought it, Claire wanted friends.

"Okay then. Jake, you'll have to team up with Claire, but the first round will be me and Molly versus Kaitlin and Max." Garrett slid two mallets across the table. "Don't worry, Sweetcakes, I'll go easy on you."

"Don't you dare, Garrett," I said. "When I win, it will be fair and square."

"I was talking to Max," Garrett said and blew Max a kiss.

Max ducked and then pretended to watch the airborne kiss sail through the air, pass the snack bar, and land on a pimpled boy picking at a plate of nachos. Max lifted both his thumbs in mock approval.

"Oh, yeah, well kiss *this*!" Garrett's puck sailed straight into our goal.

While Garrett and Molly slapped each other five, Max caught my eye and pointed toward the back of the room. Director Leavitt and Tanji were there, standing between the popcorn machine and the Whack-a-Mole. Although clearly not related, the two of them had a strange similarity, one that I wouldn't have noticed if I'd not seen them side by side. They both had the same smoky gray eyes.

And all four of those chalky eyes were zeroed in on me.

PARKER

What Parker *really* needed was proof.

His father made no secret of his occasional breach of ethics. He openly admitted to employing flattery, bribery, and blackmail to nudge people toward doing the "right thing." He used these techniques to evade getting shut down by auditors and law enforcement as well. Parker, himself, had witnessed his father greasing the palm of a very high-profile politician to not look too carefully at the facility or the cleanliness of its books.

His father had a way, however, of wrapping his misdeeds up in shiny packages and tying them with big poufy bows; no misdeed seemed that bad when wrapped so nicely. After all, it was all done in the name of the greater good—a small price to pay for a safer, smarter, and more unified world.

Nevertheless, Parker suspected that these tidy packages held only a portion of the things his father had done. The rest of his sins were hidden in steel vaults, far away, where no one could see and no one could know.

Parker was going to find these vaults, pull out his father's sins, and hang them on a flagpole for the whole world to see. Then maybe his father would pay attention to him.

His father was away on a business trip, so Parker had the perfect opportunity to search his father's den without fear of getting caught. Not sure what he was looking for, he combed through his father's computer files and then rifled through his father's bookshelf. He found nothing unusual—at least nothing he didn't already know about. Parker searched the utility drawer on the side of his father's computer desk. Pens, a stapler, rubber bands, and box of green Tic-Tacs. That was it. Frustrated, Parker slammed the desk drawer shut.

Tink.

Something had dropped onto the hardwood floor. Something small and metal-sounding. Parker sunk to his knees and inspected the ground. A key, smallish and one side of it covered in tape, lay directly under the table. It must have dislodged from the bottom of the drawer. Parker wrapped his fingers around it and thought of all the possible things it could unlock. A jewelry box? A safe deposit box? Some sort of drawer? Whatever it was, the key didn't go to anything in their apartment; Parker would have noticed. The lock had to be somewhere else, somewhere his father visited often but somewhere that not many people knew about.

Aha! The answer dawned on Parker. It would take a little field trip, but he hoped that by the next morning, he'd have all the evidence he needed to bring his father to his knees.

CHAPTER 9

KAITLIN

I didn't bother asking Molly to help me make my mask for the dance; she would've laughed, and probably spat, in my face if I'd tried. Instead I asked Sierra, who jumped at the invitation. We linked arms and walked together to the craft room at the lodge (or, for the sake of accuracy, I walked and Sierra toddled; a cracked tailbone is a gift that keeps on giving), which was equipped with multi-colored fabric, buttons, ribbons, feathers, beads, and paint.

"This will be a good start," I said and began arranging the feathers into the shape of a mask. "I'll paste the feathers onto a template, spray the whole thing with gold paint, and then put a couple of rhinestones around the eye holes."

"That'll look smokin,'" said Sierra as she dug through a bowl of small red sequins. "Max and I are making pirate-themed masks."

I dropped a feather, and it wafted to the floor. "Max? You are going to the dance with Max?" I sounded pathetic, I know, but I thought Max wasn't going to the dance and especially not with a date.

"He asked me at lunch," said Sierra. She waited for a second, frowning at my lack of enthusiasm. "Y'all okay with that?"

"Of course I am! You two will have so much fun together!" It came out a little too loudly.

"I think so, too. Actually, I was hoping that Garrett would ask me, but he asked Molly instead. I was pretty bummed until Max gave me a handful of wildflowers and asked if I would be his date. How could I say no to an offer like that? Besides, Max is hot. Sure, he's no Jake or Garrett, but he's still one fine piece of . . ."

"You guys will look great together," I interrupted and swallowed the coconut-sized lump in my throat. "So, Garrett and Molly, huh?"

"Thought y'all knew." Sierra pulled some silky red fabric off the table and measured it across her face. "Molly totally cringed when she accepted his invitation. You know, some girls didn't get asked at all, and Molly is all bummed because she has to go with only the second-cutest guy at camp. What a brat."

The craft room's door swung open, and a pair of red canvas shoes stomped in. "I should've known you two would be hanging around in the craft corner. Doing some knitting, are we?" Claire's face held the usual smirk.

"Are y'all looking for your horns and pitchfork, Claire?" said a wide-eyed Sierra. "Sorry, but they aren't in here. If y'all need some boondoggle, however . . ."

"Actually, I was looking for *you*."

"Me," I clarified for Sierra, thinking it was about tonight's rendezvous to the mystery building in the woods.

"No, both of you. I need you two to follow me."

"Like *that's* gonna happen," Sierra said and continued sorting out sequins for her mask.

"I've got to show you something. Molly and Syrup, too. Trust me—you won't be sorry."

I immediately unplugged my hot-glue gun and stowed the beginnings of my mask into an empty drawer in the cabinet. Sierra sighed and did likewise. Claire had never instigated any sort of anything with anyone before, so whatever she wanted us to see had to be important.

———

"A dead deer? Y'all made us hike all the way up here to see a stinkin' dead deer? Sierra pinched her nostrils as though her nose was a pimple ready for the taking. "What kind of psychotic freak are you?"

Molly swatted at a fly. "I think I'm going to be sick."

"I think it's cool," said Syrup and nudged the deer's bloated belly with the toe of her yellow flip-flops. "We should gut it and eat it."

"Is this what you wanted us to see?" I asked Claire, searching the carcass for something extraordinary, like a third eyeball or something.

Claire's face sustained the sneer that it had carried a quarter of the way up the Arrowhead Trail. "If you opened your eyes and looked beyond the deer, you might see something greater. You might even see revenge."

"Huh?" we all said in unison.

"I was hiking to the lake after lunch, but needed to take a leak. I pulled away from the trail and came across this deer. The idea freakin' came to me. The guys haven't been punished for messing with our stuff yet. We should pay them back in a way that they'll never forget."

"By showing them a dead deer?" asked Syrup.

"No. By *giving* them a dead deer," Claire replied. "Like an early Christmas present."

"But who would want that?" said Molly. "Er . . . besides Syrup."

"My point exactly. Can you imagine the looks on the guys' faces when they walk into their cabin only to find that Santa had left them a bloated deer in their shower?"

All were silent as we pondered the idea. The horror, the revulsion, the anger of finding an animal carcass in one's own cabin. And the smell. Oh ho ho! The idea was brilliant, and I wished so badly that I had thought of it first. "I'm in. I'm all-in!" I punched the air excitedly.

"Y'all can't be serious," said Sierra. "There's no way we can carry a deer back to camp. It weighs, like, eight hundred pounds."

"Actually, the average white-tailed buck stands three and a half feet and weighs only two hundred pounds," I said. "This one is obviously young because its third tooth from the bottom has three cusps—a baby tooth. Because this deer has not reached its maximum weight, it likely weighs only 150 to 175 pounds. But that's just an estimate."

My roommates gaped at me. "How the freak would you know that?" said Claire, looking at me as though my I.Q. might give her the cooties.

"Oh . . . huh . . . I don't really know," I said, rather perplexed myself. "Maybe Tanji lectured about it in class?"

Molly and Syrup shook their heads.

"Even so," said Sierra, "we can't carry a two-hundred-pound deer a whole mile down the trail. Especially me. Remember my tailbone problem?"

"We could drag it by the antennae," suggested Syrup.

I had an idea. "You know the buffet table that the dining staff wheels out for breakfast—it usually holds bagels and fruit and stuff? The staff cleaned it this morning and parked it outside the dining hall to dry. If we somehow got the deer on top of it, we could wheel it down the trail. It would be easy."

"And conspicuous. Don't y'all think the leaders would see us?"

My stomach did a little flip at that. Getting caught could land us in a heck of a lot more trouble than just getting sent home. I sent a worried look to Claire. "Sierra is right. If Tanji or Margaret see us . . ."

"Don't be such a baby. We'll be careful. Besides, the leaders are never out during our free time."

Sierra walked up to Claire and jammed her pointer finger angrily into the space above her collarbone. "You know, this battle is not even yours to fight, Claire. This prank war is between Molly, Kaitlin, and the boys."

Claire smacked Sierra's hand away. "This became my battle when I found my favorite pair of panties bunched up and stuffed in a bag of Syrup's salt and vinegar potato chips."

Syrup giggled.

I smacked my forehead. "Garrett!"

"Look, there's no better idea than this. The guys can't top it; they wouldn't even dare. So are you guys in or are you out?"

"Count me in," I said.

"Me too," said Molly. "But I refuse to touch the deer in any way."

"Can I keep one of the antennae for myself?" asked Syrup.

"You mean antlers? If you're truly that disgusting, it's all yours." said Claire, shaking her head.

We all looked from the deer to Sierra, the deer to Sierra.

"Fine," she sighed. "I'll do it. But I'll pin it all on Claire if we get caught."

"I wouldn't have the credit go to anyone else," said Claire, grinning from ear to ear.

"One, two, three!" We heaved the carcass into the air and swung it forward. As the deer thudded onto the buffet table, an explosion of necrotic air assaulted our noses. Molly yipped and jumped up and down on her tippy toes. Syrup clapped her hands joyously, and I dropped to the ground and put my head between my legs. If anyone ever happened to ask me what the worst smell in the world was, I would undoubtedly have the answer.

Snatching the buffet table had been the easy part. No one was anywhere near the dining hall when we disassembled the sneeze guard and wheeled the cart to the Arrowhead Trail. Pushing the table up the trail proved a bit more tumultuous. The trail was just wide enough to accommodate the table but was too rocky and steep to make it easy. The wheels wedged between rocks and refused to maneuver at narrow angles. We had to do five-point turns at every switchback. By the time we finally reached the carcass, the five of us had dispensed enough sweat to awaken the Kalahari Desert.

With the deer securely loaded, we began our slow descent down the mountain. Claire and I held the top of the table to make sure it didn't plow down the trail without us, while Syrup and Sierra walked alongside the table and held the deer steady so it didn't plow down the trail without the table. Molly volunteered to run ahead of the group (any excuse not to touch the deer . . . or maybe any excuse not to associate with me) and warn us if she spotted anyone hiking toward the lake.

We thought our bases were covered until two girl campers approached us from behind, apparently returning from an afternoon of canoeing. With no point in stashing the deer—since they saw us long before we saw them—we just let them pass. They did so in silence, staring at the deer in perplexed shock. After all, it was lounging on the same table that they had spooned yogurt from only hours before. What must've been going through their minds at that particular moment, I could only guess, but none of us could compose a believable excuse as to why we were wheeling a bloated deer toward camp on a portable buffet table.

We continued down the trail until we reached Overlook. When satisfied that our path was clear, we steered the table over the main trail and then up the smaller trail leading to the boys' cabin. We parked the deer next to the stairway, and Sierra ran up to the side window. She wiped the dusty film off the glass and peered in.

"No one's in there. They must still be playing basketball," she whispered.

Claire nodded. "Then we've got to act fast. Syrup and Sierra, grab the backside. Kaitlin and I will take the shoulders. Molly, you stand guard. Let's keep things quick and quiet." Claire didn't explain the "quiet" part, but I knew she was thinking of the possibility of hidden microphones.

With extreme awkwardness, we carried the deer up the stairs and through the doorway. As we veered toward the bathroom, I was struck by an even more brilliant idea. I cleared my throat as loudly as I dared and nodded my head toward Garrett's bunk bed—the one with a stuffed rhino and a poster of a bikini model beside it.

The mattress below Garrett's looked very empty and very lonely. Molly nodded her head vigorously, and Claire leered in approval. My insides shook with the hilarity of it. I struggled to keep my laughter inside.

We swiveled the deer toward the bed and heaved it onto the old mattress. Its stiff legs jutted off the edge of the bed, and a trickle of foamy pink fluid made its way out of the deer's nostril and onto the mattress. Otherwise, the creature appeared rather peaceful in its new resting place.

Claire slid a blanket from Garrett's top bunk and proceeded to tuck the sleeping creature in. I almost lost my composure then and there. I tried not to picture the looks on the guys' faces when they discovered their new roommate. I tried not to hear the slew of ugly words that would come from their mouths. And I tried not to think of the stink that they'd likely never ever be able to completely extinguish from their cabin.

But I did think of those things.

And then the space behind my nose got all tickly. My throat expanded and contracted, and my chest went rigid with gallons of pent-up energy. I cupped my hands over my mouth and forced myself to think of the most horrifying, revolting, unfunny thoughts possible. Hidden microphones. Puppy mills. Manslaughter. Miracle Whip.

But when Claire grabbed Garrett's stuffed rhinoceros and tucked it lovingly in between the animal's hoofs, I knew that the laughter couldn't be stopped.

Molly snorted first. Then Sierra. Syrup made a high-pitched whinnying sound. And then it was over.

"Ahhhh! Ho ho ho heeee! Ha ha ha haaaa!" I belted.

We scampered from the cabin and dove into the grass, bellowing in laughter. It took us a good sixty seconds for us to regain any semblance of composure.

I stood up, brushed myself off, and reached to help Claire out of the roughage.

"Screw the microphones," Claire said, gasping for air. "That moment was too beautiful—worth freakin' disappearing and then some."

"Maybe—hic—not worth disappearing, but it was—hic—easily the highlight of my summer," I replied.

"What's all this talk about microphones and disappearing?" Sierra pushed herself up and hinged her arm around Claire's neck—an act of truce that did not go over well. Claire stepped away and let Sierra's arm drop to the side.

"None of your business, lab rat," she said.

Sierra scowled.

"I forgot to get my antennae. I can't believe I forgot," Syrup sniffed and wiped away a disappointed tear. "Can I go back in and get it?"

"I'm sorry Syrup; we've got to jet," I said. "The guys could be here any minute. We've already pressed our luck."

"Why don't y'all just take one of Claire's horns? She'll probably sprout a new one anyway," Sierra grabbed Syrup and they started pushing the buffet table down the trail—the table's electrical cords dragging behind.

"I call the shower first," said Molly, and was gone before I saw her leave.

I turned to Claire. "Thanks. That was a really good idea."

"No. Thank *you*," she replied. She was positively beaming.

The boys were late for dinner. The anticipation of seeing them post-deer-deposit was making us all a little antsy. Molly was chewing on a clump of her hair. I was scratching itches that didn't exist. Syrup had bypassed moisturizing her lips and was simply taking bites out of her fudge-flavored Chapstick.

"Do you think they'll be mad?" asked Syrup.

"Yup," I said.

"I hope Max will still take me to the dance," said Sierra.

"He will," I sighed.

We watched as two servers wheeled the buffet table into the center of the room. It was loaded with lettuce, tomatoes, croutons, and salad dressings. We would not be eating from the salad bar that night . . . or ever again.

The dining hall door opened, and the guys walked inside. They looked pale and traumatized, except for Garrett, whose face was red and his jugular pulsing. The boys passed our table without so much as looking at us. Max, however, discreetly dropped a note into my lap. While my roommates giggled and congratulated themselves on the boys' snub, I quietly opened my letter.

Dear Kaitlin,

I think you should know that the stunt you pulled was mean-spirited and disgusting. I've never been so grossed out in my life. I will never be able to look at venison the same and should call PETA just to tell them what you did.

That being said, I'd like to give you props for the most lit prank I've ever seen.

For fear of looking like a traitor, I'll be giving you the cold shoulder for the rest of the evening. I've seen what a scalping looks like in the movies and decided it's not for me.

Garrett is the angriest; his rhinoceros is unsalvageable. I'm not sure what that means for his love life, but I question if the rhino was the good luck charm he thought it to be. Garrett asked four different girls to the dance, and only one said yes—and I don't think she was happy about it.

Because you are a cool girl, and because you and your friends' creativity deserve a reward, I'd like to pass on the general reaction to your little prank: You'd actually be surprised at how long it took us to notice the deer. When we came back from playing basketball, Jake went straight for the bathroom to rework his hair, and the rest of us started wrestling and goofing off.

My bunkmate, Stewart, commented on the smell first. Then Garrett looked up from a chokehold and saw a mule deer playing the big spoon with his boyhood rhinoceros. He screamed like a little girl.

You are a delicate lady, so I won't repeat the names you all were called, nor will I describe the colors that were left on the mattress after the deer had been removed (the mattress will be burned at the next bonfire). I will say this: NASTY.

We carried the deer as far away from our cabin as possible (except for Garrett. He refused to help us return the deer back to the wild. The guy knows how to dish out punishment but isn't very good at taking it).

A small ravine past the fire pit made a decent grave. The deer's stomach burst when it hit the rocks below. I never knew that a smell could literally knock you off your feet.

Then we came back and took turns using the shower; I scrubbed pretty hard. I hope you won't mind when I tell you I am now three million skin cells less of a man. I'm not sure I have an epidermis anymore.

Now I am writing you. I should hate you, but I don't. It helps to know that you, too, had to handle the deer. How did you girls get it to our cabin, anyway?

Do I really want to know?

Yours,

Max

P.S. See you at 1 A.M. Dress warm.

ASHLEY

"Thank you for allowing me to visit under such short notice," Dr. Forsythe said as he took the iced tea from Janice's hand. His eyes drooped with exhaustion but still managed to twinkle.

"You've had a long flight," Janice remarked and sat down on the loveseat next to her daughter.

"That I have, but for good reason." He took two gigantic gulps of tea. "But first things first; I must congratulate you on the babies, Ashley. You must have quite a bit on your mind these days."

"You have no idea," she answered, circling her volleyball-shaped belly with her fingernails. "I'm a total basket case. Twins are a lot to . . ."

"Dr. Forsythe," Janice interrupted. "On the phone yesterday, you said that you wanted to help us."

"Indeed I did. But before we get started, would you mind if I bored you with some information about myself?"

"Sure. I mean go ahead," said Ashley, smiling at this kind, old gentleman.

"Excellent, excellent." Dr. Forsythe loosened his tie and took another sip from his glass.

"I was born in California in 1950. I was blessed with everything a child could possibly need: love, food, shelter, and an extremely generous trust fund. Indeed, I lived a life of privilege. I graduated from Harvard Medical School in 1975 and returned to California for my residency.

"I worked in a small town, only an hour away from where I grew up, but it might has well have been a completely different country. The people were dirty, run-down, and extremely poor. Many of the children's teeth were rotting out of their mouths, and hardly any of them had received the required immunizations. I was also surprised by how many of the patients were young teenage girls in binds similar to your own—unwed, pregnant, and struggling financially.

"My heart ached for these young women. I settled on obstetrics and made it my lifelong mission to help them. And indeed I have done that. Last year, however, I had the opportunity to take my ambitions to the next level. I created a center to help pregnant young women fully understand their options."

Janice frowned and folded her arms across her chest. "If you are talking about abortion, Dr. Forsythe, we might as well end the conversation right here. Ashley and I have already decided—"

"I apologize, Mrs. Campbell. I didn't intend for you to think I started an abortion clinic. On the contrary, my center assists women as they journey into parenthood. We provide prenatal care, classes, and physical resources to help with the difficulties associated with young pregnancy.

"We also teach about the blessings associated with adoption. We don't push the young ladies into giving up their babies; we just present them a positive alternative to premature motherhood."

"I've thought about adoption," said Ashley. "But I also want to try to be a mother—even if I'm not ready. It's just that I wasn't expecting twins. I don't know if I can take care of two babies. I'm still in high school. I don't even have a job."

"I am aware of your predicament, and it is not as rare as you think. Just last year, I helped a handful of girls just like you." Dr. Forsythe opened his briefcase and pulled out two pamphlets, handing one to Ashley and one to Janice. The front of the pamphlet read "The Leavitt Center: A Solution for Families."

"I understand that you are struggling with the decision of adoption," said Dr. Forsythe. "You love these babies and want to be their mother. You also want to do what's best for them. You are a beautiful, smart woman, Ashley, and I surmise that you also had plans for college and a career before this pregnancy occurred."

Janice nodded smugly. "She could've been a doctor herself."

"Miss Ashley, I am prepared to offer you a solution that will no doubt satisfy your every desire for your children and for your own future."

Janice leaned toward Dr. Forsythe. "What do you mean, Doctor? What kind of solution could you offer us that we haven't thought of yet?"

Dr. Forsythe's once tired eyes positively glowed. "Ashley, you were excited to be a mother before you found out the babies were twins, right? Have you ever considered giving one of the babies up for adoption but keeping the other?"

"Oh . . . well . . . no," Ashley said.

"Dr. Forsythe, with all due respect, I don't see how the adoption of one baby would solve any of our problems," Janice said. "Ashley would still be tied down, and we'd still be in financial ruin."

Dr. Forsythe nodded. "What you are saying might be true by using the traditional adoptive route. The Leavitt Center, however, works a little differently. First of all, you'll be able to handpick the parents for your baby from a list of qualified applicants. In turn, the adoptive parents will cover all of your prenatal and postpartum medical expenses—for you and the two babies."

"Even though I will only be giving them one child?" Ashley asked.

"Yes, that's part of the agreement. Also, through the mediation of the center, the adoptive parents will pay you a monthly allotment of $1000, which will continue well into the child's teens."

"You're joking, right? That's a lot of money. That's enough to pay for childcare so I can finish high school and work a job." Ashley eyed her mother for confirmation.

"That *is* a lot of money, Doctor, but it doesn't make any sense. Why would a family spend well over a $100,000 when they could adopt through a traditional agency for thousands of dollars less?"

"Good question. Many people have difficulties adopting because they have certain . . . limitations."

"I would only want my child to go to the best parents," said Ashley. "If the agencies don't see the applicants as good parents, why should I?"

"That's where the agencies are terribly flawed. The limitations of many applicants have nothing to do with their ability to be top-notch parents. For example, some people are denied adoption because they have temporary health issues or are older than typical first-time parents. Single men and women are also sometimes denied. It hardly seems fair that a qualified applicant is deemed unfit for parenthood because of reasons completely out of their control.

"The Leavitt Center understands that these less-traditional families are often the most capable of providing loving and nurturing homes. They don't see the money as a sacrifice because you will be giving them a priceless gift, one that they could not receive any other way—the gift of parenthood." Dr. Forsythe reached across the coffee table and squeezed Ashley's hand.

"Wow. I never thought of adoption that way," she squeezed back. For the first time since finding out she was having two babies, not one, Ashley again felt all of the excitement of being a new mommy. Perhaps the twins were a godsend rather than a curse. "But will the babies be okay with the separation?"

"Wonderful question. They might sense the separation initially, but will suffer no long-term trauma. They'll adjust normally as long as they remain unaware that they have a sibling."

"And what's in it for you, Dr. Forsythe? How can you afford to provide this service?" Janice asked, ever the skeptic.

"The Leavitt Center is a nonprofit. Some of the money comes through donations, but I've also reached into my own pockets for much of the funds. Remember, I have always been a wealthy man. And while I, personally, do not receive any money back from these adoptions, I am paid richly in gratification from helping those in need." His eyes misted over.

Janice placed her hand on Ashley's shoulder. "Ashley and I will need to give this some serious thought before deciding on anything."

"Certainly. Certainly. Take all the time you need." Dr. Forsythe pulled a stack of paperwork out of his briefcase. "Here is all of the adoption information, policies, and procedures for the Leavitt Center. It is also important to know that because this is not a standard adoption, we will not be going through the standard legal channels."

"This is illegal?" asked Ashley.

"Unfortunately, yes. I look forward to the day when all good and qualified people have the option to adopt. Until then, the Leavitt Center works quietly. I will understand if this weighs into your final decision." Dr. Forsythe handed Ashley his card. "Call me with any questions, day or night. And when you are ready to start selecting a parent for one of your children, I'll send a representative to assist you in the process."

He stood up from the sofa and shook Janice and Ashley's hands. They followed him toward the front door. "Oh, forgive me, I almost forgot . . ." he said as his hand grazed the knob. "The Leavitt Foundation also provides full scholarships to all young mothers who participate in the program. I understand that you are an excellent student, Ashley. Have you considered the Ivy League for your schooling?"

CHAPTER 10

KAITLIN

I flipped on my flashlight and checked my watch—12:45 A.M. Finally! I hadn't slept a wink since I'd gotten into bed—anxiety had made sure of that. Now that the time had come, both relief and terror prickled my insides. I shimmied out of my sleeping bag and crept over to Claire's bed. I gave her shoulder a gentle tap. No movement. I poked a little harder. Claire gasped and grabbed at my arm.

"Shhh," I hushed—my heart now drumming up my esophagus. "It's just me. It's time to go." Claire's body relaxed, and she released her grip, leaving half-moon indentations in my skin. She rolled out of bed, and we changed quickly from pajamas into jeans and sweatshirts. Claire helped me thread my arms though the straps of my pack, and we tiptoed to the door. I thumbed the handle and nudged it open. The rusty hinges announced our mutiny with a tattling groan. Claire and I flinched as our roommates squirmed in their beds. Syrup's eyes popped open.

"Where are you guys going?" she mumbled.

"Nowhere. Go back to sleep!" Claire sizzled.

"Huh?" Syrup mumbled and rolled back over without another word. Claire and I passed through the screen door and cautiously closed it behind us.

A chilly blanket of clouds smothered any notion of a moon or stars. As if the evening's adventure wasn't nerve-racking enough, now we'd have to do it in pitch black. I shifted my weight from side to side; apparently, my nerves felt an urge to express themselves through interpretive dance.

"Stop that," Claire demanded, curtly. "You should've pissed before we left the cabin."

"Er . . . I'm just a little nervous."

"Now you're making me nervous, so knock it off." She looked around. A faint flicker of a light in the distance gave the sky a dangerous glow. "We better keep the flashlights off and avoid the main trail. Security Phil is on the prowl."

We skirted the campground and army crawled through the dewy meadow behind the fire pit. Our clothes and hair snagged on thorny bushes and trees and, with every snap and crackle, my blood surged in panic. True, usually I could ride horses, drag dead animals down the mountainside, and play basketball with boys twice my size, but I was definitely not cut out for this type of adventure.

We reached the official meeting spot, and Max emerged from behind a large tree trunk. "I was beginning to think you two chickened out," he said, relieved.

And then another dark figure stepped out from behind the tree. I jumped half out of my skin before I realized that it was only Garrett. "Protein bar, anyone?" he chewed, holding up the remainder of a half-eaten Power Bar.

Claire snatched the bar out of Garrett's hand and pelted it at his chest. "Who invited you?"

Max traced the dirt with his shoe guiltily and tried to explain away the new addition. "When I asked Garrett to borrow his flashlight and walkie-talkies, he wouldn't stop pestering me about why. I made up some lie about wanting to organize some night games."

"'Which was clearly bogus," Garrett intervened. "I knew he was up to something good, so I faked like I was sleeping until he tried to sneak out."

"After I confessed what we were really up to, he demanded that he come, too."

"I can't believe you guys didn't invite me in the first place! I live for this kind of stuff!" Garrett wasn't joking. Dressed in a camouflage jumpsuit and slathered in dark war paint, Garrett had evidently confused this evening's voyage for World War III. "Besides, you kiddies should be thanking your lucky stars that I'm here to babysit."

"Whatever," said Claire impatiently. "Are you guys ready to go or what?"

"I want an apology for the deer first," Garrett insisted.

"Then I guess you aren't coming."

"Then I guess you won't mind if I tell Director Leavitt what you're up to."

Claire snorted. "Try me. Come on, Kaitlin and Max; the trail starts over here."

"Hey . . . wait for me," said Garrett, chasing behind.

In addition to the blackness of the night, the temperature continued to spiral downward, making our trek clumsy and slow. We took turns tripping over rocks and divots in the trail, and after Claire face-planted on the trail and spewed out a mouthful of dirt and obscenities, we all agreed that it might be worth the risk to use our flashlights. Even so, the thinning trail and recent plant growth made the path hard to see.

Claire stopped dead in her tracks about forty minutes into the hike. "Okay, I think this is where I got turned around."

"So which way did you go?"

Claire wavered. "I . . . I guess I'm not sure. I started to panic and stopped paying attention. I might have gone any direction at this point."

"Fantastic," Garrett scoffed. "We could be out here for hours till we find the building. I should have brought more protein bars."

"Lay off, Garrett," said Max. "It can't be far from here. Maybe the best thing to do would be to split up." Max reached into his pack and pulled out two walkie-talkies. He handed one to Claire and kept one for himself. "Kaitlin and I will go to the right, and you and Garrett should go left."

Garrett yanked the walkie-talkie from Claire's grip. "Okay, but I'll be the one calling you if we find the building. And be careful with the other radio transceiver—it cost me an arm and a leg." We synced the channels of the devices, and then Garrett stomped out into the wilderness, Claire following begrudgingly. Max and I smiled at each other and began hiking the opposite direction.

"Care to take bets on who will kill the other first?" I asked as we pushed through some bushes.

"They'll be fine. They just need to figure out who's the head and who's the tail. Heck, I wouldn't be surprised if they fell madly in love by the end of the night."

"That's likely," I laughed. "And what about us?"

"What about us? Do you think we'll fall madly in love by the end of the night?"

"Maxamillian!" I scolded and twisted my body to face him. "What I meant is that I should be the head and you should be the tail." I bumped Max aside with my hip and took the lead.

"I can deal with that," he grinned. "But the name is Max. Just Max."

"Too bad," I said. "Maxamillian is a rather sensible name. Your parents should've given it more thought."

"First off, being named Maxamillian would've been a tragedy. I would've turned into a chronic booger-picker who collects funky-shaped corn flakes and then sells them on Ebay. Secondly, my parents didn't name me. When they adopted me, I came prepackaged with my rugged good looks and the senseless title of 'Max.'"

"I didn't know you were adopted," I mused.

"That's because I don't talk about it much. Don't really think about it, either. I was a newborn when I was adopted, so my folks are all I know. I like it that way; my life has turned out pretty good. I know who I am, and finding my biological parents isn't going to give me any groundbreaking perspective."

"I've never met my biological father, either," I said.

"I thought you lived with your mom and dad."

"Stepdad. He and my mom were married when I was four, but I still call him Dad. I can't remember a time when he wasn't around."

"You're lucky that you didn't have to grow up without a father figure in the house."

"I agree. I mean, my parents have been great, both of them. They could be frustrating sometimes, a bit overprotective, but they've also been really loving. But I *do* wonder about my bio dad. I've always felt a little unbalanced . . . like a ham sandwich without the mayo; I do just fine without it, but maybe I could be just that much better with it."

"I doubt that," said Max. "I like the Kaitlin sandwich as is. Besides, there's probably a reason he's not in your life. Have you asked your mom about him?"

"Yeah. She told me she didn't know him very well herself. Scandalous, huh?"

"Very."

"Maybe she knows more about him than she lets on, though. I mean, how can I trust a woman who might have exchanged me for money? I don't know for sure that's what happened, but I am really starting to freak out about it. If it's true, can I trust anything that she or my dad have ever said?"

"We don't know that's what happened," said Max. "I don't see eye to eye with my parents on a lot of things, but I'm positive that they'd never sell me off. That would contradict everything I know about them; their moral codes might as well be tattooed on their forearms. I remember this one time, when I was a kid, we were on a road trip and stopped at a diner for lunch. After, we got back on the road and traveled for two hours before my mom realized that she'd forgotten to leave a tip. We turned around straight then and drove all the way back to the diner." Max shook his head and smiled at the memory. "They could've just mailed the tip, but they wanted to apologize to the waitress in person. That tip cost us four hours and a half tank of gas."

"Your parents sound dorky . . . and pretty great."

"Yeah, they're cool. That's why I can't swallow being betrayed by them. Plus, I saw how surprised they were when they won the raffle for my stay at Overlook. They were flummoxed, but so excited for me. There was nothing sinister on their end. And I am sure that it's the same for your mom and dad. We have to clear their names so we can rest easy about them."

"Then I'm glad we're doing this. I can't even tell you how freaked out I was to come tonight."

"You don't need to. It was written all over your face."

"That can't be true. I'm a very mysterious person." I laughed.

"Oh, please! I have you all figured out, Miss Kaitlin."

"Okay then, Mr. Max. Try me."

"Alright." He rubbed his hands together. "Sometimes, when we're all in a group, I like to watch you."

"Watch me?"

"Not in a creepy, pervy way, I just notice things. I can't help it. You always have this amused look on your face, like you're telling yourself jokes . . . good ones, too. You usually keep them to yourself though—like you're either too cool to let us in on it or afraid you might get trampled if you do."

"Afraid to get trampled," I admitted. "Me and cool don't belong in the same sentence."

"Talking to you one on one is a different story, though. You light up. It's kind of like watching the fireworks on the fourth of July. It's spectacular and fiery, and I always hope it will last a few minutes more."

"Er," I said.

"Another thing about you—when you smile, you first lift up the right side of your mouth and then the left side. Oh, and you don't check yourself out in the mirror every time you pass one like other girls do. It's almost like you don't know."

"Don't know what?" My arms erupted in a rash of goose bumps.

"If I told you, it would ruin everything," Max said.

I stopped and turned around, standing less than a foot away from Max. "Ruin me," I whispered.

"If you promise not to change . . . " he hesitated and then relented. "It's like you don't know that your eyelashes go on forever and that your face is shaped like a perfect heart. It's like you don't know that your lips are the color of strawberries and that your freckles light up your entire face. It's like you don't know that I think about you all the time and I sometimes wish that . . . well, I wish for a lot of things," he said, almost wistfully.

I felt suspended in space—like I was floating in a Milky Way of dizziness. These things he was saying about me, were they true? I was flabbergasted. A change in conversation was my only hope for equilibrium. "So . . . uh . . . whatcha do for fun in California?"

Max chuckled but seemed grateful that I didn't push the issue. "Where do I start?"

As we hiked deeper into the woods, Max told me about surfing, his favorite street taco truck, and his devotion to the LA Lakers. I learned that Max would be a junior in the fall, that he played attack on the school's lacrosse team and edited the sports section in the yearbook, one day hoping to write the sports column for a big online magazine. In a lot of ways, Max was a typical guy, but in other ways, he surprised me. I'd known him for a whole month, and that night was the first time he'd let on that he was the captain of the lacrosse team or that he had a knack for writing. Max wasn't the type to need the spotlight. Instead, he quietly deferred the center stage to whomever he was with.

And every time he opened that smart mouth of his, the better looking he became. I mean, obviously he had a lot going for him to begin with—dark brown eyes, olive skin, brawny eyebrows—but his cuteness got even better as I spent more time with him. His dimple etched deeper into his cheek when he teased me. His eyes took on a determined glow when he spoke of his family. And while he wasn't tall with gigantic muscles, like Jake, I still felt small and protected while with him. How had it taken me so long to realize that Max was absolutely the most attractive guy I knew?

I liked him. There. I admitted it. I really truly liked Max. And if Sierra laid one slimy Texan finger on him at the dance . . .

"Maybe we should stop here." Max touched my arm. "We would've run into the building by now if we were on the right track. Let's find a high point and try to catch a view of the building from there."

We searched until we came to a massive boulder—several stories high—sticking out of the slope beside us. Max inspected the rock with his flashlight. A large crack, starting at the base of the boulder and zigzagging upward, would give us decent footing to climb to the top. "Do you want to go first?" Max asked. "That way I can aim the flashlight and help you if you need it."

"I don't know," I giggled. "That would give you a painfully close-up view of my . . . ahem . . . backside."

"Promise not to look." Max raised three fingers in the air, but the grin on his face was highly suspect.

I grasped the cold boulder and heaved my body onto the narrow ledge. I shimmied myself slowly along the rock's crease, careful not to slip on loose gravel or step on a sleeping snake. Max followed close behind, fixing himself on the boulder with one hand and pointing the flashlight with the other. We made slow progress up the rock. Max teased that his crippled grandma could climb quicker than me. I conceded on that point, but noted that the view of his grandma's backside would be even less agreeable than a view of my own. The image of a granny's bottom kept Max quiet, and a little nauseated, for at least a minute.

At one point, I came to a particularly steep incline. I hesitated, so Max offered me his hand. When our fingers grasped one another's, a thrill rushed up my arm and zipped through my entire body. I wondered if Max also noticed the electric energy. How could he not?

We neared the top of the boulder, and my pace slowed even more. I wasn't afraid of heights, just dying, and if I happened to slip at this altitude, without a rope, death seemed a likely consequence. Also, the crack narrowed toward the boulder's crown. The only way to reach the surface would be to pull myself up the final four feet using my own upper-body strength.

"I don't think I can do it," I told Max. "I'm not strong enough."

Max thought for a moment. "Okay. I'm going to climb around you and pull myself to the top. Then I'll reach down for you."

"Okay," I quivered.

"You sure you want to do this? We can go back down if you don't feel safe."

Under the faint glimmer of the flashlight, I could see the sincerity in Max's eyes. I pushed my chest tightly against the freezing rock to make way for him to pass. "I trust you."

Max slid the flashlight into his jacket pocket. He reached around my back and found a hold beside me. He carefully worked his body around mine, the salty aroma of his skin distracting me from my worries. All I could think about was his firm chest sliding against my shoulders and his jaw grazing the top of my head. After he made it to the other side of me, he placed his arms over the crest of the boulder and carefully hoisted himself to the top. "Child's play," he said and brushed his hands off on his jeans. He took the flashlight from his pocket, wedged it between two small rocks, and leaned over the ledge for my hand.

"Okay, Kaitlin, I need you to push up on the count of three. Are you ready?"

"Yes," I said, but my teeth were chattering.

"Okay. One, two, three!"

I pushed with all the strength my legs had to offer, but then—*gasp*—I lost my footing. It happened so fast: the sound of pebbles sliding off the edge of the cliff, a terrorizing sense of weightlessness, and then the painful jerk of my shoulder in its socket. I dangled in the air by one arm.

"I've got you!" yelled Max as I kicked for the safety of the boulder. My shin slammed into a jagged corner, but the pain was hardly noticeable compared to the panic coursing through my veins. Max grabbed under my arm, leaned back, and heaved me up and over the edge. He dragged me several feet before collapsing backward onto the face of the boulder. I fell into his lap.

"Holy crap! Kaitlin, are you alright?" He panted. I could feel his breath on the back of my neck. His arm was wrapped protectively around my collarbone, pulling me close against his body.

"Child's play," I mimicked and tried to laugh. Unfortunately, the opposite happened. I started bawling. "I'm okay. It's just that . . . I'm just so . . . it was—*sniff*—so scary."

Max moved his head forward so he and I were cheek to cheek. I tilted my face inward and let the tears flow. It was embarrassing blubbering all over him like that, but his body was warm, firm, and so comforting holding mine. I'd never experienced anything like it.

"I'm sorry," he shook his head. "That was so stupid making you climb this dumb rock. I don't know what I was thinking."

"In case you didn't notice, you didn't make me do anything." With the cuff of my sweatshirt, I sheepishly mopped my tears from Max's cheek.

"Still," he said and looked out into the distance, "we can't see the building from here. What was the point?"

Thanks to the pitch-black sky and smothering clouds, Max and I had a perfectly panoramic view of absolutely nothing. We climbed the colossal rock for nothing. I almost plummeted to a bone-crushing death for nothing.

And I would do it again in a heartbeat.

Suddenly my leg started throbbing. "Just great," I moaned as a black outline of sticky blood soaked through my jeans. "I only have one other pair."

"This just isn't your night, is it?" Max stood up and brushed himself off. He moved around me and got down on his knee. "Do you mind?"

I shook my head.

He cinched my jeans up and pointed the flashlight at my shin. Blood oozed down my leg from a huge gash five inches below my knee. He pulled a sports bottle from his pack and poured water over it. "That's not good," he said when he saw how deep it was. He riffled through his pack and found a bandana. He folded twice, vertically, turned it sideways and then cinched it around my leg. "This'll have to do for now. I don't really know what else to do. You should probably see Dr. Forsythe in the morning."

"And say what? 'Hi, Doc. I sliced my leg open after I snuck out in the middle of the night and went on a death-defying hike alone with a boy.' No, I'm sure I'll be fine."

Max offered me his hand and pulled me to my feet. I tested my leg by taking a few steps in place, but Max didn't let go of my hand. Instead, he interlaced our fingers and gave them a gentle squeeze. With his other hand, Max touched my chin and slowly leaned down closer to my face. I closed my eyes and tilted my chin upward. My body felt heavy and weightless at the same time. While the cold night air prickled my outsides, I felt deliciously warm on the inside. Instinctively, I parted my lips and felt the warmth of his breath as his mouth neared mine.

"Come in, Max and Kaitlin! Are you guys there? Over."

I opened my eyes and looked down at my feet. I had almost received my first kiss, and of course it was ruined by stupid Garrett. Max groaned and reached in his bag for his walkie-talkie. "This better be good," he said into the receiver.

"It is," Garrett replied. "We found the building. And say over, you idiot. Over."

"Great. Is there anyone inside? Uh . . . over."

"No, it's all locked up. The back window is open a crack, but it's pretty narrow. Claire tried to fit, but she's a little too va-va-voom in the chest area—if you know what I'm saying. Kaitlin might be able to wiggle her way in. There's nothing for her to brag about in that department. Ouch! Watch it, Claire!"

My face pricked in embarrassment. Did Garrett have to insult my chest to Max?

"So, where do you want us to meet you?" asked Max.

"Ahem," said Garrett.

"Over," Max remembered and grinned wickedly at me.

"Let's meet at the trail where we split up, then we'll hike back to the building together. Over."

"Fine," said Max. "Over and out." He dropped the walkie-talkie into his pack and sighed. "We're going to have to climb back down, you know?"

"As long as you don't mind if I do it grandma style."

"I'll help you every step of the way."

PARKER

Obviously, Parker knew that his father was capable of bad things. Stealing other people's babies, for example, bad. Lying and manipulating, also bad. Neglecting one's own flesh and blood, bad. But as Parker made his way through the woods, he mentally prepared himself for finding out just how bad his father really was.

The moon and stars were not at all in a cooperative mood, which wasn't a problem being that Parker could find his way to the station blindfolded. Parker had helped build it with his own two hands. Far removed from the rest of the compound, Parker had helped drag wood, brick, and other building materials for miles, without so much as a trail to guide him.

Parker hadn't minded the hard work, nor had he questioned why his father insisted the project be kept a secret. At the time, Parker was more interested in making his father proud than asking questions. Only now, two years later, did Parker realize that the station must contain secrets of the no-good variety.

Parker approached the back of the station and could see lights streaming from the window. Weird. Philip Stitchler, his father's henchman, should be out on night patrol, and it couldn't be Parker's father, because he was on a business trip till the following day. Margaret was the only other possible option, but why would she be in the middle of the woods at three o'clock in the morning? Parker walked around the station and peered through the window.

No. It couldn't be. Her. *She* was in there? The way she moved, her posture, her hair—unmistakably *her*. There were others too, but she was the only one that mattered. How would she know about the station? How did she get inside? Parker ran around to the front door and pressed the security code into the lock. The lock buzzed, warning Parker that he'd entered the wrong code. He cursed and tried again. *Bzzz.* Three more tries, and the lock finally clicked. Parker turned the knob and pushed the door open, ready to confront the intruders and finally meet the girl he'd been watching all summer.

But there was no one inside. A cool breeze whizzed through the room, calling Parker's attention to the open window. He ran outside and toward the back of the building, painting the forest in broad strokes with his flashlight. He was too late. They had escaped. *She* was gone. His heart raced and sweat dribbled from his forehead into his eyebrows as he sprinted inside to the computer. He hastily typed in commands and was able to pull up a record of the computer's recent activities. He couldn't believe the amount of information the intruders had accessed in such a short amount of time. The repercussions of this security breach would be devastating. The whole project, his father's life mission, was now in jeopardy.

A smiled crept upon Parker's lips.

He hit a series of keys, thereby erasing all evidence of any intrusion. Next, Parker walked over to the file cabinet, the same one he remembered transporting through the woods after the station had been completed. The cabinet had been heavy, and he'd torn a muscle in his shoulder when lifting it into place. Perhaps the injury is why he remembered the cabinet and the lock on the bottom drawer so well.

Parker pulled the key from his father's den out of his pocket and inserted it into the lock. It was a perfect fit, just as he had suspected. The drawer popped open. He peered inside, surprised that it only contained one thing—a manila envelope. He removed the envelope from the drawer, pinched the metal tabs together, and lifted the top flap. He slid his hand in the folder and carefully extracted a disc and series of photographs. He examined the pictures one by one.

He gasped. "Wait! No. This can't be right!" His hands shuddered violently as he moved from one picture to the next. The final photograph was the worst by far, so bloody, so depraved, and so inescapably incriminating. Parker felt like he was going to be sick. The pictures fell from his grasp and scattered across the floor. He took deep breaths and tried to calm his racing mind and upset stomach.

Parker had known his father was capable of bad things, horrible things even, but never imagined that his father was capable of mass murder.

CHAPTER 11

KAITLIN

Claire and Garrett sat on a rock facing opposite directions—Claire's hands were clenched rigidly in her lap while Garrett tinkered with the dials on his walkie-talkie. The two had obviously had their fill of each other's company.

"It's about time you got here," Claire blew a sigh of relief as we approached the meeting spot. "I was ready to Vincent Van Gogh my own ear if I had to listen to Garrett relive his numerous backpacking expeditions for one minute longer."

"Whatever," Garrett countered. "You tuned me out long before I even told you about the dog-sized squirrel I shot in Wyoming."

"Nope. I heard every excruciating word. I thought I was going to die."

"Lover's quarrel," Max whispered in my ear, and I giggled.

"What did you do to your leg?" exclaimed Garrett, his flashlight frisking my bloodied jeans.

"I cut it on a rock. It's no big deal."

"Did you clean it? I have some hydrogen peroxide in my pack. I know how to make a tourniquet . . ."

"You're such an Eagle Scout," said Claire, as if she had insulted him with the be-all end-all of swear words.

"I should be fine, Garrett. But thanks."

"But the best way to fight off infection is to—"

"She said she was fine, Garrett. Leave the girl alone."

"Okay . . . but don't look to me when your leg turns into a maggot amusement park and needs to be amputated."

"I won't. I'll look to a surgeon."

"We should get on with it, guys," Max said. "We only have a few hours before sunrise. How far is the building?"

"Not far. About fifteen minutes north."

Garrett and Claire steered us through the woods without a hitch. Sure enough, the building could not have looked more out of place amidst the backdrop of pine trees and rotting logs. It looked boxy and high-tech, not rustic and homey, like a cabin might. It was also quite small, just slightly larger than my bedroom at home. There was a door in the front of the building and only one tiny cracked window at the back.

Garrett looked from my chest to the window enough times to give himself whiplash. "Just as I thought. No bosoms to speak of. Kaitlin should be able to slide through the window opening without a hitch."

I had *plenty* of bosoms, thank you very much—though admittedly not as much as Claire. But still! I clenched my jaw and withheld my instinct to thrust my knee into his middle. If in my shoes, I doubted Claire would be so generous.

"Do you want to try, Kaitlin?" asked Max.

"I'm not sure," I said, nervously. I knew I could get in; I had a knack for tight spaces. But when I made it through, not only would I be breaking and entering, but I'd be inside an unknown dark building all by myself. The idea gave me the shivers.

"Come on, Kaitlin," said Garrett. "If you don't try, then the whole night will have been a waste. Do you really want that hanging over your head?"

Max intervened. "It's alright if you don't. We can figure out another way." While Max was trying to let me off the hook, Garrett had a valid point. The whole expedition was centered upon this very building. It would be ludicrous to call it quits. And Max. Things were just starting to get good between us. I couldn't let him down now.

"Alright, I'll do it."

"Way to grow some balls," said Garrett.

"Oh, just shut your stupid face, Garrett," I snarled in a tone that would make Claire's voice sound as sweet as red velvet cake. Garrett clamped his jaw shut, and Claire's face exhibited an expression comparable to the one on my mom's after I'd won my fifth-grade spelling bee.

"A boost, anyone?"

Garrett and Max stepped forward and lifted me up to the window. Grasping the pane, I tilted my head through the crack and slowly squeezed my shoulders, arms, and chest through. Luckily, a wide file cabinet was directly below the window inside, so I had a place to rest my torso as I wriggled the lower half of my body into the room.

"I'll open the front door," I whispered and slid off of the cabinet. I could hear the gentle hum of a power generator and smelled something akin to body odor mixed with stale cigar smoke, but I couldn't see much; a glowing computer screen gave the air barely enough light to maneuver to the front door. I walked slowly across the room, my knees feeling wobbly and weak. I grasped the door knob and twisted shakily, ushering my friends inside.

"Dude, it reeks in here," Garrett complained.

Max groped the wall and flipped on a light switch. We all looked around the room. There was the aforementioned filing cabinet next to a sleek desk with a computer and printer. In the middle of the room were two leather chairs and a peg-legged coffee table—on it an ashtray with cigars and a half-eaten sandwich. And then there was a cot with a sleeping bag and pillow.

Could this be where Security Phil slept? Was this his, for lack of a better word, lair? Gross!

As comfortably as if she was in her own bedroom, Claire went straight to the computer and started fiddling with the keyboard.

"What do you think you are you doing?" asked Garrett, skeptically.

"Shut up. I'm good with computers and systems," she replied curtly. We all moved behind her and watched as she tried to access the computer's database. She typed in codes, clicked on icons, and jiggled the mouse, but finally let out a defeated grunt. "This computer is locked down. I'd need a password to access any information."

"Here, let me try," I leaned over Claire and typed in a string of numbers and letters. My fingers knew exactly what to type, as though I was keying my email address and password or even my own name. The computer accepted my password and the screen flashed, "Welcome, Anjalie."

"Who is Anjalie?" asked Max. "And what did you just type?"

I looked at my hands as if they didn't belong to me. "Oh my gosh; I have no clue. I think I just typed a bunch of random stuff and got lucky," I said, trying to recall the sequence I'd used.

"You could spend weeks typing in random crap and never get *that lucky*," Garrett said.

"I don't know what just came over me." I scratched my head. "But it worked, didn't it?"

Claire looked at me warily, as though she was going to say something or ask me a question, but instead she looked away and began exploring the computer's files. She clicked on the file *Overlook Surveillance* and a list of camp locations appeared on the screen. She selected the *Dining Hall*, and four different angles of the dining room lined up across the screen. The room was unlit, and the chairs rested upside down on the tables. "This footage is current," Claire said, pointing to the date and time stamped on the bottom right-hand side of the image.

"Is there sound with it?" Max asked.

"Let's see." Claire minimized the images and shuffled through the options on the screen. She found an audio button for each table in the dining room.

"That's what I thought." Claire snapped her fingers. "I knew we were being bugged."

"What could be so important about our conversations that they would be recorded?" I recalled a recent dinnertime debate between Sierra and Molly about the pros and cons of hair extensions—Sierra calling them trendy and Molly calling them trashy.

"What's really messed up is that the dining hall is not the only place under surveillance." She returned to the main surveillance page and clicked on the words "Pine Oak."

"Oh, my gosh!" I exclaimed, feeling all sorts of violated. "That's our cabin! That filthy pervert is filming us in our rooms!"

"That's awful," Max agreed, his face turning pink with anger.

The screen displayed three images of our individual bunk beds. Sans Claire and myself, of course, our roommates were sleeping soundly. When Claire clicked the audio button, we could clearly decipher Syrup's trademark snore.

"Hey, I wonder if I could dive into the archives and get a video of you ladies changing into your bathing suits," said Garrett. "Ouch! Dang it, Claire!"

My heart rate slowed at the thought, but it flat-out plummeted at a new realization. "If there is an archive, that means that these images are being saved."

"Which means we are all screwed," finished Max. "If Phil sees the footage from tonight, he will know that we snuck out."

"And then we'll be the next to disappear," I squeaked.

"Not if I erase tonight's footage from all the cabins and disable the surveillance cameras. That way, even though Phil will know that the computer was tampered with, he'll have no idea who did it."

"Do *you* really know how to do that?" asked Garrett, skeptically.

"Relax. I'm an ace at this kind of stuff."

"Fine." He unwrapped a protein bar and shoved it in his mouth, chewing loudly over Claire's shoulder.

It was interesting seeing Claire in this new light. She was still as prickly as a hedgehog, but she was actually smarter than all of us combined. Without her... well, I didn't even want to think about what would happen to us if we got caught.

As Claire and Garrett focused on deleting records, Max and I took on the filing cabinets. I tried to open the bottom drawer, but it was locked. The top drawer slid open easily, however, and much to my delight, was chock-full of cell phones—probably contraband from all of the campers. Overlook went to some serious trouble to make sure nobody could call home. I rummaged through the pile until I found my blue burner phone still wrapped in the charger cord.

"Bingo," I said and slid it safely into my jacket pocket. "I bet Security Phil saw footage of me hiding my phone and knew exactly where to find it."

Max slowly opened the middle drawer, which was heavy with hanging paper files. He thumbed through the tabs at the top of each folder and finally pulled one out. "And speaking of Bingo . . . this one has my name on it." We slid down on the cold floor and flipped through the pages together.

"It's some sort of log," Max said. He pointed to a date typed at the top of the first page. "See, this is my first day of camp."

The page listed the things Max had done during the day. It detailed his health exam with Dr. Forsythe, the ease in which he made friends with Jake and Garrett, and how well he paid attention during orientation.

On the bottom of the page was a smaller section labeled *Sleeping Patterns*. It read: *Subject slept soundly for 8.3 hours. No unusual awakenings.*

"My life is way too boring to be so well documented," he said and continued thumbing through the pages. Not only did it contain his whereabouts, notable conversations, and daily doings for practically every indoor hour—his outdoor behaviors were apparently impossible to track—but it also contained a typed transcription of a few of his journal entries. His face colored as he scanned one particular entry and then quickly flipped to the next page, eyeing me sideways. I hadn't had the chance to read it but guessed it somehow referenced me.

Wednesday, two days previous, was the last day in the printed log. It noted that Max had left the dining hall with me after dinner, but made no mention of our meeting with Claire at the fire pit. No microphones there, apparently, and thank heavens for that. Wednesday's log also mentioned that Jake and Max had a disagreement before bed. I was surprised. Max was so easy going, and I had a hard time believing that he could scuffle with anyone.

"Did you and Jake have a fight?" I asked.

Max quickly closed the file. "I don't know. I guess."

"Want to tell me about it?"

"Maybe another time," he said, filing his folder and pulling out another. "This one's yours."

My file was significantly heavier than Max's, but started off similarly—my health exam, tidbits of what I'd said and done each day, scraps from my journal, and occasional excerpts from letters I'd written to my parents. Midway through the file, however, every traceable step I'd taken, every conversation I'd had, and every letter I'd written home had been transcribed in meticulous detail. Each journal entry was there, and my sleep patterns were scrutinized from toss to turn.

"This is really freaking me out, Max," I said. "It's like he's stalking me."

"It can't be just Security Phil who's watching. There's so much data here about everyone at camp. That's over eighty kids. Can you imagine the manpower it would take to watch everyone and log everything they do all day and all night? This is not just Phil being a pervert. This is way beyond that. I have to agree with Claire that all of the staff at Camp Overlook must be involved."

"But why? And why do they suddenly care more about me than they did at the beginning of the summer? Is it because Phil found my cell phone?"

"I doubt that's the reason. Maybe they know that you've figured out that something is fishy about Overlook. Have you talked about your suspicions to anyone besides Claire and me?"

"No. And I'm pretty sure we were outside every time we talked about it. No microphones."

"What about your journal? Did you write anything that might've given you away?"

"No, I just wrote about friends and stuff. That's all."

"Huh," he thought out loud. "Clearly, they're keeping extra close tabs on you. Do you remember Jason and Tanji staring at you in the rec room the other night?"

"Yeah. It was like they were expecting me to start barking and foaming at the mouth or something."

Just then, Claire clapped her hands together victoriously. "I'm almost done. I just need to send the final command before we leave, and all of the surveillance from tonight will be erased!"

"Awesome work, Claire," said Max.

"So, what did you guys find in the file cabinet?" asked Garrett.

Max filled Garrett and Claire in about the logs, and naturally, Garrett dove into the drawer and pulled out his own folder. He opened it only to find that it was completely empty.

"Not fair," Garrett pouted. "Why isn't anybody watching *me*?"

"No one cares about me either," said Claire, shutting her file.

"But what about Aya? I wonder if she was being watched and if her file says anything about her disappearance."

"That's right. Good thinking, Kaitlin!" Max said. "Do you know her last name?"

I shrugged.

"I have an idea," said Claire. "I'll look in the computer archives and pull up the footage from the night she disappeared. Do you remember the date?"

"Let's see . . . it was only a week into camp, so that would make it the fourth . . . no, the fifth of June."

She walked over to the computer and typed in the date, a time, and our cabin name. She clicked on the grainy image of Aya in her bed. She was shifting from side to side, like she couldn't get comfortable. At one point, she slid down from the top bunk and walked to the bathroom.

"I remember that," I said. "I woke up when she was coming out. She looked awful."

Sure enough, you could hear me asking Aya if she was having another rough night. We watched Aya crawl back in bed and cry quietly into her pillow.

"Fast forward a little," Garrett demanded.

Claire groaned but sped up the footage until someone appeared on the screen. It was Margaret, and she was wearing this strange gray pantsuit. Even with the volume maxed out, we had to strain to hear everything being said. Margaret was speaking so quietly.

"Hi, Aya. I hope I didn't wake you."

"It's okay. I was already awake."

"I know this is a weird time, but I have some questions I need to ask you."

"Is everything alright? I didn't do anything wrong, did I?"

"Oh, no. Everything is fine. I just need to borrow you for a sec. You can go back to bed after I'm done."

"Okay," whispered Aya. She scooted out of her sleeping bag and pulled on a robe and some slippers. Margaret guided her to the door. Moments later, another person entered the cabin. A man. Ugh! Security Phil! He reached under Aya's bed and gathered her belongings. He peeled her sheets and sleeping bag off the bed, slung the bundle over his shoulder, and left our cabin.

"That certainly didn't explain where or why they took her," said Max.

"Yes, but I think we can rule out Aya leaving camp by choice," I said. "She thought she was coming right back."

"I'm going to find her file," Max said, moving for the cabinet. "And my old bunkmate's file, too."

Bzzzz.

"What was that?" Garrett jumped, bracing himself against the wall.

"Oh, my gosh!" I screeched, panic coursing through my body for the second time this evening. "It's the door! Someone's trying to get in!"

"Quickly! We've got to go!" said Max.

Claire shook her head frantically. "But I've got to finish deleting—"

Bzzzz.

"Now!" Together, Max and Garrett forced the window open as wide as it would go. I ran to the cabinet, and Max boosted me up. I turned and slid backward out the window. Claire went next, then Garrett.

Bzzzz.

Garrett and Claire ran behind a heavy patch of trees, but I waited apprehensively until Max launched himself from the window and hit the ground, rolling several times in the dirt. He grabbed my hand and dragged me behind a large pine tree. And not a moment too soon. A dark figure sprinted from around the building and scanned the woods with his flashlight. Fighting my heaving chest and racing heart, I held my body as still as possible.

After a minute, the figure gave up and retreated back into the building, and I released the air I'd been holding in my lungs. Max also gave a sigh of relief. "We're okay for now, but we need to get away from here," he whispered.

"Pssst. Over here," Garrett and Claire emerged from their hiding spot.

"I didn't get to delete the records," Claire whispered, visibly shaken. "All I had to do was send the command, but I ran out of time."

"We can't worry about that now," said Max. "It's almost sunrise, and we've got to get back into our beds before everyone wakes up. We'll figure out the rest later."

"Come on, Claire," Garrett grabbed Claire's hand in a rare moment of kindness. "There wasn't time. It's not your fault."

I'm not exaggerating when I say we tore through the woods like deer fleeing hungry wolves. I barely noticed the shooting pain in my shin as my feet thudded against the cold, solid ground. Instead, I was a speed skater gliding urgently across seamless ice. It couldn't have taken us longer than twenty minutes to return to the spot where we'd met earlier that evening.

My lungs scavenged for oxygen, and my head felt as though it would explode if my upchuck reflex didn't beat it to the punchline. Fortunately, my stomach was empty. Garrett didn't have the luxury. He heaved half-digested protein bars all over the ground.

"Appetizing," panted Claire.

"Now what?" I asked.

"Now we go to our cabins and go to sleep like nothing happened," said Max. "We'll meet up at the dining hall for breakfast and decide what to do next."

Just then, we spotted a light moving toward us. We dropped to the ground and listened.

By the sound of the raspy voice heading up the path, Security Phil was too agitated to notice anything beyond the voice on his cell phone. "A breach of security at the station? How is that possible? I made sure it was locked before I left. Of course I am positive! What do you mean the footage was erased?! The surveillance cameras have been disabled, too? How long until they're up and running again?"

"But I wasn't able to . . . I didn't delete anything. How is that possible?" Claire sputtered.

Phil continued his conversation. "Alright, alright, I'm moving as fast as I can. I'll meet you at the lodge in less than two minutes. Fine, I'll check the boys' cabins for missing campers first. Margaret's on her way to the girls' cabins right now? Okay . . . I know . . . I'm sorry . . . " Phil tucked his phone away and began jogging toward the bunkhouse below Max and Garrett's. They'd have to sprint to make it to their beds before Phil arrived at their cabin next.

No time for mushy goodbyes, Max gave my hand a good-luck squeeze and the boys scampered away. Claire and I peeked at the main trail to be sure it was safe—there'd be no time to skirt along the edges of the camp this time around—and when satisfied our path was clear, dashed up the trail. We'd almost made it to our cabin when we saw Margaret emerge from another female cabin only a few hundred yards south of ours. She hadn't spotted us yet, but it was likely that she'd arrive at our bunkhouse at exactly the same time as us.

"You go," whispered Claire. "I'll create a diversion."

"No, I'll create a diversion. You go."

"We don't have time to argue about this, Kaitlin."

"I can't just leave you," I said, knowing full well that there was no other option.

"I can handle myself. I'll meet you in the bunkhouse in a few minutes. Do it now!" Claire pushed me forward and then ran to the left, making just enough noise to attract attention. Margaret pointed her flashlight at Claire and barked at her to stop. She chased her into the darkness.

Alone, I sprinted to the cabin, flung open the door—which actually minimized the noise of the squeaky hinges—pulled off my pack, tore off my sweatshirt, and dove for safety into my sleeping bag. Besides my suppressed wheezes and Syrup's rhythmical snore, the room was totally quiet. I couldn't believe it. I'd made it back safely without waking anybody in the cabin.

"Welcome back, Kaitlin," Molly said angelically from above me.

Almost anybody.

ASHLEY

Ashley only spent fifteen minutes with the babies before she realized that she couldn't possibly let one of them go. Their fingers and toes were too little, their baby noises were too sweet, their cheeks were too round, and their chins were too pointy. Ashley was smitten.

"Don't worry," she told the infant resting in her arms. "I won't."

"You won't do what?" asked Janice from the bassinet, swaddling the other baby.

Ashley lifted the baby in her arms vertically toward her chest. The baby's head slumped forward, and Ashley giggled. "Oops. You're a floppy little thing, aren't you? Don't worry, I'll get the hang of this soon enough. You and your sis are in good hands."

Janice looked up from her task with alarm. She left the other baby in the bassinet and quickly walked over to the doorway. "Doctor!" she called, her voice echoing down the hallway. "Come right away!"

Dr. Forsythe charged into Ashley's bedroom like there was a fire. "Is everything alright? The babies? Are they okay?"

"It's not the babies that are the problem; it's Ashley. She's having second thoughts." Janice sounded outraged, as though Ashley's desire to keep both babies was a calculated personal attack.

Is that all?" Dr. Forsythe released a sigh of relief. He pulled a chair up to Ashley's bed and wiggled his finger into the infant's tiny balled fist. "The babies are beautiful, aren't they?"

"They're the most perfect things I've ever seen. Or smelled. Do all babies smell so good?"

"I think your babies smell especially pleasant," chuckled Dr. Forsythe. "But it's no surprise that they are special; their mother is a special woman herself. I've never seen a young woman endure labor with such strength and bravery."

"When you told me I'd have to give birth at home, in my room, without an epidural, I didn't think I could do it."

"I know it was hard, but it was completely necessary. For the sake of this adoption, there can be no record of you having two babies instead of one. But you did it, Ashley, and you did a wonderful job. After thirteen hours of labor and an hour and a half of pushing—not to mention eight and a half months of pregnancy—it's no wonder you want to keep both of the babies. You worked tirelessly to bring them into this world."

"It's not just that," said Ashley. "I didn't know how much I'd love them until I saw them. I can't explain how I feel, but I know that I don't want to give one of these babies away. I couldn't."

"That's also a natural feeling; a mother's instinct to care for and protect her offspring is incredibly powerful."

Ashley ran her nose across her child's fuzzy head. "I'm sorry to bail on you, Dr. Forsythe, but I've changed my mind; I'm keeping them both."

"You haven't just changed your mind," Janice interjected, her voice shrill and angry. "You've completely lost it! Do you realize how much of a burden you'll be putting on me by keeping both of them? I'll be the one babysitting when you're flipping burgers to pay for diapers. I'll be the one bridging the financial gap when your minimum wage job barely makes a dent in our medical bills. I'll be the one getting up in the night to feed the babies because you are too tired and too selfish to do it yourself!"

"I don't need your help. I'll figure out how to do it all by myself."

"You really *are* crazy," Janice sputtered.

Dr. Forsythe raised his hand to stop the argument. "Let's keep our voices down." He leaned toward Ashley. "Your mother is wrong about you, Miss Ashley. You are not crazy, and you are especially not selfish. I knew that the moment you chose the Ericsons as the adoptive parents. Not many people can get past their physical appearance—burn victims *do* look alarming. Even legal adoption agencies refused to help them. You, Ashley, you saw beyond the idea of your child only going to parents who looked the part. You saw the Ericsons for who they are and for the love and stability they have to offer. I'd hardly call that selfish."

"But now that I've changed my mind . . ."

"Listen, I know it feels like you are losing a child. I understand loss all too well—my wife passed away just last year. Now I don't have a partner, and my newborn son doesn't have a mother." The doctor's eyes, usually so full of kindness and fun, drooped in sorrow.

"That must've been awful."

"It's a burden I struggle with every day." The doctor cleared his throat. "But the point is that you are not losing a baby, you are saving her. You are giving her a life that she'd never be able to have if you were to keep both babies. And because of that, her sister will have a tremendous, stable life with you."

"But I want both babies," she trembled, pulling the infant into her chest.

"You cannot possibly want both babies as much as the Ericsons want *just* one. After their car accident, they thought they'd never be able to have a child . . . have happiness. You should have seen their joy when I told them that you'd selected them. They fell to their knees and thanked God. You think you know loss? Visualize the looks on their faces when I tell them they won't be parents after all."

Ashley closed her eyes. For a moment, she became Mrs. Ericson, holding the very same infant in her arms—the infant she and her husband had been praying for. Oh, the love, the tenderness, and relief. The joy. Then, without warning, someone wrenched the little body away, telling her that the child was not hers, that she never had a child to begin with. She reached frantically for the baby. She pleaded. She screamed for the child. The heartbreak was unfathomable, excruciating.

Ashley opened her eyes and released a tidal wave of tears. Could she break her promise to the Ericsons? Could she inflict that kind of agony on anyone? On the flip side, Ashley had the power to give the Ericsons the most precious of all gifts, and now that Ashley was a mother, she understood the magnitude of such a gesture . . . and the sacrifice.

One party had to suffer, either the Ericsons or herself. How could a sixteen-year-old girl be in charge of such an important decision?

How could a sixteen-year-old girl take care of two babies all by herself?

Ashley knew what had to be done, and it caused her more pain than giving birth ever could. She held the baby away from her body. "Take her. Dr. Forsythe. Do it now; I can't be strong for much longer."

"Good girl," said Janice, clasping her hands together.

Dr. Forsythe gently slid the child from Ashley's arms and walked toward the door.

Ashley crumpled into her bed and wept, grief washing over her body in heavy, suffocating waves.

"You still have another one," said Janice, her arms folded at her chest.

The doctor stopped at the hallway and turned around. "The Ericsons agreed that it was only appropriate that you name their daughter. What should they call her?"

"Anjalie," Ashley sobbed into her pillow, soaking the pillowcase with tears and misery.

"And *your* baby?"

"Kaitlin. Her name is Kaitlin."

CHAPTER 12

KAITLIN

I pulled the sleeping bag up to my chin and waited apprehensively for Claire's return, but even when my huffs and puffs had thinned to a spongy wheeze, Claire's mattress remained empty. But I couldn't think about that now. Truly, I couldn't think about much of anything. My brain had turned to mush.

I was too tired to think about Claire, too tired to think about Molly awake on the top bunk, too tired to think about my throbbing leg, too tired to think about this deranged camp fiasco, and too tired to think about Max.

Okay, maybe I wasn't too tired to think about Max, but I was definitely too tired to fall asleep.

It took half an hour, but Margaret finally entered our cabin for a head count. I forced my sandpaper-dry eyes shut. They burned and tickled, and refraining from rubbing them was almost as difficult as holding in a sneeze. Nonetheless, I held strong and played dead better than a Fido or a Lassie ever could.

Margaret quietly examined each sleeping camper and then moved on to the next. She paused at Claire's side of the room. If Claire hadn't yet been caught, her identity was now as transparent as Scotch Tape; she'd have no other choice but to become a fugitive. When the light from Margaret's flashlight filtered through my eyelids, I took the opportunity to stir and groan for the sake of credibility. Molly, on the other hand, didn't make a sound from the upper bunk; either she'd fallen back asleep or was also faking it.

When Margaret finally left the cabin, I tried to make sense of all the insanity that had transpired over the previous few hours. My mind, however, kept roving back to the moment when Max took my hand. I opened and closed my fist at the memory—his hand making mine feel so delicate, his rough but gentle skin, the tingle that still lingered at my fingertips. We almost kissed. Almost. We shared a magical moment, and nothing, not sleazy security guards or disgusting surveillance cameras, could take that away.

Slowly, the morning sun tinted our cabin walls a foggy peach color. I was too frazzled to stay in bed one minute longer, so I quietly crawled out of my sleeping bag and grabbed some fresh clothing. I doubted the surveillance system was back in commission yet, but I thought it prudent to change behind the bathroom door just in case.

Max and Garrett must've also been unable to sleep; they were in the dining hall waiting for me. I quickly grabbed an apple and a carton of milk from the buffet line and walked toward their table. Garrett was guzzling a can of cola and looked in danger of falling asleep mid gulp, but Max looked even worse; he tossed his head from side to side and violently massaged his eyes with the fleshy part of his palms. Still, he managed a dimply smile as I sat down beside him. My heart jumped for joy.

"How was your sleep, Kaitlin?" he asked loudly, aware that a microphone might be recording his every word.

"Er . . . good," I said. "You?"

"Slept like a baby." *Yawn.*

"Good. And Garrett? Did you sleep okay?"

Garrett rolled his eyes, impatient with how quickly our conversation was going nowhere. "It's too warm in here. Do you guys want to eat breakfast outside?"

I nodded, even though the dining hall's air conditioning had turned my arm hairs into miniature flag poles. We carried our food to the picnic table behind the lodge, well out of the reach of any high-tech surveillance devices.

"Where's Claire?" asked Max urgently.

"Don't know. Margaret spotted her before we reached our cabin and chased her into the woods. She never made it back into bed."

"But Margaret didn't see *you*, right?"

"I don't think so. If Claire hadn't drawn attention to herself, she and I would both be on the chopping block. Who knows where she is or what they are doing to her right now."

"She's a tough girl. She'll be okay." But Max's voice was tense with worry, too.

"At least the rest of us made it back in time," said Garrett. "Phil came in for an inspection only seconds after we jumped into bed. I had to face the wall so he couldn't see my war paint, but I think we pulled it off."

Max looked at me. "How's your leg, Kaitlin?"

"I don't know. It hurts, but I haven't had the time to really check it out. I'm sure it's fine. So, what do we do from here?"

Garrett thought. "We are lucky that the footage from last night was erased—don't know how the crap that happened—but we have to keep up the show, like nothing has changed from yesterday. No one can suspect that we were out last night."

Easier said than done. Besides being barely coherent enough to form complete sentences, I wasn't sure that I could manage a regular day knowing that my every word and movement was being documented. It was hard enough playing it cool in front of my peers. Speaking of . . .

"Molly knows that I snuck out. She was awake when I came back into the cabin."

"Aw, crap. What did you say to her?"

"Nothing. What was I supposed to say?"

"You're gonna have to tell her something," said Garrett. "Otherwise, she might tattle on you."

"Molly wouldn't do that. She's my friend."

"How friendly has she been since she found out that her little Jakey is your new boyfriend?" Garrett made a pouty face.

"He's not my boyfriend," I said, but for some reason I blushed.

In response, Max's face also turned bright red. I could see the veins pulse at his temples. He looked down at his shoes.

"Yeah, right. Whatever you say," said Garrett patronizingly. "I'm just trying to warn you that Molly might try to even the score. Hell hath no fury . . ."

"I'll think of something to tell her later. I am too tired now. I'm going to skip morning classes and try to get some rest."

"Are you stupid?" Garrett exclaimed, spittle spraying everywhere. "Didn't you listen to anything I just said? You need to be alert. Go to your classes, write in your journal, and for heaven's sake, try to hide that tell-all limp of yours."

"I hate to say it," said Max, "but Garrett is right about one thing. We've got to play this day out like any other. Are you sure that your leg is okay?"

"Sure," I lied. "But what about Claire?"

"What about Claire?" Garrett snorted. "She's gone—a casualty of war. All we can do is hope that if she was caught, she has enough sense to keep her mouth shut about the rest of us."

"Nice," Max said under his breath.

"Maybe I should find a hidden place to charge my cell phone and call my mom. Maybe she'll tell me the truth about what's going on."

Garrett shook his head. "Or maybe she'll lie. Or maybe she'll turn you in. No, the best way to find the truth is to go looking for it ourselves. We'll wait until things calm down here, hopefully by next week, and then plan a midnight visit to the other building, you know, the big one. We'll find all the answers we need there."

I looked at Max. He shrugged.

"Fine," I said. "But I need to get cleaned up if you want me to look like a live human being. I dunked my apple core and milk carton into the trash can by the picnic table and started hobbling toward my cabin. Max jogged up behind me.

"Kaitlin, wait. Can I talk to you for a second?"

"Anything you have to say to the lady can be said in front of me as well!" Garrett called from the picnic table.

Max gave Garrett a stern look and then leaned in so only I could hear what he had to say. "Last night was pretty great. I mean, not the freaky cabin in the woods stuff, but, you know, the other stuff."

"Yeah," I smiled happily, remembering the almost-kiss. "It was pretty great."

"But," he said, looking remorseful, and my innards suddenly tied themselves in a knot. "Maybe we should lay low for a few days. You know, not hold hands and stuff. The dance is coming up, and we both have different dates. I know that you and Jake are a . . . well, I just don't want anyone to feel uncomfortable."

"Oh . . . yeah . . . that would be . . . er . . . bad." The knot wrenched tighter. I was finding it hard to breathe.

"We can see how things are after the dance, maybe, but let's call it quits for now."

"Sure," I managed. "I was actually . . . er . . . thinking the same thing but was afraid to say it. I, uh, didn't want to hurt your feelings." My mouth was going, but I was sure that all of the blood in my body had stopped moving altogether. I couldn't believe what he said and now what I was saying.

"Okay," he hesitated. "So then, we're done?"

"Completely."

"Alright then. I guess I'll see you later on," Max jammed his hands in his pockets and stormed away.

When I got back to my cabin, I turned on the shower and peeled the bandana off of my leg. The disruption of the dressing reopened the gash, and blood poured down my leg. The cut was deep, and the skin around it was red and raw, already hinting at an infection. I cursed and slung the bandage against the bathroom wall.

But the *real* pain was inside me, gnawing at my insides and squeezing at my soul. My chest heaved, but I couldn't cry. I wanted to, needed to, but the knot inside me was too tight.

Only hours before, Max and I were holding hands. What went wrong? What did I say? What did I do?

And then I understood.

I'd been fooling myself this whole summer. I'd somehow convinced myself that I was normal, that I was cute even. Silly me. Fundamentally, I was a loser, a social reject, a weirdo. Nothing could change that. Obviously, Max had figured it out. He'd given me compliments last night just to be nice. He'd held my hand because I threw myself on him after slipping on the rock, and he felt too guilty to say no. But really, the idea of me disgusted him. *I* was disgusting and a doggone fool for believing someone like him could go for someone like me. *Stupid, stupid, stupid, Kaitlin!* How could I give my heart away before making sure it was wanted in the first place!

There was obviously something missing in me, some key ingredient that made other humans worth loving. I mean, everyone at my high school hated me. There was a reason for that. And now I understood that it was entirely possible that I had also been rejected by my own parents. *My own parents!* They'd been paid to send me here where I'd be spied on and possibly experimented on. I had trusted them unconditionally because, hello, they were my *parents*, but even that bond could not change the fact that they'd probably betrayed me.

My mind bounced from one painful thought to another: Max's rejection, then my parents, then camp surveillance, then my throbbing leg, then back to my parents. There was too much to process, and I was starting to feel dizzy and nauseated. I stared at the showerhead and let the water pour down my body. I must've held that stance for quite a while because one of my bunkmates began pounding loudly on the bathroom door.

I quickly dried off, rebandaged my leg, and put on my clothes. Steam whirled out of the bathroom as I opened the door.

"It's about time, whore," Molly hissed meanly and then elbowed her way into the bathroom.

The only person that had ever called me that word before was Mia Bethers. But Molly? She, the first person to take a chance on me at camp, the angel, hated me, too.

I moved past Sierra and Syrup and crawled up on my bed, on top of my sleeping bag. I slowly lowered my head to my pillow. I wasn't going to take a nap; I just needed to rest a little. Just for a quick second.

I was vaguely aware of Sierra and Syrup babbling to each other as they readied themselves for the day, but then I realized the strangest thing. They were speaking in French. *French!* I had no idea that they knew another language—

and with such fluency. They giggled and laughed, the French flowing from their mouths like it was their mother tongue. Then Molly emerged from the bathroom. She had chosen the strangest outfit. It was a gray jumpsuit with these fashion-forward gray pumps. She walked over to my bed and leaned over my face. "Don't fall asleep, whore," she spat. Her eyes looked so hateful and mean, and they were such a strange color—a steely gray, like Tanji's and Director Leavitt's. Then something red dripped from her nose. Blood! She was bleeding all over my face and into my hair. I started to wipe it away but realized that once I touched it, it was no longer red but a liquid silver color, like mercury. Oh my gosh, it *was* mercury, the highly toxic, highly volatile element. And it was all over my face. My skin was absorbing it like a sponge, sucking it in with a wet, slurping sound. I closed my eyes started screaming, batting Molly away from me.

"Kaaaaitlin," she sang, like she was enjoying my terror.

I screamed more, clawing at Molly and begging her to stop dripping on me.

"Kaaaaitlin!" she repeated. "Kaitlin, open your eyes!"

I looked and realized it wasn't Molly over me, but Margaret, and I was grasping a fistful of her fluffy brown hair. There was no mercury coming out of Margaret's nose, and there was no mercury on my hands or on my face either.

"You were dreaming," Margaret said, soothingly. "but you're awake now."

"Huh?" I asked, feeling tears streaming down the sides of my face.

"You can let go of my hair now."

"Oh," I said and opened my hand. Margaret pulled away and smoothed back her hair. I sat up and wiped my face. My heart was beating rapidly—the dream had felt so real. I looked around the room. My roommates were not there. "What time is it," I murmured, still discombobulated.

"It's noon. Lunchtime."

Suddenly I felt wide awake. *No, no, no*! I wasn't supposed to have fallen asleep. I was supposed to have gone to class. I was supposed to have acted like nothing had happened last night. Max and Garrett would be so mad at me! And now Margaret was in my room. "What are you doing here," I asked, my voice cracking.

"I noticed that you missed classes this morning? I thought I'd check on you. Ya feeling alright?"

Thank heavens; she wasn't here to collect me, to "disappear" me? "Er . . . I guess I feel a little under the weather," I said, which was a cover-up for the reason I took a nap, but far from a lie.

Margaret raised her eyebrows and her forehead became a washboard of concern. "Aww, that's too bad. What are your symptoms?"

"Um . . ."

"Bad dreams, clearly," she said. "Have you been getting enough sleep at night?"

If this was her way of getting me to admit to sneaking out with Claire, I wasn't going to fall for it. If she had actual proof, she'd be here with Security Phil, primed and ready to haul me away. "I slept pretty well last night. I just have a little headache."

"That's too bad." Margaret's eyes moved to the photograph of my family that I had pinned to the wall next to my bed. "This must be your mom?" she said, tapping the photo and leaving a smudge of finger juice on my mother's face.

"Yeah."

"Pretty," she mused. "You look like her."

I nodded. Was she trying to play a game or something?

"Are you two close?"

"I guess."

Margaret laughed a little, shaking her head at me like I was a naïve child. Then, out of nowhere she said, "Did you know that Claire went home last night?"

"Um . . . no. No, I didn't. I hope everything is okay?"

"She was sick. She asked us to send her home."

"Funny. Her stuff's still here." My hand shot over my mouth. I regretted the sly remark instantly.

"She wanted us to send her belongings home through the mail," Margaret replied, not blinking an eyelash. "The reason I bring it up, though, is that I know you and Claire have been hanging out lately. I wanted to make sure that you hadn't caught her . . . bug."

"Actually, I think I'm starting to feel better," I lied again.

"So Claire didn't mention to you anything about feeling sick . . . or anything else?"

"No. Claire and I were not good friends. We were just hanging out because . . . uh . . . I had a falling out with Molly. Claire was just a shoulder to cry on."

"Right, Claire was good that way. Real soft and comforting." Sarcasm was unusual coming from Margaret, and it made me feel deeply off balance.

"Look, I'm starved. I should get down to the dining hall. If there isn't anything else . . ."

"Nope. That's all. I was just checking in on you. Make sure to visit Dr. Forsythe if you continue feeling sick, and don't forget to write in your journal today. I just love reading your entries. They are so interesting." Margaret gave my shoulder a squeeze and waved herself out of the cabin.

I knew I didn't belong at the "cool kids" table anymore. Actually, I probably never did. I lowered my head and walked past them, hoping that they wouldn't notice. As Molly and Jake were busy making kissy-faces at each other and Garrett and Max were seemingly engrossed in yet another match of paper football, I was able to slip past the group unseen.

How could I have ever thought I had a place with them? The idea was preposterous, really. Eventually, I was bound to slip back down the social ladder, knocking my chin against every preceding step. See, just look what happened: Molly now despised me, Jake was stuck going to the dance with me, Garrett thought I was stupid, and Max felt the same way about me as I felt about Security Phil.

Well, I wouldn't inflict myself on them any longer. I would eat lunch by myself, where I belonged. I slid my tray onto a table at the back of the room and pushed my fork around my plate. I thought I'd been hungry, but my sweet and sour chicken might as well have been raw sewage. The smell of it made my stomach lurch.

Sierra and Syrup stopped by my table. "Hi, Kaitlin. Why are you eating by yourself? You should've sat with us." Syrup was wearing a large percentage of her meal down the front of her shirt.

"Er . . . um . . ." I said, awkwardly.

"We're on our way to the rec room. Y'all want to meet us after you're done?"

"Oh, uh, no thanks. I have lots to do this afternoon." I did not feel like being anyone's charity case.

"I think there will be nachos there . . ." Syrup tried to tempt me. Did she have to say nachos? My eyes searched the room for the nearest trashcan wherein to toss my cookies. Instead, my eyes found Max's. He sort of smiled and waved at me, and I quickly looked away.

"Thanks anyways, guys. Maybe next time."

Sierra and Syrup left the dining hall and were quickly replaced by Max. "Hi," he said, somewhat sheepishly.

"Er . . . hi."

There was silence, so much silence that I couldn't hear myself think.

"You weren't in class today," he said. There was dejection in his eyes. No, it was pity. He pitied me.

"I know. I'm sorry. I . . . er . . . the thing is . . . I accidentally—"

"Is it because of our conversation? I completely understand; I wouldn't want to see me either if I was you." Wasn't he going to say anything about me messing up the plan? Taking a nap? Blowing my cover? Oh, the *microphones*. I forgot. He was playing a role. He was acting for the cameras. "Jake kept asking Molly where you were. He really wanted to see you."

Right, like that was likely. I wished Max would quit patronizing me.

"Are you feeling okay, Kaitlin? You don't look good at all. Is your leg okay?"

"Er, uh, it's fine. I feel great. Never been better."

Max flinched, like I'd punched him in the gut. "Look, about this morning . . . I didn't mean for it . . . I didn't want . . . I really hope that we can still be friends. I know that you are going to the dance with Jake, but there's no reason you and I can't be pals. Last night was a mistake, and I am sorry, but let's pretend like it never happened. You don't have to sit alone. You can still hang out with us."

Why? So I could continue pretending to be Miss Popular? So I could blend up what little dignity I had left and serve it to my "friends" like an orange smoothie? "Golly geez, thanks, Max! How considerate of you to allow me to sit with you guys. You're a real swell guy, a real pal, you know that?" Under the heat of my anger, my pain dripped down from my body and puddled at the dining room floor.

Good, I thought and hobbled out of the room.

PARKER

Parker no longer wanted to make his father proud.

Parker sat on his bed with his laptop perched on his knees. He read the blood tests, the CAT scans, and all of his father's notes, not just for Jason Leavitt, but for everyone who'd ever been *called upon*. No wonder his father wanted to keep these records out of the digital cloud and completely locked away. If anyone knew that being *called upon* was little more than a death sentence, they'd go running the other way. No one would enter his father's twisted world—no matter how many bows and ribbons were attached.

Poor Jason. Parker felt guilty for all of the energy he'd wasted hating him, envying him. It all made sense now; Jason's colorless eyes and dehydrated personality. Jason was turning into a human vegetable and didn't even know it.

Parker jumped half out of his skin as his father charged into the room without warning. "Parker, now would be the time to tell the truth."

Parker slowly closed his laptop.

His father continued without pausing for air. "The station was broken into last night. The surveillance system was hacked under Anjalie's name, but Anjalie had been sedated the whole night. One of Overlook's campers, Claire, was caught sneaking around the cabins, but she could not have accessed the system by herself."

Parker's heart skipped a beat at the mention of Claire. She'd been caught and was probably here, under the same roof as him, at this very moment. This abrasive, lonely, complicated, beautiful girl was at the Leavitt Center. This thought filled Parker with pleasure and panic. He was so close to her, this girl he'd watched with keen interest all summer, but she was also now in terrible danger.

Parker's father continued. "You, son, are one of the few who know about the station's existence. I'm only going to ask you once. Did you visit *the station* last night?"

Now that Parker knew that Claire's life was on the line, there was no question as to how he must answer. "Yes, Father, I did."

"And it was you who erased Overlook's surveillance?"

"It was me."

"Why the devil would you do that?"

Parker quickly decided where to lie and where to tell the truth. "I was logged on to the surveillance site and noticed Claire sneaking out. I didn't want her to get kicked out of camp."

"That's preposterous. Why would you break protocol for someone you've never met?"

"I knew her sister. She was a cool girl." Parker and Patricia used to study together. Until recently, he'd thought she was attending college. Thanks to the photographs in the manila folder, he now knew that she, along with three others, were weighted down at the bottom of Lake Arrowhead. Parker had no doubt that, unless he intervened, Claire would be joining them soon.

"You caused a tremendous amount of trouble, son. We've all been working around the clock to get the system back in working order. Why did you go to the station in the first place?"

"Because I found the key." Parker reached into his front pocket and pulled out the key to the filing cabinet. He handed it to his father.

The color drained from Dr. Forsythe's face, and he fumbled for something to grab hold of. He found Parker's bed knob and lowered himself onto a chair next to the bed. "So I deduce that you found the . . ."

Parker had never seen his father look so disoriented. It gave him a tiny thrill. "The photographs? Yes. The hard drive as well."

Pause.

"And who have you told?"

"No one. I don't intend to, either." Parker ejected the drive from his laptop and passed it over to his father. Likewise, he slid his hand under his mattress and handed over the manila folder with the photographs of the slain teenagers. "I'm sure you had your reasons."

His father seemed to gather strength from Parker's assurance. He cleared his throat and sat up straight. "Well, son, I'd hoped to spare you the truth in this situation. I'm not proud of the things I have done, of the lengths I've traveled, to keep this project moving. I've had to hide some difficult truths. I've had to silence those who might compromise the integrity of this experiment."

"Yes, Father."

Dr. Forsythe stopped and looked directly at Parker, and his eyes took on their trademark twinkle, the twinkle that won over everyone he came in contact with, the one that Parker knew to be a ruse. "But I will not apologize for my tactics. One has to make certain sacrifices to achieve greatness. Though the sacrifices seem immense now, the future will show them to be microscopic. We are going to change the world—save the world from itself, quite frankly. The greater good, my son. The greater good."

Parker had heard this speech so many times before, though given to justify much smaller infractions, that he could almost recite it verbatim alongside his father. But now it was time for Parker to give a flowery speech of his own. "I understand, Father. It's for the best. I don't blame you for what you've done. If anything, my discovery secured your place in my mind as the leader this world needs. You can do what others can't—see what needs to be done and do it. You're strong and unbiased, and I hope that one day I can be half the man you are. We differ on one point, however. I do not see your actions as sacrifices; I see them as offerings . . . offerings for a miraculous future."

Dr. Forsythe smiled proudly and reached out and squeezed Parker's shoulder. "I've misjudged you, son. For the last few years, I thought you a coward, hiding at the library and the lab, waiting for life to happen to you, waiting to be *called upon*. But even though you entered the station without my permission, you've proved that you're capable of taking initiative. You might not receive a calling this year—although that's probably for the best—but I see leadership in you yet. There is a place for you in this miraculous future, perhaps by my side."

"Thank you, Dad." Parker lowered his eyes. He'd waited his whole life to make his father proud, and now that he had, it made him positively ill.

CHAPTER 13

KAITLIN

"Please, please, oh pretty pretty please!" From the way Sierra begged to do my makeup, you'd think she had been dying to get her hands on me for a makeover since the first day of camp. Actually, that was a very real possibility.

"I don't know, I usually just wear mascara." I imagined Sierra dipping me in Elmer's Glue and rolling me around in Texas Flag-colored glitter.

"Which is exactly the problem. Tonight is y'all's first date ever, and let's not forget that it's with Jake-alicous. You need to kick it up a notch. Also, not to be rude or anything, but it looks like a tornado picked ya'll up, had its way with you, and then spit y'all out."

So I looked terrible. Could you blame me? My entire life had gone down the crapper in a matter of minutes. Max and I hadn't spoken, or even made eye contact, since I blasted him at the dining hall. My parents had sold me out. And Molly, well, Molly had basically turned into my high school nemesis, Mia Bethers.

And then there was the fact that I felt sick, and not just I-ate-one-too-many-meatballs sick, but I-think-my-leg-might-fall-off sick. My gash was definitely infected, which sent ripples of pain and fever throughout my body. I tried to sleep the pain away at night, but every time I drifted off, that feverish, otherworldly nightmare propelled me awake. I was exhausted, achy, and my head hurt something awful. I knew I needed medical attention, but I was too afraid that visiting Dr. Forsythe would expose the truth of where I'd been that night. Despite everything—feeling sick, betrayed, angry, heartbroken, and so very alone—I had to put on a brave face. I had to go to my classes, write in my journal, smile, act healthy, be alert, and pretend that my whole world hadn't just crumbled to the ground. All this because, as horrible as my life was, I could think of something infinitely worse: disappearing.

So pardon me if I didn't have the energy to groom myself. I was emotionally, physically, and socially drained. I had nothing left to give.

The mirror confirmed it. Red wires curled around my eyeballs. My hair was ragweed, and my patchy skin reminded me of a frozen toaster strudel. I was a complete mess, and nothing, save a miracle, could fix it or make it any worse. "Alright, Sierra, have at it."

Sierra clapped giddily and pulled out a case of beauty gadgets that looked more like instruments of torture and destruction. I braced myself as she plucked, chiseled, sanded, and painted. Then she tackled my hair. I had to hand it to her, that girl could work a cylinder of mousse and an iron with talent only to be described as "raw." She arranged my loose curls at the back of my neck, dusted my hair with a judicious amount of gold glitter, and shellacked everything in place with half a can of hairspray. All the while, Syrup ran around spritzing my body with fruity-smelling potions.

"Ta-da! The lady is a masterpiece!" Sierra bowed after she fastened my last stray curl with a bobby pin. "Molly, doesn't Kaitlin look hawt?"

"Sure, if she was going for drag queen chic," Molly replied, running a wand of pink gloss across her lips.

I was too busy gaping at my reflection in the mirror to pay any mind to Molly's insult. My eyes were dramatic and sultry, painted various shades of gold and rimmed with a thick black liner. My lips were strong and pouty, and my hair was soft and romantic looking. With my metallic-colored blouse and glowing skin, I felt like I could almost hold my own next to Jake . . . which was not an easy feat by anyone's standards.

A knock on the door broadcasted the arrival of the boys. Syrup, the only roommate without a date, took it upon herself to play the role of the butler.

"Greetings, gentlemen. May I take your coats?"

"We're not wearing coats," Jake said disdainfully. I didn't like that. Syrup wasn't all there in the head sometimes, but she had a heart of gold.

Molly stepped in front of Syrup. "Don't you guys look good," she said, her eyes batting only at Jake.

"You look good yourself." Obliviously, Garrett planted an obnoxious kiss on Molly's hand. But to call Molly "beautiful" was an understatement. Adorned with fresh purple and pink wildflowers, the mask around her eyes did nothing but draw attention to the radiance of her hair, lips and eyes. Molly could pass for a garden princess and next to her, Garrett—a rainforest of cheap plastic leaves hot-glued to his mask—looked more like a tall, blond garden gnome.

Jake might as well have been a Calvin Klein ad. He wore a black collared shirt, designer jeans, and a simple silver mask over his eyes. His only obvious flaw was that he smelled like he had bathed/gargled in cheap cologne. "Well, Kate, you and I make quite the couple. All eyes will be on us tonight."

I fastened my sparkly gold mask over my eyes. "Er, thanks," I muttered, unsure if his compliment was geared at me or himself. No matter. All I could think about was Max, and Max alone. He was my ideal first date, not Jake. If only I weren't such a loser, maybe things would be different for me.

I watched Max twirl Sierra around and compliment her on what a bonny pirate she made. She giggled, which jiggled the red feathers attached to her black-and-white striped mask. Instead of a mask, Max wore a black patch over his left eye and a stuffed parrot on his shoulder. The pair were major contenders for the best couple prize. Picturing them walking hand in hand to accept the honor made me want to scream. All the insecurities I had about myself were smothered by the deepest, ugliest shade of green.

I kept my eyes on the ground as we walked to the dance as a group, concentrating on disguising my telltale limp. I only occasionally looked up to sneak a peek at Max, but he was focused on his date and didn't seem to notice me at all. Jake was more attentive than ever, however, slipping his hand in mine when we arrived at the dance. Wasn't he embarrassed to be seen with me?

True to form, Overlook spared no expense in transforming the dining hall for the dance. Brightly colored tapestries canopied from the ornate chandelier at the center of the room. Strobe lights bounced from the sea of rainbow-colored balloons to the faux fog hovering over the floor.

"Want something to eat?" said Jake, sliding his hand down my bare shoulder.

"Huh?" I said, straining to hear him above the pounding music and my disgruntled feelings about Max.

"Food! Want some?" Jake motioned to a well-stocked table at the side of the room. Max and Sierra were hanging out there; Sierra was feeding the stuffed parrot a crab cake, and Max was laughing like she'd done something actually funny. He was having a riot. With her, not me.

"Let's just dance," I pulled Jake onto the dance floor.

Like I said, this was my first date. What I failed to mention, however, was that this was also the first time I'd ever danced in a social setting. I swung my arms and wiggled my hips, all while trying to balance on one leg—it simply hurt too much to put much weight on the injured one. Jake tried to keep up with me at first, but in retrospect, I realize that I looked like a complete spaz. He stopped dancing and just stared at me with a puzzled and slightly uncomfortable expression on his face. That's when I realized that I wasn't doing it right. I slowed my movement and hoped that Max hadn't seen.

Jake gave a sigh of relief as a slow song came on and washed away the residue of my horrendous dance moves. He put his hands on my waist and pulled me close. My hands dangled impishly at my side; I hadn't a clue where to put them.

"Here," said Jake as he slid my arms around his neck.

"Urm, thanks," I said and realized that an explanation might be in order. "I am kind of new at this whole dancing thing."

Or *human thing* so it would seem.

Jake laughed. "I noticed. You're so innocent and inexperienced. It's actually kinda hot." He pulled me even closer and let his hands slide to the lowest part of my back. I squirmed a little, trying to de-plaster my face from his chest. He took that as his cue to rest his chin on my head and smell my hair. We rode out the rest of the song like that, him robbing me of personal space, and me, trying my darndest not to suffocate on the fumes of his Axe body spray. At the end of the song, I unzipped myself from Jake and excused myself to the refreshment table. I seized a cookie with blue icing and polished it off in two gigantic bites.

"Eating away the sexual tension, are you?" asked Syrup, taking a sip of punch and leaving a waxy print of fudgecicle lips on the plastic cup. "You and Jake looked hot and heavy out there. Careful, he might pounce." She made her hands into paws and growled like a tiger.

True, I might be innocent and inexperienced, but even I knew what Syrup meant. Jake wanted action tonight and even some incredibly spastic dancing wasn't about to deter him.

I glanced over at Max, who was still all smiles with Sierra. My stomach dropped.

Maybe I shouldn't deter Jake. Maybe I should enjoy my attention wherever I could get it. And maybe I should show Max exactly what he was missing. I took a moment to refill my oxygen stores and then rejoined Jake on the dance floor. I kept my movements small and conservative, but gave Jake a series of sultry provocative looks while swaying my hips to the beat of the music.

He took the bait. He grabbed my waist, his thumbs riding a little lower than I thought necessary, and pulled the center of me right up snug to the center of him. When the song transitioned, Jake whispered in my ear that we should take a break and go for a walk. I felt my stomach rise into my throat. Maybe I didn't want this after all.

"Excuse me," a voice interrupted us. I looked up to see Max. "Mind if I cut in?"

"I don't think so, bro," Jake said, pulling me even closer.

"Just for a sec," said Max.

Jake rolled his eyes, but stepped away and motioned for Max to have at it. He excused himself to the food table.

Like an eight-year-old forced to dance with his great aunt Martha at a wedding reception, Max placed his robotic hands on my hips. He tilted his head so he wouldn't have to look me in the eye and swayed me noncommittally from side to side. What was his problem anyway? It's not like I asked *him* to dance.

"I should have never told you," he stated, after an awkward minute of silence.

"What are you talking about?" I stopped and his hands dropped to his side.

"Remember what we talked about in the woods? That."

I shook my head with an exaggerated smile. "I'm sorry, but I don't speak *cryptic pirate*. Why don't you just say what you're thinking?"

"You're not acting like yourself, Kaitlin. You're acting . . . I don't know . . . like Molly. She's a cool girl, but she's not you. And you're not her."

"I'm just having fun," I lied. There was nothing fun about jealousy taking hold of my mind and soul and Jake taking hold of my body. "Anyway, Jake doesn't seem to mind the way I'm acting."

"No joke! He's all over you. I can even smell him in your hair. It's like he's marked his territory." Max finally looked at me. His eye (the one that wasn't covered by a patch) was crimped in anger. Or was it hurt?

Of course I'd wanted to make Max jealous, but I hadn't wanted to cause him actual pain. I was so confused. I mean, he'd rejected *me*. He didn't want *me*. He had no right to act like I was the one hurting him. "Now you're being crude, Max. You haven't acknowledged me these last couple of days, and now you are acting like I've done something wrong!" I felt a headache coming on.

"You're the one who cut me off. I didn't ask for that. I just thought it would be rude to start dating right before the dance when we both had other dates. Plus Jake told me that . . ."

"And it seems like you are really enjoying your date . . . I mean wench," I spat.

"Listen to yourself, Kaitlin. It's not like you to talk down about people. Why would you say that about your friend?"

My face went hot. Sierra *was* my friend. She'd just spent an hour getting me ready for the dance, neglecting the last-minute details of her own costume so that I might look presentable for my first date. Not only that, I was pretty sure she would've said no to Max if she'd realized that I had feelings for him. I couldn't say the same about myself . . . ahem . . . obviously.

"Whatever," I said, somehow feeling more angered than ever. "You think you were sparing everyone's feelings by this little arrangement, but what about *my* feelings? What about what *I* wanted? Jake and I are just having a good time like *you* suggested we should. This was all your idea."

"I know you and Jake like each other, but it wasn't my idea to let him run his hands all over you." Max sputtered.

"Why am I getting in trouble for Jake's hands? That doesn't seem fair!"

"Because your hands aren't putting a stop to it! You know how much I like you, and you're throwing it in my face with Jake! Are you trying to punish me for something, or are you just that type of girl?"

Between the flashing strobe lights and Max scolding me, I started to feel dizzy. I paused before answering his question. "I'm just me. That's all."

"Well maybe you are not the you I thought you were."

A pool of nausea flowed into my gut and rushed up my spine. I needed some air pronto. I turned around and stumbled out of the dining hall to the picnic table behind the lodge.

I pulled off my mask, put my head between my knees, and waited for the sensation to pass. I breathed for a moment, mentally rehashing my argument with Max. I hated how I'd just behaved. I hated the word I called Sierra, remembering how badly Molly's name-calling had hurt me. I hated yelling at Max, accusations flying out of my mouth like flames. I'd become a jealous monster. This was not me. How did I become this way?

Max had just admitted to still liking me, but because of my insecurities, I had just demolished any possibility of a future relationship with him.

"Where'd you go, Kate? Did you decide to take that romantic stroll without me?" Jake jogged to the picnic table and flashed me his ultra-confident crooked-toothed grin—you know, the one that used to make me swoon. Now it just further aggravated my upchuck reflex.

"Sorry,"—I swallowed—"I guess I am just a modern sort of girl."

"You look pale," he ran his hand over my hair. "You alright?"

"Peachy."

"You don't need to feel bad, Kate. I know."

"Huh?" I answered.

"I figured out the problem. It's kind of obvious. You've been avoiding me all week—eating alone at lunchtime, spending your free time at the cabin. You've never kissed anyone before, and you're scared."

"I thought I was hiding it so well," I said sarcastically. "But it's not . . ."

"You don't have to be nervous about kissing me, Kate. I won't judge you if you don't get it perfect the first time. But I'll tell you what, kissing is not rocket science, just chemistry." Before I had a second to internalize the ridiculousness of what Jake just said, he pulled off his silver mask and plastered his lips against mine.

This was not how I envisioned my first kiss going. In my mind, I had always pictured the kiss with someone I actually liked. In my mind, there would have been sparks, and it would have been amazing. In my mind, it wouldn't have been so dang wet and would in no way involve tongues. And in my mind, the following would not have happened: I vomited.

Okay, so I pushed Jake off and ran to a local bush before the actual vomiting ensued, but Jake was definitely in ear shot of the retching. To make matters worse, from the corner of my eye, I saw Max charging toward us.

"What did you do to her!" he yelled. Jake didn't seem to hear or see Max. He just gaped at me as if in shock. I imagine he usually received better feedback from girls he kissed than them throwing up. Max yelled again. "What did you do to Kaitlin!"

Jake snapped out of his trance. "Nothing. I just kissed . . ."

Thwack!

Max punched Jake good and hard, right in the jaw. It's like boys are genetically programmed to fight because Jake reacted to the hit before Max's knuckles even retracted from his face. He leapt from the bench and shoved Max to the ground.

The stuffed parrot had one glorious moment of flight before bouncing on the dirt and skidding to a stop.

Max swung his body around and knocked Jake down.

I further desecrated the unfortunate shrub.

By this time, a group of people from the dance had congregated outside to see about the commotion. They were not disappointed; the show was spectacular: boys throwing punches and twisting limbs, and me puking out the remainder of my guts—which had a bluish tint due to the sugar cookie—and coming up only long enough to scream at the boys to stop. Once again, I had become Side-Show Kaitlin, the resident freak.

As a final hurrah, Jake pulled Max's eye-patch back as far as it would go and let go. The plastic snapped loudly into Max's eye, and the crowd groaned collectively. A stream of blood dribbled from his eyebrow into his blinking eye.

And then I lost it. I began sobbing like an idiot, completely unable to cope with everything that had just transpired. Suddenly the boys appeared to remember the source of their contention.

"Aw, crap. Are you alright, Kaitlin?" Max wiped his eyebrow with the sleeve of his shirt. Though a bloodied mess, he seemed to have survived the brawl.

"I'm fine," I said and motioned to Jake, who was sprawled out on the ground catching his breath. "This whole thing . . . is just . . . I'm just . . . I just don't feel good." Humiliated beyond what I'd ever thought possible, I turned toward my cabin and began staggering up the slope.

"Kaitlin, wait!" Max yelled.

"Just let me go," I bawled and, without warning, my infected leg gave way. The crowd of spectators gasped as I stumbled to the ground and slid downward a couple of feet. I pushed myself back up and continued running. I didn't have to see myself to know that nothing in the world could possibly look more pathetic than I did at that very moment.

When I arrived at the cabin, my weeping had turned to uncontrolled gasps for air. I grabbed one of my duffle bags and fumbled through the clothes inside until I found my cell phone. I turned the phone on, scrolled to my mom's name, and hit the "send" button.

"Hello."

I tried to calm myself, but a hiccup and a moan were about as much as I could muster.

"Kaitlin, is that you?"

"Yes, Mom"—*hic hic hic*—"I need you to come get me right now."

"Oh, my gosh!" Mom said, her voice turning to pure panic. "Are you okay? What did they do to you? I am so sorry! I should never have let you go!"

"Mom?" I asked, discombobulated.

"He forced me to send you! You've got to believe me. I didn't have a choice!"

I realized Mom thought I'd called about Camp Overlook and not my most recent social hurricane. Before I had a moment to respond, the phone went silent. I gave the cell phone a good shake and realized that the battery had gone dead; I'd barely charged the phone the whole summer. I shrieked and hurled the phone at the wall.

Then the cabin door creaked open. It was Molly, the icing on this urinal cake of an evening. I covered my eyes with my hands, shielding myself from the smirk that was most certainly on her face. "Oh my gosh, are you here to revel?"

"I wouldn't wish what just went down on anyone, even you," Molly said. She disappeared into the bathroom and reemerged holding my toothbrush and toothpaste.

I looked to the ceiling and ran my fingers down my face, pulling my skin and lips downward. The memory of the horrible words Max and I exchanged ricocheted from one end of my brain to the other. And only heaven knew what Max thought happened with Jake and me. On top of that, I'd now be known as "The Regurgitator" for the second time in my life. No guy in their right mind would want to touch me now. And surely not Max.

"I blew it with him. I blew it," I sniffed.

"You blew something, alright, but I think it was more like chunks." She squeezed the tube of toothpaste onto the bristles and handed me the toothbrush.

I snorted and tried to scrub away the pain of what just happened. "I threw up in front of everyone."

"One day you'll laugh about it. Maybe," she added.

I finished brushing my teeth and hobbled to the bathroom to spit in the sink. "Why did you follow me, Molly?" I said as I reemerged.

"Look, I know I've been a beast to you lately, and I want to apologize. You could use one less thing weighing you down." Molly looked to the floor. "And I kind of miss you."

"Don't say that. I am horrible for going to the dance with Jake knowing that you wanted to so badly."

"I won't disagree with you there," said Molly. "But really, I've made myself miserable by pushing you away this last week. I can't believe I called you a . . ."

that name. I'd never called anyone that before. It was so mean. You're the only girlfriend I've had in years, and I let a stupid guy get between us."

"The only girlfriend you've had in years?"

"I know, poor me . . . but it's true." Molly lifted herself up to the top bunk and situated her head on the middle of her pillow.

"Don't let this go to your head, Molly, but you seem like the type of girl people would campaign to be friends with. I'd sell my soul to be confident like you, to look like you."

"That's the problem, I think. You know the first day of camp? I walked into the bunkhouse hoping for a fresh start, but none of the girls would talk to me. It's like they made their minds up about me the second they saw me. Maybe I threatened them or maybe they saw me as competition, but that's how girls have treated me since I was in fifth grade. Tell me that you haven't noticed that Sierra or Syrup won't give me the time of day."

I shrugged.

"Kaitlin, when you arrived at camp that day looking as unsure of yourself as I felt inside, I kind of felt like God was watching out for me, sending me someone who might need me as much as I needed her—like an angel."

Huh? Wasn't she *my* angel? This was unreal. "You don't need me. Guys give you tons of attention. You're so pretty and you're really good at flirting . . ."

"My one and only talent," Molly exhaled. "I wish that I could be smart and adventurous, funny and approachable, like you. Sometimes I wish I had your green eyes and your cute freckles, too—then I wouldn't have to turn to boys to feel okay about myself."

Me? She really felt that way about *me*? "I am so sorry," I said, shaking my head. "I shouldn't have gone to the dance with Jake. A good friend wouldn't have done that."

"Yeah, well, it was a big blow when Jake asked you to the dance instead of me—not that *you're* not great, I just felt rejected. But I shouldn't have pushed you away because, really, it was the most rotten losing your friendship."

"It was hard for me, too," I said, fresh tears welling up in my eyes. I lay down on my mattress below Molly's top bunk and fastened my hands behind my head. "You know, you and I have more in common than you think."

"What do you mean?"

"This is totally embarrassing, and I can't believe I'm telling you this, but I didn't have any friends before Overlook either. Boys or girls."

"None?" Molly asked, genuinely surprised.

"Would you believe that tonight's vomiting demonstration was not my first?"

"Go on," prompted Molly.

I closed my eyes. This was the first time I had ever spoken about the incident and the memory, though years in the past, was still so tender. "I was in sixth grade. I woke up sick with some sort of flu, but my mom made me go to school anyway. She thought I was faking it. So I was sitting in my homeroom and accidentally fell asleep at my desk. And then I had this terrible, terrible nightmare. I woke up screaming and crying and ended up throwing up all over my desk in front of the whole class."

"That's not good."

"It gets worse. You know what jerks kids can be. Instead of checking to see if I was okay, everyone acted all grossed out . . . like I had barfed for the sole purpose of ruining their lives. And get this, the teacher threw me a roll of paper towels and scolded me for making a mess.

"The next day everyone made fun of me. Mia Bethers was the ringleader. That girl had actually been my best friend up to that point, but reevaluated our friendship when she saw how badly I'd embarrassed myself. She didn't want to be unpopular by association. Mia called me names and whispered behind my back. She made sure that no one sat by me at lunch."

"What a brat. I hate people like that."

"Yeah, well, the problem escalated when we started junior high and Mia became super popular. She and the other cool kids made retching sounds as I passed them in the halls and threw food and trash at me. Once, I opened my locker to find that someone had splashed actual throw-up all over my books and assignments." Another tear trickled from the corner of my eye into my hair.

"How'd they get your locker combination?"

"The real question is who'd be messed up enough to save their vomit. It was disgusting. I didn't want to tell my parents what happened. I was ashamed, and I knew they didn't have enough money to buy me new books. So I just cleaned my stuff off the best I could and carried it around the rest of the school year." I bit my lip and tried to regain my composure.

"You'd think the bullying would lose steam after a year of two, but it was relentless, Molly, relentless. Last year, someone—I'm pretty sure Mia—made this GIF. A truly horrible GIF. She'd found on old picture of me and digitally manipulated it to look like my mouth was wide open and a steady stream of green vomit was flying out. It was so horrendously gross, but it totally caught on. People passed the thing around, and somehow it hopped from school to school and then state to state. The GIF went viral, Molly. My face, vomiting, went viral."

"I know what GIF you are talking about," said Molly, quietly. "I've seen it; maybe even used it before to comment on a bad test or something. Of course, I never connected it to you. I'm sure no one could. Your face was not nearly as noticeable as the . . . puke."

"Everyone at my school knew it was me, though. Everyone. I was a joke at school. And when this summer is over and I have to go back, I will continue being a joke. I can only imagine what Mia Bethers has in store for me."

"That's awful," Molly agreed. "I would have never pinned you as the kind of girl to get bullied. You seem so normal."

"I don't feel normal. People treated me like a loser for so long that I somehow started to believe it. Can you imagine how shook I was when I came to camp and started making friends? Then Jake, of all people, asked me to the dance. I guess it went to my head."

"I can understand that."

I sighed. "But it doesn't matter anymore. Now I'm back to square one, the barf girl with no friends and certainly no boyfriend. Max will never want to date me now."

"You mean Jake, don't you?"

"No. Max."

Molly paused for a moment. "I thought you were dating Jake."

"Nope." I opened my mouth to explain, but remembered the microphones in the room. I carefully climbed to the top bunk with Molly and took my voice to a barely audible whisper. "Remember how I disappeared on Wednesday night?

I was out with Max. Well, Max, Claire, and Garrett. We were doing . . . a little exploring. While we were out, Max and I had a moment . . . or a few moments. Even though I went to the dance with Jake, it was Max that I wanted to be with."

"Oh my gosh," Molly covered her mouth and shook her head over and over. "Oh my gosh."

"What?"

"You are going to hate me."

"What?"

"I thought for sure you and Jake were together. Jake has been implying that you two have been, like, hooking up."

I gasped. "Are you kidding me? He's been saying that?" I whisper-yelled. No wonder Max got all weird on me. He thought that I liked Jake. Max thought he was coming between me and Jake. Oh, my gosh! It all made sense. My relief about the misunderstanding was suddenly replaced by fury at Jake for leading people to believe something that wasn't true. "Jake is a disgusting liar! The first time he ever kissed me was tonight and it was *not* consensual!"

"Kaitlin, I thought you snuck out on Wednesday to be with *him*. I was so jealous."

"I know what that feels like. Really, it's okay."

Molly sat up. "You don't get it, Kaitlin. When I saw you dancing with Jake tonight—you looked so pretty and Jake was so into you—I went a little crazy. So I told on you, Kaitlin. I told Margaret that you snuck out. I totally forgot what I did when I saw the fight break out between Max and Jake. I just thought of it now."

My stomach dropped, and I felt like I might pass out. I grabbed Molly by the shoulders and looked her directly in the eyes. "This is so important. Did you tell Margaret that Jake was with me?"

"No. I didn't want him to get kicked out, just you. Wait, Claire didn't go home because she was sick, did she? She left because she was with you and got caught. I'm so sorry, Kaitlin. Maybe they won't send you home. Maybe if I told them I was mistaken . . ."

"It's a little more complicated than that," I moaned. "You talked to Margaret a half an hour ago, right?"

"That's right."

I jumped off the top bunk and grabbed an empty duffle bag from under my bed. I started filling it with clothes, a flashlight, anything that I could get my hands on quickly.

"I've got to get out of here. Pass me my jacket, will you?"

"Kaitlin, what are you doing? This isn't as bad as you think! I'm sure that . . ."

"Tell Max what happened. Tell him everything. And then tell him that I'm very sorry!" I slung the duffle bag over my shoulder and threw open the cabin door. Margaret and Security Phil were standing at the entrance.

"Going somewhere?" Phil rasped.

"Um, no. I just thought I'd . . ." I madly searched my brain for some sort of excuse, but nothing came to mind.

"We hear you haven't been obeying the rules. Is that how you hurt your leg, Kaitlin?" Margaret nudged my shin with the point of her high-heeled boot. A sharp pain jolted up my leg.

"I don't know what you're talking about," I clenched my teeth, trying to hide the agony.

"So you haven't been sneaking out at night? Or making cell phone calls?" Margaret asked.

I shook my head, tears forming at the far corners of my eyes. Security Phil draped his long bony fingers over my left arm, and Margaret grabbed the other. "Why don't you come with us, Kaitlin? You don't look well. Perhaps you should see a doctor."

Before closing the door behind us, Phil turned around and smiled wickedly at Molly. "Thanks for the tip, pretty girl. You made things real easy-like for us."

Molly just stood there with her mouth gaping open.

ASHLEY

The voice on the line was friendly and familiar, but still turned Ashley's blood cold. It had been almost fifteen years since she had last heard Dr. Forsythe's voice. She'd never forget the memory of him walking away with her precious baby, Anjalie.

As promised and without fail, Ashley had received a check for one thousand dollars every month since she had given birth to her twins. Another promise kept, and a huge surprise to Ashley, near high school graduation, she received a letter congratulating her on her acceptance and full-ride scholarship at a prestigious university. She hadn't even applied.

But Dr. Forsythe had not left a forwarding address or phone number, and contacting him had proven impossible. She had spent over fourteen years regretting, wondering, and crying over the decision she had made so many years ago.

"Miss Ashley, are you still there?"

"Yes. Yes, I am." Ashley instinctively pulled the receiver closer to her mouth. "How are you, Dr. Forsythe?"

"Excellent, excellent. Thank you for asking. I trust that Kaitlin is well?"

"As well as you could expect." Ashley stopped. She had so many questions for Dr. Forsythe. Why did he disappear after the babies' delivery? What happened to the so-called Leavitt Center? Why was he calling her now? But only one question seemed to matter at that moment. "Anjalie? Where is Anjalie?"

"With the Ericsons, of course. And doing well. She made the JV Cheer squad, and from what I understand, is the apple of every freshman boy's eye."

"And she's healthy? And loved?"

Dr. Forsythe chuckled. "Yes, my dear. All of those things and more. You could not have picked a better family for Anjalie."

Ashley wiped away a tear. "Thank God."

"But Anjalie is not the reason I am calling. I wish to speak to you about Kaitlin."

"Kaitlin?"

"Yes. This summer, I am holding a special summer camp for the children of those helped by the Leavitt Center. It will be a glorious experience for them, with archery, horseback riding, canoeing . . . I want Kaitlin to be there."

"I'm sorry, what? Camp? What are you talking about, Doctor?"

"Don't worry, Ashley," Dr. Forsythe continued, seeming to ignore Ashley's question. "Anjalie will not be invited, nor will the adopted out children of any of the other recipients. Camp Overlook is only for the children who were kept; do you understand?"

"I don't understand. Why should Kaitlin go to this summer camp? What purpose would it serve?"

"We simply want to observe the children and make sure that they have adjusted properly through the years. That's all."

"Nothing's that simple," Ashley said. "No, Doctor, Kaitlin will not be attending your camp this summer."

"May I ask why not?"

"First off, we can't afford to send her . . ."

"Nonsense. The Leavitt Center will sponsor Kaitlin. Camp won't cost you a cent."

"It's not just that. Kaitlin is going through a rough patch at school with her peers. She tries to hide her feelings, but she's clearly lonely and depressed. My plan is to take her to Grand Junction, where my friend Jade lives, for a couple of weeks. Kaitlin could use my undivided attention."

"Are those your only reasons for not sending her to camp?"

"And, frankly Dr. Forsythe, I don't trust you."

"That is disappointing to hear. Have you not been receiving your checks?"

"Every month. And ever since I figured out what you really are, I have been donating every penny of that money to the local food bank."

"Tell me, Ashley, what do you think I am?"

"You sent me to a fancy school where I got a fancy education. Do you know what I studied at your fancy school? Social work. I learned all about adoption, ethics, and child-related law. I learned that you cheated me. I was young and scared, and you manipulated me into giving up my child. I have been haunted for years knowing that I handed my daughter off to a sleazy, lying baby broker. That is what you are, Dr. Forsythe."

"You may call me a baby broker if you like, but I don't deserve to be called a liar. I was open and honest with you and your mother about everything, including the legal issues of the adoption."

"How can you call it an adoption? No, Dr. Forsythe, it is called baby selling."

"You made an informed decision, and I have documents signed by you and your mother as proof. You are every bit as liable as I am for the exchange—morally and legally."

"What are you implying, Dr. Forsythe?"

"If you learned as much as you say you did at that fancy school, you also know the consequences of your actions. If found out, you'll be looking at years in prison—your mother, as well. You'll lose your job, your husband, and let us not forget Kaitlin. DCFS does not look highly on parents who sell their children so that they, themselves, can attend fancy schools. They'll take her away from you and her stepfather and send her to a foster family who may or may not have her best interest at heart. She'll hate you for what you did to her and what you kept from her. You will have ruined her life."

"If you bring me down, I can pull you down with me," Ashley's voice trembled alongside her grip on the phone.

"Both of us have much to lose, don't we?"

Ashley paused. She could take whatever consequences came her way, even prison, but Kaitlin should be spared the pain of her mother's foolish decision. Kaitlin should not suffer; she suffered enough at school already. "I just want this to go away: you, the monthly checks, my guilty conscience. How can I make it all go away?"

"Simple, my dear. Just send Kaitlin to camp. She will have a delightful time and probably come back with more friends than she'll know what to do with. I'll issue you your last check, and then you'll be done with this forever."

"But how can I know that Kaitlin will be safe?"

"You may correspond with Kaitlin via mail. Other than that, I can only give you my word. I cannot make the same promise if she doesn't come. Summer is a dangerous time and accidents happen . . . drowning, car wrecks, fires . . ."

"Are you threatening to hurt my daughter if I don't comply?" Ashley gasped.

"If you send Kaitlin to camp this *one* time, I will never bother you again, and that is a promise. I'll give you a few days to think about it, but please, Miss Ashley, don't disappoint me."

The line went dead.

Ashley stared at the phone in disbelief and then quickly dialed her mother's number. She needed someone to tell her what to do.

CHAPTER 14

KAITLIN

What else could I do but what I was told? I couldn't scream; the gun holstered to Phil's hip gagged me more efficiently than a whole roll of duct tape. Running wasn't an option, either; Margaret and Security Phil were gripping my arms so tightly that I was losing the feeling in my fingers.

Even without those obstacles, I doubted that I had the mental faculty to escape. I was completely terrified, and there was no room left in my brain for independent thought. Just fear. As I was guided down the trail and past the lodge, I robotically obeyed Margaret's every command—like she had the remote control to my body.

"Walk faster, Kaitlin!"

Yes, *Master.*

"Get in the car."

Yes, Master.

"Buckle your seatbelt."

Yes, Master.

Margaret sat down in the driver's seat and inserted the keys into the ignition. Security Phil slid into the back next to me. I flinched. The smell of him took me back to the deer carcass from earlier that week.

"Where are you taking me?" I trembled.

The two of them turned to me and smiled, but neither answered my question.

We pulled away from the lodge and turned southward onto a bumpy, unpaved road. As the sound of the dance's music dissolved into the distance, Phil cranked his head to the side and stared at me, like he was waiting for me to do something. And he was breathing loudly through his open mouth, revealing a row of yellow, disorganized teeth.

I know things about you, Kaitlin. Things you don't. Things you wouldn't want to know. And I'll be watching you.

I scooted as far away from him as I could manage.

Suddenly, my body grew heavy. So heavy, in fact, that I found myself melting into my seat. My head slumped to the side as though my neck was made of silly putty and my head, a bowling ball. I couldn't move. In my peripheral vision, I could see Security Phil watching me and nodding his head like he'd been expecting this strange occurrence. I tried to ask him what was happening to me, but my lips and tongue were made out of lead.

Seconds later, I was blasted with a full-blown migraine. Worse, my head felt like it was being crushed from the outside in. My eyes were being pushed out of my skull; I just knew it; I could feel it. My body curled into a knotty, rigid ball around my seatbelt, and spasms rippled up and down my spinal cord, causing me to convulse. The pain was excruciating.

Phil cackled. The sound of him felt like nails being hammered through my eardrums. I wanted to scream, but the pain was too encompassing. So I thrashed around and waited for my brains to explode out my ears. I begged my body to let it happen. Then I'd be dead. Then I'd have peace.

I drifted in and out of consciousness, my mind unable to cope with this unimaginable torment. I was vaguely aware of the car stopping and my body being lifted out of the car. I was being carried somewhere. I was inside a building, maybe. I was floating upward. Now, I was lying on a table. What was going on? What was happening to me? Nothing made sense, only my agony.

"This will help," someone said and inserted a needle into my arm. Relief trickled through my body. I looked up at Margaret, who was holding a syringe. At that moment, I absolutely loved her. All of my pain and worries seemed to disintegrate, as though she had injected me with the richest, creamiest cookie butter known to man. I felt light and tickly all over and could feel myself falling asleep.

"Congratulations, Kaitlin, you have been *called upon.*"

And then I drifted away.

PARKER

Some fathers exhibited their pride by extending their son's curfew or handing over the keys to the family car. Dr. Forsythe showed it by giving Parker a new job: prison guard.

Parker didn't deserve this newfound trust. He didn't idolize his father as he'd claimed, and he had no intention of taking an active role in the Leavitt Center's future. On the contrary, the moment Parker had laid eyes on the gruesome pictures from the filing cabinet, he knew he needed to obliterate the Leavitt Center and see to it that his father was euthanized like the rabid animal that he was.

Parker had originally planned to make a run for the nearest police headquarters (with the incriminating hard drive and photographs zipped up in his backpack) the very morning he returned from the station. Unfortunately, when Dr. Forsythe burst into Parker's bedroom and told him that Claire had been captured, he knew that he couldn't leave just yet. Claire would be killed, just like her sister and all the other useless counterparts.

He also knew that the only way to save her would be to infiltrate his father's circle of trust—to be put in a position with access to the prisoner. So he told Dr. Forsythe the truth about shutting down the surveillance system and lied about everything else, especially the part about being honored to have such a father. It was difficult for Parker to keep a level voice through the lies, but somehow, through the grace of God, the doctor seemed to believe him.

Prior to entering Claire's cell to deliver dinner, Parker took a breath and slowly let the air stream from his lips. It was crucial to put on a believable show in case her cell was bugged. He couldn't show an ounce of compassion. One kind word, and his father would see him as weak, untrustworthy, or worse, traitorous.

He pounded on the cell door before sliding his key card and pushing the door open. Claire was balled up in the corner of the cold room looking small and worn out—a huge contrast to the three previous days, which she mainly spent bellowing obscenities and kicking at the cell door. When Parker nudged her with his toe, however, Claire shoved his foot aside and began listing all of the obscene adjectives she felt described him best. This girl was a fighter like her sister, though Patricia had channeled her feistiness into her studies.

Claire's mother was also spirited; at least that was what Parker had heard. Rumor had it that she and his father had formed a sort of partnership, if not relationship, years back. Just after Parker's mother passed (giving birth to him, coincidentally), Dr. Forsythe began twinkle-eyeing his old medical school buddies into passing along names of qualified patients: vulnerable women who were pregnant with identical twins.

Claire's mother was one such patient.

While not nearly as young as Dr. Forsythe's other recruits, the woman was penniless and alone with a belly that ballooned out over her knees. She agreed to Dr. Forsythe's proposition immediately, proclaiming him a genius and a saint. The doctor found her flattery charming. He didn't mind her long, slender legs either, so the story went.

He visited Claire's mother frequently as she neared delivery, sometimes bringing her tulips or chocolate truffles. During their conversations, he learned that they both had a passion for righting the "wrongs" of the world. Eventually, he trusted her with the secrets of the Leavitt Center (at least some of them) and asked if she wanted to join his team.

After her babies were born, and less than a year working for the Leavitt Center, it became clear that Claire's mother was too much infatuated with the cause and too little infatuated with Dr. Forsythe. She argued with him on crucial aspects of the center and even held a secret meeting to persuade others that

Dr. Forsythe wasn't a strong enough leader. When the doctor discovered her disloyalty, he banished her from the project.

The woman fought hard to stay, desperate to be a part of the revolution, but finally agreed to leave, and keep the Leavitt Center's secrets, so long as her twin daughters could remain a part of the experiment. She left Patricia with Dr. Forsythe and took her other baby girl, Claire, to her hometown, convinced that one day her girls would be *called upon* and reunited to change the world.

This never happened, of course. Claire didn't exhibit symptoms at Camp Overlook, and her twin counterpart became a liability to the doctor. So, Patricia "went to college" and Claire was sent home from her first year of camp.

Claire's mother called Dr. Forsythe repeatedly and begged him to give her daughters a second chance (Parker knew this because he'd eavesdropped on several of those conversations). Dr. Forsythe, probably still infatuated with the woman, didn't have the heart to tell her that Patricia was dead. Instead, he agreed to give the girls a second chance—knowing full well that nothing would or could come of it—so long as Claire's mother accepted the final outcome and never contacted the Leavitt Center or Patricia again.

Without Parker's help, the woman would probably never see Claire again either, which was one reason Parker took his task so seriously. The other reason was, well, Claire meant something to Parker.

He tapped his foot and waited for Claire to finish blasting him with her awesome vocabulary before holding up a plate of food. "It's PB and J," he said.

"How sweet, the clone thought he'd bring me some dinner," Claire mocked.

Parker rolled his eyes. "I know it will be a terrible temptation, but wait at least a half hour after eating before going swimming."

She sneered but stretched her arm out for the sandwich, but Parker set the plate down on the table next to the cot, far out of Claire's reach. "This isn't room service. Stand up and get it yourself."

Claire didn't move. "When do I get my phone call?"

"This isn't jail, either."

"For sure it isn't. If this were jail, I'd get a shower every now and again."

Parker turned to leave.

"Wait," Claire said, leaping to her feet. "Do you know Sam Lukens? He was at camp with me last year. He's tall and black and has an earring. Is he here? Is he locked up like me?"

Actually, Parker *had* logged hundreds of hours watching Sam last summer at the lab. He saw Claire and Sam's romance unfold: recording when they met, their first kiss, and even the times Claire had snuck into Sam's cabin to nurse him when he began experiencing symptoms. Parker remembered how jealous he'd felt. He'd spent his whole life preparing to get *called upon*, and because of that, he'd never had time for a real relationship—not with a parent, not with a buddy, and especially not with a girl.

When Sam was *called upon* and removed from camp, Claire had been crushed. She'd stopped eating, pulled away from her friends, started mouthing off to the counselors . . . even her journal entries became dark and angry (though, technically, Parker wasn't supposed to be surveying someone to whom he wasn't assigned). But experiencing Claire's raw emotion had made Parker feel close to her, protective of her. He was disappointed when she left camp after the first summer and thrilled when she returned for the second.

When no one else was at the lab, Parker would log into the surveillance system and peek in at Claire. She was clearly miserable at Overlook, lashing out at her bunkmates, pushing them away. He understood why she behaved so abrasively. She'd been betrayed by her mother, abandoned by her boyfriend, and manipulated by the Leavitt Center. She was cynical, emotional, and deeply lonely.

Parker had felt so connected to these emotions and found her outbursts admirable and cathartic. He began to feel closer to Claire than anyone he'd ever met, and he'd never met her. He'd fanaticized about sneaking to Camp Overlook, holding and comforting her, kissing her.

But now the two of them were in the same room, a cell. Parker wanted to touch her cheek and tell her that he was working on a plan to get her out. He wanted to tell her not to be sad, that Sam was not the same person that he used to be, and that she was better off without him. He wanted her to know that he was protecting her far better than Sam ever would. But he couldn't do that yet, not with a surveillance camera recording their every word and every move. "I don't know who you're talking about," said Parker. "I've never heard of anyone named Sam."

Claire bit her lip and reached for his hand. She no longer looked strong and angry, just delicate and afraid. "Does my mom know I'm here?" she whispered, choking back tears.

Parker didn't answer.

"Are you going to kill me?"

Parker couldn't take it anymore. He pushed her away, slid his keycard through the lock, and stormed out of the room.

CHAPTER 15

KAITLIN

I woke up to someone stroking my hair. I opened my eyes.

"Good morning, Kaitlin. Or should I say good afternoon?" Margaret continued running her nails through my hair, starting at my hairline and working her way down my scalp. It felt amazing.

"What time is it?" I asked, reclosing my eyes.

"It's two in the afternoon. You've been sleeping for quite a while."

"Huh?" How did I sleep in so late? Why was Margaret in my cabin? And more importantly, why was she petting me? Wait a sec, this wasn't my cabin. The bed was so warm and cozy—the sheets must have been made of butterfly wings—and the air smelled like cinnamon and maple sugar, not stale camp fire and Syrup's mildewed socks.

Then I remembered the night before—Margaret forcing me into the car, Phil's evil cackle, the fear, the pain . . . so much pain. Then the needle.

"Stop petting me!" I slapped her hand away from my hair and quickly sat up.

The room was ornate in a way that seemed suited for a castle or a Christmas tree: a fireplace leafed in gold, marble flooring, a gigantic crystal chandelier looming over my bed, and furniture made of exotic timber. I could see that my clothing had been removed from my duffle, pressed, and hung in the closet. Beneath a large window was a table full of food: fresh fruit, bacon, French toast.

"Where am I?" I demanded.

"I told you it was a government building, but that was a fib." Margaret giggled. "Welcome to the Leavitt Center."

"And I'm here because . . . ?"

"Because you've been *called upon,* you lucky, lucky girl."

"Lucky? I almost died last night!"

"No, you didn't, silly." She moved toward the breakfast table. She ladled syrup onto a batch of French toast, poured a glass of milk, and walked the tray of food over to my bed. She slid the tray over my lap and tucked a cloth napkin into the neck of my silk pajamas, pajamas I didn't recognize or remember putting on. Of one thing I was certain, however: I was hungry. And for the first time in three days, I didn't have a headache or feel nauseated or exhausted. My only complaint was my infected leg, which still ached, though not nearly as badly as before.

Margaret read my thoughts. "Dr. Forsythe wants to take care of your leg. I'll give you an hour to eat breakfast and get cleaned up," she motioned to a clawfoot bathtub already filled with steaming, frothy water. "Then I'll return with the doctor."

"But what do you mean, I was *called upon?*"

"I'll let Dr. Forsythe answer your questions, but I will tell you this: you're a special girl, Kaitlin; more special than you could ever have imagined. Now hurry up and eat." Margaret kissed her index finger and poked me in the forehead.

I wiped the spot with the back of my hand, feeling more confused than ever.

"Well, I'll be; if it isn't Miss Kaitlin!" Dr. Forsythe entered my suite, Margaret trailing him like a puppy.

I didn't know what to say. I knew I should be furious at the man. My gut told me not to trust him, that he was connected to, if not responsible for, the pervy video cameras in my cabin, the illnesses of the vanished campers, last night's explosive headache, and everything else in between. But it was difficult to be angry while nibbling on a cracker smothered in gourmet cookie butter and lounging in a chair upholstered in unicorn hide and stuffed with angel-wing feathers (at least that's how the chair felt to me). Plus, Dr. Forsythe's eyes were twinkly, so very twinkly. He wore an old-fashioned gray tweed jacket and a pleasant smile on his face. Everything about him shouted "prime grandpa material; you can trust me."

"Do you mind if I have a look at that leg?"

"Coh ahad," I said, my mouth still full.

Dr. Forsythe perched on the ottoman across from my chair and gently lifted my leg onto his knee. He cinched up the leg of my pajama pants and frowned. "Oh my, that's quite the infection! You must be in a great deal of pain." I waited for him to reprimand me for not seeing him sooner or for him to ask me how I had hurt myself, but he didn't. Good! I would've had to tell him a lie, and he'd know I was lying, and it would be terribly awkward.

"It is too late for stitches, and there will be a nasty scar, I'm afraid. You'll need a course of antibiotics, but first I need to clean your wound." The doctor motioned to Margaret.

She handed me a clipboard and pulled a pencil from behind her ear. "Why don't you do this crossword puzzle while Dr. Forsythe takes care of your leg? It might be painful, and you'll be glad for the distraction."

Uh, weird distraction, I thought, but took the pencil and started filling in the blank for One Across. The answer was easy enough, though Two and Three Across were nearly impossible. I was able to complete about a quarter of the puzzle by the time Dr. Forsythe finished cleaning and wrapping my leg. Margaret had been right; the crossword had been reasonably distracting, though I did borrow from the library of Claire's vocabulary each time the doctor put too much pressure on the cut.

I handed the clipboard to Margaret. She read my answers, gave me a wink, and passed it over to Dr. Forsythe. He slid a pair of spectacles over his wrinkly eyes and then looked up from my crossword with the glitteriest smile I ever saw. He grabbed my hand and shook it so robustly that I could feel his excitement wrenching at the socket of my shoulder. "Good work, Kaitlin! Good work!"

Surely, he was complimenting me on my penmanship and not the crossword itself. I'd left most of the puzzle blank.

"Thanks?"

"You don't even know what you did, do you?" he said, and I shook my head. "Don't worry, that's normal." He pulled his ottoman to the side of my chair and held the clipboard between us. "One Across. The clue is: The univalent hydrocarbon C2H5 derived from ethane by the elimination of a hydrogen atom. You answered Ethyl, which is correct. Now let's look at One Down: The fourth largest of Jupiter's satellites; covered with a bright, smooth shell of ice. You answered Europa, which is also correct."

"So?"

"Where did you learn those things? Certainly, you didn't take advanced astronomy or biochemistry in ninth grade?"

I thought. I really thought. But I couldn't remember how I knew the stuff I knew. And come to think of it, while those answers had seeped so effortlessly from my brain, the questions were really advanced. "But I didn't know *all* of the answers," I reminded him.

"Here, try this." Dr. Forsythe flipped over my crossword puzzle and scribbled a math problem on the backside. He passed me the clipboard. My pen glided over the paper inscribing foreign symbols more akin to hieroglyphics or Chinese calligraphy than they were to any equation I'd ever laid my eyes upon. My hand felt like it wasn't mine, like it belonged to the ghost of Albert Einstein or Steven Hawking. I had the whole thing solved in less than thirty seconds, the whole time thinking, *Where did I learn this? How do I know this?* My hands trembled when I returned my work to Dr. Forsythe.

"Amazing! This equation is quite advanced, quite advanced indeed. Most graduate students would grapple with it for hours. You solved it in . . ."

"Um," I interrupted, swallowing hard. "You're not trying to tell me I'm some sort of genius or something?"

"No, you are not a genius," Dr. Forsythe said quietly. "You are something far better." Then, much to my astonishment, he jumped up and did what I can only explain as a spirited jig. He shuffled around the room, humming a jazzy tune, and bobbing an imaginary baton in the air. He linked arms with

Margaret and do-si-doed her around. She giggled and joined in the humming as Dr. Forsythe, even with his arthritic knees, picked me up and twirled me around the room.

I had no idea what was going on; I'd never been one to spontaneously burst into song and dance, but I was pretty sure that this musical celebration was in honor of me. And I quite liked it. By the time Dr. Forsythe sat me back down, I, too, was hiccupping with laughter.

"You did it, Miss Kaitlin! You did it! I've had a good feeling about you since the day you were born, and now, here you are, about to join my ranks. You have no idea how special you are, young lady." Dr. Forsythe kissed my hand with the pride and tenderness of a father seeing his daughter in her wedding dress. He seemed to believe that I was important. *Me.* And all I could say was, "You've known me since I was born?"

"I know you have a thousand questions," the doctor said, still out of breath from the frolic. "And I am going to answer them all, every one of them, but your mother is here and really should be a part of the conversation."

"My mother is here!" I gasped. This day was getting more and more surreal.

"Indeed. She drove here as soon as she received your frantic phone call last night."

"Oh," I said guiltily.

"Don't worry, Kaitlin. We would have called her anyway. Being *called upon* is a wonderful thing! Your mother should be here to celebrate with us."

"When can I see her?" Suddenly, my grievance with the woman for selling me to Camp Overlook seemed silly. I was *called upon*, whatever that meant, and nothing else seemed to matter. I wanted to run to her, hug her, and share the good news.

"We'll go to her right away. She's been waiting in the lobby since six in the morning. But I should warn you; she might be a bit skeptical about everything. She's confused and worried. It will take her a moment to adjust to what I have to say, but I have every confidence that she'll come around. You'll see."

From the looks of it, Mom had not been waiting patiently. As soon as I entered the lobby, she flew at me with all the urgency of a burst pipe. "Are you okay? Are you hurt? What did they do to you?" She seized my shoulders and inspected every inch of my body.

"I'm fine, Mom," I said, tucking my wobbly leg behind the healthy one. "Is Dad here?"

"He was working late, and I was frantic. I left him a note on the counter." She pulled me close to her chest. "So you're sure you're okay?"

"It's good to see you, Mom." No matter how many times I told her I was alright, I knew she'd never believe me.

"As you were informed, Miss Ashley, Kaitlin was just sleeping in." Dr. Forsythe chuckled. "All is well."

"You!" Mom yelled, wrapping her arms protectively around me and backing away from him. "I have been waiting for hours, *hours*, to see my daughter! I've been worried sick about her, and all you folks would tell me is that she was sleeping in! I was seconds away from calling the police! I still just might! Come on, Kaitlin, I'm taking you home!"

"Wait," I resisted. "Dr. Forsythe said he was going to explain everything."

"I already know enough," she sputtered.

"Mom, please." I gazed into her tired eyes, hoping I'd translate how important this was to me. Dr. Forsythe said I was special. After the ups and downs of this summer, feeling like an absolute loser, then feeling like I might be normal, and then once again learning that I was indeed a loser, I needed to know something concrete about myself. "Let's hear him out before we go."

"I give you my word, Miss Ashley, if you don't like what I have to say, you and Kaitlin can go. My original promise will stand, and you will never hear from me again. Anjalie will be a thing of the past."

There. That name again. Anjalie. And my mother started to cry. Sob, really. She covered her face and wept into her hands, her chest pulling upward, begging for air. What made her so upset? Me? The Anjalie person?

"Mom?" I asked.

"Kaitlin," she said, her voice heavy with exhaustion. "I think it's time you know the complete truth. I suppose that it's time I know it, too."

ASHLEY

Something was different about Kaitlin. The summer had changed her. The changes were subtle. Maybe only a mother could sense them, but they were there. Kaitlin held herself higher; her shoulders no longer slumped. Her skin was tan, and her freckles had doubled, but her skin took on a certain glow for which the sun couldn't claim responsibility. One thing about Kaitlin's looks, however, unsettled Ashley. It was Kaitlin's eyes. They were still a striking hazel-green, except for the very rim of each of her irises, which was now a peculiar brushed-nickel color.

"Mom, you're staring at me," Kaitlin whined, covering her face with her hands. The two of them had been sitting at a table in an office waiting for the doctor to rejoin them.

"Sorry, Potato Bug. I'm just worried about you. I shouldn't have made you go to Camp Overlook. You must've had a horrible experience this summer."

"Well, the last week wasn't so great, but it wasn't all bad. You don't need to worry."

"But I do."

Kaitlin's nose crinkled, the way it always did when Ashley got overprotective. Ever since Kaitlin was an infant, Ashley had concentrated all the energy of a mother of two babies on her one remaining child. She'd read twice as many books to Kaitlin, given her twice as many kisses, and worried about her twice as much as she would have otherwise—perhaps feeling that if she did her job doubly well, her love would also be felt by Anjalie, wherever she was. Kaitlin had basked in the attention when she was a young child, but now that she was older, she shrunk like she was being smothered. Ashley knew she shouldn't, but whenever Kaitlin fought for air, she held her daughter even tighter. She couldn't help herself; she couldn't bear to lose Kaitlin, too. "It's just that you seem different. Are you sure they didn't hurt you?"

"I'm fine. Camp was great."

"Then it's a boy, maybe? Jake? You wrote to me about him. He was going to take you to the dance. What happened with him?"

Kaitlin colored and Ashley felt herself relax. She could handle boy drama. She'd been waiting for her daughter to have boy drama for years, though up till this summer, Kaitlin hadn't had much success in that department . . . or any department.

"He kissed you, didn't he?" Ashley teased, temporarily forgetting her anxiety about Dr. Forsythe.

Kaitlin's hue deepened.

"Sooooo," Ashley prodded, "How did it go?"

"Let's just put it this way, he didn't go in for seconds."

Ashley frowned. "Oh, Sweetheart, I'm sorry. There will be other boys and other kisses. One day, you'll find the right fit." For a moment, Kaitlin looked so sad that a belt cinched around Ashley's heart. Her daughter, above anyone, deserved a little success. When was her little girl going to catch a break?

Dr. Forsythe entered the office and handed Kaitlin and Ashley each a lime-garnished soda.

He lowered himself onto his chair, crossed his legs, and laced his fingers around his top knee. "Sorry to keep you waiting. I know you're anxious, so I won't bother with small talk. I'll simply start from the beginning and steer us to where we are now."

"I'd appreciate it," said Ashley.

"Very well." He cleared his throat. "As Ashley already knows, and what may come as a surprise to you, Kaitlin, is that my medical specialty is obstetrics. In other words, I deal primarily with the care of women during their pregnancies and deliveries."

"Bet you don't use your specialty much at Overlook," Kaitlin remarked. "Boys aren't allowed in the girl cabins," she added for her mother's benefit.

The doctor chuckled. "Oh, when there's a will, there's a way. Take your fellow camper, Martin Larsen. He was caught at two o'clock in the morning in a pile of pine needles with a young lady from the Aspen cabin—covered in ticks, I'll add. We had to send the two of them home. The whole situation was rather embarrassing."

"He really *did* get sent home for sneaking off with a girl?" Kaitlin asked.

"Unfortunately, yes."

Kaitlin covered her mouth to stifle her laughter, though Ashley had no idea why. Nothing funny about teen promiscuity, not after Ashley had been swimming in the consequences for the last fifteen years.

"But thankfully, no, I haven't seen any pregnancies at Camp Overlook— though I do miss obstetrics while I'm away. I am very passionate about my work and care deeply about my patients. While in my residency, one of them changed my life forever. Her name was Stacy Leavitt. My story, our story, really, begins with her.

"Stacy was single, uneducated, and had two babies growing inside of her womb. She decided, all on her own, that it would be best to give one of those babies up for adoption."

"That must've been a rough decision," said Kaitlin.

You have no idea, thought Ashley.

Dr. Forsythe continued. "It was the right thing to do given her age and circumstances. The young woman and I kept in touch through the years, as I do with many of my patients, but I was rather taken aback when, fourteen years after the birth of her babies, she called me in a panic. It seemed that her son, Jason, had run into his identical brother on a school field trip. This caused a great stir being that neither boy was aware of the other's existence."

Ashley's palms began to sweat. She reached for her drink.

"What's more, the boys were immediately struck ill and were rushed to the hospital. I met them in the emergency room in hopes of being of assistance, but unfortunately, all the doctors, myself included, had never seen a case like theirs. The boy's symptoms quickly worsened and our only option was to sedate them."

"Did it help?" asked Kaitlin.

"Did it ever." Dr. Forsythe's eyes shimmered. "The boys woke feeling as good as new. But not just that . . ."

"What?" Kaitlin sat on the edge of her seat.

"Have you ever heard that twins sometimes share a peculiar, almost psychic connection? For example, when one twin gets hurt, the other one cries out in pain. Or both twins might say something completely arbitrary at the exact same moment."

"I've heard of that before," said Kaitlin. "Is that what happened with the boys?"

"Indeed there was a connection, but much different than anything I'd ever thought possible. Each twin woke up knowing what the other one had been learning in school. For example, Jason was taking geography and all of the sudden his brother, Douglas, had an extensive knowledge of igneous rock. Similarly, Douglas played the violin. When Jason woke up, he recognized Rachmaninoff's Concerto Number 2 playing from the overhead speakers—this coming from a boy whose only previous musical interest had been Metallica.

"You can imagine my astonishment and curiosity. What made the boys have this strange reaction, this unprecedented connection? I decided the only way to understand the phenomenon was to search for similar cases. I dove into medical journals, contacted every physician I'd ever known, and even placed advertisements in several major newspapers. Eventually, I was contacted by a family from London. Their adopted daughter, Tanji, also had a surprise run-in with a twin sister, also adopted."

"Wait a sec," said Kaitlin. "This Tanji is not the same Tanji I know from Camp Overlook?"

Dr. Forsythe laughed. "The very same one, although now quite grown up. And did you figure out who Jason had become?"

Kaitlin thought. "Jason, uh . . . Leavitt. Oh! Director Leavitt! Jason is Director Leavitt!"

"Excellent! But back to the story when Tanji accidentally met her twin sister, Keisha. Like Jason and Douglas, the girls exhibited painful symptoms. Only when they were sent to separate hospitals did the symptoms subside—if not disappear altogether. For that very reason, the girls never reconnected."

"How sad would it be to have a sibling and never be able to get to know her," Kaitlin said wistfully.

Ashley wrung her hands.

Dr. Forsythe nodded. "I thought so too. I flew to Europe and interviewed the parents in both families. Everyone agreed to reunite the twins in hopes of finding a similar connection as Jason and Douglas. The girls were brought together and quickly sedated. The next day, sure enough, both girls felt rested, healthy, and smarter than they ever had before." The doctor smiled, as though the correlation still surprised and excited him.

"I flew the girls to my clinic in California for more testing. There, they met Jason and Douglas. The odd thing was, before the group even had a chance to shake hands, they all collapsed, much as they had done when they first met their identical twins. Apparently, the connection did not stop between each twin set."

Ashley watched as Kaitlin tapped the lip of her glass with the tip of her index finger, struggling to figure out how she fit in to Dr. Forsythe's strange story, but not allowing her mind to consider the obvious answer. Ashley barely dared go there herself. The possibilities were too confusing, too consequential, too infuriating.

Dr. Forsythe pressed forward, oblivious to Ashley's flushed cheeks and quaking fists. "I admit to becoming obsessed with this new discovery. I knew I was on the brink of something with endless potential, and I thirsted for more knowledge and understanding. I searched for more separated twins, but as you can imagine, finding twin sets with such particular circumstances was difficult, if not impossible. I decided it would be far easier to create the circumstances myself."

"By tricking vulnerable young girls into giving up their babies?!" Ashley yelled. Shocked, she slapped her hand over her own mouth.

"Mom?" Kaitlin asked, eyes wide.

Ashley tried to compose herself before daring to speak again. It was difficult. Dr. Forsythe had just admitted to separating her daughters, not for the benefit of her family, but because he needed guinea pigs for a weird twin experiment. "I'm sorry, Potato Bug. I need to talk to Dr. Forsythe alone for a minute."

"That won't be necessary," Dr. Forsythe said calmly. "I believe Kaitlin should hear it all. Everything. My perspective and yours. Do you want to go first or shall I?"

Ashley paused. She was terrified of how Kaitlin would react to finding out about the adoption, but at the same time, she couldn't bear the thought of Kaitlin learning the truth from this horrible man. She leaned forward and wrapped her hands around Kaitlin's. "You know that I gave birth to you when I was a teenager; I've tried to be upfront with you about the mistakes I made when I was your age."

"Yeah?" Kaitlin said, her voice unsure and questioning.

"But I have kept one thing, the most important thing, from you. The doctor told me it would be best if I didn't . . . maybe I was afraid that if I did . . . "

"Tell me, Mom. Please."

"You have a sister, Potato Bug. A twin. Her name is Anjalie."

Kaitlin's hand went limp in her mother's. She sat very still; the color slowly draining from her cheeks. Ashley pulled her daughter's hand up to her own wet cheek. "I am sorry about everything—keeping the truth from you, making that horrible decision in the first place. I would change it all if I could go back in time. Please believe me. Please? Kaitlin?"

Kaitlin's voice was barely above a whisper. "I have a sister. All this time I have felt so alone. I didn't have to be."

"I know. I'm so sorry."

"Kaitlin," the doctor interrupted, "In your mother's defense, she was only acting in your best interest. She was in a very difficult financial spot. When a colleague informed me of her situation, I introduced myself and offered her a plan that would satisfy her desire to be your parent and also *my* need to study the twin phenomenon. Everybody benefited."

"I don't understand," said Kaitlin, coming out of her trance. "What . . . what was the plan?"

"The same plan that I offered to all the mothers."

"What do you mean? You've separated other babies from their siblings?"

"Yes. Many. Some of whom you would even recognize from camp. Two of them were in your cabin. Aya, who was *called upon* earlier this summer, and Claire, who was not *called upon*, but sent home early for breaking the rules." Dr. Forsythe gave Kaitlin an odd look, and she responded by fidgeting with the straw in her soda.

Ashley elbowed her way back into the conversation. "Dr. Forsythe arranged for Anjalie to be adopted into another family. In return, that family helped alleviate our financial burdens, making it possible for me to take care of you. I wish so badly that I could have figured out a different solution, especially now knowing that Dr. Forsythe had ulterior motives, but I was scared and under so much pressure."

"Does Dad know about this?"

Ashley shook her head. She'd never told her husband about Anjalie or the illegal adoption because she didn't want to make him an accessory to her crime. Keeping that secret from him had been excruciating, but she needed him to have zero culpability in case something went wrong and she and her mother were sent to prison. Someone needed to take care of Kaitlin if that happened.

"But my sister? Anjalie? What happened to her?" Kaitlin asked.

"I want to warn you," Dr. Forsythe said "that what I am about to say will come as a great surprise to both of you. Before you react, however, I beg of you to let me explain myself. In the end, I am confident you will support my reasoning."

"I sincerely doubt I could support anything you have done," Ashley said.

Dr. Forsythe smiled forgivingly. "I understand your animosity, Miss Ashley. You feel like I manipulated you into giving up your child for adoption, and then I forced you to send Kaitlin to Camp Overlook against your better judgment. It grieves me to admit that I am guilty of those things. Sadly, that is not the end of it. All those years back, I led you to believe that you selected adoptive parents for Anjalie. In truth, I was the one who took her on and raised her as my own. I was the one sending you the monthly checks."

"What!" Ashley cried, barely able to hold herself up. For fifteen years, she'd clung to the hope that Anjalie had been loved and cared for by the Ericsons, but now it appeared that those years were a complete sham. Her world felt wobbly and uncertain, like she'd never be able to find her footing again.

Dr. Forsythe held up his hand. "Please don't panic. You'll understand everything after I'm finished."

"Let him talk, Mom," Kaitlin pleaded, desperate to know more about her sister.

"Thank you, dear. As I was saying, I raised not only Anjalie, but all of the babies adopted out through the Leavitt Center. There were twenty altogether—twenty-one if you count my biological son, Parker, whose mother died during childbirth. Since it took about five years to accumulate these children, they ranged significantly in age. I loved them all, however, and delighted in watching them grow and change."

Like passing a horrific car accident on the freeway, Ashley could not look away from the doctor. The man was a lunatic; he'd stolen almost two dozen children! And for what? Experimentation? To satisfy some delusional fatherly need?

"I know taking care of so many children seems crazy, but I am a man of means. I purchased land, once an old campground, and erected this very building. The children grew up here. Since we were patterned after a high-end boarding school, the children received a better education here than they could anywhere else. And, oh, the fun they've had. Can you imagine growing up in the Rocky Mountains? They had a wonderfully rich childhood.

"Obviously, I did not educate and raise the children alone. Jason, Douglas, Tanji, and Keisha, now young adults, lived with us and were more than willing to help with diapers and feedings. Also, throughout the years, I was able to make very important contacts: scientists, humanitarians, professors, and philanthropists. These people, Margaret and Philip, for example, were forward thinkers like me. I could trust them. They volunteered their time, their skills, their support, and their money to this promising cause."

Ashley was bewildered. "What cause? What could possibly be so important?"

Like the sun peeking above the mountains at dawn, Dr. Forsythe's eyes filled the room with an iridescent glow. "Jason, Douglas, Tanji, and Keisha's gifts were remarkable, but it wasn't the phenomenon itself that had me enthralled, it was the possibilities of what could be done with it. In the right person's hands, such a gift could alter the course of humanity."

"But how?" Kaitlin's eyes were wide open, but Ashley couldn't exactly read what was going on behind them. Was Kaitlin horrified by the ethical breaches and exploitations, or was she excited and awestruck, like the doctor?

"Imagine this scenario," Dr. Forsythe straightened the lapel of his jacket. "Two people, such as Jason and Douglas, study two entirely different subjects. They work and study hard for several years, eventually becoming experts in their individual fields. Now, let's say that they decide to share their expertise with each other. Instead of teaching one another, which would take another several years, they simply transfer that knowledge to the other person over the course of a nap. Now both Jason and Douglas are experts in two different fields in half the amount of time it would take a normal person.

"Let's add two more people into the equation, shall we? Tanji and Keisha also spend two years in rigorous study. Like the boys, they are able to pass their expertise to one another with the simplicity of passing a note during study hall. Following the transfer, these young women meet up with Jason and Douglas, and the four of them have yet another information exchange. Miss Kaitlin, you have proven yourself quite the mathematical wonder; of how many subjects is each of these people now a master?"

"Four," Kaitlin answered, though the way she rolled her eyes clearly said, "duh."

"Excellent, excellent! All four of these people now are experts on the four different topics, although they only actually studied to be the master of one! As you can see, this is an extremely efficient way of sharing information! Now tell me this, what practical purpose would something like this serve?"

Kaitlin shrugged.

"Let me give you another small scenario, one slightly more personal. Let's pretend that your leg injury went untreated, giving way to an even more serious infection. Your fever became dangerously high, and your body went into septic shock. This was followed by multiple organ failure: your heart stopped beating, and your brain began to starve for oxygen."

"I'm sorry, *what* happened to Kaitlin's leg?" Ashley asked.

Dr. Forsythe's eyes were locked with Kaitlin's; it was like Ashley wasn't even there. "A patient in your condition would usually die. You, however, were lucky enough to be greeted at the hospital by a doctor who was a master of cardiology, pulmonology, orthopedics, and neurology. She was able to restart your heart and hook you up to complicated life-saving machinery, amputate your leg, and perform an emergency hemicraniectomy. Without her expertise, you would never have survived.

"Currently, no doctor has the skill and know-how to perform all those procedures with complete competence. They'd be almost ready to retire by the time they finished schooling and practice for four different specialties. But if that doctor went to medical school only for cardiology and was simply handed the knowledge and experience for the other three specialties, then he or she would be able to practice revolutionized medicine for years."

Kaitlin scratched her head. "But one amazing doctor, or even four amazing doctors, are not going to change the *course of the world*," she said using air quotes.

"Quite right. That's why I said my example was a small one. Let me show you the larger picture. What if it wasn't just four people who were able to exchange information? What of it was ten, twenty, or a hundred— each adding diverse and incredibly important information into the pool? Can you imagine the amount of knowledge each of them would accumulate? With so much concentrated brainpower, how easy it would be to find a cure for cancer, invent groundbreaking technologies, or revolutionize the legal system.

"And what if these people were put into positions of power? They could become super politicians, able to solve economic crises, annihilate terrorism, reverse global warming . . . do you hear what I'm telling you? The possibilities for good are endless! The world would never be the same!"

"That's so"—one half of Kaitlin's mouth tilted upward, then the other— "awesome."

"What a fitting word," the doctor agreed. "It is *awesome*. And only for a cause so *awesome* could I set aside some of my ethics, and perhaps sanity, and adopt all of those infants."

"*Steal*," Ashley corrected, trying to lure Dr. Forsythe and her child back to reality. From the floaty expression on Kaitlin's face, however, only a good taser to the rump would do the trick.

Dr. Forsythe carried on. "I could not let humanity continue to self-destruct, especially when I'd discovered the possible solution. That is why I arranged for the babies to be separated from their siblings. I hoped that one day when they were reunited, they would find that magical connection with one another and join in my cause."

"And did they?" Kaitlin asked.

"You tell me." Dr. Forsythe chuckled, his eyes crinkling good naturedly. "You're one of them."

"I guess I still feel confused. This is a lot of information all at once."

"Yes, Doctor. Please go on," Ashley's voice was an oil spill of sarcasm.

"Well, then, allow me to finish my story. I built this building and educated my children in hopes that their knowledge would one day benefit millions. Their whole lives were spent in preparation of meeting their twins. I told them that when they hit their teens, they would be tested, and if they were found worthy, would be *called upon*."

"Yeah," Kaitlin said. "You told me that I had been *called upon*, and I still don't know what that means."

"It simply means that you and your twin made a successful connection, that you are special in a very rare way, and if you choose, you may become a beacon of light to a confused civilization."

"Are you sure that you have the right girl, Dr. Forsythe? I mean, have you looked at me? I couldn't do all that. I am nothing special."

The doctor grasped his chest as though his heart had broken in two. "On the contrary, you are a wonderful, wonderful girl! I've had a good feeling about your potential for years, and just look at you now. You're blossoming before my very eyes."

Kaitlin took in a big breath of air, seeming to inhale Dr. Forsythe's encouragement and exhale the self-doubt she'd been harboring for years. The scene gave Ashley a bad taste in her mouth. "Kaitlin, I don't care if this man tells you that you bleed liquid diamonds, this so-called ability you may or may not have is not what makes you special. Who you are, who you have always been, is unique and beautiful and perfect."

Dr. Forsythe backpedaled. "I agree with your mother. It is not being *called upon* that makes you special. What makes you special is what's in your heart. Being *called upon* is more like a vehicle to set your values in motion. When I said that I had a good feeling about your potential, I meant that I thought you had both the heart and the talent."

"But why did you suspect I had the talent? How could you guess something like that?"

"Three years ago, I brought your twin, or counterpart as I like to call her, to Colorado. It was a brief trip; we took a red-eye flight and returned home early the next evening. My goal was simply to see if there would be any sort of reaction between the two of you. From a safe distance, she and I watched you walk to and from your school. Indeed, you appeared quite green that day, walking with a heavy stride. Anjalie also complained of nausea and a headache. Still, we couldn't be sure if the symptoms were a result of your proximity to each other or simply a coincidence."

"Oh my gosh!" Kaitlin gasped. "I think I know what day you are talking about. I was in sixth grade, right? I puked all over my desk that day!"

"Why didn't you tell me about that," Ashley said. "That must've been a horrible day."

"Life altering," Kaitlin muttered. "So was it just me or did you do that same test with other kids and their twins . . . er . . . counterparts?"

"Yes, I did the proximity test on others. Some exhibited similar symptoms as you did, others didn't. I didn't place too much stock in the results, though. Remember that Jason, Douglas, Tanji, and Keisha were all in their teens when they met one another. I figured that puberty played a major role in the reaction and, at the tender age of eleven or twelve, many kids had not yet entered that stage. I decided to wait and test all of the twins once they had entered adolescence."

"So that's why you opened Camp Overlook?"

"Yes. And it was a wonderful idea, if I say so myself. The old cabins were already here—left over from the old campsite. All I had to do was add some top-notch amenities: a pool, the stables, the lodge, and the chef. Maybe it was all over the top, but I needed to make sure that parents would be thrilled to send teens to summer camp."

"And if they weren't willing, you could always make terrifying threats . . ." said Ashley, tiredly.

Kaitlin didn't seem to hear her mother anymore. "Are all of the campers at Overlook part of your experiment?"

"Certainly not. Most of them aren't. We only tested six twin sets last year, seven this year, and we will test seven more next year. All the other campers at Overlook are just fillers, here to enjoy the mountain air and ropes course, and serve as a convenient control group for this experiment."

"And are all of the twin sets you separated eventually *called upon*?"

"No. Only three sets were *called upon* last year. So far, only two sets this summer. We'll see what happens next year."

"I'm not sure I want to know this," said Ashley, closing her eyes and rubbing her temples, "but I need you to explain *exactly* how the children were tested."

"It was all about location, quite frankly. The counterparts have been living here in this building, while their twins have been enjoying the activities of Camp Overlook. The twins were close enough in proximity that they would show subtle symptoms of forming a connection to their counterpart, but not so close that the symptoms would overwhelm them."

"And the symptoms are . . . ?"

"Odd dreams, headaches, fever, insomnia, fatigue, mostly flu-like symptoms . . . although some of the previously *called upon* expressed that they picked up on bits and pieces of their counterpart's knowledge before they were completely reunited—a premature transmission."

"So that's why you were making us write in the journals and filming us and stuff," said Kaitlin. "You were watching us to see if we were feeling the symptoms."

Dr. Forsythe squinted curiously at Kaitlin before giving his reply. "Yes. As the symptoms could sometimes be subtle, we needed to watch closely. We posted discreet cameras around camp so as to not miss anything. I'm disappointed that you knew about them; the cameras were meant to be a secret. We didn't want you to feel like we were invading your privacy."

"You were filming my daughter without her or my permission!" Ashley squealed, the idea sending her into a fit of ballistics. "Do you know how wildly inappropriate—"

"It's okay, Mom," said Kaitlin. "I think I can understand why now."

"I assure you, Miss Ashley, that the filming was innocent and necessary. Several weeks ago, Anjalie showed all the classic symptoms that the two of them were forming a connection. Consequently, we had to keep an even closer eye on Kaitlin. Other than a limp, Kaitlin didn't show any clear signs of feeling sick." He turned to Kaitlin. "But when you vomited at the dance, we felt certain that you'd been *called upon*. Molly's snitchery gave us the perfect excuse to take you away without arousing suspicions from the other campers."

"So, I've been feeling sick and exhausted all week, not because of my leg, but because of . . . all this?" She stretched her hands to indicate everything around her.

"Correct."

"And last night in the car when I got that horrible headache . . . ?"

"That was because you were driving closer to your counterpart. When we finally sedated you, Anjalie was also sedated, only one floor below you."

"So close and I didn't even know it."

"Anjalie is still quite close. And she's been begging to meet you two all day. Shall we continue to torture the poor girl, or shall we invite her to join us?"

"Really?" Kaitlin cried. "She's here right now? So this is happening?"

Ashley's blood turned cold. Why had the possibility of meeting Anjalie come as such a surprise? Dr. Forsythe had thrown her for every other loop, why not this one? "I—I—am not sure if I can. I haven't prepared myself. I—don't think—"

"Mom," Kaitlin begged, "please!"

Ashley felt frazzled, frazzled and exhausted. After an overnight drive, a panic-filled morning, and such an emotional, heated hour with Dr. Forsythe, she could barely wrap her mind around keeping her eyes open, let alone the idea of meeting her daughter. While she'd dreamed her whole life of a reunion, at the moment, the very idea of it was too much to handle. "It's been so many years . . . so many painful years."

"But don't you want to see your own daughter? What's wrong with you?" Kaitlin's words stung. Of course Ashley wanted to see Anjalie. She loved her more than life itself. It was just that . . . "I can't undo what has been done; I don't even have the strength to try. Not right this moment. Please try to understand, Kaitlin."

"It's not fair!" Angry tears seeped from Kaitlin's eyes. "You've kept her from me all these years, and when you finally get the conscience to tell me about her, you won't let me meet her. She's my sister!"

"Kaitlin, it's not just that. This man has wronged us in ways that you don't understand. He's a sweet talker; I should know. The more that he opens his mouth, the more you get caught in his web. I'm afraid that if you meet Anjalie, you'll never be able to untangle yourself."

"But this is my chance, Mom. This is my chance to be somebody, to be happy for once. I need Anjalie. I need her!"

"I'm sorry to interrupt," said Dr. Forsythe. "I understand, Miss Ashley, that you are not ready to meet Anjalie and you're afraid that if Kaitlin meets her, she will be committed to my cause. I promised you before, and I will promise you again, if you decide that Kaitlin doesn't belong here, I will never bother you again. It is ultimately your decision. But I beg you, for Kaitlin's sake, to at least allow her to talk with her sister. She will never forgive you if you don't."

"If you think that I am going to let Kaitlin out of my sight for one minute . . ."

"Mom, I'm fifteen; I can handle myself."

"Ashley, please. You haven't slept for two days; you look exhausted. Here is the key to the suite next to Kaitlin's. I'll have dinner delivered to you—prime rib is on the menu. Take the evening to rest up and think about both of your daughters' futures. In the morning, you can tell us what you've decided."

"But what about Kaitlin?"

"She and Anjalie will spend a few hours getting to know one another, simple as that."

"That seems fair. Right, Mom?" Kaitlin nodded, her face flush with anticipation.

It might have been fatigue. More likely it was Dr. Forsythe's appraisal that Kaitlin would never forgive her if she didn't let her meet her sister. Whatever it was, Ashley's resolve slowly began to deteriorate. "I need to know that Kaitlin is safe. I want a key to her room."

"Of course."

Ashley took the key card off the table and sighed. "Okay."

CHAPTER 16

KAITLIN

My sister was a big weirdo. But I'm ahead of myself.

After my mother retired to her suite for the evening, Dr. Forsythe and I waited for Margaret to fetch Anjalie. My mind was so overwhelmed with thoughts and emotions that my glands pumped my body with enough adrenaline to bench press a hippopotamus.

"Are you alright there, Miss Kaitlin?" Dr. Forsythe gestured to my foot, which was thumping loudly against the desk in front of me.

"Oh, sorry," I said, gaining control over my foot but losing the battle with my fingers, now twiddling with the ferocity of a knitter on speed.

"Don't worry, dear. You were given a significant amount of information in a very short amount of time. Jitter away."

I nodded, cracked my knuckles, and continued the twiddling. I simply could not believe what had happened to me. In less than a week, I had gone from less than a nobody to more than a somebody. I, Kaitlin, barfmaster extraordinaire, relationship saboteur, freakish loser of the century, had the power within me to do brilliant things. Things that most people couldn't. Things that would matter.

All that I'd ever wanted was to fit in, to be normal. Now, clearly, I could never be just that. Nor would I want to. I had been *called upon*. I was special. And one day, if I did things right, my name would be immortalized in biographies and history text books. One day, people like Mia Bethers would brag that they'd once known me. One day, nobody would remember how I tossed my cookies on my desk at school or that I tossed them again into the bushes at Camp Overlook. One day, my heart would be too occupied with the task of saving the world to notice the throbbing ache of losing my first love.

Max. Oh, Max.

Then I chastised myself. How dare I give pause for a boy at a time like this? I was mere seconds away from meeting my twin sister, Anjalie. This would be the most important moment of my life! Not only was Anjalie the key to my calling in life, she was the reason I'd never be lonely ever again. We were going to be best friends. We would understand each other in a way that only sisters could, root for each other, and laugh hysterically at each other's jokes.

I pictured our reunion in my head. We'd meet each other's eyes and fall into each other's arms. It would be like we already knew each other heart to heart and soul to soul. We'd have no need for words but wouldn't be able to stop talking. Dr. Forsythe would leave us, and we would spend hours braiding each other's hair and revealing our deepest darkest secrets, later falling asleep with our heads on the same pillow. That's how I pictured it.

Here's what really went down. Margaret opened the door, and Anjalie stepped inside. For someone who looked *exactly* like me, Anjalie looked absolutely *nothing* like me. I mean, she had my face and body and stuff, but nobody would ever confuse the two of us. She held herself like a stuffy librarian, her posture so straight that her shoulder blades almost overlapped. She wore a gray business suit over an even grayer blouse—the collar so high that it met up with her earlobes—and the bun at the back of her head was so taut that her temples bulged out like elevator buttons. Her eyes were dull and skin was pale and flat and, I'll be darned, without a freckle to its name.

"Hi," I said, standing up, my heart pounding.

Anjalie took a step closer to me, and I opened my arms. Instead of hugging me, however, she leaned forward and sniffed me. The me-sniffing was the first indication that my sister was a big weirdo.

"Just as I hypothesized," she said, wasting no time explaining the hypothesis or her methods. Instead, she grabbed my hand and shook it as though she were meeting an assigned lab partner for the first time. "I suppose you and I will be working with each other for the next while. So you're aware, I don't tolerate slackers. I expect you to work every bit as hard as me; heaven knows you have a lot of catching up to do. I've spent my whole life preparing for this opportunity. I've specialized in science and mathematics—and am quite versatile in both. From the looks of it, you've spent your whole life specializing in freckles—you must be so proud."

I shrugged.

Anjalie continued. "It's hardly fair, all the work I've put in and all the work you have not. Being *called upon* is the highest honor, one that I have earned and one that you have stumbled upon as clumsily as a sockless foot stumbles upon a fresh pile of dog scat. I will try not to hold it against you, but I will not congratulate you, either. I will be civil to you so long as you hold up your end of the bargain."

To say our first exchange had been anticlimactic would be generous. This wasn't how it was supposed to go. Didn't the doctor say Anjalie was excited to meet me? I tried to smile at my sister but barely managed to lift the right side of my face a fraction of a centimeter. I was so disappointed.

Dr. Forsythe, reading the quiver of my lips, moved between the two of us and placed his arms around each of our shoulders. "Anjalie, what's gotten into you? It is not Kaitlin's fault she hasn't prepared herself for this. If anything, you should be thanking her. Without her, you'd never have been *called upon*. All those years of study would've been a waste, and you'd be little more than a useless counterpart."

"I know, I know, but—"

"No buts. I want you to apologize to Kaitlin. You owe her everything."

"I apologize, Kaitlin," she mumbled nasally.

Dr. Forsythe looked to me in a way that made me feel like a kindergartner caught in rift over stolen crayons. "It's okay," I mumbled back.

"Excellent, excellent!" Dr. Forsythe clapped his hands together. "Now, take a seat, ladies. I want to answer any questions you have before I send you two off for some womanly bonding." He walked around the desk and adjusted his jacket before sitting down. "Miss Kaitlin, what would you like to know?"

"Tons of stuff, I guess," I said, eyeballing my sister as she picked away at some imaginary lint on her blazer. "But mainly I want to know how our connection works. And why."

"The *why* I am still trying to figure out. As you remember, I drew your blood at the beginning of camp—not just yours, but the blood of every camper and every counterpart. So far, I haven't been able to make a correlation between blood types and this phenomenon, but I have detected a subtle chemical variance in the blood of the twins after they have been *called upon*. Last night as you slept, I collected fresh samples from the two of you. The samples now contained that variance, though they didn't earlier this summer. I theorize that the combination of being separated and then reunited with each other—during an extreme hormonal phase in your lives—caused a chemical reaction in your bodies. This reaction is the reason for the connection.

"The *how* question is a little simpler to answer. As your bodies began forming a connection, you both started feeling ill in response to the chemical changes in your blood. As I've implied, the only way to feel better during the reaction is to have an information transfer, and the only way to transfer information is while you are asleep. The difficulty is that one of the symptoms of the reaction is trouble sleeping. So if you are unable to sleep, you are unable to transfer information, and if you are unable to transfer information, you continue getting sicker. That's the reason for the sedation. Does that make sense?"

I glanced at Anjalie. She looked bored, no doubt having heard Dr. Forsythe's explanations of this her whole life. I, on the other hand, was enthralled. "It makes sense. I just don't understand how the transfer works—mechanically, I mean."

The doctor smiled. "The easiest way to explain it is by likening your brain unto a computer. As you learn new things during the day, your brain records the information onto a Word document. At night, when you are asleep, your brain opens an email account, attaches the document to a new message, and sends the message to Anjalie's brain. She receives the message in full instantaneously. Pretty nifty, eh?"

I shifted in my seat uncomfortably. True, I thought the whole concept was insanely cool, beefing up each other's brain power in a matter of minutes, but I was beginning to realize that there were some things in my head that I had no interest in sharing with anyone else. Things that embarrassed me. For example, I didn't want Anjalie to know about the time when Mia Bethers squirted a bottle of ketchup on the front of my jeans so that it looked like I'd had a volcanic menstrual problem. I didn't want her to know about the countless fantasies I'd had about Max and the way his mouth may or may not taste against mine. And for the sake of Anjalie's feelings, I didn't want her to know how badly she fell short of my expectations and that I thought she was, I'll say it again, a big weirdo.

"Um, Dr. Forsythe?" I said. "Does that mean that all my . . . personal thoughts will be out in the open?"

"Not necessarily. Ideas that have been studied and committed to memory are the things that transfer. Passing thoughts and occurrences, things that you don't place much stock in, don't. Many of the *called upon* have trained their minds to not mull over the things they don't want others to know. You will learn to do the same over time."

"But my thoughts right now . . . my secrets . . ."

"I am afraid you're an open book, my dear."

"So after last night, Anjalie knows everything I know, and I know everything she knows?"

"Well, if it were just you and Anjalie in the picture, that is how it would work. Last night, however, twelve other people—twelve other *called upon*— were also staying here: Jason, Douglas, Tanji, Keisha, the three sets of twins who connected last summer, and Aya and her counterpart."

"Holy crap! I know everything they know, too?"

Anjalie laughed out loud. "What an ignoramus. Don't you think you'd notice if you had that sort of brain power? And also, you wouldn't be asking so many idiotic questions. You'd already know the answers because the information would've already been transferred to you." In my mind, Anjalie was transitioning from a big weirdo to a big jerk. Maybe it wouldn't be so bad if she knew exactly what I thought of her after all.

"Imagine this, Kaitlin," Dr Forsythe said, barreling through the tension between me and Anjalie. "Imagine you were on the brink of starvation and someone put a bowl of spaghetti in front of you. What would you do?"

"I'd eat it."

"Alright. Now let's say you were on the brink of starvation and someone put, not just a plate of spaghetti in front of you, but a table full of food: honey-glazed ham, mashed potatoes, corn, blueberry pie—a real feast. Would you eat it all?"

"I'd probably try."

"But *could* you eat it all?"

"Realistically, no. I'd probably take a bite or two from every dish, but after all was said and done, I'd only have grazed the surface of it all."

"Even though you were starved?"

"Even though. I could only eat as much as my belly could hold."

"Right. Let's liken that scenario to your experience last night. As you drove closer to Anjalie, your brain starved for the information in her head. Anjalie represents the plate of spaghetti. Do you follow?"

"Yes."

"But upon arrival at this building, not only was your brain offered that plate of spaghetti but a whole smorgasbord of knowledge. You tasted a bit of Anjalie's expertise, a little of Jason's, a little of Aya's, etc."

"Your example is starting to gross me out."

"But do you understand what I am trying to say? You took in enough information to be satiated, but not so much that you got indigestion."

"So, what you're saying is that my brain took bits and pieces of knowledge from a bunch of people, not just from Anjalie."

"Exactly. That is why you were only able to complete a fraction of the crossword puzzle earlier on. Had you been transferred everything all at once, you would've been able to finish the whole thing."

Something still didn't make sense to me. "If what you're saying is true, how come I don't feel sick right now? I mean, I am sitting right next to Anjalie, but only have a small percentage of her knowledge. Shouldn't my brain be thirsting for more? Shouldn't I be flat on my back, writhing in pain?"

"Like we discussed, your mind partook until it was full. It is still content. But just as your body feels hunger pangs when it's ready to be refueled, your body will let you know when it is time for another transfer."

"So I'm going to get sick again?"

"Don't worry, we will sedate you as soon as you start exhibiting symptoms."

"But how many times will I have to go through this until I've got all the information I need?" My voice verged on panic, but I couldn't help it. The pain yesterday was excruciating. I never wanted to feel that horrible again.

"Quit your whining," Anjalie griped. "I'm experiencing all the same inconveniences you are, and you don't hear me complaining."

Not helpful.

Dr. Forsythe ignored Anjalie. "I estimate it will take a couple of weeks for the two of you to catch up with all of the others. Let us not forget, however, that everyone will continue studying and learning after that. You will too. Realistically, as long as you share a roof with the *called upon*, you will experience unpleasant symptoms leading up to the nightly information transfer."

"And it will hurt the same way as it did last night?"

"After you've caught up with everyone else, the pain should lessen . . . but yes, it will always hurt."

"Oh," I said.

Dr. Forsythe reached over the table and took my hand. "I know all this is difficult to swallow. Change, my blessed girl, never has come cheap. Remembering what you are fighting for, the lives that will be saved, and the hope that will be restored will give you the strength to rise above your trials and push forward in this tremendous cause."

I sighed. "Do you really think I can do this? That I am good enough and strong enough?"

The doctor's eyes misted, and he gave my hand a gentle squeeze. "I have never met a young woman so wonderfully qualified."

———————

Suffice it to say my sister didn't like me much. She grimaced when Dr. Forsythe asked her to show me around the facility. By the way she kept three feet in front of me the whole tour, paying no mind to my slight limp, Anjalie evidently regarded me more as an unsightly wart than her identical twin.

I wish I could say that it didn't bother me because, heck, I didn't think much of her either, but it did. Even after Dr. Forsythe, perhaps the most amazing man I'd ever met, had spent the previous three hours indoctrinating me on my own greatness, the only opinion that seemed to matter was that of my big weirdo twin sister. Hadn't she been waiting her entire life to meet me? We were flesh and blood. Family. She and I had been nourished by the same placenta, for heaven's sake. Screw unconditional love, shouldn't she love me because of those very reasons?

Anjalie hastily pointed out the lounge, the kitchen, the cafeteria, and the classrooms. While obvious that no expense had been spared in the building's finish work, it all looked a lot like Camp Overlook's facilities to me—it even had a Le Cordon Bleu smell to it. But the building was familiar in a way beyond that. I felt like I'd known this place all along, that I had even once lived here.

We took an elevator to the second floor, riding in silence for ten tedious seconds—me, looking at the ceiling and Anjalie, the floor. We both breathed a sigh of relief when the doors slid open and let in a fresh supply of personal space. We practically tripped over one another to be the first out.

The second floor was quite different from the first, though it gave me an equally nostalgic feeling. And for the first time since arriving at the Leavitt Center headquarters, I saw people—not just Margaret, Dr. Forsythe, my mom, and Anjalie, but *actual* people. There were kids my age, but also tons of adults, whom I assumed were staff members. Everyone walked down the halls with a sense of urgency, purpose, and they were all wearing gray—gray shirts, gray slacks, gray skirts, and if I were a betting girl, I'd say gray underpants.

"Felicidades, Kaitlin y Anjalie," said a short, Hispanic-looking guy as he passed us on our right. I turned my neck to follow him, surprised that he knew my name.

"Congratulations on being *called upon*, you two," said another teen as she passed us going the opposite direction.

Three more people gave us their well wishes as we walked down the hallway, although I got the distinct impression that the last two didn't really mean it.

"They're jealous," Anjalie remarked. "They'll be tested next summer and probably won't be *called upon*. The odds are, mathematically speaking, against them." I saw a discreet smile creep across her face.

We came to an ornate doorway, and I caught a heavenly whiff of leather, paper, and ink. *Books!* I thought, feeling an immediate pep in my step. I pushed open the door and almost cried for joy. Big enough to fit a Boeing airplane (well, almost), this room housed more books than most public libraries. Shelf after shelf after shelf!

"Pretty amazing, isn't it?" said Anjalie, her eyes glowing. And for just a second, I felt a spark of warmth between the two of us. She took a book from a shelf and held it up to my nose. "This is a book. Maybe you could read one sometime and make an actual contribution to the knowledge pool."

And the spark turned into a bubble and floated away.

"I spend most of my time studying," Anjalie continued. "When I'm not at class or the lab, I'm here." She motioned to the dozen tables situated at the front of the library. Each table housed one or two people, each person deep in study. I recognized some of them. Director Leavitt . . . er . . . Jason was there. He was reading a book called *Media and the Law*. His twin sat next to him, or was his twin Jason?—couldn't tell—taking notes from another gigantic textbook. A few tables behind him sat a girl who looked like someone from the Wildflower cabin—a counterpart hoping to be *called upon*, no doubt. Then I saw Sam— Claire's Sam. He was picking a book from the shelf of the Science section. I wondered if he was too busy with his studies to think about Claire every now and again. I hoped not.

"Kaitlin," someone tapped my shoulder.

I turned around to see my old roommate, black eyeliner and all. "Aya!" I squeaked and gave her a massive hug. I was tremendously happy to see her!

"You did it. I hoped you would. Isn't this crazy? Guess what? My counterpart is fluent in Portuguese, and French and Spanish and, like, ten other languages. And now I am. You will be too soon enough. Can you believe it? How are you feeling?"

"Good," I said. "Overwhelmed."

"I understand. When I was *called upon*, I was worried that I'd let everyone down. I didn't believe that I could handle so much responsibility. But I don't feel that way anymore."

"How come?"

"Because of Dr. Forsythe, of course. He is such an amazing person. His vision, his kindness . . . he is a genius. Do you know that he believes we'll be able to prevent and cure autism and Alzheimer's? He thinks we can obliterate hunger, terrorism, and even all crime. Dr. Forsythe has taught me that, although I am small, that if I think big, I can be a part of it. Oh, Kaitlin, I am so happy."

And Aya *did* look happy, but she also looked very tired. Her voice was robotic, and her words dragged on slowly. Plus, something about her eyes was off; they were dull and chalky. Were they like that at camp? Then again, I suppose anyone's eyes would appear that way if they were dressed in all gray.

"Aya, can I ask you a question? How did your mom react to all this? I mean, was she happy about it?"

"Of course. She was so proud of me and my gift and was ecstatic to meet Izumi, my counterpart."

"And your mom wasn't mad at Dr. Forsythe?"

"Why would she be? He made it possible for her to raise me; she couldn't have done that without his help. And now, he is giving Izumi and me these life-altering opportunities. When Mom sends me and Izumi cookies in the mail each week, she makes sure to include an extra dozen for him." She gave a strained, throaty chuckle.

"Ahem!" Anjalie coughed. "I know you're, like, so popular, Kaitlin, but we're in the library. Save the gossip for cheerleading practice or, like, the mall."

Aya gave me a rueful wave and sat down at a nearby table. Anjalie pulled me out of the library and into the hallway to continue the tour. We turned a corner and entered a medium-sized room full of computers, shelves, and more busy people.

"This is the lab."

"Is this where you check your Insta and stuff?" I asked.

She threw her head back in disgust. "No, it's where we view and record data. Look, I'll show you." She walked over to an empty computer and typed in a password. *Welcome, Anjalie* flashed on the screen followed by an all-too-familiar list of camp locations. She clicked on the dining hall, and we watched Overlook campers trickle in for dinner. I saw Max. He was hunched over the table, rubbing his temples and looking very stressed out. I touched the screen wistfully.

"The lab is where we observe the campers who might be *called upon*. We follow their every move and listen to their conversations, making sure to record anything that might suggest they are experiencing symptoms. It's a big, complicated job, so several people are assigned to one individual camper. We are all required to log at least two hours of data each day. Some brownnosers log more, but I don't. I like to spend my time studying."

"Were you assigned to me?"

"No. It's against the rules to watch your own counterpart. I've been observing a girl from the Wildflower cabin. She's boring as dirt, and there's almost no chance she will be *called upon*."

"Were boys watching me?" I thought of the hundreds of times I'd changed my clothes in the cabin's main room and the time I had excavated my nose without a tissue.

"Females are assigned to females and males to males, nothing inappropriate going on here." But the wicked smile on Anjalie's face seemed to hint that she cheated the rules once in a while.

"After we've recorded the data, we print it and file it in these binders. We also include entries from the camper's journals and excerpts from letters they've exchanged with their families—we don't want to miss any crucial piece of information."

She walked over to the shelf and pulled out a binder with my name on it. "This is your file. Notice how detail-oriented your data gets toward the end. That's because I was beginning to experience symptoms."

I didn't mention to Anjalie that I had already seen a copy of my file in Phil's lair.

"Anyhow, every morning, Dr. Forsythe stops by the lab and reads the camper's files. He likes them in hardcopy because he's old, and old people like paper, despite it being a terrible waste of resources. He spent a lot of time reading yours."

I blushed, thrilled that Dr. Forsythe took such an interest in me.

"But I don't know how he could stand it," Anjalie said. "You're also boring as dirt." She ushered me out of the lab and back to the elevator, which we rode to the third floor. The doors slid open, revealing a long hallway of doors, patterned carpet on the floor, and fancy sconces on the wall. "These are the living quarters. The faculty and staff stay in suites on the north end of the building, and the rest of us have rooms on the south end."

"Where's Dr. Forsythe's suite?"

"He lives on the fourth floor, across from your VIP suite, with his son, Parker."

"Dr. Forsythe's son lives here?"

"Yeah. And he's a real skunk."

"What's wrong with him?"

"All of the above. He's rude and strange and he goes around spreading fanatical conspiracy theories about his dad. Can you imagine saying bad things about Dr. Forsythe? The man's a saint."

"So where's your room?"

Anjalie motioned down the hall. "I used to share the room with this girl named Patricia. She was tested last summer, but wasn't *called upon*. Ha, no surprise there. She left for college after that, so now I have the room to myself. I guess that changes now that you're here; you can't stay in a fancy fourth-floor suite forever, pampered princess. We'll probably move your stuff in after your mom goes back home."

And then a realization washed over me. I'd probably be living here, not till the end of the summer, but for a really long time. The thought overwhelmed me, so I quickly convinced myself that it would be like going away to college, just a few years earlier than I'd planned. I mean, it would be awful not to live with Mom and Dad, but I'd never have to see Mia Bethers and her flock of evil wannabes ever again. That reason alone would make the sacrifice worth it.

"Can I see your . . . er . . . our room?"

Anjalie huffed. "Just keep your mitts off of my things."

I hobbled behind Anjalie to a room near the end of the hallway. It was large with oodles of natural light, although the gray walls sucked the warmth right out. Other than a stack of textbooks next to bed and a small framed photograph on the night stand, the space had about as much pizazz as a celery stick. And she said *I* was boring as dirt.

Perhaps the drabness of the room is why the button stood out so much. Bright red and mounted on the wall next to the door, it practically begged to be pushed. I lifted my finger . . .

"I told you not to touch anything!"

Sheepishly, I lowered my hand and walked over to her bed and sat down. "So, what do you do for fun?" Because I couldn't imagine anyone spending a moment longer in this room than they had to.

"I already told you. I study."

"But when you're not studying?"

"What are you talking about?" Anjalie snorted. "Why would I want to do anything else?"

So there it was. Anjalie's monochrome complexion was not a result of copious amounts of sunscreen, but because the girl never got out . . . literally. No wonder her social skills were even less developed than my own. The poor girl didn't know how to do anything but study. I bet she never went for a hike or played a game of Monopoly, let alone touched a book that was written by a person without a PhD.

"Never mind," I said.

Anjalie took a seat on an uncovered mattress across the room—the bed that would likely become my own—and opened her mouth as if to say something.

"What?" I asked.

"Oh, nothing."

"Really, what?"

She sighed. "Not that it matters, and not that I care, but did you pick up anything from me . . . any of my knowledge, while you were asleep last night?"

I thought for a second. "Well, I was able to answer some pretty crazy math and science questions with Dr. Forsythe this morning, and I've been having some serious déjà vu while walking around this building, but honestly, I don't know if all that information came from you or from somebody else. Part of me feels like I don't even know what I know. Like, I've got all this new information in my head, but since I have no immediate use for it, it's just sitting up there waiting for me to trip over. How 'bout you? Have you picked up anything from me?"

"Well, I know for a fact you spend a disturbing amount of time thinking of cookie butter."

"I won't deny it."

"I also have learned a lot about her."

"Who?"

Anjalie pointed to the framed picture on the nightstand. "Her."

The girl in the photograph looked about my age. She wore an unbuttoned plaid flannel over a white tee. The shirt would have had to be pretty stretchy to accommodate the dinosaur egg of a belly beneath it. The pregnant girl looked done enough to stick a fork into but smiled happily at the camera anyway. She was beautiful. "This is my mother," I said, picking up the frame.

Anjalie cringed, though at the moment I was too dense to realize why. "Dr. Forsythe took the picture a couple days before she gave birth. He gave it to me when I was three. Since then, she's stayed right there on the nightstand, looking over me."

Anjalie moved next to me and took the picture from my hands. She traced my mother's outline with her pinky finger. "She always seemed so magical to me, like a fairy or mermaid or something. I've always wondered what she was really like, my mother, but today . . . today I woke up knowing. Her favorite color is orange. She puts sour cream on everything, even pancakes. She loves autumn but hates snow. Her best friend is named Jade. She worries obsessively about you—and you wish she wouldn't—but that's because you worry about her, too, I guess. You smell like her, you know. Like salt and peppermint. I don't smell like that."

So that's why Anjalie sniffed me.

Her voice suddenly caught in her throat. "Why didn't she want to see me today? I was right there. Why wouldn't she see me?"

I had been wrong about Anjalie, and it hit me like a soccer ball to the gut. Here I'd been all put out that I wasn't the center of Anjalie's world, that she hadn't been overcome with joy to meet me. Of course her world hadn't revolved around me, or studying, or even being *called upon*. All of those things were only paths to lead her to what she wanted most. She'd waited her whole life to meet her mother, and after all her hard work, after so many years of hoping, after getting so very close to her happily ever after, Anjalie's mother wanted nothing to do with her.

And *I* must've been an incredibly painful reminder of the mother who had given her away. No wonder she was keeping me at arm's length. "I'm sorry. I am so sorry," I said.

Anjalie cried so deeply, so honestly. She cried with the tears of a scared, lost child. She cried with a loneliness that made me understand how little I actually understood loneliness. I wanted to cry with her. I wanted to put my arm around her shoulder and to be a sister to her. But I didn't. I just sat there and watched her sob.

Suddenly her eyes widened. In a frenzied movement, she clenched her fists to the sides of her forehead and began thrashing from side to side. "Oh no! Not again!" she moaned. "I hate this!"

I didn't have to ask to know what she was talking about. I was feeling the same thing. The pressure behind my eyes might as well have been formed by Niagara Falls, it was so intense. My muscles seized. My limbs contracted until I turned into a human gerbil ball rolling spasmodically around the floor. It was happening again!

"The button!" Anjalie gasped. "Press . . . the . . . button!"

I tried to force myself out of my ball, but the room was caving in on me; the air was too heavy. I wanted to scream, but the pain smothered me. I was drowning in it.

Anjalie staggered off of the bed and toward the door. Her foot caught against my body, and she stumbled to the ground. Pulling herself across the floor arm over arm, she finally made it to the entryway and snaked her arm up the wall. She fell short of the red button by only a few inches. Slowly, as if it weighed more than a bag of bricks, she extended her finger and grazed the button with the tip of her fingernail. An alarm sounded, and Anjalie dropped back to the floor in agony.

The alarm screamed louder than hell in surround sound—a torture beyond anything anyone could endure. Just when I thought my head might pop, splattering my brains across the walls, Anjalie's door burst open. Margaret ran into the room carrying syringes full of purple fluid. I felt a needle slide into my arm and then relief, sweet relief . . .

PARKER

Tonight was the night. Claire, now refusing to eat anything, was quickly losing strength. Parker feared that if he waited one more day, she wouldn't have the energy to escape with him.

In the dark, Parker slid his camera, water bottles, and a few granola bars into his backpack. He'd have to pack light if they were to travel quickly. In a matter of hours, his father would roll out of bed, take his morning coffee, and notice that Parker was nowhere to be found. So he'd take the elevator down to the basement to check on Claire himself, and, of course, he'd find her missing. Putting two and two together, Dr. Forsythe would send a small army into the wilderness to hunt the pair down. That's why it was imperative that Parker and Claire got a respectable head start.

Parker picked up the keycard to Claire's chamber and fumbled through the dark apartment, walking on the balls of his feet as to not wake his father. He froze midstep, however, as the lights from the master suite suddenly cast a yellow glow from below the door. Parker tossed his backpack behind the suede recliner just before the light poured into the living room. His father stood at the doorway with disheveled hair and a pinstriped pair of pajamas. "Goodness gracious, son! Have you any idea what time it is?" He scratched his head, eyeballing the keycard in Parker's hand.

"Um,"—Parker thought quickly—"I had a dream that Claire escaped. I wouldn't be able to sleep unless I made sure she was still in her cell."

"But you're in jeans and a sweatshirt."

"Would you have preferred that I go in my tighty-whities?"

Dr. Forsythe chuckled. "Well, no. Wait here, I'll put on my jacket and join you. We have some important business to take care of, and there's no point putting it off."

"Okay . . . alright." Parker felt as though he'd swallowed a bowling ball. What business could they possibly have with Claire in the middle of the night? His father returned wearing a jacket over his pajamas. "Shall we?"

The duo made their way down the hallway to the elevator, which took them to the basement of the Leavitt Center. Cold air surged into the elevator when the doors opened. The men stepped into the hallway. Parker shivered but not because of the cold. Something awful was about to happen, though he didn't dare imagine what. They made their way down the main hallway and then through the labyrinth of passageways and pipes. When they reached the cell door, Dr. Forsythe held out his hand for the keycard.

Claire was in her favorite spot of the cell, the corner, her arms wrapped around her knees and her body rocking back and forth. Her hair was matted and oily, and her face was beginning to sink inward. She glanced up at the two men but didn't say anything. She was in worse shape than Parker had thought. The last two days of starvation and dehydration, not to mention her less-than-ideal living quarters, had sucked the fight out of her completely.

Parker almost went to her, almost took a step forward, but stopped himself just in time. Now, more than ever, he needed to show his father how much he didn't care about Claire.

Dr. Forsythe spoke. "Stand up, Claire."

Claire didn't move.

"You heard him; stand up!" Parker flinched at the grating resonance of his own voice.

She slowly pushed her body off the floor, but refused to meet her captors' eyes.

Dr. Forsythe spoke, but not to Claire, to his son. "It has come to my attention, Parker, that you have not been entirely honest with me. You told me that you saw Claire sneak out, and you implied that she was alone."

"I was being honest with you. That's all I saw. The surveillance system is limited in its—"

Dr. Forsythe held up his hand. "You are my son, so I chose to believe you, but I admit that I was not entirely without suspicion. Your story was too convenient, too simple. That's why I detained Claire instead of sending her home. I needed to make sure that she didn't know too much about the Leavitt Center—that she couldn't compromise the integrity of this outfit."

Parker tried to remove any hint of compassion from his reply, but the pleading tone of his voice absolutely reeked of it. "Look at her, Dad, she doesn't know anything. Let's make her promise to keep quiet in exchange for her freedom. We should let her go. She won't talk, I swear it—"

"Stop it, Parker. Just stop it. Claire's little buddy, Kaitlin, admitted knowing about the surveillance system. How could she know about that unless she'd seen it? She logged into the system under Anjalie's password—which I assume had been prematurely transferred to her—and Claire must've been with her. Tell me, Parker, were you with Kaitlin and Claire when they broke into the station?"

"No, Father. I promise. Things happened just as I said. I don't know how Kaitlin did it. Maybe she broke in after I erased all of the data and left, while the system was still down. Maybe she—"

"There are a lot of holes in your story, son. Too many holes." Dr. Forsythe shook his head, but rested his hand on Parker's shoulder. "But once again, I am willing to give you the benefit of the doubt. You are my son, and I love you. I believe you are trustworthy. I believe you are invested in this cause. I believe you would do anything to preserve it."

"You know I would," said Parker with relief. He saw Claire, still staring at the floor, take in a breath of air as well.

"Yes," Dr. Forsythe continued, "I believe you. And now is your chance to prove yourself." He lifted his jacket, reached behind his back and pulled a pistol from the waistband of his pajamas. "Kill her."

Parker gasped and vehemently shook his head no. Claire, for the first time during their visit, lifted her face. Sheer terror pierced her eyes. Dr. Forsythe took Parker's hand and laced it through the gun, sliding the safety to fire.

"You said you admired me. You said I see what needs to be done and then I do it—no matter how difficult. You said you wished you were half the man I am. Well, here's your chance, son. Here's your chance."

"But Dad, don't you think someone's going to notice that Claire's missing? We'll get caught. Her mom will—"

"Her mom has been taken care of. Apparently, she was involved in a horrific car accident yesterday morning. Sadly, she didn't survive." There was a weightless glow to Dr. Forsythe's eyes, like he was finally free of an emotion that had plagued him for years.

"Please, no!" Claire sobbed, falling to her knees.

"What are you crying about, little girl?" said Dr. Forsythe. "She died on impact; didn't feel a thing. Let's hope my boy here is a good shot so you'll share her good fortune."

"I can't. I won't." Parker flipped on the safety and lowered the gun to his side, his fingers and voice quivering.

"But you must. Philip called me right as you were sneaking out a few minutes ago. He let me know that we'll be having some unexpected guests this evening—a rescue party, if you will. We need to clear this place out if we want them to have accommodations suitable for their welcome."

"No," Parker whispered.

Dr. Forsythe snatched the gun out of Parker's hands. "Then you are a coward!" He pointed the pistol at Claire.

"Please!" Claire shrieked, her tears forming trails through the grime that had accumulated on her face during the week. "Please don't kill me! I promise I won't tell a soul about what I know. If you want, I'll even help you. I'll do whatever you want! I'll pay you. If you want money, I'll find a way to get it. Anything! Please!"

Bam!

For a moment, Claire held very still. Her eyes bulged out in horror, and the color drained from her face and lips. Then she wheezed. It was the most horrible, wet sound Parker had ever heard. The bullet had gone straight through her lung.

Bam!

This time Claire's torso flew backward, her knees buried awkwardly beneath her body. A puddle of red pooled around her back and into her hair.

Parker stared at her lifeless body in shock. The one person that he ever cared about—even though he'd never really known her—was dead.

"See, that wasn't so bad." His father smiled and tucked the warm pistol back into his pajama bottoms. "Tomorrow night, you will have another opportunity like this, and if I were you, I'd aim to please."

Parker barely heard his father's threat, smelled the metallic scent of warm blood, or felt the sting of his fingernails digging into the flesh of his palms. He was filled with a fury so consuming that it blunted all of his other senses.

Dr. Forsythe turned to go back to bed, but as an afterthought, leaned in and whispered into Parker's ear. "And don't even think about trying to escape again. I've got armed men posted at every exit, and they're not as afraid to fire weapons as you are. Goodnight, son."

CHAPTER 17

KAITLIN

Sure, it was only a bland gray dress, but the sight of it tickled me beyond belief. I kicked off my silky covers and jumped out of bed, swooping the new dress off of the chair and holding it up to my body. The color did nothing for my complexion, and the cut looked more formfitting than I was accustomed, but the dress seemed to make it official: I was a bona fide member of the Leavitt Center club. Yippee!

I twirled around, letting the dress's pleats swish against my legs, and wondered who had left it for me. Then I wondered how many new brain cells I'd accumulated during the night. And then it hit me that I was doing all my wondering in Spanish. Que bueno! Habla Espanol! Tengo que decirle a mi mamá

I ran out of my suite, still wearing my pajamas and the dress hanger around my neck, and pounded on the door next to mine.

"Your mom's not there," said Tanji, emerging from the elevator with the usual bored-stiff frown on her face.

"Donde est—I mean, where is she?"

"She went to town for the day. She said she needed some time to herself."

"But I thought that we were going to have breakfast with Dr. Forsythe, and she was going to give us her decision about all this."

"Didn't you look at the clock when you woke up? It's 10:00. Dr. Forsythe and your mother met earlier this morning, before he had to report for duty at Camp Overlook. You couldn't be roused."

"Oh. Well, what did my mom decide?"

"You've got a new gray dress, don't you?" Tanji yawned.

"Oh my gosh! Mom said yes? She said I can be a part of all this?! This day just keeps getting better and better!" I grabbed Tanji's shoulders and jumped up and down like a tween who'd just been given tickets to a boy-band concert.

Tanji stood there and waited for me to contain myself. "If you're quite done . . ."

"Oops. Sorry." I stopped jumping and brushed off Tanji's shoulders where the delicate fabric had bunched under my grip.

"Look," said Tanji testily, "I need to get back to camp to teach class. I simply came up to make sure you were awake and tell you to meet Anjalie for brunch in an hour. She'll help you create an action plan for your education and future role with the Leavitt Center." She pressed the button for the elevator and tapped her toe impatiently for the whole three seconds it took for the door to slide open. "By the way, everyone at the Leavitt Center is expected to present themselves in an undistracting manner. I know this will be difficult for you; I saw the way you groomed yourself at camp. You should know that the dress so sloppily slung around your neck is an Armani. Don't disgrace it."

I scratched my head as the elevator doors closed in front of Tanji. My friend, Molly, would really come in handy right about now. She'd gladly roll her eyes with me about Tanji's cantankerous attitude, and she'd certainly be able to tell me what the heck an Armani was.

I readied myself for the day and went to the cafeteria. The room was littered with people, but no one seemed to be interacting. Instead, people were reading textbooks, typing at the laptops, or practicing flashcards—only occasionally taking breaks to shovel forkfuls of food into their mouths. It was like the dining room was a mere extension of the library.

Though sitting across from one another at a table, and not a book in sight, Anjalie and I weren't exactly communicating, either. I was eating my breakfast, but she was forking a poached egg back and forth across her plate, ingesting absolutely nothing. Did she wake up knowing how weird I thought she was? Did she wake up knowing how weird *I* actually was?

The egg forking was driving me nuts, but the silence between us was worse; I had to do something about it. "So . . . eh . . . that really hurt last night. You know, the onset of symptoms . . . in your room . . . last night. It hurt. Good thing you had that button in there. Does everyone have a button? I mean, does everyone who's been *called upon* get sick at the same time and whoever pushes a button first . . . like . . . wins. Did we win? I mean, we got sedated, and woo-wee, that sure felt like winning."

Anjalie punctured the yolk on her egg and looked up at me—orange goo seeping all over her pancakes and sausage links.

I continued rambling. "I mean, I noticed a few red buttons in the hallway, and there's even some in this dining hall. There must be buttons all over this place. Am I right?"

Anjalie sighed loudly and dropped her fork on her plate. "Whenever your symptoms flare up, you push the nearest button, and an alarm sounds. That's how the staff is able to find and quickly sedate you."

I knew I was annoying Anjalie, but I couldn't seem to stop myself. "So do all of the *called upon* feel the symptoms at the same time every day and the same time as everyone else?"

"Well, the time it happens varies from night to night, but everyone feels the symptoms at approximately the same time. Chaos takes over when the *called upon* get sick; the whole Leavitt Center staff—the faculty, the janitors, the guards, the cooks, everyone—drops everything and runs around like chickens without heads until every last person has been sedated. It used to be pretty hilarious to watch, before I was *called upon*, but it's not funny anymore—now that I know what the pain feels like."

"Yeah," I said.

And then there was silence again.

I nibbled my buttered toast and tried to act as though the toast-nibbling itself was so interesting that a conversation with Anjalie would be unnecessary and even distracting. But the silence was bad, really bad, and inwardly I scrambled for a suitable way to break it.

Luckily, Anjalie broke it first. "About last night . . ." she said in a way that made me think that last night was the real reason she'd been avoiding looking at or speaking to me for the last quarter hour. "Before we started feeling the symptoms. I got a little emotional for a moment. I don't usually do that."

"Oh. Well, it's okay to cry every once in a—"

"No, it's not. Dr. Forsythe teaches us to be strong, to hold our emotions—that crying is a sign of weakness. Then, the first real opportunity I had to prove myself, I completely lost control, like a coward. What you must think of me."

"Are you kidding me? What *you* must think of *me*! I just stared at you and let you cry. Who does that? I don't blame you for being upset. I'd be upset too if my mother didn't want to . . . well, you know."

"Please don't tell her, your mother, about how I reacted. Don't tell her about the photograph on my night stand, either. I'm so embarrassed."

"I won't," I promised.

Anjalie whistled a gust of relief. She slowly lifted one side of her face and then the other—a weak smile at best, but the first one I'd seen on her face since I met her.

I giggled.

"What?" she asked.

"I do that, too, smile with one half of my face before the other."

Surprised, Anjalie pressed her hands against the sides of her lips.

I laughed again. "I didn't know I did it either until last week. One of my friends told me. I thought he must've made it up, but you just did it, too. How funny!"

Anjalie's smile grew. "Looks like you and I have something in common after all."

"Maybe so."

Anjalie took a sip of her coffee and pushed her breakfast plate to the side of the table, a subtle indication that she was through with the chitchat and ready to get down to business. "Well, Tanji told me that I needed to help you decide on a specialty. I've been brainstorming and thought of the perfect idea. Want to hear?"

"Bring it."

"Since you like to read so much, I thought you could specialize in literature and writing. You're already better read than all of us, and I hear your journal entries were incredibly well-written, too. All of the *called upon* are learning important, practical things, like math, science, politics, and economics, but without the ability to write about it—the ability to write well, I mean—our effectiveness is lost in translation. We could really use your brain to fine-tune our grammar and writing style. What do you think?"

"Yes! Yes! Yes!" I exclaimed. "And maybe I could read a bunch of good stories, too—you know, like, fiction. That way, I could transfer you all a little entertainment; heaven knows this place needs some form of diversion." I motioned to the next table over, where a guy was salt and peppering his napkin because he was too engrossed in his Radiology textbook to nail the exact coordinates of his scrambled eggs.

"You might have a point," Anjalie nodded. "Should we head over to the library right now?"

"Can I meet you there in ten minutes? I need to run upstairs and take care of something really quickly."

"Sure. See you in a few."

————————

Thanks to Tanji's blatant stab at my self-grooming skills, I felt more anxious about how I looked that day than I would walking the red carpet for the Oscars. I was afraid that if she caught me with so much as an eyelash out of place, she might overheat and blow a saline boob or something. So there I was in my suite, applying my fifteenth coat of lip gloss and manically smoothing down my eyebrows with my pinky fingers.

As I gave myself a final inspection in the mirror, Dr. Forsythe's chuckle drifted from the hallway into my room. I grabbed my purse and reached for the doorknob to tell him good morning, but stopped short at the nails-on-chalkboard sound of Security Phil's cackle. Even though I now knew that technically Phil was one of the good guys, he still gave me that icky-crawly feeling inside. I intended to avoid him at all costs.

"You're a good man, Philip," I heard Dr. Forsythe say from behind my door. "I always know I can count on you when in a bind."

"I do my best," said Phil in his gross, raspy voice.

"If you don't mind my asking, what did you do with it?"

"I put it in the auxiliary freezer in the basement storage room, just temporarily; I'll relocate it to the designated spot during my night shift. There simply wasn't time to dispose of it properly this morning."

"Excellent, excellent," said Dr. Forsythe. "I might have another load for you tomorrow as well."

Phil cackled again. "You've been a very busy man, Dr. Forsythe. This job gets more interesting every day."

And then the men must've gotten into the elevator because their voices disappeared completely. I slowly turned the door knob and walked into the empty hallway, feeling uneasy about the conversation I'd just overheard but not knowing exactly why. I decided to take the stairs to the library.

Row after row after row. My unease forgotten completely, I could hardly contain my glee as I strolled along the aisles and ran my fingers across the countless book spines. I didn't want to be too hasty in selecting my book; this book would be my first official contribution to the Leavitt Center knowledge pool. This book needed to make a statement about who I was and what I had to offer.

Anjalie was studying at the front of the library and, as far as I knew, I was the only one perusing the stacks. But I was mistaken. Out of nowhere, a hand clasped itself tightly around my mouth and dragged me down the aisle. Any scream I may have made was stifled by that hand; no one could hear me. Still, I squirmed, wiggled, and kicked, even while being lugged into a dark, musty broom closet.

"Shush," whispered a male voice as he closed the door behind us. "Don't worry, I'm not going to hurt you." He flipped on the light and released his hand from my mouth.

My heart skipped a beat as I slowly turned to face him. I'd know that voice anywhere, just as I knew those chocolate eyes and bottomless dimples.

"Max! What are you doing here?" I threw my arms around him, completely forgetting our little spat last week. All of that seemed years ago. Max seemed years ago. I was so ecstatic to see him that I squealed with delight and pawed him into a shelf of all-purpose cleaners.

"Cool it, lover girl." Max peeled me away from his body like a stubborn Band-Aid and reshelved a bottle of Lysol. "I'm not who you think I am."

"What are you talking about?" I wondered why Max would tease me after everything that had happened between us. And especially after I'd just mauled him like bear during mating season.

Max just looked at me. "I'm not Max. I am his counterpart. My name is Parker, and we have a serious problem."

ASHLEY

Well past midnight the previous night, Ashley had woken with a start. The sound, like a firework popping in the distance, was faint enough to cause her to question what she'd heard. But a second muffled boom left no doubts. Someone in this building was firing a weapon.

"Kaitlin!" Ashley jumped out of bed, rushed to the room next door, and slid the keycard through the lock. "Thank God," she sighed. Kaitlin was snug in bed—gentle snores singing relief into her mother's soul.

But then Ashley thought of Anjalie, and a claw of apprehension gripped at her insides and squeezed until every last drop of calm was forced from her body. Where was her other daughter? Was she in danger? Were the gunshots for her?

Ashley hadn't come to a decision about Kaitlin before falling asleep the previous evening. She hadn't even taken off her shoes before collapsing onto her bed in physical and emotional exhaustion. But now that Ashley had heard gunshots . . . well, the decision was made. This place had terrible secrets. It was not safe. Not only did Ashley need to get Kaitlin out of here, but she also needed to rescue Anjalie. And she needed to do it now.

Don't you dare go to the police, Ashley! You will ruin your life. You will go to prison, and so will I. We will lose everything. Is that what you want? After everything I've done for you?

Janice's words ran through Ashley's mind on a loop. Her mother had used these words against Ashley thousands of times since the adoption. But after a lifetime of heeding her mother's advice and receiving nothing but misery in return, Ashley knew what she must do. She needed to tell the truth to the authorities. All of it. Forget her mother. Forget the consequences.

"Potato Bug?" Ashley shook her daughter at the shoulders, but Kaitlin's rhythmical breathing didn't miss a beat. She was sedated, out cold, and clearly, there'd be no waking her.

Ashley tried lifting her daughter's body from the bed, but quickly realized that she barely had the strength to carry Kaitlin across the room, let alone to the nearest police precinct. She'd have to leave both of her daughters here, at this terrible place, and pray that they'd still be safely in bed by the time she arrived with the police.

Ashley grabbed her car keys from her room and ran into the hallway, gasping as the elevator doors opened wide and Dr. Forsythe stepped out. He was wearing a jacket over his pinstriped pajamas and an expression of surprise that equaled her own.

"Miss Ashley?" he said, fumbling with the back waistband of his pajamas. "Having trouble sleeping?"

"Um, yes. I thought I'd go to the kitchen downstairs and see if I could find something in the cafeteria to settle my stomach. I always feel a little queasy when I'm stressed out."

"Yes, yes. I just came from the cafeteria myself; I had a thrashing case of the midnight munchies," he chuckled. "There's leftover prime rib in the fridge—would make an excellent sandwich. Help yourself."

"I will," Ashley stepped nervously past Dr. Forsythe and into the elevator. "I'll see you tomorrow for breakfast?"

The doctor laughed again. "Today is tomorrow, Miss Ashley. It's almost four in the morning. I'll see you in a few hours. With your decision." And the doors closed in front of him, but not too soon for Ashley to see him reach into his jacket and pull out a cell phone.

Ashley made it to the first floor, ran through the lobby and out the front entrance, passing a security guard who tipped his gray hat to her as she ran to her car.

———————

Ashley's mind raced at the speed of her car as she plowed down the bumpy mountain road. Her encounter with the doctor so soon after hearing gunshots added an extra ten pounds of worry to her right foot. Was Dr. Forsythe responsible for the blast? Was that red spatter on the hem of his pajamas blood? Whom did he call on his cell phone?

But most importantly, where was Anjalie, and was she safe?

These thoughts swirled around her mind until she was almost too dizzy to notice the dark SUV rumbling behind her. But she did notice it. And with it having no headlights to speak of, Ashley had a sinking feeling that the car was up to no good.

With a squeal of tires and a shower of dirt and gravel, Ashley made a sharp turn off of the unmarked dirt road and onto the main highway. The SUV followed, slicing through Ashley's dust storm like a hot knife through butter. Ashley stomped on the gas, praying that somewhere on this unlit highway, a patrol car would turn on its lights and pull her over for speeding.

No such luck. The mountain highway was all but deserted.

After five miles of being trailed, Ashley began to panic—gripping the steering wheel to within an inch of its life. That's when the SUV made its move. It accelerated forward and rammed the corner backside of Ashley's sedan. She screamed as her car spun out of control, round and round till she slowed and found herself pointing the complete opposite direction.

Knowing there wasn't time to right herself and continue her path toward town, she stepped on the gas and screeched past the dark vehicle, hoping to get enough of a head start in this direction to lose her pursuer. But her car had taken a severe hit to the rear—and the engine was never very powerful to begin with—

and it was only a matter of seconds before the SUV had flipped around and was right behind her again.

Tauntingly, the vehicle nudged her bumper two or three times, and each time Ashley cried out in terror. The SUV fell back for a moment, and then accelerated—not ramming her backside like before, but pulling up next to her and driving parallel to her. Both cars were traveling at well over eighty miles an hour.

Ashley glanced into the passenger window of the attacking car. The moon gave just enough light to illuminate a silhouette of the car's driver. Because of the frizzy nature of her pursuer's hair, Ashley quickly identified her assailant as Margaret, Dr. Forsythe's peppy assistant—hardly someone she'd expect to find herself against in a high-speed race.

But Ashley didn't have time to dwell on the fact, or dwell on anything, really, because Margaret swung her steering wheel to the right, thrusting the side of her SUV into the side of Ashley's car. The impact wrenched at every joint in Ashley's body.

She heard the squeal of metal folding around her body. She felt her car jump the guard rail and roll thunderously down a slope. But then Ashley didn't feel much of anything.

CHAPTER 18

KAITLIN

"Parker?" I squinted at him, blinked my eyes, rubbed them a little, and squinted again.

"Parker, as in Dr. Forsythe's son, Parker?"

"In the flesh." He did a complete 360-degree turn—which wasn't easy considering the size of the broom closet—so I could better visualize where he fit into the Forsythe family tree. I didn't see much of a resemblance to his father, but to Max . . . well, Parker's hair was shorter and his face slightly rounder, but all in all, the two brothers were hardly distinguishable.

Oh, yeah, except that I had a serious thing for one of them, and this one was not him.

I must've worn my disappointment like lipstick because Parker frowned and put his hand on my shoulder. "Sorry I'm not Max; I know you and my brother were involved in some hot and heavy love triangle . . . that is, until you ralphed all over him at the—"

"I did not ralph *on* him," I insisted. "But you're right about one thing: he and I are over. A relationship, or whatever we had, doesn't rebound from something like that."

"No offense, but I have no desire to hear about your summer fling with my brother."

"Oh," I muttered.

"So, it looks like they have you fully institutionalized. Welcome, friend." He motioned to my new "nondistracting" look: the designer gray dress, the freshly plucked eyebrows, the overly coiffed hair.

But really, who could think of French twists at a time like this? "So, if you are Dr. Forsythe's son and you are Max's counterpart, then that would mean that Dr. Forsythe is Max's . . . biological father?"

"Unfortunately for him."

"Are you kidding me? Having Dr. Forsythe for a father would be like winning the genetic lottery! The guy is amazing, a genius, a saint. He'll do more for the world than all of the—"

"Great humanitarians combined," Parker finished sardonically. "I know. I've heard it all before."

"I just can't believe it!" I shook my head. "Max's father was right under his nose this whole summer, and he didn't even know it! I bet Dr. Forsythe was going crazy seeing Max every day and knowing he couldn't say or do anything about it."

"I doubt he even noticed or cared. My father only cares about one thing, and his children don't fall under that category—unless we happen to get *called upon*, which is unlikely at this point."

"That's quite the thing to say about your own dad."

"Oh, really? I thought it was pretty tame compared to the things I could've said. My father is a psychopath and narcissist, and those are some of his more flattering qualities."

I inched away from Parker. One could be struck down by lightning for voicing such sacrilege.

"Let me tell you a story about the paternal instincts of the man you seem to think is so great," Parker continued.

"If you think you're going to change my mind about him, then—"

"Just humor me." He rubbed his hands together. "So, when my dad and mom got married, they agreed that they would never have children. Not ever. Both of them were ambitious to the extreme, and they thought a kid would suck the fun right out of their self-centered lifestyle."

"Wait a second," I interrupted. "How would you know that? Like any father would tell his own kid that kind of stuff."

Parker rolled his eyes. "I'm trying to tell you; Daddy Forsythe was not a typical father. Anytime I so much as colored outside the lines when I was a kid, he pulled me aside and reminded me that it was a miracle I existed in the first place. He was excruciatingly upfront with me about not having wanted kids. Maybe that's why I spent my first sixteen years trying to convince him that the night of my conception was worth the effort."

"Nope. I don't buy it." Sure, Dr. Forsythe wasn't perfect, no one was, but of one thing I was certain: the man didn't have a lick of cruelty in him. Quite the opposite. Dr. Forsythe was compassion personified.

"Do you want me to finish my story or what?"

"Whatever." I folded my arms across my chest and gave my best go at a blank stare.

"Alright. So, my folks stuck to their plan, and my mother's prime child-bearing years sailed past them unnoticed until my father discovered Jason's paranormal abilities. Suddenly, his need to become a dad surpassed a junkie's need for another hit of cocaine. He pined for kids. A pair of them. Immediately. At any cost.

"Okay, so here's the part of the story where I don't have all the details, but am smart enough to fill in the blanks. My mother, almost forty-five and with a serious heart condition, was probably less than thrilled to jump aboard the mommy train. I don't know how my father changed her mind. I'm guessing he threatened her, but soon enough the two of them declared war on Mother Nature. My mother began taking a cocktail of fertility drugs and treatments—ones that drastically multiplied the chances of conceiving twins. Obviously, she got pregnant. And it killed her. Her heart gave out only minutes after squeezing Max and me out of her tired, middle-aged body."

"Poor Dr. Forsythe," I whispered. "To lose your wife and the mother of your children that way. I can't think of anything worse."

"Poor Dr. Forsythe?! He was responsible for my mother's death! She was in no condition to have babies, and he knew it!"

"I'm sure it wasn't black and white like that. Like you said, you filled in a whole lot of blanks. Your mother could've been the one who pushed for children for all you know."

"Alright. Well, how's this for concrete: even before my mother's embalming, my father had given Max up for adoption—ironically the only legal adoption in history of the Leavitt Center. And that's a fact."

"So?"

"So?! Does splitting one's family in half sound like something a normal father would do?"

I shrugged.

"Of course not! Even if my father didn't want to care for two children himself, he had enough money to hire Mary Poppins herself to help. He had no good reason to separate us, just like he had no reason to create us in the first place, unless he wanted us for guinea pigs. Which is precisely how he's treated me my whole life. Like a good-for-nothin' guinea pig!"

I didn't know what to say. Parker was dead set on believing his father was some sort of tyrant, and nothing I was going to say would change his mind. Still, I couldn't resist pointing him toward the bigger picture. "I'm sure you have your reasons for feeling how you do, and I am definitely in no place to judge. Maybe Dr. Forsythe is a crappy dad, and maybe your childhood kind of sucked, but Dr. Forsythe is going to lead the charge to change the world—save the world from itself. Can he really be that bad?"

"Ugh!" Parker flung his arms in the air, knocking over a broom, mop, and from the looks of it, his last few tablespoons of composure. He grabbed me at my wrists and pulled me forward, spittle flying from the corners of his mouth. "Do you think I pulled you in here so I could hear a pep talk about my father and the Leavitt Center?"

I shook my head, now afraid for my safety. This guy was a noodle short of a tuna casserole, and I was alone with him in a very tight space.

"I brought you here because you're the newest recruit, and I thought maybe, just maybe, you hadn't been completely indoctrinated. I thought you'd be able to help me out. Clearly, I was wrong. You're just as loony as everyone else."

"*I'm* loony?" I retorted, pulling my hands away from his grasp. "Anjalie told me that *you're* a crazy conspiracy theorist, willing to say anything to get people riled up. You're a pot stirrer, Parker. Don't make me your spoon!"

Without breaking our gaze, Parker reached into his back pocket. He lifted a digital camera, so I was looking straight into the screen. And on it was the most grotesque image I had ever seen.

"How's this for stirring the pot?" he snarled.

I took the camera from his hands and looked more carefully. Lined up along the shoreline of what was clearly Lake Arrowhead were four lifeless human bodies—each sporting a matching bullet hole in the center of their forehead.

"I . . . I . . . don't understand," I quivered, almost dropping the camera on the ground. "Who are these people?"

"Last year's useless counterparts," said Parker.

"Wh-what?"

"The counterparts who didn't pass the test. The ones who weren't *called upon*. They'd become a liability to the Leavitt Center, so they were exterminated."

"Why would . . . ?" I gasped. "Who would . . . ?"

Parker grabbed the camera and scrolled to the next picture. It was similar to the first but with one dynamic difference. Posed like a fisherman showing off his latest catch, Dr. Forsythe crouched down next to the bloodied bodies with a proud-as-punch smirk on his face.

"This can't be right! This is a joke!"

Parker scrolled to the next picture where Margaret and Philip were heaving a body, weighted down by a large stone, into the lake. This picture had been taken at a strange angle—I couldn't see much besides the corpse's lank hair and her blue Converse shoes—but something about the girl was familiar to me.

Parker sighed. "Because there was no legal record of the counterpart's births, no one outside the Leavitt Center project even knew that these kids existed. Dr. Forsythe told the rest of us that they had gone away to college, and we didn't question him."

"No." I said. "No, no, no! I don't believe you! I don't believe any of this! These pictures aren't real! Dr. Forsythe couldn't do something like this; the only bad thing he's ever done was give life to a son as conniving and horrible as you! Stay away from me, Parker. I mean it!" I flung myself out of the broom closet, roped the nearest book off the nearest bookshelf, and stomped all the way to Anjalie's table at the front of the library, sinking into my chair and opening my book with a huff.

Anjalie looked at me with a perplexed expression. "Everything alright?"

"Fine!" I said, loud enough that three different people looked up from their studies and put their finger to their lips.

I gave them all a nasty look and then crouched over my book. How dare Parker try to pull me into his little revolution against his father! And to use such malicious and disgusting methods: forcing me into a closet, fabricating gruesome pictures, and then shoving those photoshopped pictures down my throat! What audacity! I knew that Dr. Forsythe could never hurt anyone, just as I knew I could not have been fooled by a man who could. No! Dr. Forsythe was great. *I* was great! And Parker . . . well, Parker just sucked.

"Uh, you sure you're alright?" said Anjalie.

"I said I was fine. What's your problem?"

"No problem. I'm simply confused why you chose to study a book about amphibians of all things."

I looked down at my book, which was titled Newts, Salamanders, Frogs, and Toads. "Because amphibians are awesome," I growled, turning to a page featuring a poison dart frog whose hue was almost identical to blue shoes worn by the corpse in the picture . . . which were identical to the shoe Garrett had found in Arrowhead Lake the first day we'd been there.

No! I thought again. Not possible! Dr. Forsythe would never. Security Phil, not such a stretch, but Dr. Forsythe, no way.

But even though Dr. Forsythe was superior to Phil in every way, the men worked together, didn't they? Only a half an hour before, I had heard them bantering in the hallway. What were they talking about again? Something about a freezer in the basement?

I quickly stood up. "Here, treat yourself." I handed Anjalie the book on amphibians and quickly left the library.

My finger wobbled as it hit the "B" button on the elevator. My lungs felt light and tickly, but in the worst possible way. I was nervous. I mean, it's not like the basement was off-limits to me or anything. At least no one had told me that it was. I wasn't knowingly breaking any rules. So why did I feel like I was doing something I shouldn't?

The elevator doors opened, and I stepped into a dark, musty hallway. I walked forward slowly, pulling my feet from behind me as though they were tied to twenty-pound bags of flour. *You have nothing to be afraid of, Kaitlin. All you're going to find in that freezer is some ground beef past its expiration date, that's all. Nothing to worry about.*

I knew that the storage room couldn't be too terribly far from the elevator, and sure enough, there it was, right after I'd rounded the first corner. I stepped inside the fluorescent-lit room and looked around. Rows of silver shelves held bulk containers of dehydrated potatoes, powdered milk, and dried peaches. There were flashlights and batteries, blankets and jugs of water—all stuff you'd expect to see in a storage room in the mountains.

I walked around the shelves until I came to a stainless steel, commercial-grade freezer about the size of a large refrigerator. The freezer's center handles were roped together tightly by padlocked chains.

Well, that's that, I guess, I thought and turned to leave, for some reason feeling a tremendous sense of relief. With the contents of the freezer unavailable to me, I had no choice but to trust my original instincts and continue on my path with the Leavitt Center.

But were those really my instincts anymore? I mean, something had compelled me to come to the basement, even though my knees knocked the whole way down. Maybe, deep inside, I needed to confirm that following Dr. Forsythe was the right thing to do, that nothing was in that freezer. Nothing bad at least.

I turned back to better examine the padlock. It was small, functioning more as a deterrent than an actual safeguard. My locker padlock at school had more clout than this rusty shard of tin. *A temporary solution*, I remembered Phil saying to Dr. Forsythe.

I looked around the room until my eyes caught sight of the row of flashlights. I grabbed the biggest, heaviest one and walked over to the freezer. I gently hit the corner of the flashlight against the lock, my heart taking off at a steady gallop at the high-pitched clink.

I paused and listened, waiting for someone to charge into the room, extricate the flashlight from my fingers, and give me a reproachful bop on the nose with it. When no one did, and after I'd actually begun breathing again, I hit the lock six or seven more times, finally winding up like Babe Ruth at home plate and swinging the flashlight with all my might.

Home run.

The lock busted open. Slowly, with trembling fingers, I lifted the shackle off the chain links and unwound the chain from the freezer handles. The chain slid from my grasp and coiled onto the concrete floor. I reached for the cold handles and, once again, reassured myself that whatever was in the freezer was nothing to be afraid of. Then I pulled.

And screamed.

A cold, stiff body tipped onto the floor in front of me, landing with a sharp thud.

The body belonged to my friend, Claire.

"Kaitlin!" Parker exclaimed after he opened the door and saw me standing in the hallway. "What are you doing here? If my father were here . . . if he saw me with you . . . "

"Claire is dead. My friend is dead," I shuddered, still in a dazed shock from discovering Claire's body. "She is frozen solid. So much blood."

Parker grabbed my hand and dragged me across the hallway to my suite. He sat me down in the comfy chair and retrieved a water bottle from the mini refrigerator.

"You look pale. Here, drink this."

I reached for the bottle but didn't have the strength to unscrew the lid. "Did you know about Claire? Did you take a picture of her dead body, too?" My voice was quiet, detached.

"You think *I* took those pictures—that I had something to do with all those deaths? No way! I may have inherited my father's Y chromosome, but he kept his sociopathic murdering genes all to himself!"

"Then why do you have those terrible pictures?"

"I found photographs in a filing cabinet at the station—ironically, only minutes after I discovered you and your friends there surfing Camp Overlook's surveillance system. I turned the photographs over to my father, but I took pictures of them before that."

"So that was *you* at the station . . . or whatever you call that place?"

"You're lucky it wasn't Philip or my father. I erased all the evidence from your midnight adventure, although it did little to save Claire." He crinkled his face to keep himself from showing emotion, but didn't work. He looked as traumatized as I felt. "Look, I know this is hard to hear, but my father is not the hero everyone thinks he is. The Leavitt Center isn't about solving world hunger or curing cancer. The Leavitt Center is about power. My father is obsessed with it and will say or do anything to get it: lying, manipulating, killing, anything." Parker's choked voice sent me the clear message that he took no pleasure in passing along this information.

I sat in silence as all the emotions from the past week began forming a thunderous mosh pit in my head. Pain, fear, surprise, elation, pride, and shock collided violently with one another, sending sparks of horror into my blood and heating it to the temperature of molten lava. "And what about me? What about all the *called upon*? Are you trying to tell me that Dr. Forsythe is using me? Using all of us? That we are nothing to him—just a means to an end?" My body jerked in a wild spasm of anger. "Claire is dead! Dr. Forsythe is a monster! And now I'm . . . I'm . . ."

"You're going to help put an end to this." Parker put his hand on my knee.

I pushed it away. "Look at me, Parker! I am good for nothing! The gifts I thought I had . . . they're only evil weapons in the hands of Dr. Forsythe. Me personally, I don't have anything to—"

"You've got your anger, Kaitlin. Use it. Use it to save it."

"To save it?"

Parker grabbed my hand. "Listen. Have you noticed anything fishy about Jason or Tanji or any of the others who've been *called upon*? Have you looked at their eyes?"

I remembered the night in the rec room when Tanji and Jason watched me play air hockey with my friends. Their eyes were gray, murky, and incredibly unsettling. Come to think of it, Aya's eyes had a similar sheen when I talked to her in the library yesterday.

I nodded.

"Their eyes aren't the only things that have lost their luster. Would you believe that Tanji was a cheerleader in high school? And Jason, I'm pretty sure he once had an actual sense of humor. That was before they'd met their twins and before all the Leavitt Center garbage. Since then, their intellects have grown, but their personalities have slowly fizzled like opened cans of soda. A month ago, I chalked their personalities up to changed priorities, but that night I found the photographs I also found a hard drive. Now I know better."

"What was on it?" How could Parker have more horrendous news?

"Health records of all the *called upon*—blood work, urinalysis, eye-color observations, all that jazz. The periodic brain scans are what stood out, though."

"Brain scans?"

"Now, I'm no brain specialist, but even I could see that the brain images showed irregularities. In all of the *called upon*, the frontal lobe of the brain, the part largely responsible for intellect and personality, became progressively blotchy and swollen in certain places and shrunken and shriveled in others."

"But what does that mean?"

"I assume that it means that the brain has trouble accommodating all the information transfers—that it is not equipped to handle so much knowledge so quickly. As a result, the parts of the brain that are responsible for intellect swell, while the parts of the brain that handle emotion and personality shrink. Maybe that's why the information transfer is so incredibly painful."

"And that's why Tanji and Jason are . . . the way that they are?"

"I guess so."

"Why on earth would they consent to be a part of Dr. Forsythe's plan if they knew that they'd lose their emotions and personalities?"

"I don't think they do know. I bet that the brain scans were done while they were sedated; maybe you've already had your first scan, too. The point is that I don't think anyone, besides Margaret and Philip, knows a thing about the true nature of the man they worship. They are all just as starry-eyed as you were an hour ago."

With that, my anger blossomed into spectacular bloom of fiery-pink panic. I grabbed Parker's arm and shook it. "We've got to get out of here before I undergo another information transfer! Oh my gosh; do you think I have brain damage already!?"

"Go look in the mirror."

"What?" I wheezed.

"Go check yourself out."

I jumped out of the chair and ran over to my sink. Pulling my cheeks downward, I leaned in as close as I could to the mirror. So subtle that I didn't catch it while getting ready this morning, yet so obvious now that I couldn't believe I'd missed it, my once radiant irises were rimmed in a waxy grayish hue. "You've got to get me out of this place! We've got to get everyone out of here!"

"What do you think I've been trying to do? No one believes me, Kaitlin! Everyone thinks I have a vendetta against my father and make up lies to debunk him. They sure won't trust a newbie like you, either."

"Anjalie might."

"I doubt it," he shrugged, "but I think you should try to talk to her anyway. Go find her. While you're pleading your case, I've got some unfinished business with my father. Let's meet back in your suite in an hour and then make a quick escape."

"Why don't we just call the cops? Surely they'll—"

"With what phone? The only people with links to the outside world are my father, Philip, and Margaret, and it's unlikely they'll loan us their cells so we can turn them in."

"What about the internet?"

"The Leavitt Center has computers and a surveillance service, but no access to the worldwide web. Almost all of our learning comes from the books in the library. There is no way to send an email."

"That's insane! Then how will we—"

"Don't worry; I have a plan. It will be difficult, though. There are armed guards stationed at every doorway. Plus, we'll have to make an inconvenient detour to a hidden part of the basement before we go."

"Why?"

"Because that's where your friends from Camp Overlook, the ones who snuck out last night to rescue you, are being imprisoned. And I am pretty sure they are the next people on my father's hit list."

PARKER

Parker found Dr. Forsythe in the lab flipping through the folder of one of Camp Overlook's participants. He was, much to Parker's satisfaction, alone. Parker locked the door behind him and gripped the roll of duct tape behind his back. He'd have to be relentless while holding his father down and wrapping him up. The man's salt and pepper hair and slack skin merely disguised the sturdy and willful muscles underneath.

"Hello, Father."

"Oh, Parker, my boy! I was just looking at Isaiah Aku's file. He's been complaining of a headache for three days straight. This is a most excellent development, don't you agree?"

Parker raised his brows. After the murder and threats of the previous night, was his father really planning on playing the chummy card? "Yes, that's just splendid."

"I thought you'd agree. The Leavitt Center is certainly headed in the right direction. I trust that you've given some thought to our conversation last night?"

"Plenty."

"And you're willing to do anything to protect my cause?"

Parker narrowed his eyes. "I used to think I understood the cause I was protecting. But I don't anymore. Tell me, Dad, do you really plan on saving the world, or do you just want to become the king of it?"

Dr. Forsythe tucked the binder back into the bookshelf and scratched his chin. "Most ambitious people work their whole lives to become wealthy. I was born wealthy, so naturally I had no choice but to aspire to power."

"You didn't answer my question. Are you really planning on doing all those things you said you would? All those good things?"

Dr. Forsythe chuckled. "If some of those things happen to get done on my way to the top, excellent. If not, well, I will still be on top."

Parker found it disconcerting that his father was being so candid with him. "But what about the *called upon*? You made it sound like—"

Dr. Forsythe placed a stern index finger over his lips. "The *called upon* think that I am a god. To me, they are nothing more than stepping stones. With their limitless knowledge, they'll be able to slide into slippery places of power, and I'll be able to walk across them until I have steady footing as the world leader . . . no, world dominator." Dr. Forsythe's eyes no longer twinkled but blazed with an insatiable, inhuman hunger. And Parker felt truly afraid.

"Aren't you worried about g-getting found out?" Parker stumbled, nearly dropping the duct tape clutched behind his back. "You've already taken so many lives. At some point someone's going to figure out . . ."

"People only see me the way I want them to," Dr. Forsythe cackled, for once seeming to lose a sense of decorum or self-awareness. "Take, for example, the time I slipped my hand over your mother's air passages after she gave birth to you and Max. Everyone assumed her death was linked to her heart problems? Ha!"

Parker took a step backward.

"And then the useless counterparts last year . . . no one asked a single question when they went to university in the middle of the school year."

Parker fell back another step.

"Claire, her mother, and now Kaitlin's mother, Ashley—they are all dead. And I will get away with it. I always do!"

"But the campers in the prison cell downstairs, the ones that you want me to kill tonight, when they end up missing, people will notice. And they will suspect you. Killing them would be a huge mistake."

"You are a foolish boy if you thought I'd waste my bullets on those brats. They don't know diddly about the Leavitt Center, and after I've had a civilized chat with them about the consequences of breaking Camp Overlook's rules, I will send them home to their mommies and daddies—no harm done."

"Then who did you intend for me to kill tonight?"

"Simple," Dr. Forsythe said. "Yourself."

Parker felt his blood crystallize below his skin. He now understood why his father had been so open with him.

"You, Parker Forsythe, are nothing to me but a useless counterpart. Since the day you were born, you have been a thorn in my side and a detriment to the Leavitt Center. I am ashamed of you. If you really believe in this cause, you will prove it once and for all by removing yourself from this project . . . permanently."

"But there's still a chance I might be *called upon*; the summer is not over yet. I'm far too valuable to be taken out."

"Parker, at this point, even if you were *called upon* you would still be a dangerous liability. I cannot risk it."

Parker turned around. He wrenched and yanked at the doorknob behind him, forgetting that he'd locked it on his way in. He pulled and he tugged, but the door wouldn't budge.

"Parker, stop."

Parker turned around and found himself staring into the barrel of his father's pistol. "Don't worry, son, I've accounted for your cowardice. You've been a disappointment to me your entire life; why should I expect any different at your death?"

At the click of the gun's safety, Parker flung his arm upward and hit his father's jaw with the edge of the duct tape. Dr. Forsythe's head flew back, pulling the rest of his body with it. The gun slid out of his hand, and he turned to the side and scrambled for it. Parker quickly stomped on his father's hand, and Dr. Forsythe yelped in pain. Parker, still standing on the hand, bent over and picked up the gun. He could shoot his father and prove once and for all that he could do *exactly* what needed to be done for the greater good. A simple pull of the index finger is all it would take—the Leavitt Center would be destroyed, and his father would never be able to hurt another human ever again. Patricia, Claire, Claire's mother, Kaitlin's mother, the useless counterparts, and all of the other victims of Dr. Forsythe's scheme would be avenged.

Hands shaking, he raised the gun, aimed it, but instead of firing, he swung the butt of it into the side of his father's head. With a bone-crushing crack, Dr. Forsythe went limp. Parker held his breath, watching for the rise and fall of his father's chest. He hadn't wanted to kill his father; he'd just wanted to knock him out. But had Parker used too much force? Was his father too old to handle such a powerful blow?

But wait. Dr. Forsythe made a small sound. A groan. He was unconscious, but definitely still breathing. Parker sighed in relief. He was not like his father. He didn't want justice this way. Not now.

He pulled out the duct tape. Everything would have to move quickly from this point forward.

CHAPTER 19

KAITLIN

I paced my suite nervously until Parker returned. When he did, the pained expression on his face did little to ease my stress. "Um, how'd everything go with your dad?"

"As well as could be expected." He tried not to meet my eyes, but clearly his were webbed in a red, profound sadness. He sniffed. "And Anjalie? Is she coming with us?"

I paused before shaking my head. "She made fun of me when I told her about my meeting with you. She couldn't believe I trusted you after she'd specifically warned me."

"But didn't you tell her about the photographs?"

"Yes. She said you had used Photoshop. Then she got all huffy and marched away to her room. Parker, I still believe you, but I can't leave without Anjalie. I mean, thank heavens my mom is safely in town, but Anjalie is family, too. If something were to happen to her . . ."

Parker swallowed. "You're right. She's your family, and you're going to need her. We'll make sure she comes with us one way or another."

"What do you mean I'm going to need her? Is something wrong, something that I don't know about?"

"Look, my father is unconscious and tied to a chair in the lab. We've got to get your friends and get out of here before he wakes up and wiggles loose. Time is of the essence here."

He peeked his head into the hallway, and seeing that no one was around, motioned for me to follow. He led me to the stairwell and down five flights of stairs to the basement. I shivered at the familiar gust of cold, musty air. We moved down the hallway and turned the corner, passing the closed door of the storage room. Was Claire's body still on the floor, thawing out, blood and water pooling beneath her?

We continued forward until we came to a series of dark passageways. Parker reached for my wrist, and we ducked under low piping and zigzagged through narrow spaces. Finally, we stopped at what appeared to be a random door. Parker slid his keycard through the lock and pushed it open. And there, in the bathroom-sized cell, were a tousled-looking Garrett, Molly, and Max.

"Kaitlin!" Max rushed forward. "I'm so sorry about everything! I thought that you and Jake . . . well, I completely lost my head. I was such an idiot!" In one fluid moment, he hinged his arm around my waist and lowered his face toward mine.

And just like that, the world and all its chaos shrunk to the size of a nickel and tucked itself deeply into my pocket. All I could feel was Max's soul and mine—connected at the lips—whispering apologies, it's okays, and relief. The kiss was so simple and tender. Max's lips held mine with the care one would take while handling a precious painting but with the urgency of one who'd thought he'd lost something priceless. My whole body felt light and peaceful, almost drowsy, like I could breathe him in, feel his warmth, and absorb him in for all time.

Now *that* was a kiss.

"Eh-heh-heh-hem!"

With great reluctance, Max and I pulled apart and turned to Parker, the source of the interruption. Max's daze evaporated as he registered that the face smirking at him was not his own reflection. "What the . . . ?" He scratched his cute, rumpled hair.

"Oh," I said, rising above the daze myself. "Max, meet Parker. Parker, Max."

Garrett, dissatisfied by his current lack of importance, stepped forward and pointed his finger accusingly at Parker. "You! Care to enlighten us on what's going on here?"

"I would, but thanks to Kaitlin and Max's make-out extravaganza, there's no time left for explanations."

"I don't think so!" yelled Molly, whose face was caked in both dirt and fury. "We risked our butts last night sneaking out to find Kaitlin. Then we were accosted by Security Phil, *Phil* of all people! To top things off, I have been sharing a toilet, publicly, with two guys for the last twelve hours, and I would like to know why! Start talking, Max . . . uh . . . that is, Parker!"

I quickly stepped into the middle of the group. "I can't believe you guys risked everything just to make sure I am okay. Thank you so much! But the truth is that I'm not okay. None of us are. We are all in serious trouble. We have to get out of here as quick as possible."

"Trouble? As in real danger?" Molly quivered.

Parker unzipped his backpack and distributed a small stack of papers. "Listen carefully, I only have time to go through this once. These are maps of the building. I have marked a specific pathway on each of your maps. Max, your pathway leads to the fourth floor. Kaitlin and I will go to the third floor, Garrett will cover the second floor, and Molly will hit the first. On each floor, there are a series of red buttons on the wall. I have marked the buttons with an X on each of your maps, see?" Parker touched the five Xs on Molly's map.

He continued. "When you reach your designated floor, locate and push as many buttons as possible. An alarm will sound each time, so you'll need to move on quickly so no one sees you."

"How is button-pushing gonna help anything?" asked Garrett, feeling his self-appointed alpha-male status threatened.

"When the alarms go off, all the staff members drop whatever they are doing and rush around to help those who pushed the buttons. My hope is that the security guards stationed at the building's entrance will also abandon their posts and lose themselves in the chaos—giving us a brief moment to escape."

"I still don't get the point of the—"

"Dude, aren't you listening? The buttons aren't important. What matters is getting out of here."

"Okay," said Garrett grudgingly. "So after we've pushed a few buttons, what do we do next?"

"Head back to the stairwell. We'll all meet on the first floor and, the moment I give the signal, we'll book it out the front doors. Simple as that."

"It doesn't sound so simple," said Molly, biting her lower lip. "What if someone sees us? You said we are in danger. I—I don't think I can—"

"Molly," I said firmly, "I know you've felt your whole life that you weren't equal to the tasks in front of you, but I also happen to know that you are. You've let what other people say and do bury your hidden strength, but now is the time to dig it out. You can do it. You have to do it."

Molly simply nodded and whispered, "Okay."

Parker led the four of us out of the cell and through the basement passageways. When we reached the stairwell, he unbuckled his watch and passed it to Max. "Kaitlin and I will need a head start. Once three minutes has passed, go ahead and follow the maps to your buttons. Good luck."

"Parker?" said Max, a slightly desperate tone to his voice. "Take care of Kaitlin, alright? I can't lose her again."

"Sheesh," Parker groaned and gave my wrist an impatient tug.

Parker and I ran upward, the echo of our feet bouncing across the concrete walls, until we reached the third floor. Rounding the corner to the hallway, Parker tucked his thumbs into the belt loops, and we strolled casually down the hall. We tapped lightly on Anjalie's bedroom door.

"Leave me alone," said a gruff voice from within.

We let ourselves in anyway.

Anjalie was propped up on her bed clutching the framed photograph of our mother. She quickly stashed the picture under her pillow and yelled, "didn't you hear me? I said leave me—"

"Didn't you hear Kaitlin?" said Parker. "She told you that you're not safe here. We need to leave right now."

"Kaitlin has been misinformed," she cleared her throat loudly, raising her brows at Parker. "This is our home. We belong here."

"No, we don't," I said. "Dr. Forsythe is doing horrible, horrible things. He killed—"

"Shut up!" she screamed, causing me to jump backward. "Don't talk that way about him! You've known him, for what, two months? I've known him my whole life. He's all I've known. This is all I've known!" she motioned to the building around her.

"What you know about my father is an illusion," Parker said. "If you just let me show you the pictures—"

"I don't want to see your phony pictures or hear your crazy stories. You're a liar, Parker! And even if you weren't, I still wouldn't go with you. I have been *called upon*; I belong with the Leavitt Center. I have nothing in the outside world—no home, no social security number, and especially no mother!" She reached under her pillow and frisbeed the picture of our mother across the room, denting the drywall and shattering the glass insert in the frame.

And then the first alarm went off. Distant and echoing, it sounded like it was coming from the first floor. *Good work, Molly*, I thought, just as a second alarm sounded from upstairs. Instinctively, Anjalie curled in a ball and prepared for the excruciating pain of an information transfer. I pitied her for reacting like a trained zoo animal, but I also understood the overwhelming desire to brace for it.

Parker clapped his hands sarcastically. "Pavlov would be so proud."

"Please, Anjalie!" I begged, scooting close to her bed and clasping my hands together. "Please come with us! Don't you see? I can't leave without you!"

Anjalie looked up and shook her head. "This is my life. I choose this."

More alarms rang from within the building. The sound was loud and shrill, tightening the anxiety in my chest. I looked pleadingly at Parker. He immediately pitched forward, scooped Anjalie in his arms, and moved toward the hallway, hitting the red button beside the door on his way out. "Come on, Kaitlin!"

"Let go of me!" Anjalie screamed and thrust her body outward so she was wedged inside the doorframe. Parker pushed her through, but she'd been able to dig her fingers around the frame and hold tight. I ran to the other side of the doorway and helped Parker pull Anjalie by the legs. She squirmed and kicked, making the job surprisingly difficult.

"Hey! What's going on here?!" Margaret had just stepped into the hallway holding a syringe full of purple fluid, no doubt responding to the alarm we'd just pushed. Parker and I let go of Anjalie's legs. She scurried back into her room and slammed the door behind her. Margaret pulled out her cell phone, dialed with one hand, and held it up to her ear. "Phillip!" she yelled into the receiver, trying to be heard over the alarms, "I need backup! I'm on the th—"

"Drop the phone!" yelled Parker. I gasped when I saw he was holding a gun. So did Margaret. She dropped her cell but quickly stomped down on it—cracking the dial pad and rendering the phone completely useless. She smiled defiantly.

"What are you doing?" I said in Parker's ear. "Are you going to shoot her?"

"No way! I can't shoot her; she's a girl!" He forced the gun into my hands. "You do it!"

"What?" I squealed, holding the gun away from my body like it was an infectious disease. "I can't shoot her either; what's *wrong with you?*"

Taking advantage of our indecision, Margaret ran forward and plowed into Parker. Surprised by the attack, he tumbled to the ground, and she jumped on top of him. I watched in horror as she lifted the syringe into the air and plunged it downward toward his chest. Parker grabbed her wrist just before the needle pierced his skin and twisted her hand until the needle was facing her bicep. Margaret's scream turned into a soft whimper as the sedative penetrated her flesh and circulated through her system. She was asleep within seconds.

Parker pushed Margaret's body off, grabbed the gun away from me, and fired two shots at the lock on Anjalie's door. Then he kicked the door open, ran inside, and reemerged with Anjalie. She still thrashed in his arms, but with less enthusiasm than before. Clearly, the gunshots had helped her realize how relentless we were about getting her out of that crazy, brainwashing place.

We ran through the hallway and into the stairwell—which thankfully muffled the shrieking alarms—two steps behind Garrett and two steps in front of Max. Molly was already waiting for us all on the first floor.

"Who's that?" Molly said, but after getting a good look at Anjalie's contorted face, jumped half out of her skin. "Kaitlin, you have *a sister?*"

"Cool!" gasped a sweaty Garrett. "This means I have a twin, too, right?"

Max pulled me in at the shoulder. "You okay?"

"I will be as soon as we get out of here."

"Was anyone seen?" Parker asked loudly, wrapping his fingers over Anjalie's yelping mouth.

Garrett shrugged. "When I was running down the hallway for my first button, someone called to me from one of the rooms. He said he was tied up and needed help. He sounded like an old dude. I ignored him and kept going."

Parker sent me a panicked look. "My father's awake! It's only a matter of time before he gets out." He nudged open the stairwell door and peeked into the foyer. Sure enough, Leavitt Center staff members were buzzing around like a molested beehive.

"This is bad!" Parker backed away from the door. "The guards are still at their post. My father must've changed their orders yesterday. We'll never be able to get past them."

"Then what are we going to do?" I panicked.

Parker passed Anjalie over to Garrett (who slung her over his shoulder like a wriggling sack of potatoes) and thought for a moment. He narrowed his eyes at me, nodded his head, and then pointed toward the top of the building. "Up! We've got to go up."

"But that makes no sense!" Garrett spat. "If we want to get out of here . . . Ouch!" Anjalie had grabbed a handful of his arm flesh and twisted it as hard as she could.

"If you want to get out of here alive, you'll follow my lead!" Parker turned and began running up the stairs. Bewildered, and still out of breath, the rest of us struggled to keep up—especially me, whose leg throbbed with every step, and Garrett, who now had a writhing hundred-and-ten pound disability.

We had passed the second floor and were approaching the third, when the stairwell door swung open and Molly screamed. In the blink of an eye, Security Phil had darted forward and hooked the nearest person, which happened to be her. He held her, facing out, against his chest and nuzzled his nose into her hair. "Hey there, pretty girl. I take it that your basement accommodations weren't to your liking?"

Molly responded by clamping her teeth into his forearm. Phil threw his head back and cackled, as though her teeth were tickling his funny bone instead of ripping his flesh in two. He reached down to his holster and then gently tapped the side of her forehead with his shiny, black gun. The color drained from Molly's cheeks and she released his arm.

The rest of us froze in place, afraid if we tried to help Molly, we would actually be doing her a grave disservice.

Philip grinned, his crooked teeth looking more yellow than ever. "It seems that my associate, Margaret, is taking a little nap. Since Dr. Forsythe is not answering his phone, I take it that I'm the new boss man. I don't claim to be the crowd pleaser he was, but I can still get the job done."

Molly closed her eyes and moved her lips in silent prayer. I did, too.

Bam!

I almost fainted as the sound of a gunshot echoed up and down the stairwell. Another friend; another horrible tragedy.

"Molly, move!" Max yelled and I opened my eyes. I cried out in relief as Molly scrambled away from Phil and ran into my arms. Philip was hunched over, blood flowing from what was left of his kneecap, and Max dove for the gun on the ground.

Confused, I turned to Parker. He was holding his father's smoking pistol. "I've never shot anyone before," he said, staring bug-eyed at the weapon.

"Well, you got great aim, dude," Garrett lifted one hand from Anjalie's backside to smack Parker on the back.

"I was aiming for his heart," Parker admitted.

We all jumped as Philip moaned. He lifted one bony hand in front of the other, crawling toward Molly and me, leaving a crimson trail behind him. I screamed as he clutched the bottom of my jeans and tried to pull himself up. Max rushed to my side, lifted his foot, and jammed it down onto Phil's forehead. Phil was forced backward and began rolling down the stairs toward the second floor. None of us waited to see how he landed.

We continued our path upward, Anjalie still hollering. We ran past the fourth floor and only stopped to rest while Parker opened the hatch that led to the roof. He climbed the ladder and then reached down for Anjalie. She squirmed and thrashed, but with Parker pulling and the rest of us pushing, we were able to get her up. Then, one by one, the rest of us climbed into the sunshine and squinted at the bright blue aircraft in front of us.

"A *helicopter*? We are going to escape by helicopter!" Molly cried. "Is it yours?"

"It's my father's," said Parker. "One of the staff members, Keisha, flies him to wherever he needs to go."

"But do you know how to fly it?" asked Max.

"Of course he doesn't!" cried Anjalie. "What's wrong with you?"

"Then who's going to fly that thing?"

Parker pointed at me. "Kaitlin is."

ASHLEY

"Miss? Miss! Are you okay?"

Ashley opened her eyes and groaned. Everything was so bright . . . and up-side-down.

"What's going on?" she whispered, her head throbbing from being inverted.

"I've already phoned an ambulance. They told me not to move you; they're on their way." The man was crouched on his knees, leaning sideways to see into the crushed driver's side window. "Do you have any idea how long you've been out here?"

"What happened?" she repeated.

"It looks like you were in an accident . . . a really bad accident. It's a miracle I found you; your car is completely hidden from the highway. You went over the guardrail and rolled down the ravine. I don't know how you survived it. If I hadn't been out hiking . . .

"Everything hurts," Ashley moaned.

"I'd imagine so. Can you tell me your name?"

"Ashley."

"Ashley. Is there anyone I can call for you? A spouse? Some sort of family member?"

Huh? Spouse? Family member? Oh! Kaitlin! Anjalie! My babies! Ashley reached though the shattered window and grabbed the man's shirt. "The police! I need to talk to the police!"

CHAPTER 20

KAITLIN

"*What?* Have you completely lost your mind? I can't fly a helicopter!" I gaped at the shiny blue aircraft in front of me. It seemed to double in size and grow venomous fangs before my very eyes.

"You don't know that." Parker insisted. "Keisha can do it. Maybe the ability has been transferred to you already."

"But maybe not!" I cried. "Do you realize what you are asking me to do, the risk you want me to take?"

"Yeah, man. What are you thinking?" Garrett asked, still gripping Anjalie. "Kaitlin would kill us all!"

Parker scratched his head thoughtfully. "Kaitlin, what model is this helicopter?"

"It's a Bell 407," I answered before I even had the chance to think about it.

"Aha! How would you know that unless the information had been transferred to you?"

So I knew the name of the helicopter. I could label all its parts and recite how they all worked together, too. Big deal. Knowing how to fly a helicopter and actually flying one were two different things. I needed a way out of this mess. "Wh—what about Anjalie? If I know how to do it, she probably does, too."

The five of us looked at Anjalie. She flipped us off.

Parker placed both of his hands on my shoulders and looked me squarely in the eyes. "My father will be up here in a matter of minutes, and he will shoot. He'll kill us, Kaitlin, just like he killed your—um—just like he killed last year's counterparts. If you don't do this, if you don't take this risk, we will all die for sure."

As Parker released my shoulders, Max slipped his hand into mine. "Look. I don't understand what's going on here and, other than the fact that this dude looks just like me, I don't know a thing about him either. It's clear that now is not the time for an interrogation, so I'm only going to ask you two quick questions. First, do you trust him?"

I looked at Parker. His eyes held enough anger, pain, and determination to ignite an Olympic-sized swimming pool. On anyone else, so much emotion would scare the socks off me, but on Parker, well, it looked heroic. "Yes. I trust him."

"Okay," said Max. "Second question, do you trust yourself?"

It was only a question, I know, but I felt like I'd been slapped in the face—the sting of it bringing tears to my eyes. "I . . . I think I might know how to fly a helicopter, but just because I know how, doesn't mean that I should. I've never done it before. I'll probably have crappy instincts. I might mess up, and we'll crash."

"Kaitlin, just answer me. Do you trust yourself?"

"Do *you* trust me?" I whimpered.

"That's it!" Molly marched up to me exasperatedly and flicked my cheek with her index finger. "You listen here! I know you've felt these last few years that you weren't special or anything. You've let what other people say and do bury your hidden strength, but now is the time to dig it out! It doesn't matter if anyone else thinks you can do this; it only matters what *you* think!"

These were basically the same words I'd used on her only ten minutes before. I couldn't believe that she was throwing them back in my face. My first instinct was to grab Molly by the ponytail and propel her over the edge of the building, but my more rational instinct was to give a moment of consideration to the words. And when I did that, I realized that they were indeed true.

"I . . . I can do it," I quivered.

"That's right," said Molly, folding her arms. "You can do it because you have to do it."

"So let's go then!" said Garrett, picking Anjalie up by the armpits and dragging her toward the chopper.

Max brushed my forehead with his lips and smiled. "You've got this, Kaitlin; it's all you." He then turned the handle to the cockpit door and boosted me into the pilot seat. I turned back toward the cabin and watched Max climb in and reach down for Molly and then Anjalie, who finally seemed resigned to her fate. Garrett hopped in last and pulled the door closed behind him.

As they fastened their seatbelts, I was struck by how very calm everyone looked. Even Anjalie sat quietly with her hands folded in her lap—apparently finally at peace with her own kidnapping and impending death.

Was I the only one who understood the gravity of this situation?

Parker slid into the seat next to me and handed me a headset. I placed it over my ears and inspected the control panel. I knew what everything was and how to use it, like I'd memorized a dozen textbooks on piloting, but as I began running through the startup checklist, the knobs and switches felt clammy and foreign under my touch.

I switched on the battery and checked the Caution Advisory System. I ran a haphazard BIT Test and watched as the gauges swung to the top of their displays and then back down. I checked that the twist grip throttle on the collective was in the governed position and reached upward to lift the Start switch, jumping half out of my skin when the helicopter made a low rumbling sound.

"Engine's on," I said shakily, and Parker nodded. As the rotors gathered speed, a whining sound grew louder and shriller—narrating the accelerating panic in my chest. I was seconds away from lifting this puppy off the roof, and once I had, there'd be no turning back.

My hand was unsteady as a grandpa with the shakes as I pushed in the circuit breaker and rolled the throttle to the FLY position. I raised the collective stick tentatively, pushing down the left pedal with my foot at the same rate. "Whoa!" I gasped as the aircraft slowly began to lift and jerk to the right like a windblown balloon.

Anjalie reached into the cockpit and jiggled my shoulder. "Use the cyclic stick!" which I barely heard over the roar of the rotors. I quickly grabbed the center lever and applied a careful counterpressure, stabilizing the helicopter at a four-foot hover. I exhaled about a bazillion gallons of air, held the cyclic steady with my left hand, and gave my friends in back a quick thumb up with my right. Though I couldn't hear their response, from the excited expressions on their faces I could tell they were cheering me on.

"I did it! We're really up!" I squealed, shocked by what I'd just accomplished.

"What'd I tell you!" said Parker into his headset. "You're a natural!"

I laughed manically, only to be interrupted by a muffled crash to my left. I turned my head to see that a bullet hole had punctured the passenger window.

"It's my dad! He escaped!" Parker pointed at the open hatch of the roof. Dr. Forsythe was standing next to it, and three of his guards were crouched in front of him, pointing their guns straight at the helicopter. He signaled angrily for me to lower the aircraft.

"What do I do?" I cried.

"Just hold the hover!" Parker motioned for everyone in the cabin to duck down and pushed open his door. He wedged himself against the helicopter and lifted the gun over the window, firing several shots at the guards. Unsurprisingly, they fired back, bullets sliding through the chopper's body like a hot knife through butter.

"Aargh!" Parker moaned as he pulled himself back into the helicopter, another bullet sailing through one window and out another. He squeezed his shoulder, and blood leaked through his fingers.

"You're *shot*?"

He removed his hand and flinched. "Just grazed, but . . . uh . . . you should probably get us out of here."

Almost without thinking, I rotated the helicopter, applied a gentle forward cyclic pressure, and increased the collective. The nose of the aircraft tilted, and we began moving off the building. As we reached a speed of twenty knots, the helicopter began to climb and roll slightly to the left. I allowed us to follow that path until not only were we out of the bullet's range, we were soaring smoothly over Camp Overlook.

"Are you okay?" my focus was torn between the blood trickling down Parker's arm and the balancing act of flying a helicopter.

"It hurts like a mother," he groaned, "but it's just a surface wound. Deserved it . . . trying to be a hero. How's everyone in back?"

I snuck a glance. Everyone appeared to be hole-free, although in various states of shock. Molly was rocking back and forth in her seat. Garrett was clenching his chair so tightly that it was only a matter of time before he'd burrowed a hole into the Italian leather. Anjalie was weeping—the man who'd raised her like his own had just ordered a firing squad against her.

Max caught my eye and gave me a brave smile, though I bet inside he was a bowl of mashed potatoes.

"Where should I go?" I asked Parker queasily.

"Let's put a hundred miles or so between us and my father, and then we'll find a field or something to land in. Sound good?"

But I was distracted. "Look down there," I said, referring to a squad of flashing police cars charging up the road toward the Leavitt Center. They'd be there in less than ten minutes.

"You don't think my mom called the cops on Dr. Forsythe while she was in town, do you?"

"Um . . . sure. Sure she did. Good for her." Parker cringed, but something told me that it wasn't in response to his pain.

"Parker? What is going on? You're acting really strange."

Parker contorted his face. "How's a guy who just got shot supposed to act?"

"It's just that both times I mentioned my mom, you got all . . . *oh no, oh no, oh noooo!*"

Parker lowered his eyes sadly. "You figured it out? I'm so sorry, Kaitlin; I was going to wait till we landed to tell you about your mother."

Truthfully, not a single word Parker was saying registered in my mind because my "oh nos" had very little to do with his strange behavior and everything to do with the fact that my head suddenly felt like someone had taken a hammer to it.

Anjalie and I were ready for an information transfer.

At that very moment.

While I was flying a helicopter.

Really high up in the sky.

"Parker!" I gasped. "It's happening; it's happening now!" A spasm zipped up my spine and exploded in my skull. The helicopter dipped sideways.

"You guys are having a transfer *now*?"

I moaned.

Parker turned to look at the commotion in back. "Anjalie looks pretty bad, too; your friends are trying to help her. Now tell me how I can help you!"

"You've got to take the controls," I mustered, while another sharp pain sucked my entire body inward.

"I can't do that, and you know it," said Parker, bracing himself against his door.

"Ahhh!" I gripped my hands over my ears and screamed, only vaguely aware of the helicopter jerking around in the air.

"Kaitlin, get a hold of yourself!" Parker grabbed my hands, unclenched my fingers, and placed them back around the controls. "There's a meadow about a mile ahead; see it? You can land this thing in a matter of minutes."

"It hurts, it hurts!" I cried.

"I know it does, but we only have a few options here! Either we open the back door and toss your sister out of the helicopter, or you push past your pain and save us all! Make your choice!"

I forced my eyes open and began working my body out of its knot, every nerve and muscle wailing in opposition. *You've got to do this! You can do this!* I repeated to myself until my body had completely righted itself. I squinted out the windshield. That's when everything became quiet. Or maybe numb would be the right word. No longer aware of the whining rotors or Parker's frenzied shouting, all I could hear was the subtle rhythmic exchange between my heart and lungs—although I even felt detached from that sound. In a way, I had departed from my body entirely, leaving behind my fear, my friends, and especially my pain. I felt like I was in a cloud or a dream, a hazy place when only my thoughts, the sky, and the helicopter existed.

I took the helicopter's speed to sixty knots and lined up my landing spot—a grassy clearing behind a pond. I adjusted the collective, then the cyclic, then the collective again, and the helicopter gradually relinquished altitude and speed. I could see the grass beneath me swivel against the wind of the rotors. By then, I'd decelerated enough that the aircraft began to settle and roll lightly to the right. I made the necessary adjustments until I'd taken the aircraft into a smooth hover. I lowered the collective and gently set the helicopter down on the ground.

The moment I shut off the engine, the pain once again washed over me—pressure crushing my body like an avalanche of knives. My chest pulled for air, but the heaviness around me refused to give. Starved for oxygen and compressed by an unseen force, my body screamed in agony. Certainly, I would not survive this time.

"Take her and go!" someone called.

"I've got you!" said a far-away voice. Like a spatula to a pancake, my body was scooped from my seat and pulled from the helicopter. And then there was running. Fast running. I was being carried away from the helicopter and away from Anjalie, through the meadow and into a patch of trees. There, we met up with a stream and followed it down a slope, running and running and running. And with every step, the pain in my head lessened and my body felt lighter. And after a while, ten minutes maybe, the pain was gone completely and was replaced by a sense of peace, happiness even, because the person who was running with me in his arms was Max.

My Max.

"You can stop now," I said, tugging on the shoulder of Max's sweatshirt. "I think I am okay."

Max took a few more steps before collapsing to his knees. He lowered me to the ground and rolled backward onto the grass, his chest rising and falling in steady heaves. His face was splotchy and beaded in sweat, but despite this, he sat up, flashed me his one-of-a-kind dimples, and patted the grass next to him.

I complied, mopping his forehead with the arm of my jacket before resting my head on his shoulder. We sat there quietly and watched the crystal water rush down the valley.

"I am thirsty enough to suck that stream dry," Max said, his breathing almost steady. "Do you think the water would give me gonorrhea?"

"You mean giardia?" I sputtered, exhausted, but nearly falling over with laughter.

Max smiled sheepishly. "Probably shouldn't risk it either way. I've had enough excitement for the day. So, uh, looks like you can fly a helicopter."

"I can speak Spanish, too," I said and then nuzzled my way deeper into the space between Max's collarbone and chin.

"Ouch," Max flinched, pulling a protruding bobby pin from my hair. "No wonder you had such a gnarly headache; you've got a ton of metal thingies in your hair." He began removing the pins one by one, my hair slowly falling against my shoulders.

I tilted my head to the side and enjoyed the sensation of Max's fingertips grazing my neck. "If only the cause of my headache was so simple. I guess you have a lot of questions, starting with your long-lost twin brother, Parker, and ending with how I almost killed all of you guys while flying the helicopter. Oh, and I bet you're simply dying to know who your biological father is."

"Yup, got lots of questions," Max mused, leaning forward and placing a gentle kiss on my neck. "But they can wait. Right now, all I want to do is to hold you for a few minutes."

I leaned back and Max pulled me in tight. "Hey Max, thanks for saving me today."

"Hey Kaitlin, thanks for saving *me*," he replied.

PARKER

Parker hated his father, truly and indisputably hated him.

But now, as he finally had the opportunity to tell his side of the story, Parker wondered if he could stomach doing it.

It's not that he didn't want his father to pay for his actions; there was nothing Parker wanted more. But turning his father in to the authorities seemed so impersonal, passive almost. Dr. Forsythe needed to understand the magnitude of what he had done, and he needed to suffer for it. Parker doubted the legal system could be creative enough to handle the crimes appropriately.

Molly and Garrett were already talking to the police in the ER's waiting room and, as soon as the nurse returned with Parker's discharge papers, he and Anjalie would have to join them. If only he'd run off into the woods with Kaitlin and Max.

They were still somewhere out there, far away from hospital rooms and men with shiny badges, but it was only a matter of time till the police found them and brought them in, too.

"So, uh, that was a whole lot of blood for only seven puny stitches," Parker grumbled to Anjalie, who had volunteered to keep Parker company while the doctor stitched him up.

"And that was a whole lot of whining for only seven puny stitches. You're such a weakling." Anjalie stuck her thumb against Parker's fresh dressing and pushed. Parker slapped her hand away. "First a liar, then a weakling. What will she call me next?"

"Shut up, stupid head."

"Stupid head it is then. Very mature."

Funny, the two of them had practically grown up together, but had hardly exchanged these many words the whole time. Now, all of the sudden, they were acting like siblings—bickering, yes, but with an undertone of understanding of those who'd been raised under the same crazy roof.

"So, um, your dad tried to shoot us today," Anjalie said quietly, picking at a hangnail. "I guess you were right about him after all."

"Ya think?" Parker said, but once he saw that Anjalie was holding her breath to keep from crying, he softened his voice. "I'm sorry. You must feel really bad right now."

She sniffed. "What are you going to do once all this is over?"

"Thumb a ride to anywhere but here. You?"

She sneered. "You know, I can tell you the chemical components of gasoline, but have no clue how to use a gas pump. I'm pretty much lost in this world."

"Me too," he agreed.

"Maybe I could go with you? Hitchhike. I *do* know how to extend my thumb."

Parker opened his mouth to respond, but was interrupted when a nurse peeked inside the curtain. "I am sorry to bother you two, but it is my understanding that someone named Anjalie is in here. I am assuming that is you, young lady?"

"Yes, that's me," Anjalie narrowed her eyes, curiously.

"You have a visitor." The nurse pulled back the curtain and there sat a pummeled-looking woman in a hospital-issued wheelchair. The woman's forehead was bandaged, as was her right arm and both of her legs. Her bottom lip was starting to scab over, and her right cheekbone boasted twice as many stitches as Parker's arm, but even with all that, there was no mistaking her identity.

Greenish eyes, honey-colored hair, freckly skin—this woman was Kaitlin and Anjalie's mother, Ashley. Alive, yes, but Parker wouldn't go so far as to say "and well." But alive was good enough.

Anjalie and her mother froze, locked in place by the moment they had both envisioned for fifteen years. Ashley broke the silence with a whisper. "I could teach you how to use a gas pump. All you do is slide your credit card, select your fuel grade, and insert the nozzle. My car is totaled, but the insurance should take care of it. We'll get a new one, and then we'll practice together. I could teach you other things too—like how to grow herbs or how to hem a pair of jeans. That's a mom's job, teaching the simple things, the things you can't learn from a textbook."

A tear rolled over the rim of Ashley's eye, almost completely in sync with the one that had just fallen from her daughter's.

"But mostly, I could teach you what it feels like to be loved. If anyone could teach you that, oh my goodness, it would be me. My beautiful girl, my Anjalie, I have been loving you so completely, so heart-wrenchingly your entire life. Please be mine again."

Wiping her eyes, Anjalie took a step forward, then another, then another, and before the nurse had a moment to advise against it, she had climbed into the wheelchair on Ashley's lap. Like a tiny child, she wrapped her arms around her mother's neck and sobbed. They both did.

Ashley stroked Anjalie's hair and whispered into her daughter's ear, and whatever she was saying made Anjalie cry harder and pull her mother closer.

Parker felt overwhelmed. Thanks to his father, he would never have a moment like this one. He would never have a mother to love him. Never.

He took his bag and showed himself to the waiting room. Police were everywhere. One of the officers, who had a fluffy mustache and watery eyes, flagged Parker down.

"You're Parker Forsythe, correct?"

Here we go, he thought as he shook the officer's hand.

"I am Officer Partridge. I have a couple of questions about the whereabouts of your father."

"Excuse me? Hasn't he been arrested already?"

"We've searched the Leavitt Center. No one was inside."

"But . . . but that's impossible . . . " Parker scratched his head. "When we were in the helicopter, I saw squad cars. They were only ten minutes away from the Leavitt Center. My father couldn't have possibly gotten away."

"When we arrived, the place was a mess. We found plates of uneaten food in the dining hall, still warm, books scattered across the library, and even a wet trail of blood in the stairwell. But no people. Surely you have some idea of how everyone disappeared so quickly."

"I . . . I . . . " and then Parker started to laugh. His father had escaped. Of course he had. Someone so smart, so ruthless would have had an emergency evacuation plan—something that could be executed at a moment's notice.

Officer Partridge frowned. "Do you have any information that might help us?"

At the moment, Parker could show Officer Partridge the photos on his camera. He could tell him *everything* he knew, *everything* Dr. Forsythe had done. But the cops would never find his father. Dr. Forsythe had too many resources, too much help. He could outsmart just about anyone. Parker remembered seeing his father sliding money into the hands of a government official at a fundraising event. It was likely that even Officer Partridge and the entire police precinct had already been compromised.

"I've got to go." Parker veered away from the cop toward the hospital doors, nodding to Garrett and Molly on his way out.

Parker had neither resources nor help, but he did have a genetic connection to his father—an innate understanding of the man and his capabilities. Now it was up to him to find his father and issue a punishment equal to his crimes. Especially the crime of killing Parker's mother.

Because now, for that reason, Parker hated his father the most.

CHAPTER 21

KAITLIN

"My turn!" I reached under the Christmas tree and grabbed the present that looked like it'd been wrapped by an elf with epilepsy. I steered the gift across my living room and lowered it into Syrup's outstretched arms. "You're going to love it!" I tittered.

Everyone else leaned in close, curious as to what this long, jagged present could be.

Syrup stuck her tongue to the side of her mouth, tore a small piece of snowflake wrapping from the leftmost corner of the package, and unwound the paper like ribbon from a spool. "Deer antennae!" she gasped. She stood up and carefully displayed the antlers for everyone to admire. "I've wanted some of these for as long as I can remember. Thank you, Kaitlin!"

I gave Syrup a hug and skittered back to my comfy spot on Max's lap. He rested his hand casually on my waist and my heart gave a not-so-casual jump for joy.

Mom walked into the room with a tray of cookies and, when catching sight of Max and me, bit her lip to suppress a grin. I was just glad she didn't jump up on the coffee table and tap dance herself silly. It had been years since my mom had seen me having any sort of successful social interaction, and me sitting on a cute boy's lap, surrounded by friends . . . well, that definitely qualified as such.

Actually, this whole post-Christmas get-together had been her idea. She made the invitations, helped my friends find cheap airfare, and had been in the kitchen cooking up a storm for days.

She'd finally told my father about the adoption, the blackmail, and all of the lies she'd had to tell to cover up what was *really* going on with Camp Overlook. While this had been a heavy load off of my mother's heart, it had come as a shock to my father. Understandably, he was hurt, confused, and angry—she hadn't even given him the opportunity to love and comfort her, to help her through the threats, and help protect me from Dr. Forsythe. He stayed to help Mom with her rehab, but moved out of the house and into an apartment when she was well enough to get around without his help. This separation was painful for both of them. It was incredibly painful for me as well, but I had a feeling they would make their way back to each other when the time was right.

I'd like to say that when I returned to school in the fall, with two new pairs of jeans and a fuzzy coat of self-esteem, that I was openly embraced by Mia Bethers and the rest of my high school peers. Not so. In fact, my first day back, I was welcomed to school by a can of ravioli being dumped into my backpack. I'd also like to say that the constant teasing no longer bothered me. Also not so. Even though I knew what people were saying had no basis whatsoever, it still stung.

But in my heart, I knew the truth. My worth was not dependent on the opinions of my high school peers or my fellow Overlook campers. It was not dependent on being considered "special" or having been *called upon*. It was not even determined by the fact that I had flown *a freaking helicopter*! My worth came simply by being a human being. And I could realize that worth simply by accepting, loving, and celebrating myself.

Sometimes I felt like waving my three-ring binder in the air and yelling, "Can't you guys see that I am awesome? And you all are awesome, too! We are all awesome, so let's be nicer to each other!"

But I never did that. I just hung my head low through my classes and counted the minutes until I could run home and dial one of my Overlook buddies on the phone. And when they answered, well, they were flat-out thrilled that I'd called.

They liked me. They got me. We could talk for hours about our parents, school, hair products—although of one subject we steered clear like a skunk on a frontage road: Dr. Forsythe and his miraculous escape.

Perhaps the subject was too terrifying. I mean, the man left no clues as to where or how he went. Really, he could be anywhere. Maybe even outside this very house, at this very moment, just waiting to launch a grenade through the window and finish the job he started on the roof of the Leavitt Center.

The police have been unhelpful through this whole ordeal. After searching the building and finding no evidence of the horror I'd described—Claire's body, for instance—and then after the fruitless scuba search in Lake Arrowhead, the police seemed to put as much priority into this case as they would a kitten stuck up a tree.

"No evidence, no case," Officer Partridge had said, mindlessly running his fingertip along the bristles of his mustache.

No evidence?! There were truckloads of evidence! Camp Overlook and all its participants had been completely abandoned when Dr. Forsythe and the rest of the staff disappeared. What about that? And what about the campers who'd been *called upon*? Where'd they disappear to? And let's not forget about all the young mothers who had turned their babies over to Dr. Forsythe. Couldn't the police interview them?

My mother, for one, was finally more than willing to answer questions, even if it meant incriminating herself. But the cops kept downplaying her answers. They waved off the illegal adoption as a mistake that "anyone could make" and admonished her to "not let it happen again."

Then they insisted that her car accident—you know, the one that nearly claimed her life?—was merely that. An accident.

There were so many leads. So many! And while the police said that they intended to follow up on some of them, the way their eyes wandered to the cold-cuts table at the back of the room seemed to imply otherwise.

To me, it was obvious. Somehow, someway, Dr. Forsythe had gotten to them. He had bribed, blackmailed, and threatened whoever it took to keep his operation under the radar.

Between my worries of Mia Bethers and Dr. Forsythe—and really, it was a toss-up between the two as to who was eviler—was it any wonder that my stomach could hardly even manage to properly digest oatmeal? I was a jumbled mass of nerves, leaping out of my chair at the tiniest unanticipated noise and giving myself whiplash from looking over my shoulder, like, every five seconds. After the sixth night of my mother waking up to find me curled in a sleeping bag next to her bed, well, that's when she suggested that I invite my friends to Colorado to help ring in the New Year.

As far as medicine goes, my friends were the best. I scooted farther into Max's lap and took in the happy scene of my living room. Sierra, who was sitting next to the Christmas tree, giggled girlishly as Garrett crammed an eighth snickerdoodle into his mouth and reached for a ninth. On the opposite couch cuddled Molly and her new boyfriend, whom she'd only started dating a month prior but insisted she couldn't possibly survive the holiday without.

Then there was Syrup, sitting alone by the fireplace . . . yet not alone at all. She lovingly caressed the curvatures of her new deer antlers with an awestruck gleam in her eye, and I was glad for her.

Several key players from our summer adventure were missing, notably. First and foremost was Claire. I couldn't go an hour without feeling a throbbing ache in my chest at her memory. She had been grouchy and stubborn, prickly and condescending, but in our few days together, I could see that all those qualities were only a hard exterior shell. Inside, she had a gooey, cookie-buttery center, I was sure. She and I would have been great friends, I think, given the chance. I would never forget her.

Jake was also absent. Fact was, he hadn't been invited. After I'd been *called upon*, Max had invited him to join the rescue party. Not only had Jake refused, but he'd threatened to sic Security Phil on them if they went after "that barfing barracuda." Making good on his word, Jake was responsible for my friends' capture, imprisonment, and putting them in a whole heck of a lot of unnecessary danger. He was a stinker, and I would never do him the honor of calling him "my first kiss." Nope. I reserved that right for Max.

Parker, however, would have certainly been invited had I been able to find him. Though I only knew him for several hours, my fate would've been very different without him. But before I got the chance to thank him, he had taken off. I didn't blame him. He had some serious baggage to sort through, but it would've been nice of him to lend a helping hand in the investigation. He had more inside knowledge than anyone else, not to mention honest-to-goodness photographic evidence.

Max had seemed remarkably okay that Parker had disappeared before they'd gotten to know each other. He didn't freak out when he learned that his biological father was a murdering psychopath, either. I guess he wasn't kidding when he told me that his genetics didn't define him; that his parents were the ones who raised him, and the ones who created him were not. Max sure had his ducks in a row.

Obviously, Anjalie couldn't be at the party with us right now. She and I valued our brain cells way too much to spend time under the same roof. That's not to say we washed our hands of one another; I spent more time on the phone with my sister than anyone else. I still thought she was a big weirdo, but a very interesting, very smart big weirdo. I liked her. She talked a lot about science and math and about her research on ways we could spend time together without frying our brains. She occasionally talked about what it was like to grow up at the Leavitt Center and, surprise, it wasn't the "wonderfully rich childhood" that Dr. Forsythe had described.

Anjalie had been staying in Grand Junction with my mom's childhood friend, Jade, since summer. During the week, she home-schooled herself and learned how to do normal-people tasks—like ordering Chinese takeout and using an iPhone. Every weekend, without fail, my mother drove three hours to see her. It sucked having to share Mom with someone else, but truthfully, I'd never seen my mother as happy as she was now. She laughed easily and sang cheeseball Disney songs as she washed the dishes.

And our mother–daughter relationship had never been better. Mom didn't seem to take it personally when I had a bad day at school. Actually, she reacted very rationally to my everyday woes—patting my back, kissing my nose, and reassuring me that everything would work out in the end. Because of this, I felt like I could open up to her in a way that I couldn't before. I could tell Mom about Mia Bethers and my daily torment. I could tell her about the nightmares I had about finding Claire's body or being shot at by Dr. Forsythe's guards. I could tell her pretty much anything. It was a tremendous relief, that.

I gave Mom a little wink as she loaded empty hot chocolate mugs onto the tray and lifted them off the coffee table. Mom squeezed my shoulder as she passed me on her way out of the room.

Sierra then reached over the arm of the loveseat and scooped up a present from under the tree. "For you," she handed a gift to Garrett and gave him a hopeful smile.

Garrett, cheeks still bulging with Christmas cookies, yanked the ribbon away and lifted the lid off the box. Out of it, he procured a neon pink hippopotamus with plastic rhinestone eyes. He examined the stuffed animal with a perplexed crest between his brows.

"It's a replacement," Sierra volunteered, "for y'alls lucky rhino."

"But it's pink."

"I thought a different color of pachyderm would bring y'all a different kind of luck." She batted her eyelashes hopefully.

"Here, Sierra," said Molly, handing Sierra a gift. "I saw this at the mall, and it just screamed you. I had to get it."

"Thanks?" said Sierra, surprised because she and Molly hadn't bonded at camp. After the unwrapping, however, Sierra jumped up, pushed aside Molly's boyfriend, and tackled Molly with the kinship of a long-lost friend. "Texas flag nail-decals! Thank you so much!"

"Sure," said Molly, hugging Sierra back with equal gusto. With one simple present, Molly had doubled her collection of girlfriends. She now had two.

"There's one more present under the tree," Max whispered in my ear. "See it? I think it's for you."

The gift was small and long with a tiny red ribbon stuck to the top.

"Allow me," said Max, taking the box from my hands. He scooted toward the edge of the cushion and looked up at me with that dimply grin of his.

"Kaitlin, over the summer, you proved yourself to be lots of things: funny, brave, adventurous, smart, and cute . . . really cute. But there was one moment, before I got around to discovering all that other stuff—except for the cute thing; that was apparent from the get-go—when I knew that I was in serious jeopardy of losing my wits because of you."

Max held out the box in front of him, facing me, and slowly opened the lid. There was a silver chain with a dainty charm on the end.

I placed my hand over my chest. "It's a . . . it's a . . . pinecone?"

He laughed.

"Max!" I screeched. "Tell me the moment you decided to like me wasn't when I babbled on and on about pinecones and their sap?!"

"The very one. You looked so nervous and vulnerable, could you blame me for wanting to take care of you?"

"In case you didn't notice my brilliant and brave helicopter piloting, I don't need caring for."

"All the reason to like you more. I hope you'll let me try anyway."

"What can I say?"

"Say you'll accept this pinecone charm as a token of my devotion."

"I will wear it always," I sighed melodramatically and gave Max a great big kiss. He reached behind his back and pulled an envelope from his back pocket. "And what's that, mister?"

"Another present. It's a roundtrip ticket to California. I was hoping you would be my date to prom?"

I pulled away in shock. "Um, you've seen me dance before, right? Your friends will think I am a total—"

"Who cares what anyone else thinks," he reminded me, standing up, twirling me around, and dipping me backward. "We would have fun, and that's all that matters."

I giggled. "I'll say yes with one condition."

"Okay?"

"That you'll limit yourself to one squirt of cologne. I have a very sensitive gag reflex."

"Noted," Max nodded soberly.

"Come on, guys; thirty seconds to midnight!" Garrett grumbled, as though our flirting was somehow delaying the New Year.

Max and I laughed and joined our friends in the countdown.

"Nineteen . . . eighteen . . . seventeen . . . "

But as we fast approached the glorious moment of "Happy New Year," something happened. I felt my excitement for the upcoming year harden to rock-solid apprehension. Just like that. I mean, I knew there would be good stuff: café lunches with Mom, a relationship with my sister, prom with Max . . .

"Ten . . . nine . . . eight . . ."

But I just couldn't shake the sinking feeling in my chest. It was the feeling of dread. It was a feeling of fear. It was a feeling that my journey with Dr. Forsythe and the Leavitt Center had not yet ended . . .

"Three . . . two . . . one!"

It had just begun.

ACKNOWLEDGMENTS

Writing my first book was a thrilling act of creation, hours spent crouched over my computer, chewing on my index finger as I imagined the next line of dialogue. My best ideas came with my head against the pillow, eyes closed, ready to fall asleep. The next plot twist would pop into my brain, and I was suddenly wide awake with excitement. Writing *Called Upon* was, simply put, a joy.

Getting this book across the finish line, however, took many champions, whom I would like to thank right now. First of all, I thank my momma, Adrienne Robinson, who offered gentle suggestions and corrections that were always exactly right. Likewise, my mother-in-law, Cindy Lee, read each chapter as it came and reassured me that this book was worthy. In fact, many of my favorite people read this book in its infancy and helped me fine-tune my characters and word choices: Sierra Penrod, Jared and Kristy Robinson, Josh Lee, Zell Lee, Richelle Lee, Katie Bateman, Anne Driggs, and my dad, Thomas Robinson. Thank you!

So much gratitude goes to handsome husband, Ryan Lee, who picked up the slack when I neglected the kiddos, house, and bedtime so the words could flow without interruption. He was always endlessly encouraging, especially so while my manuscript was buried deep in the slush piles of countless literary agents and I feared this book would never see the light of day. Thank you, Pooh Bear. I love you.

A special shout-out goes to Anissa Holmes, who introduced me to Nick Pavlidis, a wonderful book coach. Thanks to him, Ethan Webb, and Jennifer Harshman for loving the book, helping me with edits, and getting my manuscript to the top of the stack at Morgan James Publishing. Thank you so much to Morgan James who saw my story's potential and wanted to be a part of its journey! I am so lucky to be a part of their family now!

ABOUT THE AUTHOR

When Bethany Lee isn't writing, she is elbow deep in garden soil or covered in dust from a mountain trail. She is decidedly an "outside girl" and loves biking, hiking, and basically any activity that can be done in yoga pants—clearly, she was born to write a book about an adventure in the mountains. Bethany is a communications graduate who has a soft spot for young adults and all of the cringy moments they experience every day (It gets better, friends). A creative writer since early childhood, she uses humor, honesty, and whimsy to pull readers in and invite them to laugh, relate, and introspect. Bethany currently resides in Lehi, Utah, with her husband, three kids, and garden.

Please visit bethanylee.com.

CPSIA information can be obtained
at www.ICGtesting.com
Printed in the USA
JSHW030514250221
12032JS00001BA/22